THE SCHUMANN
FREQUENCY

THE SCHUMANN FREQUENCY

CHRISTOPHER RIDE

JAVELIN BOOKS

JAVELIN BOOKS

First published in 2007 by Javelin Books Pty Limited
Level 6, 468 St Kilda Road, Melbourne 3004, Australia.

Copyright © text Christopher L. Ride, 2007

The moral rights of the author have been asserted.

All rights reserved. No part of this book may be reproduced or transmitted in any form or by any means, electronic or mechanical, including photocopying, recording or by any information storage and retrieval system, without prior permission in writing from the publisher. The *Copyright Act 1968* (the Act) allows a maximum of one chapter or ten per cent of this book, whichever is the greater, to be photocopied by any educational institution for its educational purposes provided that the educational institution (or body that administers it) has given a remuneration notice to Copyright Agency Limited (CAL) under the Act.

National Library of Australia Cataloguing-in-Publication data:

Ride, Christopher L., 1965- .
 The Schumann frequency.

 1st ed.
 ISBN 9780646467801 (pbk.).

 I. Title.

A823.4

Front cover image based on waveform data, Schumann Frequency, from the North California Earthquake Data Centre website: www.ncedc.org/ncedc/em.intro.html (Earth-ionosphere cavity resonance at Parkfield, California)

Cover design by Andrew Cunningham, Studio Pazzo
Text design and typesetting by Andrew Cunningham, Studio Pazzo
Edited by Sally Moss, Context Editorial
Printed in China by The Australian Book Connection

This book is dedicated to Natasha and Jessica.

Special thanks goes to all those who have in some way contributed to the writing of this book.

FACTUAL INFORMATION

The Schumann Frequency

The Schumann Frequency is a real phenomenon. The data in this novel relating to its discovery, measurement process and continuing increase is entirely accurate. A Google Internet search on 'Schumann Resonance or Schumann Frequency' will return over 696,000 positive matches—websites, measurement stations, discussion groups, scientific papers and university studies. The phenomenon is officially recorded by the North California Earthquake Data Centre (NCEDC) at two telemetry stations: in Arrival Heights, Antarctica; and in Parkfield, California.

To date, the United States Navy has conducted the most comprehensive research on the Schumann Frequency. The increased resonance has had a detrimental effect on the performance of the ULF (Ultra Low Frequency) sonar equipment used for the navigation of military submarines.

Zero Point

The earth moves into a new phase every two thousand years, due to the precession of the equinox—the 26,000-year cycle of the earth's wobble on its axis and the resultant view from earth of the twelve star constellations of the zodiac. This fact is recognised by many ancient cultures and is popularly depicted in modern astrology with the coming of the Age of Aquarius, due around the turn of the twenty-first century, and the leaving behind of the Age of Pisces—an era said to be of great religious significance. Before the Age of Pisces was the Age of Aries—a time of war and conquest, which ended around the birth of Christ.

In the ancient Mayan culture, the turn of the twenty-first century is said to be the completion of Great Cycle Number Five and the beginning of an entirely new 26,000-year cycle—hence 'Zero Point'. Mayan legend has it that, at Zero Point, the magnetic poles of the earth will momentarily flip, causing the resonance of the earth to be recalibrated back to normal levels. Like the Age of Aquarius, Zero Point is said to herald an age of new light and friendship in which fear-based concepts are dissolved.

Scientific Information

The information in this novel relating to the process of time travel is based on the theories of Albert Einstein, Kurt Gödel, Frank Tipler, Hugh Everett III, Michael Talbot, David Bohm and Stephen Hawking.

Historical Fact

The information in this novel relating to the Dead Sea Scrolls, Copper Scroll, Mayan pyramids, Egyptian pyramids, Stonehenge, Judea, Josephus and General Flavius Vespasian is based on historical data—which includes construction dates, architecture, monuments, culture, texts, people and events.

1

> 'The destined are fortunate; they lack
> the burden of alternatives and therefore the
> distraction of retreat.'
>
> —Barton Ingerson

Houston, Texas
Post Oak Towers, Building 2, Rooftop—Level 35
November 25th 2012
Local time 6:51 a.m.

Mission of Isaiah—Day One

AN INTENSE GLOW saturated the morning sky, washing it with pink, yellow and orange. The vivid splash of colours was fading quickly, just seconds away from a new dawn. Beams of gold suddenly burst upwards from the horizon as the last remnants of darkness were vanquished and the sun rapidly crested the landscape. The metropolis of Houston, the fourth-largest city in the United States, was waking from its slumber. Cars and trucks filled the streets. People hurried along the sidewalks. Things moved quickly. It was just like any other day.

High on an inner-city skyscraper, an unfamiliar breeze swirled.

With a flash a time portal opened.

Two red electrons appeared from thin air and orbited each other, silently hovering above the floor. Growing in size and brightness, they multiplied into four, then eight, as the pattern of the rotation increased in complexity. Over and over they doubled in number and velocity, until they swarmed together in their thousands.

On the thirty-third floor of Building 1, Post Oak Towers, an office worker lowered a mug of coffee from her lips. A red glow was radiating from the roof of the skyscraper opposite. Fascinated by the strengthening brightness, she walked towards the plate-glass window and stared outside, her mouth agape. She had never seen anything like it. She squinted, trying to focus more clearly. *What is that?* she wondered.

The mist of swirling electrons rumbled as fingers of highly charged electricity spun from the core. A metal handrail nearby began to glow as the gusting wind reached super-heated temperatures. Everything on the rooftop vibrated furiously. Paint peeled. Scorch marks appeared on the concrete. The red electrons massed ever more closely, building themselves into a luminous tornado. The phenomenon pulsated with a monstrous energy until, at last, with the roar of a dozen thunderclaps—it detonated.

The woman watching from her office window was stunned as the heat of the explosion slapped at her face. She threw up both hands as a shield, letting the coffee mug go. In slow motion, the mug fell, taking a lethargic path downwards before bouncing off the carpet in front of her feet. Boiling droplets of brown liquid—small perfect spheres—were propelled from the cup in leisurely arcs and splashed across the floor.

Everything in the city moved at one-quarter of normal speed, to the sound of a low-pitched drone.

Meanwhile, the by-now millions of red electrons were blasted thousands of metres in all directions. One by one, they swung back on a predetermined path towards the flashpoint and fused together into a molten mass. Something started to take shape. The construction—a human form—began from the inside out: marrow, bones, muscles, skin, then clothes.

With every electron finally assimilated, a man dressed in black was revealed. He was suspended in mid-air, his arms splayed outwards. The super-heated wind swirled around him chaotically, holding him aloft somehow and tossing his hair this way and that. Yet he was unaffected by the blistering temperatures.

With a flash of golden light, the wind dropped away and the figure fell unceremoniously backwards onto the smouldering concrete. In an instant, *time* surged back to its normal speed, the sounds of the city rising to a familiar pitch again.

The transport was complete.

Inside her office the woman looked, perplexed, at the fallen coffee mug on the carpet. What just happened? Her focus shifted to the top of the building opposite. The red glow was gone. She pressed her hand against her forehead—her skin was burnt and blistered.

ON THE ROOFTOP, a time traveller lay pale and motionless. White smoke hovered above him in the still morning air. Suddenly, spiderwebs of electricity rippled across his lifeless body, causing his eyes to dart from side to side under his eyelids. His left hand twitched, then the right. With a mighty heave of his chest, he gasped and opened his eyes.

Wilson Dowling had successfully made a leap of almost seventy years backwards in time. He felt no pain and his breathing quickly settled into a rhythm. Numbness clouded his senses, making it difficult to think, and he continued to rest the back of his head against the rooftop pavement. He stared through the smoke at the blue sky above him, trying to put everything together in his mind.

He just lay there.

Memories slowly began connecting together. He recalled seeing GM and Jasper in the command centre, just seconds before the final transport. There was no doubt that things had become overly complicated at the last moment. *An understatement.* And somehow Wilson knew he was lucky to be here, in the past.

If they could have stopped the transport, they would have.

Anyway, all that mattered now was that he was *here*. The Mission of Isaiah was his new focus: completing the tasks assigned to him was the only way to get back home. Gingerly lifting his head, he gazed about. The rooftop was scorched. Hundreds of streamers of smoke, like burning incense, wafted into the motionless air. From this perspective it was impossible to tell where 'here' was.

With his senses gradually coming back to him, he began to feel the radiant heat of the concrete through his clothes. Sweat trickled from his face and he knew it was time to get up. A headache throbbed behind his eyes. Using all his strength, he struggled to one knee, then to his feet, and stumbled towards the railing.

He was high up—very high up—on a structure of some kind.

Layers of reddish smog blanketed the skyline before him. In the distance, sunlight filtered through the rows of tall buildings clustered at the city centre. Everywhere he looked there was traffic. The pavements were busy with people. It was exactly like the old movies and photographs he had seen; exactly as his research had said it would be. Wilson felt a strange sense of comfort as he smelt pollution for the first time and tasted it on his tongue. The city was loud; much louder than anything he had ever heard before. At that moment he realised that Barton had done it. *They* had done it! This was certainly Houston—Houston early this century. The transport had worked successfully; there was no doubt about it.

A clunk echoed from the air-conditioning system as the large cooling fans on the rooftop began to turn clockwise. At the same time, Wilson's thoughts became clearer. This was potentially a hostile world, he remembered. He would need to remain composed. Remember what he had learnt. Stay focused, stay positive, be in the moment. It was all quite simple, he told himself.

Joints cracking as if his body had not functioned in an eternity, he made his way across the blackened concrete towards the fire escape. For some reason the situation seemed funny now. He had travelled through time—*Wilson the time traveller*. It was almost impossible to comprehend.

After taking one last disbelieving look at the smouldering rooftop, he walked down a dusty flight of steps and opened the door onto a lift lobby. There were six elevators—three on each side of the landing—and a sign saying 'Level 34'. It was a large building, he realised. Its magnetic signature must be strong. That was certainly the reason he had been recreated at that very location.

A chime sounded and one of the elevator doors slid open. Soft classical music wafted towards Wilson. With great curiosity, he approached a mirror at the back of the lift and carefully studied himself from different angles. His longish light-brown hair was in disarray and he drew it back through his fingers to create some semblance of neatness.

The reflection he saw made him smile; nothing had changed at all. His eyes were their usual dark blue, his skin deeply tanned from days spent in the sun before his transport.

'This is all going rather well,' he said to himself. His headache seemed to be intensifying, but he chose to ignore it. A computer-generated voice emanated from the wall speaker: 'Going down.'

Wilson turned and pressed the first-floor button and waited for the doors to close. This was all too easy. Barton Ingerson was certainly a genius, he decided. It seemed the time-travel process was a complete success and there was cause to be optimistic.

Little did Wilson realise, everything was about to unravel and there was nothing he could do to stop it.

A date scrolled past on the liquid-crystal display:

November 25th 2012

The first real indication of his dire predicament had appeared. According to the date, he had arrived more than six years behind schedule.

AS THE ELEVATOR DOORS were closing, a tired-looking policeman appeared from the toilets, adjusted his gun belt and plodded across the top-floor landing with a newspaper tucked under his arm. His shift was due to end in the next hour. Noticing a burning smell in the air, he stopped for a moment, gathered his thoughts, then sprinted up the dusty stairs into the morning sunshine.

Officer Frank McGuire's face went pale as he scanned the rooftop. The concrete was peppered with scorch marks and a layer of smoke hung in the air. He had been gone for only fifteen minutes. He fumbled for his gun, drew it from its holster and nervously turned full circle, searching for any sign of movement. Somehow, the paint had peeled off the walls, he realised. The steel hand-railing had melted. McGuire's plastic chair had been reduced to a pile of green goo on the ground.

His heart pounding so loud that he could barely hear himself think, he pressed the talk button on his walkie-talkie. 'This is Lookout Nine.' He turned another full circle, almost dumbstruck. 'Something's happened. An explosion of some kind ...' The radio crackled in his hand.

'This is Base. Repeat your transmission.'

'Lookout Nine!' he repeated more emphatically. 'An explosion of some kind! On the roof!' He struggled to stay calm. 'I don't know how. I can't explain what happened!'

'Lookout Nine, did you see anyone?'

'I'd have been killed if I'd been up here,' he replied. There was a moment of silence, then the radio crackled again.

'Lookout Nine, hold your position. We're scrambling a response unit. Repeat: hold your position.'

WILSON STARED AT the date scrolling past every few seconds. Soft elevator music played in the background. He was trying to work out whether arriving six years late would affect his mission. The Schumann Frequency would probably be higher, but what would the ramifications be? He concluded that Barton had made a critical error. The temperature of the transport pod must've been too low.

Unexpectedly the elevator halted.

Level 24

The doors slid open. An armed security guard stood in the foyer outside, staring intently in Wilson's direction. The man was chunky, with a thick neck and bulging jowls. His pale-green uniform clung to his barrel chest and his black pants were a little too short for his squat legs, revealing a pair of white sports socks.

He has a face like a bulldog, Wilson thought. There were badges on the man's shirt—'Security' and a company name. His freshly shaven skin and neatly combed hair suggested he was just beginning his day.

Wilson looked away, trying to appear casual, but he could feel the man's gaze still locked upon him. The elevator doors will be closing, he told himself. *It'll be okay.* A revolver was strapped to the security guard's belt and Wilson stole a brief glance—it was the first time he had ever seen a handgun close up.

'Going down' echoed from the speaker.

The sound was a trigger.

Without provocation, the guard leapt through the doorway in attack.

There was no room to manoeuvre! No way to escape!

Barton's words echoed in Wilson's head: 'You'll have a weakness after you've travelled through time. Your eyes will make you vulnerable. This is very important. Not doing what I say could cost you your life.'

The guard's full weight hammered Wilson into the back wall of the elevator with a crunch, smashing the wind from his lungs. Wilson gasped for air as he tucked himself into a ball to deflect the frenzied onslaught of punches and kicks. In some way he felt like a spectator; it was impossible to conceive that this was *actually* happening to him. He was being beaten to death!

Both men tumbled to the floor between the closing elevator doors, which sprang open in response. Coming to his senses, as if awakening from a bad dream, Wilson began to fight back. Clothes began tearing, muscles quivered. He clumsily struck out, but felt a heavy blow to the head in reply, then another. The pair groaned with exertion as the inelegant melee continued. It was primal combat in its simplest form. Spit flew from the guard's mouth as he repeatedly drove Wilson's head into the carpet.

The guard was too strong!

Wilson forced a command from his lips: 'Activate Overload.'

A familiar chill quaked through him as a mixture of adrenalin, testosterone and endorphins flooded his body. The tables were about to turn. Feeling his strength multiply twenty-fold, Wilson effortlessly flung his attacker out of the elevator into the foyer. He expected the guard to retreat at this sign of newfound strength, but that was not the reaction. The man merely regained his balance, snarled and charged fearlessly once again. Wilson hurled him away, this time with such force that he was slammed into the elevator doors on the other side of the foyer and fell in a heap on the floor.

But in just seconds, the guard gathered himself yet again, as if possessed by an unstoppable compulsion, and sprinted forward, screaming at the top of his lungs. In one quick movement, Wilson leapt into the foyer in a counter-attack, grasping his adversary in a headlock and holding him tight. The solid man thrashed about, scratching and trying to bite, but Wilson's grip was like a vice. Seconds ticked by and the struggling inevitably gave way to unconsciousness.

Wilson concluded that the man's reaction had certainly been caused by an optical trackenoid response. It had to be. His contact lenses—worn to prevent this very effect—weren't working. A pair of dark sunglasses protruded from the guard's breast pocket. Deciding that he needed them to cover his eyes, Wilson snatched them up.

The doors slid closed and he was once again in the confines of the elevator. Calm music continued to play in the background in total disregard for the situation. It was almost annoying. Stretching his shoulders from front to back, Wilson felt profoundly tired. The after-effects of the Overload command were coming. He was filled with dread—he had always likened the feeling to having his spine ripped out of his body with all the nerve endings attached. First, there was a cold sweat, and his body began shaking. That was the easy part. Then the excruciating pain began—like acid flowing through his veins. He clenched his teeth and suppressed the urge to scream.

It was difficult to know how long the pain lasted, but it always felt like an eternity when in reality it had only been seconds. Wilson took a moment to compose himself and assess the situation. His clothes were torn and saturated with sweat. He was so weak he could barely stand. Blood was trickling from his bottom lip. The only good news was that his headache appeared to be gone. He looked at the dark sunglasses in his palm; they were his only hope of avoiding further confrontation.

The elevator stopped again.

Level 14

'Oh no,' Wilson whispered. Slapping the sunglasses over his eyes, he straightened his clothes, wiped the blood from his mouth and nervously backed away to the far corner of the compartment. If he was attacked now, he certainly wouldn't have the strength to fight.

The doors hissed open and an office worker loomed just outside. Of average height and wearing a white shirt with a blue tie, he gave Wilson a cursory glance before shifting his attention to the ream of papers in his hand. The man stepped into the confined space, the elevator descended a floor, the doors hissed open again and he stepped away without incident.

To Wilson's great relief, he was alone again. He watched the red digital numbers descend one by one. When the doors eventually opened on level 1, a murmur of voices filtered towards him. An impressive marble atrium spanned the building lobby. Bright morning sunlight beamed through the glass ceiling. The air was warm, heated to an uncomfortable temperature.

Wilson cautiously made his way towards the railing. Below, at ground level, an endless stream of workers poured in through the double doors, making their way towards the elevators. Hundreds of people, all potential killers, he thought.

A receptionist glanced at Wilson from behind her desk. An attractive woman. When she ignored his presence and continued with her telephone conversation, he surmised that the sunglasses were actually protecting him. Walking with a slight limp now, he wound his way down the white marble staircase towards the crowd. The situation made him anxious, but there appeared to be no negative reactions to his approach. Strangers bumped and jostled him as he made his way outside, but it was nothing out of the ordinary. Stepping into a sunlit forecourt, he felt the cool morning air on his face and breathed a well-earned sigh of relief.

But a high-pitched chirping sound snatched his sigh away.

Police sirens echoed off the walls as four squad cars simultaneously screeched to a halt in the car park, roof lights blazing. A gaggle of smartly dressed officers jumped from their vehicles and raced from ground level up a single flight of steps towards him. Wilson didn't immediately understand what was happening, but he instinctively turned back towards the building, moving with the flow of the people. Nothing about the situation made any sense. It had only been moments since the incident with the security guard—surely not enough time for the police to arrive in these sorts of numbers.

The officers bustled past and took up position at the entrance.

'No one is allowed inside!' one of them bellowed.

'Everybody move back!' yelled another.

The growing crowd was forced away and Wilson was herded down the steps with the throng. Two more squad cars appeared at either end of the street as all local traffic was diverted away from the building. Sentries, carrying rifles, were now posted at each corner. The operation appeared well organised.

An unmarked sedan with tinted windows stopped next to the curb and a policeman uniformed in black hurried to open the rear door. Seconds later, a giant of a man with red hair climbed out. He was enormous, easily dwarfing the officer beside him. Everyone in the crowd, police included, appeared to be distracted by his presence. Sensing the opportunity to slip away, Wilson dashed across the street into a narrow alleyway.

His expression stern, Commander Visblat stared towards the rooftop. He was the most senior law enforcement officer in the city.

Almost two metres tall, he was an imposing figure in a loose-fitting black suit. Aged in his mid-forties, he had a full head of distinctive wavy red hair and an overbite that magnified his strong jaw. His skin was pale and he was a little dark around the eyes from habitual lack of sleep.

Visblat carefully studied the building. *So it happens here*, he thought to himself. Scanning his surroundings he momentarily caught a glimpse of Wilson's shadow stencilled on a wall across the street. One second it was there; the next, it was gone.

A voice suddenly interrupted his concentration, 'This way, Commander.'

Visblat stared down at the man next to him.

Officer Benson pointed in the other direction. 'The entrance is this way, sir.'

'Have SWAT gone to the roof?' Visblat said in a gruff voice.

'Not yet, Commander. They're on their way. We were the first to arrive. Apparently, it was an explosion of some kind. I've requested the bomb squad attend.'

The last thing Visblat needed was the bomb squad, but it was of no consequence. His quarry was close—he could feel it. 'No one is to leave here until I've seen them, do you understand?' He gestured imperiously across the street. 'Get that alleyway checked out. I think I saw something over there.'

'Yes, Commander.' Officer Benson immediately directed one of the sentries to investigate.

Visblat stared at the crowd. 'Quarantine the entire area. I don't care how much they complain. No one is to leave here.'

'Yes, Commander.'

'I want to see the trooper who was assigned to watch the rooftop.'

Officer Benson leant closer. 'I've given orders to keep Officer McGuire isolated, as you requested.'

'I want to see him, *alone*,' Visblat said under his breath. 'Not a word to anyone about this. Do you understand?'

'Yes, Commander.'

Visblat waited at the top of the stairs as a group of uniformed men dutifully surrounded him, three deep. He was giving orders left and right: '... Get that crowd further away. *You*, check the loading bay.' Armed men set off periodically to complete their tasks. 'I want a one-mile checkpoint perimeter from these doors.' Visblat waved his arm in a giant circle.

An officer raised his hand and spoke, 'Commander, there are dozens of streets and laneways. We don't have the manpower to cover everything.'

Visblat gave him a burning gaze. 'Just do the best you can.'

The sight of Visblat's eyes somehow made the officer's skin crawl.

'Yes, Commander,' he said compliantly.

Visblat stood tall. 'Men, this is the moment we have been waiting for. Find the fugitive and bring him to me. *Move it!*' The remaining officers scurried in different directions. Visblat looked once more towards the alleyway, pondered what he thought he had seen, then entered the office building.

WILSON'S PACE SLOWED. He needed more time to think. The failure of his contact lenses, his *special* contact lenses, would have cost him his life if not for his Overload command. How could Barton have made such a critical error? And the police, why were there so many? Could they possibly be looking for *him*?

At the end of the laneway, a steady stream of cars rumbled past towards the city.

The security guard's furious expression flashed into Wilson's mind once more. Wilson had never been in a fight before, let alone suffocated someone into unconsciousness. The Schumann Frequency was seriously out of balance here—the security guard's reaction was testament to that. Wilson felt sick in the stomach; the thought of being set upon again was playing on his mind.

The sound of running footsteps unexpectedly filled the laneway. Wilson's worst fears were realised as he turned to see a policeman approaching at full pace, gun drawn. It took a moment for Wilson to react—he just couldn't process what was happening.

'Police! Stop right there!' the officer yelled. 'Stop!'

Stunned into action, Wilson sprinted for the corner. If his sunglasses were removed, which would surely happen, he was in even more trouble. The traffic was moving quickly and he ran the full length of the street waiting for the opportunity to cross without slowing. The Overload command had stripped much of his energy and he was going as fast as he could. Seeing an opening, he threaded through the traffic, dodging a car that came within a fraction of ending his escape.

But even so, the officer's footsteps drew closer.

A shop doorway was open and Wilson ducked inside. The smell of fresh doughnuts filled the air. People reeled as he dashed past them. He ran to the back of the store, jumped the serving counter and bolted out the back door. A wooden fence. Wilson launched himself over. A steep embankment. He hurled himself down. Another tall fence, chicken-wire. He scaled it, landing heavily on the other side. A bustling freeway lay before him like a river of moving steel that defied being crossed. Vehicles were sweeping by in both directions, four lanes each side, moving at insane speeds.

The policeman made it to the fence. He was puffing. 'Stop … right there! I mean it!' he yelled as he awkwardly poked his gun through the wire.

'Why … are you … chasing me?' Wilson spluttered, raising his hands in the air.

The officer coughed, trying to catch his breath also. 'Get down … on your stomach! Hands … behind your head!'

Wilson was aware of the incessant drone and whoosh of traffic hurtling behind him.

'I said—lie down!' the officer yelled again.

With only one hope of escape, Wilson turned and ran along the freeway apron. There was suddenly a gap in the traffic. Taking the opportunity, he sprinted across the smooth pavement. Horns blared. Tyres squealed. A fender almost collected him. Someone screamed a curse from an open window flashing past.

The police officer scaled the fence and landed on his feet.

Wilson made it to the relative safety of the guard rail in the middle of the road.

A torrent of vehicles continued in either direction.

'Stop, or I'll shoot!' the policeman yelled, at the same time taking aim through the traffic.

Wilson jumped the waist-high rail to the other side. One lane at a time, he told himself. The city-bound traffic was more heavily congested—seemingly moving even faster. A car streaked by only centimetres away. The mere rush of air nearly knocked Wilson from his feet. Car horns blared. He shuffled forward. Vehicles swerved by on either side.

The officer sprinted forward, making it to the guard rail.

Wilson took yet another step. The sound of screeching tyres suddenly dominated his senses. There was nowhere to go! A side mirror clipped his lower back, catapulting him into the air. Strangely, the impact was painless. With a crunch of steel on bone, the police officer was simultaneously struck down just behind him.

Glass shattered. Metal splintered.

Wilson found himself face-down on the pavement, out-of-control vehicles bearing down upon him. A series of images flashed through his mind: the magnificent Rembrandt in the Enterprise Corporation boardroom—a painting of a sleeping baby, so peaceful in her crib, being watched over by her mother. Faces of friends: Professor Author, Jenny Jones, his grandfather. Another image: the ominous Dead Sea scrolls, each and every parchment so impressively spread out in custom-made glass cabinets. Then another: the view from Mount Whitney—a series of mountain ranges of ineffable beauty. White puffy clouds swept past, high above. Barton Ingerson was there, looking like a god. He was wearing his mercury team labcoat, telling Wilson how important his mission was.

'There is no room for complacency,' Barton said. 'If you fail—*this* reality will be gone forever. A parallel universe will take its place.'

At the point of impact, Wilson's mind went blank.

And with him went all hope for the future.

2

Houston, Texas
Memorial Apartments, Level 16
November 25th 2012
Local Time 7:11 a.m.

Mission of Isaiah—Day One

WARM SUNLIGHT FLOODED in through the tall bay windows.

Helena lay on top of the bedcovers, her flannel pyjamas twisted awkwardly around her legs from another restless night's sleep. Lifting a glass of water from the side table, she threw a red pill into her mouth and gulped it down. *I hate pills*, she thought. Her night-time medication made her groggy—this tablet was to help wake her up again.

Tucking her fringe behind her right ear, Helena remembered the unusual dreams she had endured through the night. Grabbing a pillow for comfort she hugged it to her body like a favourite doll. The images were so bizarre, yet so real.

A telephone began to ring. The number on the call display was all too familiar and Helena composed herself before picking it up. She tried her best to sound alert.

'Good morning, Dad.'

'How are you, my dear?'

'Really good.' The truth was quite the opposite. 'How are you?'

'Fine, fine.' Lawrence always said that.

'Is everything okay?' she asked.

'Yes, yes. Can't complain. I just called to find out how you were doing.'

'I'm fine,' she said curtly. Helena wanted desperately to tell him what she was going through, but she knew it would only make things worse.

'Are you coming in to the office today?' he asked.

Helena hadn't been there in more than a week and her voice was uncertain, 'Yeah, I guess so.'

'Great!' He sounded pleasantly surprised. 'We can finalise the plans for the Recida Village project. Friday is the deadline. You realise that, don't you?'

'Is that why you called ... to tell me to come to work? That's just *terrific*!'

Lawrence's tone hardened also. 'Helena ... *relax*.' There was a long silence. 'I'd appreciate it if you wouldn't react like that. That's not why I called.'

'Then, why *did* you call?'

There was another long silence. Her father's voice was gentle again as if he'd coached himself into restraint. 'Well ... to ask how your therapy sessions with Dr Bennetswood are going.' His tone was unusually tentative.

The question caused Helena's irritation to bubble, but this time she kept it inside. Eventually she said, 'I feel much better. Really, I do.' It was an unconvincing reply and she knew it.

'When do you see Dr Bennetswood again?'

'Friday, I think.'

'Are you sleeping?'

'Not much.' There was another lengthy silence.

'Do you think the sessions are helping?'

'What is this, Dad, some kind of inquisition?'

His reply was firm. 'Why are you always so evasive?'

'You've never been interested in my therapy before.' Helena quickly checked herself. 'I'm not being evasive.' Getting angry with her father was not the answer. 'Look, I have to go. I'll see you in the office soon.' Without waiting for a response, she hung up. That was the easiest way to deal with the situation.

Helena spent the next few minutes going over their conversation word by word. She was annoyed that her father would call to discuss business and, when she got upset about it, immediately start asking about her treatments. He thinks I'm being silly, she concluded. He has no idea what I am going through. No one wants to help me. She amended the thought: no one *can* help me.

Helena tossed her pillow away and jumped out of bed.

She felt alone.

The view from the sixteenth-floor windows of her high-rise apartment was superb—the expansive green lawn of Emerald Park, dotted with trees, and black tarmac bicycle tracks lacing their way through. The morning sun was low in the sky, casting long shadows towards the west. In the distance, a cluster of skyscrapers marked the central business district of Houston.

Helena stopped at the window and gazed outside. She wanted answers—that was all—answers to why she was having these persistent and unexplainable dreams.

Unbeknown to her, the cause of her bizarre hallucinations was running for his life just a few kilometres away—Wilson Dowling had time-travelled into Helena's world. And, as a consequence, things were about to become even crazier.

Suspending her gaze, Helena climbed the steps to her bathroom. She unbuttoned her pyjamas and let them fall to the ground. Helena Rainsford Capriarty looked at herself in the mirror. Rainsford was her mother's maiden name and Helena evoked it with pride whenever the opportunity arose. Her hair was blonde, quite light in colour, cut shoulder length—like her mother's used to be—and her symmetrical smile, if she ever had the unlikely cause for merriment, displayed perfect white teeth. She cast a critical eye over her naked skin, searching for imperfections. But there were few to be found. Years of swimming and running had toned her 29-year-old body to a peak level. Yet her fitness was genetic as much as anything else; she ate whatever she liked, junk food included. She turned and studied her backside: a few more hours a week on the treadmill were what was required, she decided.

The air was scented with the perfume of fresh flowers as she reached into the glass cubicle and turned on the water. It gushed, instantly hot, from the shower rose, fogging up the cubicle even before she immersed herself in the spray. Helena didn't like to admit she had problems—*ever*. So she manufactured a way of thinking that suited her. They weren't problems; they were questions, she decided. In the same way, she saw herself as determined, rather than stubborn. Strong-willed, instead of short-tempered. Colourful, rather than crazy.

Steaming water pounded her shoulders as she considered her situation once more. The constant dreams made it impossible to relax. At times her visions were terrifying. For weeks she hadn't slept more than three hours at a stretch. She turned the water temperature up a notch so that it was almost scalding her skin. Not sleeping made her irritable and everyone close to her was affected. Her relationship with Jensen was on the rocks—and, as a result, her sex life had wound down to non-existent.

Helena appeared from the bathroom minutes later wearing a black flannel dressing gown, her hair neatly combed back. Dr Bennetswood's theory was that her hallucinations were caused by post-traumatic stress. Removing herself emotionally from the situation, Helena understood that it was a logical conclusion for him to make, but she knew that wasn't the problem. She was sure of it. It was a conscious choice to block out the incident with her mother. Helena was in control of her own life—that was her belief—and she resented anyone who suggested otherwise.

A tray of food was now sitting on the bedside table—muesli, fresh fruit, wholemeal toast. It was there every morning just after 7 a.m.

Helena whispered to herself, 'Maybe I am going crazy.'

'You are no crazy,' a woman's voice unexpectedly replied.

Helena spun round in shock.

'I no mean to alarm you, Bambina.' Julia Jimenez's accent was a rhythmic Spanish, her attitude habitually buoyant. 'But—you *are* one person short of a conversation. That is why I am here now, to save the day.' Julia was a homely-looking woman, short and hefty. In her late fifties, she had long dark hair, streaked with grey, tied in a neat bun. She wore a black maid's uniform with a plain white apron.

Julia had worked for the Capriartys for more than twenty years. 'I look after you when you were just a baby,' she would always say. 'You had chubby little cheeks.' When Helena moved out of the family home, Lawrence decided Julia would accompany his daughter. That was more than three years ago now. Julia had no children of her own and treated Helena as if she were family. Helena felt much the same way, but Julia could often get on her nerves and at times the atmosphere was edgy. They knew each other too well to stand on ceremony. And, like family, when they disagreed, things occasionally became heated.

Helena reacted abruptly, 'Why do you do that all the time?' she yelled. It was unnerving when Julia appeared without warning. Helena immediately thought better of her outburst. 'I'm sorry ...

please forgive me for shouting,' and she pressed her hands to her face in embarrassment.

'No apologise to me!' Julia replied sternly. 'No!' she shook her head.

'I didn't mean to snap at you.'

Julia pulled Helena close. 'Is no your fault. What is happening is no your fault.' Helena was as rigid as a post; she didn't like being touched. There was an uncomfortable silence, as always, until Julia released her grip and pointed to the tray of food. 'You must eat, *si?*'

Helena straightened her gown. 'I'm going to work today.'

'You go to work today?' Julia seemed surprised.

Helena nodded. 'That's what I'm doing.'

'You must *relax*. *Sleep*. Watch some television.'

'No sleep. I'm going to work today.' Helena walked quickly to her dressing room. She was forcing herself to think of the Recida Village project. Her father was right—she was way behind. That was okay; Helena liked being under pressure—it deprived her of the curse of thinking too much.

She studied her own face in the mirror. *I look tired*, she decided. 'But I'll be okay,' she whispered. 'Make-up fixes everything.' She refocused her steely gaze. *I can do this.*

Helena gathered her clothes, walked down the stairs and threw them on the bed. As she pulled on a shirt and did up the buttons, she glanced at the clock. It read 7:27 a.m. If the traffic was okay, she could be in the office by 8:15.

Unexpectedly, Helena began to feel disoriented.

It was just a dizzy feeling at first, but gradually her legs went to water and she found herself falling to her knees, her hands pressing into the carpet just to steady herself. A red haze had overcome her senses, and then vivid hallucinations appeared. A thoroughly frightening revelation. She tried to fight the images, but the more she resisted the clearer they became.

In her visions, through a red haze, Helena was fleeing—trying to escape. Panicking, she opened her eyes to gaze at her bedroom. It was hard to focus. The pictures in her mind overlapped what she saw around her. *How can this be happening?* she thought.

A policeman was chasing after her! Helena was running for her life.

How could this be possible?

'Help me!' she screamed. Helena pressed her hands to her face trying to erase the images plaguing her. 'Help me!'

Julia heard the cries of distress and ran back into the bedroom.

The policeman was gaining, his gun drawn! In response, Helena was hyperventilating. 'I'm seeing things,' she whimpered, sensing Julia's presence beside her. 'Jay Jay, I'm seeing things. Oh my God!' In her visions Helena climbed a tall wire fence and fell heavily on the other side.

Julia held on tight. 'Breathe, Bambina. Breathe.' She rocked Helena's quivering body backwards and forwards. 'You are safe with me, Bambina, just breathe.' She repeated the mantra over and over in a steady, soothing voice.

The words echoed in Helena's ears, calming her.

She was making her way across a busy road—a freeway. Traffic sped by on both sides, missing her by inches. She stumbled and fell! Helena cried out in fear. At that moment she realised she was seeing images through someone else's eyes, a man's eyes; she saw his legs and feet. He wiped his face; blood covered his hand.

Vehicles suddenly spun out of control towards him.

Death was certain.

As abruptly as the visions began, the red haze was gone and so too were the images.

Helena tentatively opened her eyes.

'He's dead,' she whispered. As if she understood everything.

'Who?'

'The man.'

'What man?'

'The man I saw in my dream.'

Julia dragged Helena's limp body onto the bed and pulled the covers over her, as if trying to protect her with the soft cotton sheets.

Julia's voice was strong and assured, masking her worry. 'You are safe now, Bambina.' She straightened the blankets and tucked them in tight. 'It is only a silly dream. *Si*. We no mention it again.'

Helena stared at the ceiling. Up to this point, her dreams had been confined to her sleep, but now they had invaded her waking mind. Strangely, she felt quite calm. There was something tangible about what she had seen. And if it was tangible, she could deal with it.

Julia opened an orange glass bottle and emptied two white capsules into the palm of her hand. 'Take them. They make you sleep.'

Helena turned away. 'No, I don't want pills.'

Julia was firm. '*Si!* You must.'

'No, Jay Jay, I don't want any!' Helena needed time to think. She recognised the place where the car accident had happened. She was sure of it. Was it possible that everything she had witnessed was real? Was it a telepathic link she was having? Was she psychic?

Julia held out the telephone receiver. 'Then I call the Doctor Bennetswood!'

Helena focused on Julia's resolute expression; her housekeeper meant business. 'I'll take the pills,' Helena said, grabbing them, and she threw them into her mouth.

Julia replaced the receiver. 'I no call, *but I should*! You rest, *si?*'

Helena took a big gulp of water. '*Si.*'

'Good.'

When Julia turned away, Helena spat the tablets under her pillow. *No pills*. Right now she needed all her wits about her. There was something in her visions she was supposed to figure out; she just knew it.

With a flick of a switch, motorised curtains gradually shifted across the windows, carving away the bright morning sunlight. The room became darker by the second, almost pitch black. Julia pulled a chair to the side of the bed in the murky light, sat down, and gently stroked Helena's forehead. She used to do that when Helena was a little girl.

At the same time, Helena was pondering the image of the freeway. She knew where the accident happened; she was sure of it—near the Westheimer Overpass. Helena took a deep breath and closed her eyes. In many ways she felt relaxed for the first time in weeks.

3

Houston, Texas
Memorial Apartments, Level 16
November 25th 2012
Local Time 5:52 p.m.

Mission of Isaiah—Day One

HELENA OPENED HER eyes and scanned the spacious bedroom, then the clock on her side table. She had been asleep for more than nine hours. *Nine hours.* That was the first time she had slept without medication in a month. Julia was asleep in the chair beside her. Judging by her appearance, she had been there for some time. Carefully planting both feet on the carpet, Helena took a moment to get her balance, then entered her wardrobe and selected her clothes. She pulled on a pair of faded blue jeans and a black polo neck, then sat again on the edge of the bed to put on her shoes.

Julia stirred. Her voice was groggy, 'You are awake?'

'I can't believe I slept that long,' Helena replied.

'Good medication, *si?*'

The comment triggered a rare smile. '*Si*, Julia. Good medication.'

Lifting her solid frame from her resting place, Julia attempted to brush the creases out of her black dress. 'Your father, he call. I tell him you are sleeping.' She made for the door. 'Come, I make you some dinner.' At the press of a button, the curtains slowly motored open. The late afternoon sun was low and had swung to the west.

'I have something important to do,' Helena replied.

Julia stopped in her tracks, her expression unhappy. 'I no want you leaving. *No!*'

Helena strutted past, tucking her fringe behind her right ear at the same time. 'I'm just going for a drive ... to clear my head.' She grabbed a black leather jacket from the wardrobe and slid it on. 'I won't be long.'

Julia waved a finger, disapprovingly. 'No, no, no—we cook dinner together.' She pointed in the direction of the kitchen.

Helena unlocked the wall cabinet and the smell of gun oil wafted out. The drawers had been specially built: there were at least twenty handguns of different makes and models inside. Each one was handle-up, with the required ammunition and cleaning kit in a drawer underneath. Helena made her selection: a black Colt pistol, one of a pair. She inserted the magazine into the rubber-gripped butt and it locked into place with a decisive click.

Julia was getting frustrated. 'I no let you go—'

'Half an hour, that's all. You can start making dinner if you want.' She picked up her car keys from the side table.

Julia attempted to block the doorway. 'You stay! You promise you would!'

Pointing her gun at the floor, Helena looked down the sight. 'I never promised I'd stay in bed *forever*.' She tucked the weapon into her jacket. 'It'll be all right, Julia.'

'What if you are dreaming again? While you drive your car, maybe?'

Helena eased Julia aside. 'I won't be long. I promise.'

Julia stood alone in the bedroom. 'I am old woman!' she called out. '*Si!* You will give me a heart attack!'

There was no response.

Julia picked up the telephone and dialled a number. 'Mr Capriarty, please,' she said. '*Si*, it is Julia. I speak with him urgently. *Si*, urgent. It has to do with Helena.'

TURNING THE IGNITION key, Helena brought the Mercedes to life with its familiar throaty roar. She watched the red needle bounce up and down on the rev meter as she pressed on the accelerator. As always, she slid the barrel of her gun under her left thigh. The pistol was easy to reach and she could feel it against her body at all times.

The clock read 6:14 p.m., but it was a few minutes fast.

Helena was still trying to decide whether or not to leave the parking lot. It would be dark in less than twenty minutes. But if she didn't go, she would be wondering all night long if her visions were real.

The wheels of the black SL55 squealed as it darted up the ramp towards the guardhouse. An Asian-looking man in uniform waved from behind his bullet-proof window as it sped past at a dangerous speed. Helena didn't return the gesture. Her Mercedes jarred onto the main road and accelerated towards the city. All around, the clear evening sky was turning a pale shade of crimson.

Helena was remembering what she had seen in her visions. Deep down she knew they had to be real. They just had to be. A steady stream of vehicles poured out of the city, their blazing headlights forming a vivid chain of light. Houston wasn't a safe place after dark—a fact Helena was all too aware of. Drug dealers, gangs, angry homeless people, that sort of thing. The thought of it made her drive even faster.

In the distance, across the urban sprawl, the sun seemed to blaze as brightly as ever, before disappearing behind a thin band of stratus clouds near the horizon. *It's so beautiful*, Helena thought. Seeing the beauty in things was something she had not felt for a long time. Today, everything was different somehow. Yet she was unsure why.

As her destination approached, her heart beat more quickly. Only two more corners, then a straight run to the crest of the bridge, along which she accelerated to maximum speed. She hit the brakes hard and skidded to a stop. There was not a moment to lose.

Leaving the engine running, Helena gripped the handle of her gun, flung the door open and cautiously took the seven or eight steps towards the railing. She flicked the safety off. Looking over the edge, she peered down at the multi-lane freeway below her.

The surface of the road was covered with the scars of a tremendous car accident. Skid marks laced the concrete like strands of burnt spaghetti. A constellation of glass fragments sparkled against the glow of the traffic going the other way. It somehow proved to Helena that she was not going mad. If this was the place, she could be certain of one thing: the man she had seen—the man from her visions—was dead. No one could possibly have survived an accident like that. With that revelation, a mixture of fear and relief overcame her.

Why did I see this? she wondered. *Why now?* There were so many questions.

The sun vanished below the horizon and the streets darkened quickly, a copper hue taking possession of the sky. In response, only the brightest stars appeared. Behind Helena, the headlights of the black Mercedes continued to burn faithfully into the gloom. Her mobile phone started to ring, but she was oblivious to the sound.

Every now and then a car rumbled past, but no one dared to stop. Helena was standing in plain view, tapping the barrel of her gun against the waist-high steel railing, the metallic sound clanking into the night.

Staring towards the lights of the city centre, Helena was thinking: *What am I supposed to do next?* That single question had her unable to leave.

4

California, The Americas
Enterprise Corporation, Mercury Building, Level 2
May 9th 2081
Local Time 4:52 p.m.

14 Days before Transport Test

A THREE-DIMENSIONAL hologram of a human DNA strand hovered in mid-air. The complex image was made up of thousands of colourful spheres—red, blue, yellow, green—connected together with tiny white battens. The entwined mass formed a swirling, twisting fabric of information that told Barton he had a serious problem on his hands.

There has to be another way, he thought.

Barton Ingerson sat below the hologram wearing a neon-white labcoat. Made of pressed Egyptian cotton, the slim-fitting garment was angular and modern, with a high military-like collar. Every member of the mercury team wore one. On each of Barton's lapels was a small black square with a white star in the centre, designating that he was the leader. Feverishly typing away on his computer, Barton modified the hologram, then shuffled the digital papers on his desk in an effort to make sense of the puzzle that confronted him.

In his early fifties, Barton had been a scientist at Enterprise Corporation, the world's largest company, for more than forty years. A child prodigy, he had been enrolled in the Enterprise Corporation advanced learning program when he was only eight years old. Some of the inductees were as young as six; but, on reflection, Barton was one of the few successes of that program. Some said the unseasoned mind could not handle too much knowledge, others said it was the expectation of high achievement; but either way the failure rates were always high. The early induction program had since been modified and intakes were restricted to children twelve years and older.

Barton attributed much of his professional longevity to his passion for fishing. He always said that it relaxed his nerves so that he could concentrate on what was important, and thus he travelled the world to its most remote corners in search of crystal-clear streams and his favourite fighting fish—the magnificent rainbow trout.

Barton's build was slim, as is often the case with a thinking man. He was handsome too, with clear, hazel eyes. Ask anybody who knew him and they would agree. They'd also add that he was calm, extremely calm. That was imperative in his profession, because Barton was the leader of the famous group of scientists known as the 'mercury team'. Over the years their discoveries had changed the world, it was said, but to the billions of people whose lives they had enhanced they were an anonymous group. Barton was Enterprise Corporation's number-one scientist, assigned to solve problems of the most complex and unusual nature. His position was one of power and prestige. But success never comes without a price, and he wore the marks of his dedication in his brittle white hair and the deep wrinkles on his tanned face.

As he looked up from his desk, Barton scanned his surroundings. One wall of his enormous office was floor-to-ceiling glass, affording views of lush green forests as far as the eye could see. At the other end of the room were six blue couches arranged in a generous circle—Barton's discussion area. To the right was a hexagonal boardroom table with twelve chairs, one for each member of the mercury team. Indoor plants lined the walls. The floors were polished black granite. The environment was always quiet, except for the soft hush of waves gently lapping a tropical beach: white noise that helped Barton think.

Barton took a moment to clear his thoughts, then looked once more at the colourful DNA strand. There had to be an answer. Moving the digital pages around on his desk yet again, he hoped that he could soon make progress.

Silently, the glass door to the office swung open and two dapper men, wearing identical pinstripe suits, entered the room. The distinguished older man with the ivory walking stick was Godfrey Martin Tredwell, the chairman and major shareholder of Enterprise

Corporation. To everyone other than his wife, Godfrey Martin was known as 'GM'. Some called him 'God', but never to his face, fearing he might not appreciate the irony. It had been said that he was so revered that his mere approach sent junior staff into a panic. Easily more than one hundred years of age, he had been in charge longer than anyone could remember, and those years had been prosperous ones for the company. It was he who had masterminded the purchase or demise of nearly all of Enterprise Corporation's competitors—'predatory acquisitions' were his specialty. As a result, GM was now one of the richest men in the world—a business figure beyond influence or corruption.

The old man was a maverick turned statesman—that was how he had transformed Enterprise Corporation into what it was today. He had it all: excellent logic, exceptional instincts, impeccable political skill. There was once a time when he would bend the rules if it suited him, but those days, and the need for them, were gone. The only thing *not* in his favour, or under his control, was his advanced age. And all the money in the world—which afforded him a blood transfusion every single day, to improve his quality of life—could no longer stop him from getting older. He was a truly successful leader in the twilight of his long career.

GM and Barton had known each other for more than four decades. Barton liked his chairman, always had. They were friends—as much as that was possible with one of the most powerful men in the world.

The man tagging behind GM was his grandson, Jasper Tredwell—the president and heir apparent to the throne of Enterprise Corporation. While the pair were more than fifty years apart in age, the family resemblance was striking; in dim lighting they could easily be mistaken for each other. Jasper was GM's eldest daughter's eldest son. He was a few centimetres taller than his grandfather, with the elongated Tredwell torso. The facial features, especially the nose, were sharp, the eyebrows dark and bushy. His hair, brown and cropped in the same short style, was a little thicker on top.

In spite of their similar appearance, the pair were quite different in temperament. Jasper was not a 'people person' and he had a habit of using threats to get what he wanted. Barton often theorised that working with GM on a day-to-day basis drove Jasper to seek some sort of edge, however undesirable. It had been said that there was no darker place on earth than in GM's shadow. As a result, Jasper used his considerable power unhesitatingly, and if his ambitions were thwarted, he would fly off the handle. It was safe to say that Barton's relationship with Enterprise Corporation's second in charge was icy at best.

But Jasper was not without his strengths, Barton willingly admitted. He had the discipline of an army officer and a keen eye for profit, and he showed caution where his grandfather generally had little or none. They were a good team in so many ways. Good guy, bad guy. Optimist, pessimist. Philanthropist, auditor. Together the Tredwells—the old master and the domineering protégé—were a world-class alliance under any circumstance.

When Barton finally realised the Tredwells were standing in his office he immediately terminated the laser image floating above him. The sound of lapping waves also dissipated to silence. Barton kept his wits about him and his voice calm.

'I wasn't expecting to see you today, GM. To what do I owe this impromptu visit?' Barton stood from his seat and dutifully directed the Tredwells to the pair of visitors' chairs facing him. GM tapped Barton aside with his cane and eased past.

'I'm here about your mercury project,' he said, making his way to the far side of the desk and taking Barton's seat. Barton wasn't surprised. GM stamped his authority on everything. What *was* concerning him was Jasper, who was carefully inspecting the stack of confidential documents strewn across the table.

GM picked up a digital marker and suspended it between his frail fingers. He was straight to the point, his voice silky smooth, elocution perfect, as always. 'Jasper believes the time has come for us to terminate mercury project 81-07. It is regrettable.'

Barton stayed calm.

'I think he's right,' GM continued. 'Yes. I think we need to re-deploy the mercury team to an obstacle we've encountered at Plutonium Plant 27.' He shifted his gaze to the marker. 'We need to get more electrical power. It's overloaded. And I'll be damned if I'm going to rebuild it. That will be project 81-08.'

'Can't you send someone else?' Barton replied, his lips pasted with a smile of disguise.

'I need the best.'

'There are other teams better equipped than the mercury team to deal with a power problem. And anyway, I have a few things on the go at the moment.'

'I'm not comfortable with project 81-07 any more,' GM said earnestly.

Barton was prepared for just this eventuality—he had been from the very beginning. It was only ever a matter of time before the Tredwells reacted this way. 'Why would you want to close the mercury project down,' Barton offered, 'when *you know* it represents something of unparalleled importance?'

GM sat back.

'The concept of *time travel*,' Barton continued, 'is—well, it's something that warrants more research. You know that. Think of the things we could learn if we—'

GM raised his slender hand and Barton immediately stopped talking. The pair locked eyes.

'It's too dangerous,' GM said.

Barton's gaze didn't waver. 'It's in the Dead Sea scrolls for a reason.'

The old man's grip tightened around the marker. 'Two years.'

'Important research takes time.'

'You've spent billions.'

Barton rolled his eyes. 'This can't be about the money, so why the sudden change of heart?'

There was a pause. GM eventually replied, 'You're creating a mechanism to *travel time*, Barton. The way I see it, that puts *me* in jeopardy. And in doing so, it puts Enterprise Corporation in the same position.'

Barton gave a subtle smile. 'You've never been one to be afraid.'

The old man feigned offence. 'So you think I'm being stupid?'

'I would never think that.'

Jasper spoke for the first time, his tone direct. 'There's a reason why Enterprise Corporation is the largest business on the planet,' he said. 'It's because we always manage our downside. This experiment has a poor risk profile.'

'I agree with Jasper,' GM added. 'There's nothing in it for Enterprise Corporation, besides colossal exposure.'

'I'm just a scientist,' Barton said meekly. 'The company's risk profile is for you and Jasper to work out. And I know you already have.'

The old man smiled in response; he was expecting a more vigorous argument.

Barton rubbed his chin. 'And you're right to be concerned, GM. I am too. But one day you'll need this time-machine, for some reason.

Its presence in the Dead Sea scrolls has a purpose—a godly purpose, I expect.' He shrugged his shoulders. 'I'm just building it for you.'

The discussion waxed and waned for the next ten minutes. Every time GM tried to corner Barton into a confrontation, Barton skilfully eased himself out of trouble. And all the while he was being gradually more forceful.

'The best time to plant a tree is twenty years ago,' Barton said. 'The next best time is *now*. There's no point deferring the test. It only means we'll have to come back to it later.'

GM was impressed by Barton's composure. Avoiding an argument with the chairman, when he wanted one, was a difficult thing to do.

'We have destiny on our side,' Barton said confidently. 'We could build a hundred time machines and in my opinion that would not change anything. All time exists simultaneously. It is not like a length of string ... that can be cut. It's a multi-dimensional ball that is affected just as much by the future as by the past.'

'You know I hate philosophical discussions,' GM replied.

Barton ran both hands through his thick, white hair. 'Everything regarding this project is philosophical.'

'That's why I hate *every* discussion we have about this. It's esoteric garbage! Just tell me how much money I can make out of it. That's how I operate.'

Barton was again at his most serious. 'We're not in this to make money, GM. Look—I'm very close to conducting a transport test. I'm close. And you already have an investment in this project, other than money, that is impossible to question.'

'What investment is that?'

Don't come on too strong, Barton told himself, the Tredwells will sense desperation. He cleared his throat, then said, 'Knowing that you were the one that made it happen.'

'Oh my goodness!' GM exhaled, a look of surprise on his face.

Barton raised a finger. 'I'm serious! Together we'd be solving one of the great mysteries of humankind. Imagine that. We'd be unquestionably proving that Einstein's theory of relativity is flawed. That it's missing a dimension. We'd be proving that time travel *is* possible.'

'Better salespeople than you have attempted to play to my ego,' GM said, unwavering. 'I should be offended by your clumsy approach.'

Barton interlocked his fingers, realising he had gone too far. 'Stop playing games, GM,' he said, trying another tack. 'I've spent two years on this. You *must* let me see it through. I've come too far.' He stared out the window, the look of a scorned child in his eyes. 'Much too far.'

The silence grew.

Jasper eventually leant over and whispered in GM's ear, summarising options, until they both nodded in agreement. 'All right, we'll give you two weeks,' the old man said.

The suggested timeframe brought Barton out in a cold sweat. 'Two weeks is not enough.'

GM shook his head. 'It's two weeks or nothing. You said you were close. Now make your choice.'

Barton's heart was thumping as if he'd just run up ten flights of stairs without stopping. His legs felt numb, his stomach hollow. There were so many secrets, and so much pressure. He knew, if he agreed to terms that were simply unworkable, that the ramifications were endless. 'If you are worried about the risks,' Barton said, 'then why rush me? That's a foolish decision to make.'

'We want this to be over,' GM replied. 'Make your choice,' he said coldly. Both Tredwells appeared to be in complete agreement about their course of action.

Barton asked himself a question: was it possible to launch the Mission of Isaiah in just fourteen days? He considered as many variables as he could in the short time there was available. In the end he had no choice but to go with his gut. He replied, 'If that's what you want … then you win.' The reality was, GM could shut the project down immediately and Barton couldn't risk that. And the more he fought, the more likely that would be.

'No extensions,' Jasper reiterated, as if that was not already obvious.

Barton maintained a façade of calm detachment. 'I'll conduct a transport test, document my work, then close it down.' There was a positive to all this, Barton realised; rushing things would at least make it easier to break the rules.

'I'm glad to see you will co-operate,' GM said.

'But I must have total authority,' Barton insisted. 'You guarantee me that and I'll shut it all down on time.'

GM seemed puzzled by the comment. 'You'll have the same authority you've always had, which is just about everything anyway.' He pressed his cane to the floor and slowly lifted himself from his chair. 'And when your time is up,' he pointed with the marker, 'we pull the plug, finished or not.' As he approached Barton, a smile unwound on the old man's face, deep wrinkles creasing his skin. He gently placed the digital marker in Barton's hand. 'I trust you, my friend. Make sure the project is finished by the deadline. Now, get back to work.' As usual, GM had made the ground rules absolutely clear. Pointing his index finger in the air, he said finally, 'Remember, Barton, two weeks,' then hobbled out the door with Jasper close behind.

The large office was cloaked in silence.

Barton remained where he stood. Fourteen days was all he had. It would take an incredible effort to complete the Mission of Isaiah in that time. A miracle, in fact. But he was renowned as a miracle worker. And the upside was clear: soon, all the secrets and the lying would be over.

Pressing the intercom on his lapel, Barton talked into the small microphone, 'Karin, assemble the mercury team right away. Bring everyone back from leave.' He released his finger, then thought a moment. He pressed the talk button a second time. 'Contact Andre Steinbeck and get him here also. I'm going to appoint him to the team. Phone his mother. Make a big deal out of it. She's going to need to sign some papers to make it official.'

'No problem,' a crisp female voice replied. 'By the way … what did the Tredwells want?' Karin never missed a trick, and Barton expected nothing less.

5

California, The Americas
Enterprise Corporation, Mercury Building, Level 2
May 9th 2081
Local Time 5:30 p.m.

14 Days before Transport Test

THE SOUND OF DISTANT waves was again gently pulsing in the background.

Barton looked at the digital papers sprawled across his desk. There wasn't time to address all the issues any more. Reaching out, he pushed the loose pages into one of the empty drawers and closed his eyes again. *Focus.*

An attractive brunette wearing a white mercury labcoat confidently entered the room. Her posture was perfect. 'Everyone is on their way,' she said purposefully. 'Now tell me, what did the Tredwells want? I hate secrets, you know that.'

Karin Turnberry was a tactician on the mercury team. She was in her mid-thirties, a tall 177 centimetres, voluptuous. Her cunning eyes observed everything and she had the ability to listen to three conversations at the same time if it was in her interests. Originally, she had come to Enterprise Corporation from their major competitor, General Electric, where she worked in the research department. Divorced at twenty-eight, she applied for a job as secretary to Barton Ingerson. Since then, with Barton's help, she had advanced all the way up the corporate ladder to be on the mercury team herself. An astonishing achievement for a girl with only a high-school education.

'They never visit the mercury building without a good reason,' she said. Not getting an immediate reply, she continued, 'Do you want Data-Tran activated?' Barton nodded and she walked to the far end of the room, placed the receiver on her lap and typed the activation command.

Data-Tran was a worldwide network of mainframe super-computers matrixed together to create a total knowledge database. Most of the information was highly classified but the mercury team had unlimited access across all platforms. It was their major simulation tool.

A holographic three-dimensional screen flashed to life above the boardroom table. The image stretched up to the ceiling and blocked out the view of the plants lining the far wall. No matter from which direction you approached the screen, it appeared to be facing towards you.

'I need your authorisation,' Karin said as she approached Barton with the grace of a cat and placed the receiver on his desk. Barton rubbed his eyes, then typed the security password. The image at the far end of the room became active and a charming male voice announced: 'Authorisation complete.'

Karin glanced towards the door, then back at Barton. 'Are you okay?' There was genuine affection in her voice. Karin had worked for Barton for more than six years, and she had been his mistress from the very beginning. It was a relationship based on intellect as much as sex, but more importantly it filled a void in Barton's life that he just couldn't satisfy in any other way. To him, Karin was his everyday companion, confidante and friend. The risk to his reputation, and his marriage, had always been worth it. For Karin, it was the perfect arrangement: she was with the man she loved, every day and most nights. In her opinion, Barton's marriage merely allowed someone else to have his children; something she never actually wanted for herself.

Barton focused on her. 'We've got a big problem.'

'What did the Tredwells want?'

'To shut down 81-07,' he answered.

'You're kidding.'

'We only have two weeks to finish everything up.'

'We'll never do it,' she said seriously. It had always been Karin's dream to be part of the time-travel program. And if things were perfect, she hoped *she* would be the candidate chosen for transport. 'Surely they can't stop you now?'

Barton gazed into thin air. 'GM can do whatever he pleases. He's worried about the risk.'

'Rushing you will only make it *riskier*.'

'I said the same thing. But they are seeing it as a window of threat. They close the window and the problem is solved.' He shrugged his shoulders. 'Apparently, they can live with two weeks of risk.'

'That's a short-sighted approach.' Karin's green eyes focused on a single point on the wall. There were a few seconds' silence. 'Is Jasper behind this?' she asked.

'I'm not sure.'

'I could get him to reconsider.'

The comment filled Barton's mind with images he'd rather not think of. 'I don't want you dealing with him, directly. I've told you before: keep your distance.'

'But it's going to be impossible to get everything done in two weeks!'

Barton hated the word *impossible*. 'We have no choice, Karin. And there won't be any extensions, either. GM made that *very* clear.'

'We need more time.'

Barton sized up the challenge. 'We have two weeks. And you know what? I think we can do it.' He had no choice but to be positive.

Karin stood behind Barton's chair and massaged his shoulders. 'That's why you want Andre Steinbeck?'

'I'm going to take your advice, Karin. We're going to need all the resources we can get. A fresh outlook might make all the difference.' Andre had been working well with mercury tactician Davin Chang on a couple of smaller projects and Barton had been watching his progress for some time. 'Under the circumstances, I think he's worth taking a chance on. His results on the three-dimensional Zion Systems were amazing.'

The glass door to Barton's office swung open. In reaction, Karin immediately removed her hands from Barton's shoulders and stood beside him looking casual. Two people entered the room: a middle-aged Asian man and a teenage boy.

Davin Chang was upbeat. 'So, what brings us here today?' He wore a white mercury labcoat exactly like Karin's, with thin black bars on the lapels designating that he, like Karin, was one of the tacticians. Davin was a small man, a little podgy, thirty-nine years old, with thick spectacles and long black hair tied in a ponytail. He came from a strict

Chinese family in Hong Kong. After being awarded a genetics scholarship he had moved to Enterprise Corporation at twenty-one. He was a veteran of the mercury team, a stalwart. He had an apartment inside the mercury research building, and this was his life. One of the top genetic scientists in the world, he was a free thinker and Barton's permanent number two.

The teenager next to him was Andre Steinbeck: young, gangly, fourteen years seven months old. As a party trick, in an instant, he could tell you the exact number of days, hours and minutes since his birth. He had been born to an unmarried Jewish woman, Jane Steinbeck, when she was just eighteen. Jane was ambitious for her boy and together they worked hard to ensure that Andre's brains took him as far as he could go. Andre was at that awkward-looking stage that all boys go through where their hands and feet seem out of proportion to their bodies. A hint of acne had begun to spread on his cheeks. Wearing a brown tracksuit, he looked a little underdressed, but his eyes were sharp and he appeared ready for anything.

Barton's greeting was warm, 'Thank you both for coming so promptly.'

'I knew it was important when Karin said I'd get cookies, if I was quick.' Davin scanned the room for his reward.

Barton smiled. 'Take a seat, I'll be with you in a moment.'

As promised, Karin produced a packet of chocolate biscuits. Davin opened them immediately and popped one straight in his mouth. His response was typical. 'Only one box?'

Karin shook her head. 'You're such a pig.'

Davin grinned even wider.

One by one, the other members of the mercury team, eleven in all, gathered in a circle around the Data-Tran display. Barton pulled out the last remaining chair at the head of the table. 'Can I have your attention please ...' Everyone became silent. 'I'm appointing Andre Steinbeck to the mercury team. For the first time in our history we will have thirteen members.'

Expressionless, Andre stood up and gave an abbreviated bow. 'You won't regret it.' The mature reply seemed odd coming from such a young boy, but Master Steinbeck was anything but ordinary.

'I'm appointing him as our third tactician,' Barton continued. The tacticians were the grade-one staff. They led the projects and ultimately received the credit, and significant royalties, if things went well.

Davin reached over and pinched Andre's arm. 'It's a great honour. Well done.'

'Yes,' Barton added. 'Well done, Andre. You deserve it.' The room was filled with polite applause, which halted when Barton spoke again. 'Unfortunately that's the only good news I have.' Barton took a deep breath. 'The current mercury project is under threat. We now have time restraints. We need to assemble a Gen-EP candidate, then conduct a transport test within fourteen days.'

'You can't be serious!' Davin blurted, pieces of half-chewed biscuit flying from his mouth. 'It would take two weeks just to *activate* a Gen-EP, let alone prepare a candidate for a test.' He swallowed. 'It took almost a month to convert that tiny mouse. *And* we got it wrong.'

'What's the hurry?' asked one of the other scientists.

'You know how dangerous it is when we try to rush things,' another said.

Karin cut in, 'We're being redeployed to a new project. 81-07 is being shut down.' Barton glared in her direction. That wasn't how he was going to approach it. 'You don't have a choice,' she added, under her breath.

Barton inhaled deeply once more—she was right to cut to the chase and he knew it. 'In two weeks we have to shut it all down,' he said. 'We don't have any other option.'

Davin muttered to himself, 'Hmm, that's different.'

Andre was puzzled. 'What's a Gen-EP?' Details of each and every mercury project were highly classified. Davin looked to Barton before answering.

'It's all right,' Barton said. 'You can tell him. That's why he's here.'

Davin wiped the crumbs from his fingers, picked up a laser pen and began drawing on the Data-Tran image, speaking rapidly at the same time. 'I'll start from the beginning. As we all know, a living organism is made up of chromosomes—twenty-three pairs for a human—arranged in the form of a ribbon, called DNA. The DNA contains the genes that dictate the shape, form and function of all living things.' A small albino mouse appeared on the screen. 'A Gen-EP is one of the billions of genetic protein structures that make up the strands of DNA. Or the acid chain, as we call it. Which are essentially four types of protein—adenine, guanine, cytosine and thymine. A Gen-EP is a living organism with a DNA ribbon that has protein building blocks arranged in a very specific pattern.' The molecular form appeared in great detail.

'And why do we want a living organism like that?' Andre replied.

Barton answered, 'So that we can separate their DNA atoms with a Particle Atomizer—then put it all back together again.'

Andre still didn't understand. 'Yeah, but why?'

'That's what's required if you want to send something *through* time,' Davin said.

The young boy looked more confused than ever.

Barton continued, 'Mercury project 81-07 is about *time travel*.'

Andre's doubting expression prompted Davin to confirm the extraordinary claim. 'That's right, Andre. *Time travel*.' The image on the screen broke down into a molecular form, then recreated again.

Andre was overwhelmed by the mere suggestion of it. 'I thought time travel was supposed to be impossible—because, well, matter can't exceed the speed of light.'

Barton shook his head. 'Apparently it can.' He looked at the faces of the other scientists circled around him. 'We're pretty sure we can do it.'

A look of sudden clarity appeared in Andre's eyes. 'This is what I want to work on!' he said, as if it all made sense to him now. 'You made the right decision, bringing me here.' For the first time that day he appeared happy. Every other scientist in the room felt the same way about *this* project. It was otherworldly and they loved the challenge. The ramifications were something they did not consider. They focused on the process. And the goal.

Barton watched the boy's face. 'We are here to prove the *theory* of time travel,' he counselled. 'And, ladies and gentlemen, we have only fourteen days to make this project happen. That's going to require something special.' There was a hush as they collectively considered the situation.

One of the other scientists spoke, 'How can we create a Gen-EP candidate in just a few days when normally it would take months?'

'We'll have to find a way,' Barton responded.

Andre raised his hand. 'Can't you send another protein type?'

'It's called Humpty Dumpty syndrome,' Karin answered. 'We can disassemble anything we like … we just can't put it back together again. Even a Gen-EP's not perfect. We found that out with the mouse.'

'How does the time machine work? Tell me.' Andre wanted the basic information.

Davin gestured towards the simulation screen and a detailed set of blueprints appeared.

Collider ➡ Imploder ➡ Inflator ➡ Differentiator[1]

All of the corroborating technical algorithms were detailed across the screen. There were thousands of lines of data. 'Like you said before,' Davin said. 'The key to time travel is getting matter to travel *faster* than the speed of light.'

'But,' Andre said, 'I didn't think that was possible.'

Barton continued, 'Neither did we, or Albert Einstein for that matter—his time dilation formula states that matter can *not* exceed the speed of light. It appeared to be a magical barrier that could not be penetrated.'

'So how do you do it?'

'We now know that we can get matter to travel at .99999 times the speed of light by de-particalising it,' Barton explained. 'But that is still not enough to warp time. It merely slows time down in accordance with the time dilation effect.'

'Let me give you an example,' Davin said. 'Let's say we were to send Karin here in a spacecraft—a hypothetical one of course—at 0.99999 times the speed of light, on a journey to the nearest star, *Proxima Centauri*, 4.22 light years from here. For *us* it would take her roughly five years to get there and five years to get back. Logical, of course. But this is where it gets interesting—for Karin, travelling at *almost* the speed of light, the trip would take only 8.5 days. That is known as time dilation due to speed.'[2]

The time dilation formula appeared on the screen.

Square root of: speed, divided by the speed of light, squared, subtracted from 1 = Time Dilation

Barton added: 'Einstein theorised *that* more than 120 years ago. Time is relative to speed. The question is how do you break the speed of light, and what happens when you do?'

---

[1] *How to Build a Time Machine*, Paul Davies, Allen Lane/Penguin, 2001, pages 78–9.
[2] ibid, page 16.

'We have now learned something new,' Karin said. 'That by introducing a strong magnetic field, combined with the rotation of the universe, we could stretch the distance matter travelled, therefore causing it to exceed the speed of light because the distance it travelled becomes elongated.'

'It's called the "black hole effect",' Davin said. 'Kurt Gödel, the Austrian logician, theorised it back in 1947 but had no way of proving it in a practical sense. To quote Gödel, "In theory, you can travel any-*where* and any-*when* you want, provided you can get matter to exceed the speed of light."'

'Now we understand how,' Karin said. 'We have learned that we can take a particle atomiser and a laser strobe, about five terawatts, and fire it at the subject in an orchestrated sequence and *Z-pinch* it inside a magnetic field. This crushes the matter into muons, sub-atomic particles called 'quark-gluon plasma', travelling at just below the speed of light. That's the process of Colliding and Imploding.'

'Then we transport the gluon plasma,' Barton continued, 'using an applied encryption frequency, through the magnetic field of the earth, and stretch space to increase the speed.' He pointed at the screen again. 'The Inflator and the Differentiator. When the frequencies of the molecules match with the external frequencies of the earth—you are anatomically reassembled.'

'You've time-travelled,' Karin concluded.

'The only molecular structure that can handle the reassembly is a Gen-EP,' Davin said. Popping another cookie into his mouth, he stared at the information-filled screens. 'Amazing, isn't it?' Crumbs dropped out of his mouth onto the table.

Andre was astounded. 'How on earth did you figure that out?'

'We didn't,' Barton replied. 'The blueprints for the transport sequence came from some ancient Hebrew writings.'

'Ancient writings?'

'Yes, from information contained within the Dead Sea scrolls.'

'The *Dead Sea scrolls* have blueprints in them?' Andre's mouth hung open. 'You can't be serious!'

'For the moment, Andre, you are just going to have to take my word for it.' Barton rubbed his chin the way he always did when he was serious. 'What we need right now is a Gen-EP candidate.'

'Time travel,' Andre muttered to himself. 'I can't believe it. I mean, I knew you guys worked on some amazing things, but *this* is incredible.'

'It's possible,' Davin said, 'to recreate a single DNA ribbon in about a week, but to completely reassemble a living organism would take at least two months. I just can't see how we can do it in time. Not the normal way.'

Karin brushed away the crumbs from the tabletop. 'How about scrambling the protein pool? Maybe we can rush the Gen-EP process if we play around a little bit.'

One of the older scientists, Stuart Gamin said, 'I've done some genetic simulations.'

'That's a good start,' Barton acknowledged.

Stuart explained what he had done.

Another scientist raised her hand. 'I have some research on the molecular breakdown sequence.' The process was thrashed out at length—positives, negatives, more new theories. Davin led the conversation while Barton sat thinking, in silence.

After a good thirty minutes of animated discussion, Davin said, 'I think we have enough to go on.' The group was broken into three units and they began furiously typing away on their palm devices, the details appearing on the Data-Tran screen in small individual segments. 'The whole is greater than the sum of its parts,' Barton always liked to quote. That was why the combined mercury team was such a powerful problem-solving tool. Individually they were all geniuses in their own right—together they formed *super-genius*.

Simulations and algorithms were being run, numbers were being crunched. The Data-Tran system was constantly comparing one segment against the other, speeding up the process. It was so complex that for a normal person it appeared like unreadable strands of useless information. Questions were being asked left and right. The energy in the room was palpable.

Andre sat in his seat, motionless—his Data-Tran segment was empty. Barton watched carefully, wondering if he was out of his depth. Was this all too much for him?

Eventually Andre spoke. 'What about someone or something we don't have to recreate?' The typing and the questions suddenly halted. Everyone turned away from their palm devices and stared at the boy. 'I mean, isn't it possible there's a natural Gen-EP out there somewhere?'

Barton felt a shiver run up his spine. 'Has anyone thought of that before?' he said seriously.

There was silence.

Davin handed Andre a cookie. 'That's an excellent idea, my boy.'

It was such a simple solution, and one tailored precisely to Barton's requirements. Recreating a Gen-EP would take a miracle in the short time they had available—and Barton needed a human, not a mouse. This could be the best solution he could hope for. Barton turned to Davin. 'What are the chances?'

'Of finding a human Gen-EP? Are we prepared to use a human?' Davin asked, dubiously.

'That was always going to be the final test,' Barton replied.

Someone said, 'Human genetic data is available on Data-Tran.'

'You're prepared to send a human?' Davin said again.

'We have no choice,' Barton replied. It was perfect.

'Off the top of my head,' Davin answered, 'there are roughly nine billion different human DNA ribbons. That, mind you, is the maximum extent of the DNA capability. In reality there are probably around two billion, because many of the basic ribbon types are associated with human deformities. They've been eliminated in the pre-birth scanning. So we can discount them.'

'Is a Gen-EP a rare DNA ribbon?' Karin asked.

'No more than any other. It's totally random.' Davin looked up at the ceiling. 'Let's see, the earth has a population of about eight billion people. Two billion DNA ribbon types. That gives us roughly a one in four chance.'

'Yeah,' Karin added. 'But we might find a Gen-EP candidate that's 120 years old. Or three years old.'

Barton smiled in Andre's direction. Either way, the boy had come through for him.

'Well,' Karin said. 'What are we waiting for?' Her fingers hovered over the Data-Tran receiver. Davin sent a simulation model to each member of the mercury team and within minutes they had nearly completed the entire criteria breakdown.

'There's no doubt the subject will have blue eyes,' Davin said. He knew this from the analysis he'd already conducted. The eyes were the most complex component of the chromosome table—in the mouse that had been converted, the eyes changed from red to blue.

Detailed information again flooded the screen. A list was slowly coming together. Karin stopped typing and pointed. 'Data-Tran has collated the Gen-EP models we've simulated.' The physical characteristics were listed down the left side of the screen.

Barton found himself staring at Karin's body for a fleeting moment. There was something about her that lured him—particularly when they were working and under pressure. He shook his head, as if to be rid of the thought. Now wasn't the time to be distracted.

'Here are the details,' Karin said excitedly. 'Blue eyes. Blood type AB negative. That's the rarest blood group, by the way. That'll help.' The list went all the way to the bottom of the screen, detailing attributes right down to molecular checkpoints. The next piece of information really surprised her. 'According to the Data-Tran simulations, a Gen-EP will have a mark on the left eye.' She was dumbstruck. 'Two faint stripes in the lower radial of the iris.'

The comment caused Barton to sit up straight. It was an amazingly precise indicator. He had never seen anything like that before. He followed the information flow back to one of the mercury scientists, Dez Lewis. She was a young molecular biologist who had been with the mercury team for about four years. 'Well done, Dez. That's an excellent simulation.' He turned to Karin. 'Run the eye colour and blood match through Data-Tran. Then cross-reference that against the optical records. Let's see what that brings up.'

'I'm already doing it,' she replied.

Because the human iris is fundamentally unique, an optical register system was used to catalogue all newborn babies. Data-Tran had access to all the hospital systems. Therefore, if a match existed they would surely find it.

There were 1,235,000 matches to the eye-colour and blood-group search. The optical records would narrow that list down even further. A clock indicated that the search would take one hour and twenty-seven minutes to complete.

'Start with employees of Enterprise Corporation,' Barton instructed. 'If there is a candidate, hopefully they already work for us.'

'We have a breakdown of the employee search,' Karin announced quickly. 'Bad news I'm afraid—no one at Enterprise Corporation fits the optical criteria. The search is continuing.'

Andre typed in a command on his palm device and transmitted it to Karin. 'That should speed things up a little,' he said smugly. The search would now take just one hour and six minutes.

Barton smiled. 'I've heard you're a whiz with Data-Tran.'

Each mercury-team member continued to run simulations on their palm devices, but even so the next hour passed slowly. The suspense was agonising as the Data-Tran computers filed through the tens of thousands of optical records searching for an identical match.

Finally Karin said with great anticipation, 'A result is coming through.'

Barton turned away, not wanting to look.

There was a collective gasp.

'We have *two* candidates,' Karin said. 'Both men. The first is a thirty-one year old in the Pacifica Region. The second, a forty-five year old in the European Region. Amazing!'

There were smiles all round.

Hands were pumped in congratulation.

Barton wanted to run around the room screaming in delight, but instead he counselled: 'Let's not get carried away.' He realised there was a huge amount of work that still had to be done. 'We have to confirm the mark in the left eye. We have to be sure.'

'Which candidate do we want?' Karin said.

Without hesitation Barton replied, 'Get them both. Go and see them yourself, Karin. Bring them back to Enterprise Corporation if they have the genetic mark.' If Barton could convince just one of the Gen-EPs to help him, he would be on track again.

Karin stared into Barton's eyes and he held her gaze for longer than normal. He just wanted to look at her and enjoy their moment of success. It was a common ritual between the pair that no one ever seemed to notice. Barton smiled, then headed for the door. 'Davin, get everyone working on the transport systems.' Barton stopped in his tracks. 'By the way, what are their names?' Photographs and historical data flashed up on the screen.

'The thirty-one year old is Mr Wilson Dowling. He's studying law at the University of Sydney, in Pacifica. He's in the fifth year of his degree.'

'That's a long time to complete a thesis,' Andre said. He himself had graduated from university in just six months.

'Mr Dowling's hobby is flying vintage aircraft,' Karin added. 'He's healthy. Average academic results.'

Dez Lewis tilted her head. 'He's handsome.'

'And the other?'

'The forty-five year old is Mr Magnus Kleinberg. He's a political criminologist based out of Prague. Healthy. Good academic results. Very tall.' Karin nodded. 'This is good.'

'Kleinberg,' Andre said. 'He sounds like an excellent choice. My mother says the Jewish people are the chosen ones.'

'They both look capable enough,' Karin said.

Barton stared at the photograph of Magnus Kleinberg. Then Wilson Dowling received equally close scrutiny. Barton rubbed his chin and announced, 'Get them both here as fast as possible. Let's not take any chances. The more options, the better.'

Barton was the only one who understood the full story; not even Karin knew what was really going on. The translations from the Dead Sea scrolls had been very specific; he was to keep the truth about the Mission of Isaiah to himself, for now.

6

Sydney, Pacifica
Frazer House, University of Sydney
May 10th 2081
Local Time 11:01 a.m.

13 Days before Transport Test

BRIGHT SUNLIGHT BEAMED through the holographic television on the wall of Wilson's study room. The computer-generated image made the small area look much larger than its meagre dimensions. There were no windows in the room and the air was cool. Wilson sat in the glow of artificial sunshine, slumped in an old leather chair. All around him, every available space was stacked with books—hundreds of them—in piles on the floor and tables.

Classical music played in the background.

Wilson closed the novel he was holding and studied the binding. Without moving from his position, he cast the book on the floor and randomly reached out for another. When he realised he'd selected a leather-bound copy of *A Tale of Two Cities* by Charles Dickens, his eyes lit up. He had always intended to read it.

Wilson opened the cover and recited the first few words out loud.

'It was the best of times, it was the worst of times ...'

As he scanned each page, he didn't move in his seat, not a muscle. Occasionally his face betrayed a hint of a smile and sometimes a gentle frown as he absorbed the thousands of perfectly crafted words printed in front of him. Over the course of two hours he read constantly, totally involved in what he was doing.

A knock at the door broke his concentration. He ignored the sound, but the knock came again, this time louder. Reluctantly standing, his legs a little numb, he wove his way through the maze of books and furniture to the door, to see who it was.

As Wilson looked out into the corridor, a broad smile of yellowish, crooked teeth met his gaze. The owner of the less-than-pretty grin, Bernie Muhandis, the courier/postman, stood proudly in his grey university uniform. By his side, a three-wheeled trolley bulged with letters and packages. Originally from Central Asia, Bernie's real name was Bagwan, but he had changed it to Bernie when he emigrated to Pacifica; it was much more Australian to be a Bernie than a Bagwan, he decided.

'Valentine's Day!' Wilson said, as always, arms outstretched as if to receive the entire trolley-full.

Bernie raised his hand in mock defiance. 'Mr Wilson, it is certainly *not* Valentine's Day! How many times must I be telling you!' Although Bernie had been in Pacifica for more than thirty-five years, his accent was still very much Hindi.

'What have you got for me then?' Wilson said in anticaption as he studied the packages.

'There is no mail for you, my friend, not a thing.'

'Then why did you knock?' Wilson asked.

'I am finding out what you are up to,' was the response. Wilson attempted to block the doorway but Bernie poked his head inside and scanned the small study room. 'My goodness gracious, it's true, half the library *is* checked out in your name! You must be out of your mind.'

'I'm just doing some research.'

Bernie placed his dark-skinned hand on Wilson's shoulder. 'Mr Wilson, no one, not even your incredible self, could read that many books. What are you up to in there?'

Wilson looked back inside. 'I like reading, that's all.'

Bernie chuckled. 'Have it your way, Wilson-the-mysterious. I know you are just pretending to read them. So don't expect me to take them all back for you when you are finished. You will have to get a truck, I think.'

It was true: Wilson had more books than any normal person could possibly read in a month. But lately he had been able to plough through as many as two or three per day without any problem. His capacity for absorbing information had increased at an astonishing rate.

Bernie motioned towards his mail trolley. 'Anyway, no Valentine's Day card for you,' he said happily.

'I'm expecting quite a few of them next February, you'll see,' Wilson said, appearing confident.

'You will probably get *none*, like last year.'

'I told you, they were lost in the mail, that's all.'

'I am understanding your problem,' Bernie announced, preparing himself to give some father-like advice. 'You are too particular about the fairer sex. This is my educated opinion. In my country we once had arranged marriages. Terrific! Yes. It is by far the best way for young men and women to meet and fall in love. It still happens in some places, you know. It is a far, far superior and more civilised way to get young people together. It would be good for a man like you.' Bernie smiled and his lovely teeth appeared again.

'That sounds very advanced,' Wilson said quietly.

'That is how I met my wife,' Bernie continued. 'She was such a pretty thing. Gorgeous!' He was lost in reminiscence. 'My father came and said to me, "I have found a girl for you." He was so right.' Bernie placed his hand on his heart, his head tilted up and to one side, as if he were Julie Andrews in *The Sound of Music*.

Wilson looked at his wristwatch, finding it difficult to conceal his boredom any longer. 'Bagwan,' he said, emphasising the name. 'Look, I'd love to chat, but I have a lot of studying to do, you understand?' and he pointed inside. 'Lots of books to read.'

'I am talking too much?' Bernie said, with some embarrassment.

'No-o-o ...' Wilson said, backing away. 'I'm just busy, that's all. Tell me all about it next time. I can't wait.'

'It will be my pleasure—' Bernie called out, the door closing in his face.

Then the door opened again and Wilson appeared.

'And Bagwan,' he said, as an afterthought. 'Next time ... only knock if you *actually* find those lost Valentine's cards for me.'

Bernie grinned. 'You are very cheeky, Mr Wilson.'

Wilson glanced at his watch a second time, suddenly realising something; he was late for his lecture with Jenny Jones! The class had already started.

A string of expletives escaped Wilson's lips as he ran inside, wove through the books, grabbed his identification tag from the table and bolted outside, slamming the door behind him.

He flew past Bernie in the corridor.

'You've made me late, Bagwan!' Wilson called out. 'Jenny will be angry with me!'

'Then, Mr Wilson,' Bernie called back, 'everything is perfectly as it should be!'

THE UNIVERSITY QUADRANGLE was exactly one square acre of immaculately tended grass. It was surrounded on all sides by open-air walkways. People were sprawled out on blankets enjoying the autumn sunshine, some reading quietly, others chatting in groups. The atmosphere was calm and idyllic until Wilson leapt the stone wall and sprinted across the grass—dodging and jumping people as he bisected the lawn at a rapid pace.

A sensor detected his security pass and the glass doors opened as he approached. Breathing heavily, he ran down the empty hallway, his footsteps echoing in the void. He glanced at his watch one more time, then stumbled through the double doors, immediately sensing the gaze of the students peering down from the tiered seating above him. The digital blackboard was covered with notes, and Jenny Jones—the wicked witch of the west—was standing next to the podium with her hands on her hips.

'Nice of you to join us,' she said, her words barely tepid.

Jenny was an attractive 35-year-old brunette with a postgraduate diploma in law. She was witty and opinionated, with a good body and a flirty smile—and if Wilson had it his way, he would never see the bitch again as long as he lived.

Wilson could tell by her expression that she was upset—not an unmanageable situation—and he turned his gaze to the fifty-odd students staring blankly in his direction. About four rows back, Jenny's boyfriend came into view. It seemed that Alfy—Alfred Souza—was sitting in on the class yet again.

Wilson *liked* Alf. Yes, he *liked* seeing him in attendance in the same way that he liked having his nails pulled out by the roots—with a pair of blunt pliers. The situations were comparable, Wilson decided; only seeing Alf was probably worse.

The reason?

Jenny and Wilson had once been an item. Professor Author said Wilson's lingering feelings for her were solely based on the fact that Jenny was good in bed, but he wasn't so sure. It had to be more than that. So, Wilson elected to despise her now that they were no longer together—it had to be one way or the other, he decided. There was no middle ground. What made things so difficult was that their combined thesis on commercial law required Wilson and Jenny to teach classes together as part of their degree. Therefore, they spent ten agonising hours per week lecturing first-year law students.

'Important to make an entrance,' Wilson announced to the class. 'A *composed* entrance. You should all pay attention. I'm teaching you a valuable lesson in how not to panic when a colleague is angry.' Wilson gave Jenny a tap on the backside to ease her away from the podium.

'You bastard,' she whispered.

'Come on, you love it,' he whispered back.

Adjusting the microphone, Wilson said, 'Notice how calm I'm being,' his voice now amplified through the sound system. Wilson's gaze locked on Jenny for a moment, narrowed, so that he could rub it in, then shifted back towards the group. 'But seriously, everyone,' he said. 'I'm sorry I'm late. There was a terrible accident with an ice-cream truck. It hit the front door of my office and I had to eat my way out.' He rubbed his stomach and gave a small burp, the sound amplified around the room. 'The things I do for you people.'

Smiles broke out on the students' faces—only Jenny and her boyfriend seemed immune to his humour.

Wilson glanced at the notes written on the digital blackboard. He knew the material well.

'Commercial Law,' he said. 'Let's get right into it. How do we ensure that two countries, with different laws and systems of law, can resolve disputes when they arise? A very good question …'

KARIN TURNBERRY WAS seated three rows from the front. She had been waiting patiently for Wilson to arrive for the last twenty minutes. *A comedian*, she thought to herself, how interesting. Now that she had positively identified the suspected Gen-EP candidate, she strutted confidently down the stairs towards the podium.

'Mr Dowling, my name is Karin Turnberry.' She gestured towards the double doors to her right. 'I need to speak with you a moment.'

Wilson glanced towards Jenny questioningly, as if this were all a hoax, then back at the stranger standing in front of him. He hadn't seen her before, ever; he would have remembered. She was attractive, smart-looking, with an hourglass figure corralled into a white jumpsuit that seemed almost militaristic, except for the colour.

Wilson moved closer to Jenny and whispered in her ear, 'A stripper! Is this your idea of a joke?' But judging by Jenny's hostile reaction, she had nothing to do with it.

Wilson gazed at the stranger once again, at all times aware that the entire law class was watching his every move. The woman reached out and handed Wilson a business card. Embossed on the surface were just two words:

Enterprise Corporation

'Please, Mr Dowling,' Karin repeated. 'I'll be very brief.'

'I'll be right back,' Wilson said distractedly to the class.

Jenny seethed. 'Should I hold my breath, Wilson?'

'Go ahead,' he whispered back at her.

Wilson followed the curvaceous brunette into the empty corridor. Enterprise Corporation meant only one thing: trouble.

'What was your name again?' Wilson said, having not listened properly the first time. And it wasn't written on the card.

'My name is Karin Turnberry,' she said professionally. 'I work for Enterprise Corporation.'

Wilson held up the card. 'Discreet … I like it.'

Looking Wilson up and down, Karin circled him, at the same time producing a small black device from her bag. It had an optical lens on the front. 'Do you mind if I take a look into your left eye?' she said sweetly. 'It will just take a moment.'

The request was so unusual that Wilson took a step back. 'Why would you want to do that?'

'It's a random genetic test. It will only take a second.'

Wilson didn't need his law degree to know that she was lying. A woman like Karin was not sent to do anything *random*.

'Mr Dowling?' she said impatiently, breaking his train of thought.

He gazed at the strange black device once again. 'Tell me why.'

'There is no time to explain.'

'*You* might not have time. But, I assure you, *I* have plenty. And I'm the one in the middle of a class.' He pointed back inside. 'So, humour me …'

Karin dutifully produced a digital document from her folder and handed it to him. It was from the University of Sydney, addressed directly to Wilson. It was three lines long and it strongly suggested that he co-operate with Ms Turnberry's request. He could read between the lines: his scholarship would be revoked if he didn't co-operate. The entire situation didn't seem quite that random any more.

'I just need a few moments of your time,' Karin said, smiling disarmingly. She motioned to a bench against the wall. 'I assure you, it will be over in seconds. The procedure is completely painless.' With no choice, Wilson sat down and Karin stood between his legs, gently raising his chin with her index finger. 'Look straight ahead.'

A red beam of light pierced Wilson's left eye, but he was momentarily distracted by the scent of Karin's perfume and the closeness of her body. Suddenly the light was gone and Karin stepped back, her eyes fixed firmly on the display. There was no expression on her face at all—good or bad.

At that moment, her mobile telephone rang. Karin unclipped the wafer-thin receiver from her belt and glanced at the display. It was Barton, presumably calling to find out how things were going. She casually pressed the power-off button and the phone was once again silent. Karin's gaze lifted to meet Wilson's.

'How would you like to take a trip to our head office?' she said. 'Do you like travelling?'

Wilson was trying to figure out what Karin could possibly have been looking at in his left eye. It just didn't make any sense. 'What is that device for?' he asked.

Karin packed the small mystery computer into her bag. 'Enterprise Corporation needs you, Mr Dowling.'

'Really? Well, I don't *need* Enterprise Corporation.'

'It will be worth your while.'

Wilson chuckled, 'This is ridiculous.'

In response, her tone hardened, 'Mr Dowling, I'm sorry, but you don't have any choice.'

Wilson glanced around in a state of mock surprise. 'Please, Karin,' he exclaimed, returning her gaze. 'For God's sake call me Wilson. Every time you say "Mr Dowling", I start looking around for my grandfather.'

'My orders are to take you to head office,' she said firmly.

'It was very nice to meet you,' was his dismissive reply. 'Have a nice day.' Wilson began to walk back to the lecture hall, but Karin blocked his path. 'I have a class to teach,' he said.

'You're coming with me.'

'No chance.' He sidestepped her.

Karin grabbed Wilson's arm. 'Imagine never having to work again as long as you live.'

Alarm bells immediately began ringing in Wilson's head—Enterprise Corporation must know about his secret!

'Come with me to head office, in the Americas. There's a private shuttle waiting at the airport. I need you to meet with a man called Barton Ingerson. He's very important.' She gave Wilson a smile that was more than a little seductive. 'We have the finest vodka on board the shuttle. This will be worth your while, I assure you. And I make a terrific vodka Martini.'

She knows I drink vodka, Wilson thought.

'Enterprise Corporation can be very generous if it wants to be,' she said. 'Or quite the opposite, if that is required.'

It seemed Wilson's greatest fears had materialised: this was definitely about Professor Author's omega programming. A cold sweat duly flushed his body.

'Do you agree?' she asked.

'I'd love to come with you,' Wilson said with a manufactured smile.

Karin seemed pleased. 'Good ... I'm glad.'

'I've never been on a private shuttle before.'

'You'll enjoy it. The trip only takes four hours.' Her tone suggested they were now the best of friends. 'The stars are really worth seeing.' Airbus shuttles were the latest form of supersonic transport. They accelerated just outside the ionosphere, into space, to shorten the journey. By far the quickest way to get from A to B, from one side of the world to the other. Even if you flew during daylight hours, once you were outside the ionosphere the stars could always be seen sparkling brightly.

'I can't wait,' Wilson said, masking his true feelings. *I'm going to kill Professor Author when I get my hands on him*, he thought. *He's the one responsible for getting me into this.*

'It'll be fun. We'll drink Martinis.' Karin's small talk was even more painful than her negotiating style. 'I'll meet you at the main entrance in an hour,' she said. 'A car will be waiting for you.' Karin glanced at her palm device. 'And, Wilson, I know you're quite often late, so why don't you try to be there in forty-five minutes?'

It seemed they knew everything about him already.

Wilson thought a moment, then said, 'Can you do me a favour, please?' and pointed towards the lecture hall. 'It would mean a lot to me.'

Karin hesitated, then replied, 'I guess I could.'

'It's only a small favour. Go in there and tell the other lecturer, Jenny Jones, that I won't be coming back today? Tell her I'm leaving with you. She'll appreciate knowing what's happening. Tell her about the shuttle.' Karin flicked back her shoulder-length brown hair in a manner suggesting the stripper Wilson had first imagined.

'I suppose I could do that,' she said confidently.

Picturing Jenny's reaction to the news—and her reaction to the woman who was delivering it—Wilson concluded that every cloud has a silver lining.

7

Houston, Texas
County Ambulance #33, Corner Kirby Drive & McNee Road
November 25th 2012
Local Time 8:02 p.m.

Mission of Isaiah—Day One

A PIERCING SIREN echoed through the streets as an aging white ambulance appeared, red and blue roof lights slicing the gloom. It was early evening and the roads were deserted. Not slowing for the red traffic light ahead, the ambulance rattled along, hit a bump, then made a sharp right-hand turn and sped off into the night.

Inside the rear cabin, the jolt snapped Wilson back into consciousness. Confused and in a great deal of discomfort, he tried to open his eyes, but all he could see was darkness, and he could taste something familiar in his mouth. It was difficult to move, and when he did, pain speared through him. His hands appeared to be restrained. There was motion all around. He began to struggle.

'Don't exert yourself, boy,' a male voice called out. 'You'll only make it worse.' The accent was American, with a distinct southern drawl. Even so, Wilson attempted to sit up and the pain became even more intense. Then he recognised the taste in his mouth: it was blood—sticky blood.

'I told you,' said the voice. 'Don't move.' The paramedic tightened the Velcro straps across Wilson's chest, securing him even more firmly to the stretcher.

Numerous layers of soiled bandages were wrapped around Wilson's torso, head and legs. His clothes were mostly shredded. He had several broken bones—ribs, upper legs—and his thighs were braced with heavy plastic splints. An intravenous drip was attached to his right arm. More than half his skin was lacerated from being dragged along under a car during the accident.

The paramedic prepared to inject more sedatives.

'I can't see,' Wilson said.

'What's your name?' the voice asked. 'Tell me your name.'

'I can't see,' Wilson repeated.

'That's just the bandages. You took a blow to the head. Now tell me. This is important: do you have health insurance?'

'Insurance?' Wilson muttered in reply. He smiled to himself—his policy wouldn't come into effect for at least fifty more years. It seemed funny somehow.

'Do you have insurance?' the voice asked again.

A wave of pain flashed through Wilson, more concentrated than before, like a thousand knives being plunged into his back and legs then slowly being twisted. The whole situation didn't seem quite so amusing any more.

'You're gonna wish you did,' said the voice.

The ambulance took a sharp turn and Wilson was slammed against his restraining straps. Acute pain jabbed him in a dozen extra places. He flirted with the serenity of unconsciousness again.

The paramedic looked his patient up and down; it was surprising he could still talk considering the amount of morphine he had already been administered. Another 15 ml should do the trick, he decided. Tapping the syringe to free the air bubbles inside, he worked against the motion of the cabin and stabbed the needle into the tube hanging from Wilson's left arm.

Pain was coming and going in waves, stronger and stronger, forcing Wilson to take short, shallow breaths. It was all he could do to stay in the moment. A part of him just wanted to be free of this constant torture. Anything that could release him, he would accept.

'I shouldn't even be here,' he winced.

The ambulance hit a rut, jolting the cabin.

The agony was too much …

THE SCHUMANN FREQUENCY

Sydney, Pacifica
Billboard Nightclub, Glebe Point Road, Glebe
May 23rd 2080
Local Time 11:27 p.m.

281 Days before Transport Test

LOUD MUSIC THROBBED in the background. The club was smoky and crowded. Wilson sat on a bar stool next to Professor Julius Author. In the shadows around them, dozens of people danced. Disco lights flashed from the ceiling. They were playing 'Bony M'. It was *20th Century Nite: hits from the last millennium.*

Without asking, the bartender filled two more glasses with vodka and slid them forward. Wilson could feel the interactive credit card in his pocket vibrate, letting him know he'd been billed for two more drinks.

'Why do I always have to pay?' he said.

Professor Author replied, 'Cause you get the pleasure of my illustrious company.'

'You're drunk.'

'Yes, Wilson—I think you are correct.'

Julius Author was a regular here at Billboard. Three nights a week he could be found sitting in the same seat drinking double vodkas on the rocks, glass after glass. 'The professor', as he liked to be called, was a brilliant man. But with brilliance often comes eccentricity, and he had both in ample quantities. The University of Sydney, where he worked as a neurological researcher, had a love–hate relationship with him. They figured he was too gifted to do without, but far too strange to be teaching students. If asked, Wilson would be the first to agree.

The professor was in his early fifties and not exactly the most handsome bloke in the world. 'Unbeautiful' was the term Wilson used to describe him. His frizzy dark hair, streaked with grey, stood straight up, as if he had just stuck his fingers into a power socket.

Albert Einstein—to whom Professor Author bore an incredible resemblance—was the little man's role model. Like Einstein, he always wore the same clothes. Dark blue pants, white button-down shirt, white sneakers, white socks. Even his underwear was the same. He had seven sets of everything—all identical. Quoting the Nobel Laureate, the professor said it was one less decision he had to make every day and when you multiplied that out over a lifetime, that was millions and millions of thought processes that could be expended on something much more worthwhile.

Wilson had known the professor for many years. They'd met when Wilson went for a job as a lab assistant. At the time he needed to earn a little extra money and applied for a position in the neurology department. He didn't get the job, but the two became firm friends from that day. Friendships are funny like that. The two were different in so many ways. More than twenty years apart in age, they had different skills, they came from different backgrounds and their interests were mostly unrelated—yet here they were. Every Friday the pair would meet at Billboard, drink the same drinks and have the same conversations and arguments.

Wilson held his glass in the air. 'This is my last drink, and then I'm getting out of here. I have an assignment due tomorrow.'

'Law is *s-o-o-o* boring!' the professor announced. 'How do you even stay awake?'

'I have that kind of mind,' Wilson replied, and placed his empty glass on the bar.

'Yes, you do,' the professor nodded. 'Yes, you do.' It was by no means a compliment. 'Everybody hates lawyers, you know that? They're parasites!'

'That's my cue,' Wilson said, standing. 'I'm outta here!'

'No!' The professor said, emphatically. 'We have much to talk about,' and he dragged Wilson back into his seat.

'I can't afford to drink with you any more, Professor. It's not the money; it's just too hard on my ego.'

'The next round is on me,' the professor slurred.

'You wouldn't *shout* if a shark bit you.'

'That's crap! I shout all the time!' and he indicated to the bartender to pour Wilson's drink.

'Look, I have to go,' Wilson said. 'Really, I need to get some studying done. I'm way behind.' But a fresh drink slid forward anyway.

The professor leaned closer, a goggle-eyed stare in his eyes. 'Situation normal, mate. You know what ... we could fix that.'

Wilson had a feeling he was about to get another 'the world according to Professor Author' sermon.

Then it began ...

'Do you know what a *god box* is?'

Wilson cringed—not the god box!

'It's located inside your right temporal lobe.' The professor pointed at Wilson's forehead. 'It's active in people who are *brilliant*. Everybody has one, it's just that only the *very gifted* have the ability to engage it.' The professor reached out and tapped Wilson on the skull. 'Your god box is *there*, in the front of your brain.'

Wilson pulled back, annoyed by the contact.

'Did you know,' the professor slurred, 'that the average human only uses ten per cent of his brain capacity? That leaves ninety per cent with nothing to do. That's a lot of vacant real estate.'

Wilson predicted the next few words. The god box is the key ... It's a fount of mental power ...

'The god box is the key,' the professor said. 'It's a fount of mental power.'

'It's illegal, remember!' Wilson blurted.

The professor looked dismayed. 'Who told you it was illegal?'

'You did.'

'The god box is well named, Wilson.' The professor didn't even break stride. 'It's so *powerful* that anyone who learns how to harness it will have capabilities beyond comprehension.'

'Yeah,' Wilson said, butting in, his patience worn through. 'And three years ago the medical community banned experiments on that part of the brain. *You* mentioned that as well.'

The professor surveyed the room, shiftily. 'When has that ever stopped us?' Wilson went to stand up, but the professor pulled him back into his seat. 'I have a new theory. Yes, a new theory!'

Wilson swallowed the last of his vodka and slammed the glass on the bar. His credit card unexpectedly vibrated again—the barman had already poured another round. Wilson leant forward and made a cutting action with his hand against his throat. 'This is my last one! Close my tab!'

'I'm making you the greatest offer of your life,' the professor said, jabbing his finger insistently into Wilson's arm.

'It could get us both thrown in jail. Or worse.' Indicating the other strangers in the nightclub, Wilson added: 'I'm the only friend you have! If you turn me into a vegetable, you'll have to sit here all on your own. Yep, *alone*.'

'I'll bring you with me, anyway.'

'Oh, that's comforting.'

'I will!' The professor's eyes darted around the room again. 'It's not dangerous, you know.' He leant forward and whispered in Wilson's ear, 'Because I've found a way to stimulate the god box without any surgery.'

Wilson strained to hear. 'Why are you speaking so quietly?'

'The university has spies everywhere,' the professor whispered.

'Who do you think is going to hear you in this place?' The music was so loud it was throbbing. 'And anyway ... back off a little—your breath isn't so flash.' It was a hideous mixture of stale alcohol and onions.

In response, the professor pulled Wilson even closer. 'I did some non-invasive omega programming last week,' he continued. 'On a *rat*, Wilson. You should have seen what happened.'

'I don't want to know—'

'You'll have physical abilities you can't even begin to imagine.' The professor sculled his drink, then went on to the next glass. 'Anyway, this isn't like anything I've ever done before. It's not like anything *anyone* has ever done before. It's a cerebral program—which means no danger of rejection.'

'Do you remember what happened the last time I agreed to help you with one of your experiments?' Wilson nodded his head up and down in an exaggerated fashion. 'I had a headache for a month! Yeah, you remember that, don't you? *I* sure do!'

The professor waved his hands as though he was trying to swipe away a persistent insect. 'That was a mistake, I admit it! But this ... this is the real thing. Don't you see? The god box is only the power source this time. You'll be able to control your physical performance just by saying a couple of commands. I've done the research! There'll be no side effects—nothing too bad anyway. Come on, Wilson. I wouldn't ask again if I didn't think it was safe.'

'Let me consider it.' Wilson looked towards the ceiling. 'Hmm.' He paused. 'Okay, Professor ... the answer is definitely *No*.'

Disappointed, the little scientist pressed his forehead down on the bar.

'I'm your friend,' Wilson said. 'But not this time ... no way.'

The professor gripped Wilson's arm. 'Mate, I know this will work!' He tried to smile, but he was too drunk. 'I can't exactly go out into the street and get a volunteer!' His face scrunched up even more than usual. 'Those bastards at the university,' he lowered his voice again, 'are trying to steal my work. I know it!' He refocused. 'I'm asking you for a favour, Wilson.'

'Why can't you ask a normal favour?'

'A favour is a favour.'

'This is a brain experiment!'

'So what?'

Wilson shook his head. 'You're even more drunk than I thought.'

'Will you do it?'

'I thought we were friends,' Wilson said, trying to get the moral high ground.

The professor stood up. 'Maybe we're not friends after all!' He was a little unsteady on his feet. 'You know what? There's a reason why Jenny Jones left you. I know why. I'll tell you what it is, since friends should be honest with each other. You're *ordinary*, Wilson! You're *dull*! You've been on a scholarship for …' He counted his fingers. 'Five years! Take a look at yourself, mate. Jenny Jones was right to leave you for that other bloke.'

The music continued to throb in the background.

'It's 'cause that other guy is more *interesting* than you are,' the professor added.

'He's studying law as well!'

'I can't believe I've spent the last six months listening to you talk about …' he made inverted commas with his fingers, '… Jenny Jones the love of your life! It's been torture, mate. So she was a great lay, *so what?*'

'I'm not dull!' Wilson countered. 'Take that back.'

'I give up, Wilson. I do.' The professor disappeared into the crowd.

Wilson stared at the ice cubes suspended in his glass. Minutes ticked by. Was it possible there was some truth to what the professor had said? A frown took over Wilson's expression. Maybe it was time to reflect on his place in the world. He was in a rut—he knew that—like a skipping record that played the same lyric over and over. Deep down, if Wilson looked into himself, he knew something was missing, something significant; he just didn't know what, or possibly who, it was.

HOURS LATER WILSON walked back to his apartment. He lived near campus in a former office building that had been converted to student accommodation. Everything was so familiar that he didn't even look towards the elevator, which had a sign 'Out of Order' hanging across the doors. It had never worked since he'd lived there.

Wilson headed straight for the staircase and climbed the fourteen flights to his floor. When he opened the door to his room he found Professor Author sitting inside smoking a cigarette.

'*Oh, great*—' Wilson tried not to look surprised. 'How did you get in?' He checked the lock, but it appeared to be in working order. 'I see … a small part of my ego is still intact—therefore your work is not done yet.'

The professor spun round in the swivel chair. 'This is a great view.'

Wilson scanned the Sydney skyline glowing in the distance. 'Yeah, it's almost worth having to trudge up those bloody stairs for.'

'Let's not go that far,' the professor said. 'But it keeps you fit, I guess.'

The spacious one-bedroom apartment was partially furnished. There was one sofa, one flat-panel satellite television and a fridge full of beer. On the floor was a stack of pizza boxes and magazines. On top of the bookshelf were three picture frames—one holding a picture of Wilson's foster parents, Jean and Ian Stradbroke, standing in front of Uluru. The second held a picture of his grandfather—his birth grandfather—William Dowling, taken just before he died. Wilson treasured that photograph. The third frame was empty. It used to hold a picture of Jenny Jones, which had since been torn up and thrown in the bin.

The professor tapped his half-burnt cigarette on the edge of a small dinner plate. 'This place is a dump. My point is,'—he wasn't slurring any more—'thank heavens for the view.' He inhaled another puff.

'You're full of compliments tonight, aren't you?'

'Look, I came to apologise.'

'Great. Apology accepted. Now get out.' Wilson pointed towards the door, but the professor didn't move a muscle.

'Seriously—I'm sorry about what I said. I went too far.'

'You said I was dull!'

'Yeah, I'm sorry about that.'

'Dull?'

'I'm sorry!'

Wilson shook his head. 'You know what pisses me off?' He paused, thinking about how honest he should be. 'I'm worried that you're probably right. It's really annoying.'

'Life is funny like that.' The professor smiled. 'It makes me laugh, actually.'

'It makes *me* wanna cry.' Wilson took two beers out of the small fridge, one for each of them.

'My omega programming,' the professor said calmly. 'I need you to test it for me.' Smoke drifted from his lips. 'I swear to you, the university is suspicious that I'm close with my research. They want to take it away from me. The bastards.'

'You know,' Wilson flashed a smile, 'you're much more compelling when you're sober.'

The professor spent the next thirty minutes, and six cigarettes, explaining to Wilson how the process worked. It was *non-invasive* programming—that meant no incisions—and it activated the god box by targeting the frontal lobe of the brain with high-frequency ultrasonics. He got the idea from a navy radar operator who, due to a malfunction of his equipment, had been unexpectedly exposed to coded ultrasonics while he was at sea. When he returned after three months, his IQ had increased dramatically. An interim study had been conducted by the navy, which was common knowledge, but since then, as a result, the GHO—Global Health Organization—had banned all cerebral testing.

The professor took up the research where the navy had left off. He had the equipment, the funding, the skill, and most importantly the anonymity to do just about anything he wanted. So for the last two years he'd been working on how to program the ultrasonics to get the results he needed.

Wilson knew it *was* possible that the university could try to steal the idea. Especially if they thought there was money to be made and the risks had already been taken. It sounded like it certainly had military applications. Wilson didn't normally smoke but he grabbed a cigarette and put it in his mouth.

'It's a good thing these aren't bad for you,' Wilson said. 'I can smoke a whole pack when I'm stressed.' Only twenty-five years earlier, cigarettes had been causing cancer, before the Enterprise Corporation scientists removed the dangerous chemicals from the formula.

'I liked them better when they were bad for you,' the professor replied. 'For me, the appeal of smoking something *carcinogenic* was a real buzz. But I guess it's a terrible business when you're killing off your best customers.'

'Apparently they still taste the same,' Wilson said, before inhaling.

'Those bloodsuckers at Enterprise Corporation have taken all the fun out of it. They've destroyed smoking's soul. They should all be locked up. They made it innocent and nice. What a waste.'

'Why do you hate them so much?'

The professor didn't even have to think. 'They represent the establishment, Wilson. Take my word for it—they are *not* to be trusted. They want us all to live in cotton wool, like morons, so we keep our medical expenses down, live perfect lives, have 2.3 kids and never cause any trouble. It's disgusting! I subscribe to the *chaos theory*—live, laugh, be bold, get on the edge. *Carpe diem*.' He paused. 'Which is why I need you to do this omega thing for me. Don't you see—this is our chance to stick it up the bureaucracy. And, I wouldn't ask you if I didn't think it was going to work. We, together, can make a difference.'

'What if it *doesn't* work?'

'It'll work. Trust me!'

'I love your confidence, Professor, but sometimes it's misplaced.' In truth, Wilson was astounded by the little man's self-belief. He used to joke that Professor Author's self-image was so good that he believed he had the looks of Errol Flynn and the body of an Olympic athlete. Unfortunately, the truth was some way off. In fact, so far off you couldn't locate it with binoculars.

'You should do this for me,' the professor said seriously. 'It's your fate to be my friend. And believe me; I can appreciate that's a difficult thing to do, at times. Maybe it's also your fate to help me with this.'

Fate … The comment triggered something and Wilson's mind filled with unexpected memories. He walked to his desk, slid open the top drawer and produced a large silver coin. 'My grandfather gave this to me when I was a boy. He said it was my *fate coin*.' Wilson stared at the shiny object, more questions surrounding its purpose than answers.

The professor snatched the coin away.

'It's an Egyptian pound,' Wilson said. The pyramids of Giza were etched on the front surface. The other side of the coin was badly damaged, indented, like it had been hammered with great force.

'What happened here?'

Wilson looked on. 'I'm not sure. I don't think my grandfather knew either.' Wilson pointed at the disfigured outline. 'That's the Queen of England. Elizabeth II. She's a little mangled.' Wilson took the coin and affectionately rubbed it between his fingers. 'My grandfather used to say "If you need the hand of fate to show you the way, the coin will guide you." Strange, huh?'

'Let's flip it and see what happens,' the professor said enthusiastically.

Wilson stared at the Egyptian coin and his heart beat faster. Up to now, its most important application had been helping him decide between pizza and Chinese food. Not exactly life-altering stuff. It was odd, but his grandfather had always said the coin would never fail—and to trust in the destiny it would deliver.

'If I win,' Wilson said, 'never ask me to do this omega thing again. I mean it. Never!'

'And if I win,' the professor replied, 'you go through with the programming.'

Wilson didn't want to think too much about the consequences of losing—that was his way with just about everything. For some reason, however illogical, he trusted the coin, and his grandfather, and was deeply convinced they would both be looking out for him.

'The Queen is heads,' Wilson said. 'Pyramids are tails. You call.' He spun the coin upwards and the professor's voice cut the silence …

'Tails.'

The coin seemed to hang in the air for a long time, light flashing off the shiny surface. End over end it spun. Wilson wondered for a fleeting moment if this was a significant crossroads in his life, but before he had a chance to decide, he caught the coin easily and slapped it against the back of his hand. There was no time to think any more—his destiny was now set.

'Tails, Tails, Tails,' the professor chanted.

Wilson lifted his hand—the pyramids of Giza were facing upwards.

Houston, Texas
County Ambulance #33, Stirling Drive, Harris County
November 25th 2012
Local Time 8:16 p.m.

Mission of Isaiah—Day One

THE AMBULANCE WAS slowing as Wilson emerged from his dreamlike state. Intense pain came and went in waves and he still couldn't see anything. In a moment of mental clarity, he engaged his omega command with a whisper: 'Activate Nightingale.'

It felt like being submerged, instantly, in a very hot bath. Wilson's blood pressure multiplied to three times its normal rate as a cocktail of amino acids, dopamine and protein flooded his system. Endorphins numbed his senses as his body's production of red and white blood cells went into overdrive. The excruciating pain that was previously tearing away at him had magically faded to almost nothing.

'This is your last chance,' the voice said. 'I need you to tell me your name.'

The ambulance began to reverse—Wilson could sense the change in motion. Then the back doors swung open and cool night air flooded the cabin. The wheels of his stretcher locked down with a click. In the distance, he could hear a child crying.

THE AMBULANCE HAD arrived at Harris County Hospital. The paramedic looked outside and saw queues of people waiting at the emergency entrance. Many of them were covered in blood, from what appeared to be small-calibre gunshot wounds. Men, women and children were among the injured. A young child about four years old was crying out for his mother, wailing desperately.

A tired-looking doctor approached the ambulance, wearing a blood-splattered plastic apron.

'What's going on?' the paramedic asked.

'We had a shooting at the mall,' the doctor replied. 'Third time this month.' He pulled off his plastic gloves and threw them to one side. 'It's a shit-fight. Anyway, what have you got here?'

The paramedic went to sign the paperwork, then suddenly realised something was wrong. The form read: 'Ms Winter, Sex: F, Age: 42 years, of no fixed address.'

He looked hastily at the tag around Wilson's right wrist. It read: 'John Doe.'

The paperwork was wrong!

'Well ...?' the doctor said impatiently. 'I have people waiting.'

The paramedic looked at his watch; it was almost knock-off time. The paperwork error certainly meant another trip back to Mercy Hospital to sort it out. And if they had the correct paperwork and the *wrong* patient—well, that was even worse.

'Everything's fine,' the paramedic replied confidently, as he crudely altered the details on the form with a blue biro: 'John Doe, Sex: M, Age: unknown, of no fixed address.'

It didn't matter anyway; neither of them had health insurance. 'A John Doe transfer from Mercy Private,' he said directly. 'As I understand it, John Doe here has been refused treatment at three hospitals in the last twelve hours.'

'Isn't he lucky,' the doctor said sarcastically, 'getting sent to *this* hellhole.'

'He has no ID and no health insurance.' The paramedic handed over the forms. 'From what I can gather, from the orderlies at Mercy, he was hit by a car this morning. Appears to have a fractured skull. His legs are broken. The nursing staff—I can only assume—did a good job with his thigh splints. He has some broken ribs, lacerations, but he'll live. He's been prescribed saline, nutrients and 25 ml of morphine every thirty minutes.'

'Any internal injuries?'

'Not sure. All I know is, he hasn't had any X-rays or an MRI. The poor bastard momentarily regained consciousness in the ambulance on the way over. I tried to get his name, but he didn't appear to be lucid, so I gave him another hit of morphine—15 ml.'

The doctor clipped the paperwork to his notepad. 'Well, I hope it's enough to keep him unconscious, because at this rate, it's going to be a long wait before we get around to him.'

'There's nothing we can do about that,' the paramedic said dismissively.

In the background the young child continued to wail for his mother.

The doctor gestured to get a nurse's attention, then pointed to

Wilson's stretcher. 'Get this patient,' he looked up at the waiting list and allocated the next available ID number, 'Patient 456, to a waiting room on level one. He'll have to wait there until we've cleared this backlog.' The doctor gazed towards the chaos in the emergency room. 'Will somebody take care of that crying kid!' he yelled out. 'He's driving me fucking crazy!'

The paramedic closed the back doors of the ambulance and jumped in next to the driver. 'What a screw-up,' he said. 'We got the wrong patient again.' The pair gave each other a knowing look. 'Let's get out of here before someone wants us to sort it out.'

8

Houston, Texas
Sam Houston Parkway
November 25th 2012
Local Time 8:17 p.m.

Mission of Isaiah—Day One

A PAIR OF BRIGHT-WHITE Zeon headlights pierced the gloom. Engine roaring, the black Mercedes was travelling at high speed, tyres squealing, as it rounded the corner and accelerated up the empty parkway. There were no other cars on the road and everything outside seemed as still as a snapshot. Helena was in a daze, streetlights flashing by against the blackness of the night sky above her, the whistle of the wind against the tightly closed windows.

The silhouette of her apartment building appeared in the distance as she dropped through the gears and came to a stop on the wide sloping driveway, the corrugated steel door glowing in the headlights. Helena pressed the remote control, flipped down her visor and looked at herself in the mirror. Her eyes were red and she looked exhausted. Lost in her own image, she didn't notice time drift away. The giant door had risen all the way to the top and was beginning to close again. She slammed her foot on the accelerator, the engine screamed and the Mercedes sped down the ramp in a plume of tyre smoke, barely squeezing under the sharp edge of the door.

The throaty sound of the high-tech V8 was magnified as her car descended the various ramps, one after the other, past some of the finest vehicles money could buy. An empty parking space appeared—

with the word *CAPRIARTY* stencilled in bright yellow lettering on the concrete—and she swerved towards it at ridiculous speed, testing her reactions in a bizarre effort to amuse herself. All four wheels locked simultaneously, the ABS stuttering, and the car ground to a halt just a few centimetres from the wall.

An old man sat in a security booth next to the elevators, behind bullet-proof glass. His uniform was freshly pressed. On the surveillance cameras, he'd watched Helena drive past and he wanted to tell her she'd been driving dangerously, but didn't dare. Instead he stood and gave her a sharp salute. Helena didn't acknowledge him, which was unusual, but he thought nothing of it.

THE ELEVATOR DOORS opened and Helena was once again in the familiar surroundings of her apartment. To her dismay, there were two bodyguards standing in the marble foyer, handguns bulging under their jackets. It meant her father was inside. Hearing his voice coming from the living room, she considered whether or not to eavesdrop on his conversation. Normally she would, but Lawrence's men were watching her too closely to try. Passing them with an unbroken stride, she let out a whispered profanity in their direction. She wanted them to know that she was unhappy.

Helena's appearance was met with a gasp and Julia and Lawrence jumped from their seats in surprise. A log fire was burning in the fireplace, soft music played. Outside, through the tall bay windows, the lights of Houston sparkled in the darkness.

Helena's father, Lawrence Capriarty, was an older man with a full head of thick brown hair, greying at the temples. Quite long, it was parted to one side. He had a sharp nose and the trademark Capriarty blue eyes. His black Brioni suit was a perfect fit, slim and tailored, and his Italian shoes were new and shiny.

Lawrence was a confessed control addict—both personally and professionally—and getting worse every day. He was a self-made man and his property development business stretched across the globe, with offices in every major city—thirty-seven, to be exact. Originally he had come from a middle-class Texan family; just a Houston boy made good, he would often proudly say. The key to his success was refusing to let anything get in his way; and he used all his resources, legal or otherwise, to achieve the outcomes he desired. That's what it took to succeed in property development. He was a product of his industry—crooked, aggressive and predatory. But when it came to Helena, Lawrence was a model father, because that's what he set out to be, and he worried about his only child in a way that even the most honest man would. Maybe more.

'What are you doing here, Dad?' Helena said.

Lawrence pointed an outstretched finger in her direction. 'We've been ringing you for more than an hour, young lady! I've got people out there looking for you!' He gave her no time to answer. 'Julia and I have been worried sick about you! It's just not good enough!'

'I can look after myself,' Helena replied dismissively.

'Christ, Helena, have you gone mad?'

'That comment is not helpful, Dad.'

'What *would help* is if you did what I asked for a change!'

'I said: I can look after myself!' And she headed for her bedroom.

Lawrence cut off her exit. 'You're not going anywhere—'

'Don't lecture me, Dad. I'm not in the mood right now.'

'You will do as I ask!' he yelled.

She pulled the handgun from her jacket and held it in the air. 'You told me to carry a gun ... and I'm doing that!' Her emotional intensity was at least equal to his. 'You're always telling me what to do. *That's not helping!* "Be more careful!" "Do this! Don't do that!"' She waved her pistol in the air like a toy.

As Lawrence looked at his daughter, his heart became heavy. She reminded him so much of her mother, in so many ways. And strangely he loved Helena's stubbornness—it was just that it made him mad with worry. But he would rather she was stubborn than timid. The world had a habit of crushing people who were not so strong. Lawrence did his best to calm himself and lowered the tone and volume of his voice.

'I'm just glad to see that you're okay,' he said. 'And yes, I'm happy you're carrying that gun.' If Lawrence had his way, he would assign a bodyguard to her day and night, but Helena would have nothing of it. Instead he would have to be content that she was well armed and well trained in her own protection. 'I know how much you've been through,' Lawrence said softly. 'But you *must* be more careful.' He reached out for his daughter's hand and led her to the sofa. 'Helena, I know I'm not a doctor, but we need to talk about these dreams you've been having.'

Helena shot a glance in Julia's direction. 'What did you tell him?' she seethed.

'She did the right thing,' Lawrence announced.

'You told him!' Helena shouted. 'How could you betray me like that?'

'I worry!' Julia said, stamping her foot. 'I panic! You run off and leave me!'

'Julia did the right thing,' Lawrence said again.

'You shouldn't have told him!' Helena yelled.

'When you run off,' Julia said, 'and say nothing. I call him! I tell him! *Si!*'

Lawrence stood between the pair. 'That's enough, both of you!' he roared.

An uneasy silence descended.

'Julia, get me a scotch on the rocks,' Lawrence said sternly. 'Even better, bring three glasses and we'll all have a drink.' It was his way of getting Julia out of the room for a moment.

'She shouldn't have told you!' Helena continued.

'I call him!' Julia snapped back defiantly. '*Si!*'

Lawrence pointed one hand at the sofa, the other out the door. 'Helena, sit down! Julia, get the drinks! Listening to the two of you argue is more than I can God-damn stand right now!' Helena plonked herself down on the sofa and Julia stomped out of the room.

Alone with his daughter for the first time, Lawrence said, 'I'm worried about you.'

'Don't worry, Dad.'

'I think you should spend some time at Dr Bennetswood's clinic. It'll be good ...' He didn't even have time to finish his sentence before Helena had leapt from her seat.

'You think I need to spend time in a *mental institution*?' Her face was crimson with anger. 'Have you considered that maybe *you're* the problem! Your need to control my life, that's my problem!'

Lawrence stood back and watched as Helena paraded around the room. She had always reacted fiercely to his demands, especially regarding her treatment—and the outburst was strangely reassuring. It had been that way since Camilla's death. A calm response would probably have been more worrying. Lawrence raised his hand and Helena stopped yelling immediately.

'It's for your own good,' he said in a resigned voice.

Helena knew that a head-on confrontation with her father was no solution. 'Please don't make me go to Conroe, Dad. That's not the answer.' Her eyes became misty—and for once she wasn't acting. It was all the emotion she was trying desperately to keep inside. 'I don't want to go there. That place is full of crazy people. Things are improving. I slept fine this afternoon.'

'Then *explain* to me what's going on,' he said sincerely. 'Maybe I can help.'

'I'll try to explain, Dad, but let me be clear. I'm not going to Conroe. I won't do it.'

Lawrence looked into her eyes. 'Tell me ...'

'This will sound crazy, I know it will.' She took a deep breath. 'I'm seeing visions—through someone else's eyes. I saw a car crash—in a dream, I guess it was. I went to the freeway, the 610 loop at the Westheimer Overpass. There were skid marks and glass fragments everywhere. *Exactly* where I saw it in my dream.' Helena sensed her father's doubt and her voice hardened, 'The accident happened this morning, Dad. A man was killed. I just know it.'

Lawrence kissed his daughter on the forehead and motioned for her to sit down. She seemed lucid enough. He paced up and down in front of the fireplace. Orange flames were licking over the wood and the scent of burning pine was in the air. It reminded him of his cottage at the lake. He had not been there since Camilla had died. He missed her, he realised. Then Lawrence began reprimanding himself; they were *weak* thoughts he was having, *stupid* thoughts that he did not often let penetrate his armour.

'Aren't you going to say something?' Helena asked.

Returning to reality, he said, 'When do you see these visions?'

'At first, they were only when I was sleeping. But *today* it happened while I was awake. It's like I'm watching a movie with no sound. The pictures, with a kind of red haze, they *overlap* what I see through my own eyes.' Helena wiped her cheeks dry. 'Please work with me, Dad. Please.'

Lawrence stared down at her. He loved Helena so much, and that made him feel vulnerable.

'The car accident happened today,' she reaffirmed. 'And that proves that what I'm seeing is real. I know it does. Look Dad, I understand this is all very unusual. But I'm not mad. I'm not going crazy. I'm sure of it. It really happened.'

'Where did you say the accident was?'

'On the 610 freeway, on the south side of the Westheimer Overpass.' At least he was listening to her, Helena thought. 'A man was killed,' she added. 'The police were there, in my dreams.'

Lawrence grabbed his mobile telephone. 'What time?'

'Just after 7:30 a.m.'

Julia entered the room holding a silver tray. '*Si*, Mr Capriarty, just after 7:30 a.m.'

Lawrence keyed in a number and held his phone to his ear.

'Captain Olsen, please,' he said. Lawrence waited for a moment. 'Hello John, it's Lawrence Capriarty here. How are you? I need a small favour. Some details of a car accident that happened this morning. Yes, the 610 freeway, under the Westheimer Overpass, at about 7:30 a.m.' He waited, then said, 'That would be great.'

Helena gulped at her scotch to ease her nerves. She would soon prove to her father that she was not going crazy.

Lawrence held his hand over the receiver. 'John's a detective with the HPD. He owes me a couple of favours.' Eventually Lawrence's pacing stopped and he said, 'I'm here, John. What have you got?'

Helena grabbed Julia's hand, pulling her on to the sofa next to her.

'*Nothing* ...' Lawrence said softly. 'Are you sure?' He turned to his daughter with a doubtful expression, and judging by her appearance she was equally perplexed. 'Could there be a chance it wasn't reported?' He paused. 'Okay. Yeah. Thanks John. Call me if anything comes up.'

'The skid marks are there!' Helena erupted. 'The broken glass is there! You can check it for yourself. Let's go there now, together—I can show you! The accident happened. I know it did!'

'Helena,' Lawrence said calmly. 'Those skid marks could have been there for weeks. How could we tell?'

'Because I saw it,' Helena said, her every muscle shaking. 'That's why! *Please* ... let's go there together. Now!'

'This is crazy, Helena. There's no point. I want you to relax—'

Before he could finish his sentence she had already disappeared into her bedroom and slammed the door. After downing his scotch in one shot, he dialled another number.

'It's Lawrence Capriarty here. Page Dr Bennetswood and get him to call me on my mobile as soon as possible.' He turned to Julia. 'Have you spoken to him about what happened today?'

'She no want me speaking with the doctor,' Julia replied.

'Helena has to talk with someone,' he said. 'Doctor Bennetswood is the best there is.'

Julia poured them both another scotch.

'Julia, why is this happening?' Lawrence asked. 'I mean honestly, what do you think? Her visions, are they real?'

'She misses her mother very much,' Julia said sympathetically.

That wasn't the answer Lawrence wanted to hear. He strolled towards the window and felt the radiant heat of the fire against his legs. In the distance, the lights of Houston were burning brightly. Lawrence had lost his wife to a terrible tragedy, something he himself was trying to forget—and, as a result, it seemed he was losing Helena as well. This was the worst situation he could imagine. Witnessing his daughter's self-destruction was tearing him apart. She was all he had left—all that he loved. He would do anything to protect her; kill for her if he had too. And it seemed all the money and the power that he had amassed over his lifetime could do nothing. He was helpless—a situation that did not sit easily with him.

9

Houston, Texas
HPD Headquarters
November 25th 2012
Local Time 9:26 p.m.

Mission of Isaiah—Day One

COMMANDER VISBLAT APPROACHED the briefing room. Stay calm, he told himself. His hands gripped a thick stack of papers which he held behind his back, out of sight. The suit he wore was now wrinkled, his tie loose and off centre. It had been a long and frustrating day.

When he appeared in the doorway the murmuring ceased immediately.

The large auditorium was filled with more than sixty senior officers from every department of the Houston police. It was standing room only. Some were in uniform and others were dressed in plain clothes. Visblat walked quickly to the front of the room and stood behind the duty officer's desk. His massive frame loomed just below the height of the ceiling—the fluorescent lights accentuating the colour of his hair and the scowl on his face.

For a moment he merely stood and stared. Then, jamming his huge foot against the edge of the solid wooden desk, he kicked it over and it slammed against the floor with a resounding crash. No one even flinched as pens and papers scattered into the crowd.

'Catch one man, that's all I ask!' He strutted up and down in front of the assembled officers. 'We had our chance this morning, didn't we —but it seems we let him get away.' His agitated voice resonated all the way to the back of the room. 'You know what I think? I'll tell you. I don't care how long we've been waiting for this ridiculous situation to take place. It's finally happened—and just like I said it would.'

Everyone gazed in Visblat's direction, but no one looked directly into his eyes. He had a way of making even the most senior officer feel uncomfortable. There wasn't a person on the force, and that included the Mayor, who wasn't wary of him. Although Visblat generally seemed rational, over the last few months his actions had become more and more extreme, as if he was going to crack.

'Everybody take a copy,' Visblat said sternly, as he held out the stack of papers towards one of the officers in the front row. 'This is the fugitive we're looking for.' It was an identikit picture of a dark-haired man in his early thirties, even-featured, with blue eyes and brown hair—Wilson Dowling, the exact likeness of him.

Commander Visblat continued to pace up and down as the sheets were handed out.

'Everyone take a copy,' he repeated. 'Memorise *this* face, ladies and gentlemen.' One by one, he began to stare at each officer as he passed, his piercing gaze ensuring their full attention. 'We have a positive ID of this man. So let's all be clear about our situation. Between us—if any of you fail me again, you'll be off the force for good. Do you understand?' He waited a moment, letting his words sink in. 'And for those of you who *do* catch him, there will be accolades beyond your wildest imagination.'

Looking over the top of the group, he interlocked his sweaty hands behind his back. 'Let me tell you all about the odd sequence of events that unfolded this morning. The fugitive detonated a bomb on the rooftop at precisely 6:57 a.m. The officer assigned to watch *this* building was in the bathroom taking a crap.' There were seven buildings in the Post Oak area that were all under 24-hour surveillance.

'Isn't that just terrific. The officer—who shall remain nameless—was having a dump and reading the paper. Terrific! Meanwhile, the fugitive goes to the twenty-fourth floor and viciously assaults, and almost *kills*, a Chubb security guard; then he casually takes the elevator to the first floor and walks down the stairs to ground level and straight out the front door.'

Visblat raised his hands in the air like an evangelist.

'He then disappears! Can you imagine how I feel about that? Fourteen hundred men on duty across this city and we are blind.'

There was silence for a few moments.

'But I have good news, at last,' he said sarcastically. 'We figured this out *ten hours* after it happened. What a terrific team you idiots are!' He did his best to compose himself, then continued. 'One of our men, Officer Tolle, set out on foot in pursuit of our fugitive, just after 7:30 a.m. *Yes*, this morning! He had no backup—didn't tell anyone what he was doing. Thought he would be a hero.'

Visblat made a clicking sound with his tongue. 'Ladies and gentlemen, Officer Tolle was killed in a car accident at 7:36 a.m. He tried to cross the 610 freeway, on foot, in pursuit of our fugitive, and was struck down in a car pileup. More than ten vehicles were involved. It appears the fugitive was injured in the accident, also.'

Visblat wiped the accumulated spit from the corners of his mouth.

'He was taken to hospital, we believe. The only problem is—we don't know which fucking one! It's a comedy of errors ... *but I'm not laughing!* Due to an administration fault of some kind—someone screwed up the forms, I'm told—he was transferred from one hospital to another, because he couldn't be identified. So far we've had raids on three emergency rooms, and still nothing. So, until we find him, I've ordered that all information relating to the car accident—the pileup on 610—is to be kept confidential. No one is to leak the details out of this precinct. I don't want reporters all over us. Do you understand?'

Detective John Olsen stood at the back of the room, thinking: that was the very accident Lawrence Capriarty had asked him about less than an hour before. It explained why there was no information about the accident on the system. It was all restricted.

Commander Visblat paced about the briefing room like a caged tiger; his hair was a mess, his mannerisms were wild. And his strange eyes, it made Olsen shiver just to think about them. As a result, Olsen decided to keep Lawrence's enquiry to himself. Anyway, there was no way it could be related to the manhunt. That would be almost impossible. And there was certainly more to be gained from protecting Lawrence Capriarty than implicating him.

'What is it going to take,' Visblat asked pointedly, 'to convince you people that I want this madman caught? I don't care what you have to do to get him.' He jabbed a finger into the palm of his other hand. 'I want you to catch him! Alive! Do you understand?'

Corporal Jeremy Bishop, standing three rows back in the group, scratched his nose and Visblat immediately picked up on the tiny movement. It was just what was needed, an opportunity to display how serious this all was. Pushing through the front row, Visblat loomed menacingly over the young officer. 'So, there are more important things to worry about than listening to me?'

Bishop stood rigidly at attention, his nervous gaze fixed on some distant point on the far wall. 'No, Commander,' he replied.

'Will you do everything I ask?'

'Yes, Commander,' he said quickly.

Visblat moved closer, nose to nose with the corporal, drawing his stare. Their eyes locked and Bishop's muscles involuntarily began to quiver.

'Tell me,' Visblat said. 'Why do you think the fugitive got away? Tell me what you think.'

'Sir—Sir,' he stuttered. 'I'd rather not say.'

'I want to know what you think.' The accompanying gesture indicated everyone else in the briefing room. 'We all want to know!'

The corporal was having difficulty forcing out his words. Beads of sweat had formed across his brow and upper lip. At last he replied, 'Sir, we've been waiting there. Downtown, I mean, for—for years. I don't think we were, well, I don't think we were prepared …'

'Why is that?' Visblat said with a measured tone.

'I—I don't think any of us thought he would turn up the way he did. I think that, *maybe*, the situation caught us off—off guard. I mean, none of us could understand why he would be up there on one of those buildings. What his motive was—'

Visblat unclipped the corporal's revolver, took one step back and raised the weapon, pointing the barrel at the young officer's forehead.

'You don't trust me, do you?' the commander said.

Every person in the auditorium looked on in horror.

At the back of the room, Detective Olsen stood off to one side just in case the gun fired. His heart beat furiously in his chest. He had heard that Commander Visblat's actions had been getting increasingly unstable over the past six months—there was talk of it within all ranks of the HPD.

Should I do something? he asked himself. Can I say something to stop this? Olsen swallowed, his throat dry as if it were filled with sand. But no one else moved in opposition to what was going on, and neither did he. They all stood rigid. Olsen decided he had two things to be thankful for: one, he'd kept his mouth shut about Lawrence's call; and two, he wasn't in Corporal Bishop's shoes.

Visblat cocked the hammer of the gun and the click pierced the silence of the room. 'I need people I can trust!' he called out. He stared down the barrel at the officer in front of him. 'What have you got to say for yourself?'

Bishop's skin had turned pale and the beads of sweat were now streaming down his face. He was paralysed with fear. He couldn't even muster the will to beg for his life.

Lifting the gun upwards, Visblat fired a single thunderous shot, over Bishop's head, into the roof. The echo reverberated off the walls as chunks of ceiling plaster fell to the floor at the back of the room.

The smell of a discharged firearm hung in the still air.

Someone coughed in the background.

'What have you got to say for yourself, now?' Visblat asked.

'I trust you, Commander,' was Bishop's listless reply.

'That is the correct answer.' Visblat sheathed the handgun in Bishop's holster, clipped it down and gave it a pat of paternal affection. 'Now, where was I?' He made his way to the front of the room. 'That's right. The fugitive is not to be harmed. His sunglasses are not to be removed under *any* circumstances. That is a *direct* order. They *must* remain in place. A direct order!'

No one understood why Commander Visblat would make such a request and no one was game to ask why. It only served as further proof of his deteriorating mental state.

The doors to the auditorium suddenly opened and a uniformed officer hurried to Visblat's side to whisper in his ear. Everyone looked on. They were all still stunned by what had just taken place.

'That's good news,' Visblat whispered back. 'Tell CIP I want everything to be kept confidential. Quickly!' The officer ran out the door again.

Visblat addressed the gathering once more, a new sense of urgency in his tone.

'We've narrowed down the list of hospitals. You are all to remain on standby. We're very close.' He grabbed one of the identikit pictures and held it up for everybody to see. 'Let me make this clear.' He pointed at the image. 'I want this man alive! Don't take any chances. *Alive!* He's badly injured, but you must still approach him with caution.' Visblat scanned the auditorium one last time. 'Get to your standby positions.'

There was a slight pause because no one wanted to be the first to move, but a sharp gesture from the commander was enough to spur the gathering into motion.

As the room emptied, Visblat gazed at the image on the piece of paper in front of him. 'Soon this whole nightmare will be over,' he whispered to himself. 'I'm tired of this, Mr Dowling. You've kept me waiting far too long.'

10

Houston, Texas
Harris County Hospital, Level 2
November 26th 2012
Local Time 1:01 a.m.

Mission of Isaiah—Day Two

JUST SEVENTEEN HOURS after his accident, Wilson peeled the wrapping from his eyes. Gradually his gloomy surroundings came into focus. He was flat on his back in a hospital bed with an intravenous tube hanging out of his arm, the smell of antiseptic heavy in the air. Soiled bandages were wrapped around his torso. His legs were braced in heavy plastic splints. What was left of his clothing was crusty and shredded.

The hospital room was dark, the only light coming via a small viewing window cut high in the middle of a single closed door. Through the tiny window Wilson could occasionally see the shadows of people passing outside in the corridor. Thankfully, nothing was hurting, but Wilson knew he was partially numbed by the effects of the Nightingale program; his only sensation was the constant burning feeling that always accompanied the command. When he pinched the skin at his waist he could tell that all his body fat had been eaten away. The healing program had stripped him of his reserves. And if it continued, before long he wouldn't have the energy to walk, let alone escape.

Searching his pockets, he realised his sunglasses were nowhere to be found.

'Terminate Nightingale,' he whispered.

The burning gradually subsided and Wilson braced himself for what followed. He was expecting something excruciating, but the effects appeared to be only minor—twinging nerves in his lower back and legs and some aching muscles, probably caused by a build-up of lactic acid. The question was: had he given himself enough time to heal?

He wriggled to the edge of the bed. Layers of dry blood tightened against his skin as he gingerly dangled his legs over the side. Tugging the intravenous needle out of his arm, he tentatively sat up and proceeded to unclip the plastic splints from his thighs. He placed his bare feet on the floor, tested his weight, then stood up.

Although he was unable to confirm it, Wilson felt pale—profoundly tired. And though not conscious of being in any serious pain, he knew by the blood-encrusted bandages wrapped around him that he had sustained significant injuries. The moment of impact, when the car struck him on the freeway, flashed into his mind and he winced.

He was lucky to be alive and he knew it.

A red wire was attached to his wrist with a sticky electrode—it led to a heart monitor sitting on the side table. A small light indicated a rate of about one hundred beats a minute. Taking care not to let the electrode disconnect, in case it triggered an alarm of some sort, he limped to the door and peeked through the glass. Across the hall, two women were sitting behind a tall counter. Wilson could just see the tops of their heads and hear their distant voices. Dropping to one knee, more from exhaustion than any attempt to avoid detection, he cracked the door open just as a telephone began to ring.

'Nurses' station,' a woman's voice answered. There was a long pause. 'I'll just check,' she said. Wilson could hear tapping on a keyboard. 'Yes, patient 456 is across the hall. Why do you ask?' Wilson gazed at the paperwork clipped to the end of his bed—it read: 'Patient 456.'

'Yes!' the woman said in a surprised voice. 'Ward 22a. He's across the hall from me, on the first floor of B-wing.'

Someone was asking questions about him, Wilson realised. He looked around the hospital room, hastily trying to plan a form of escape—anything that would get him out of here alive.

The female voice continued, 'I'll bring his vitals up on the screen.' There was another pause. 'I understand. Yes, he's alive. Just get up here as fast as you can.'

If anyone looked into Wilson's eyes, he would certainly be attacked.

Again, he frantically looked around the small room. There was a single bed, one side table, a heart monitor sitting on it, and a chair. The ceiling tiles were too high for him to reach, even if he put the chair on the bed. And anyway, he didn't have the strength to pull himself up. Wilson considered putting a pillowcase over his head and making a run for it. But the more he thought about it, the stupider it seemed. His gaze locked on the power points on the wall, then the intravenous tube dripping onto the floor.

He had an idea.

Wilson limped to the bedside table and eased it out of the way. Half the power outlets were coded with blue panels, the other half red—two independent power systems. Grabbing the intravenous tube, he inserted the needle into the blue power socket and squeezed the saline bag, letting the solution pour into the wall for a few moments, then moved the tube to the other side of the panel and did the same thing again, with a red socket. With a finger on each switch he closed his eyes and flicked them both on.

A brilliant white flash erupted from the wall, momentarily scalding his arms. With a yelp, he jumped back as the lights in the corridor extinguished and everything went pitch-black.

'Activate Possum,' he commanded.

The blood flow to the light-sensitive cells in the back of Wilson's eyes—the *macula lutea*—increased to maximum pressure. His irises dilated fully as natural reserves of vitamin A stimulated the optic nerve. Night vision had been engaged and the room slowly came into focus in greyscale black and white.

Time was of the essence. Peering through the viewing window into the corridor, Wilson saw the two nurses clutching each other in total darkness. Silently he opened the door and limped out into the hall.

'Did you hear that?' one of the nurses said, detecting his approach.

'He was too badly hurt to move,' whispered the other, in reply.

Wilson was passing by only metres away, towards the stairs at the end of the landing. It all felt like some bizarre dream. Time-travelling to this strange place was *absurd*; the coils of soiled bandages wrapped around him, ridiculous. His shredded clothing, the night vision—it was crazy, like a silly game. But even so, Wilson tried desperately to keep his situation in perspective. Stay focused, he told himself, over and over. Just stay focused.

Moving as fast as he could, he made it to the staircase and approached the railing. As he did, a husky male voice came bellowing up from the ground floor.

'Move it! Move it!' The sound of footsteps followed in an ever-increasing clamour.

Wilson glanced over the side as beams of bright light, dozens of them, danced in the darkness below.

'Up to level one!' the voice yelled. 'On the double!'

It was a group of soldiers approaching, their footsteps growing louder by the second. Each man carried a rifle and a high-powered torch, the beams of illumination cutting through the dark like lasers. Utterly helpless, Wilson backed away from the railing into an adjacent corridor and pressed his depleted body into a small alcove next to a water fountain. He couldn't run even if he wanted to. The torch light swept ever closer. There was no choice but to put his hands over his eyes to protect them from the brightness.

A shrill voice called out and the torchlight suddenly swung in the other direction.

'This way!' a nurse yelled. 'Hurry!' She was pointing across the hall. 'He's in there!'

The police sergeant gathered his troopers in a semi-circle around the door to Ward 22a. 'Remember, he's not to be harmed,' was the directive. 'No shooting!' All the flashlights beamed against the entrance, with the exception of a single beam that held steady on the face of the nurse pointing the way. The sergeant sought confirmation, 'Is he in there alone?'

'Yes, he's alone.'

The sergeant held three-fingers in the air. 'On my mark. Three … Two … One!'

With a crash, the door was kicked open.

EVERY MUSCLE IN WILSON'S body was hurting as he shuffled down the last flight of stairs to ground level. The longer he had been out of bed, the worse he felt. The glass door facing him had a sign across it, painted in red lettering:

> Warning. Door is Alarmed.
> Use Only in Emergency.

'This is definitely an emergency,' he whispered to himself.

As he thrust the barrier open, an alarm bell began ringing. An irritating sound, but it stopped after he slammed the door closed behind him. Outside, in the coldness of the night, his breath turned to mist as he selected a fist-sized rock from the garden. Suddenly, specks of light inside the hospital began to flicker—then all at once the building was again fully lit. The brightness hurt his extra-sensitive eyes and he had no choice but to cancel his omega command.

Breathing heavily, Wilson stumbled away into the parking lot—there were at least eighty cars there. Summoning his remaining strength, he threw the heavy stone against the passenger window of the shiniest car he could see. With a crash, the glass shattered into a thousand tiny fragments and exploded inside, across the seat. Police sirens wailed in the distance as he rifled through the glove box. To his great relief, he found what he was looking for: a pair of dark sunglasses. The wallet, which he took also, was a bonus.

Wilson backed himself out of the vehicle, closed the door, and dropped to the ground. Staying low, he frantically stripped away the bandages from around his arms, head and neck. Amazingly, there were no wounds on his body. None at all. The only sign of his recent injuries was dry, blackened blood caked all over his skin.

In the distance, across the parking lot, beams of torchlight were approaching. He scanned in each direction—they were coming from everywhere! Everything had happened so quickly, Wilson had not yet found even a moment to ask himself why. Bundling the crusty bandages together, he tossed them away as far as he could. He wanted to run, but the lights seemed to cut off every avenue of escape.

A SWAT TROOPER quietly made his way through the parked cars. He was wearing a black uniform—Kevlar vest, cargo pants with pockets on the thighs, beanie and gloves. A powerful torch was mounted on the barrel of his assault rifle. Suddenly, his boots crunched on broken glass.

He pressed the mike on his headset. 'This is Alpha Three,' he said in a hushed voice. 'I've found something.'

A dozen men converged on his position in seconds, a combination of SWAT and local police officers. Alpha Three pointed his rifle at the broken car window. 'There's blood on the seat,' he said.

Captain Ronald Hall, leader of the elite SWAT taskforce, burst through the crowd and peered into the vehicle. With an abrupt hand gesture, he directed his men to continue onwards. They obeyed without question and sprinted into the darkness. Under a full deployment, like this one, he was in command. Catching the fugitive was his responsibility.

'The rest of you,' Captain Hall yelled, 'back to the hospital—now!'

There were police everywhere.

Hall's headset crackled, 'This is Alpha Five. I've found something.'

Searchlights swung towards a trooper not more than ten metres away. He was motioning towards the ground with his rifle. 'Bandages,' he said. Removing one of his gloves, he pressed the back of his hand to the material. 'They're still warm.'

Hall knew it meant the fugitive had to be close.

A local police officer, watching from nearby, casually leant against the back of a rusty white Ford. Under his weight, the trunk clicked shut!

To Wilson's horror, the mechanism locked directly above his head. There had been no time to close the lid of his hiding place properly beforehand. Had they found him? In the cramped confines of the boot, he lay completely still and tried not to make a sound.

'Concentrate the search towards Alpha Five,' Captain Hall said into his headset. Releasing the talk button, he angrily swung towards the local officer nearest to him. 'I said get back to the hospital—that's an order!' He didn't like the Harris County police—they were arrogant and soft and they were always getting in the way.

The local officer nervously pointed to the back of the white Ford, gazing at the lock questioningly. 'I think there's something you should—'

Captain Hall angrily grabbed the officer by the shirt to make sure there was no misunderstanding. '*I said*, get back to the fucking hospital! I know what I'm doing,' and he shoved him away. 'That's an order!' He was in no mood to be screwed around.

As directed, the Harris County officer disappeared towards the building complex.

Wilson didn't dare move as shards of light pierced through tiny rust holes in the rear panelling of the car. Seconds ticked by. For some reason, it seemed they were yet to detect him being there. The boot was crammed full of small cardboard containers. Silently, he angled a box into a stream of light. The label read: 'Pharmaceutical-Grade Morphine, fifty vials per box.'

OUTSIDE, ALPHA-TROOPERS swept across the parking lot towards the industrial area at the rear of the hospital complex. They moved with great stealth and speed—and yet they found nothing. The fugitive is supposed to be badly injured, Hall thought. How could he be moving so quickly?

Lieutenant Goodman, his second in charge, suggested, 'We need to search these cars. He must still be here somewhere.'

Hall glanced at his watch, then nodded. 'Quickly,' he said. 'We're running out of time.'

MINUTES LATER, POLICE officers, standing in pairs, were strategically stationed at every corner of the main hospital building, weapons at the ready. Through the double doors, a group of men and women, at least sixty of them, were herded out into the cold night air.

'Why are you dragging us out here?' asked one man.

'Who's looking after the patients?' shouted another.

The gathering was a mixture of hospital staff—everyone who was on duty in the Emergency Wing—including doctors, nurses, orderlies and various administrative personnel.

Lieutenant Goodman addressed the gathering, 'We have to clear this area, ladies and gentlemen.' He pointed towards the employee parking lot. 'You will identify your vehicles and we will search them. This is for your own safety.'

The door to the hospital again swung open and a skinny black man wearing a Houston Astros baseball cap was forced outside. George T Washington had shoulder-length dreadlocks and gold earrings in both ears. He wore a purple T-shirt, grey orderly's jacket, blue jeans and sneakers. His most distinguishing feature was his missing front tooth.

George had never seen so many police at one time and quickly concluded it was a trap. This was certainly due to the fact he had enough stolen morphine in the back of his car to sedate half the population of Houston. Thirty-two boxes, to be exact. He had taken it from the infirmary the day before yesterday. 'I told y'all, I don't drive!' he said in a bothered tone. '*Kapeesh?* No car! Who's in charge? I want to know who's in charge!' But despite his antics, he was pushed into the crowd with everybody else.

'I hate cars!' he continued. 'They cause pollution and stacks of other bad stuff. They're putting a hole in the ozone layer, man.' Grimacing ferociously, he strutted his way through the group. 'Yeah man! Pollution! Ya know, there are *two* things I hate: cops who oppress minorities, and gas-guzzlin' automobiles! They're both products of capitalist hypocrisy.' One of the other orderlies, Jethro Nixon, grabbed George by the arm.

'What are you doing?' Jethro said under his breath.

George's wary gaze shifted to the 300 pound black man above him. Jethro was huge, shaped like a giant basketball. George then turned his attention to the crowd of people gathered around him—they all knew who he was.

'Your car is over there,' Jethro said with a confused expression. He motioned towards the severely rusted white 1979 Ford Impala with the bald tires.

'Jethro,' George whispered. 'Y'all win the "fat-and-stupid award". Yes, you do.' There was now no choice but to cover his tracks. 'I don't own a car,' George announced. 'I own a *Ford Impala*! If a cop asks me if I drive a car, I tell him: no man, I drive a Ford, *Kapeesh?*' When it came to spinning bullshit, George T Washington was a self-proclaimed master. That's why he always claimed the 'T' in his name was for 'Truthful'.

Lieutenant Goodman stood at attention, his arms behind his back. Spotlights flashed across the dark sky behind him. 'We are tracking a runaway killer,' he announced. 'The fugitive was in your hospital just fifteen minutes ago …'

'Terrific,' George muttered. 'A runaway killer—just terrific.'

'We have reason to believe he escaped in *that* direction.' The lieutenant pointed across the parking lot into the night. 'Everyone—go to your vehicles and identify them. Your car will be searched. Then you'll be asked to move it to the other side of the building. We must clear this area as quickly as possible.'

The group of employees slowly began to disperse, with the exception of George. He stood perfectly still, hoping no one would notice him.

'It's over here!' a familiar voice suddenly called out. Jethro was pointing towards George's rusty white Ford—smack-bang in the middle of the commotion.

George wanted to slap Jethro across his stupid, black head.

A policeman immediately doubled back. 'Where's your vehicle, sir?'

George scratched his chin. 'I can't remember.' He looked the other way. 'Over towards emergency, I think.'

The officer pointed at the white Ford. 'Is *that* your vehicle?'

George put on his most confused expression. 'Man, there it is!' he said softly. 'I get lost sometimes. I'm new here at Harris County.' It was another lie. At that moment, George decided he was going to kill Jethro when he was released from prison—because at this rate that was exactly where he was going.

The view ahead was worrisome. Police officers were all around his car. It definitely looked like a trap and George nervously pulled a cigarette from behind his ear. 'I should get a job at 7-Eleven,' he whispered to himself. 'Selling Slurpys and that sort'a stuff. Something honest, at least. Runaway killers are giving this hospital a bad name.'

One by one, the vehicles were searched then driven away.

Police were everywhere.

George nervously sucked on his cigarette. 'I should have dumped it,' he said to himself. 'I should've.' Jethro—the stupid fool—was the one who helped him load the stolen morphine into the back of his car.

'Open it up,' a trooper said, prodding George with a torch. 'Quickly!'

He reluctantly dug into his pockets. 'Hold on, hold on, I'll just find my keys, man.' Turning full circle, he tried to look confused and disoriented, but the trooper became annoyed and slapped the cigarette out of his mouth. 'What did you do that for?' George whined.

'Open the vehicle, sir!'

'Damn cops,' George muttered.

'What did you say?'

'I said, damn *locks*!'

Before the trooper had a chance to retaliate, George produced a bunch of keys, at least thirty of them, tied together with an old piece of string.

'Well ... which one is it?' the trooper asked.

'I tell ya, there's nothing inside.' With no other choice, George reluctantly pointed to a well-worn car key.

After struggling with the lock, the trooper opened the driver's door and scanned the interior with a flashlight, just as Captain Hall walked past.

'Check the trunk,' he said.

'There's nothing in there—' George reacted.

'Shut up!' the captain snapped back.

The trooper opened the glove compartment and repeatedly pressed the boot release button, but nothing happened. He stepped outside again. 'Which key opens the trunk?' he asked.

George was confused.

The trooper held out the string of keys. 'Which one—?'

'That lock's been broke for years,' George explained, happily. 'Someone tried to steal from me, you understand. You'll see, you'll see,' and he ran to the back of the car and pointed at the disembowelled keyhole.

Captain Hall inspected the lock also—the centre of the mechanism was missing. 'I want this trunk searched!' he yelled, pounding his fist on the metal. 'Open it!'

'This ve-hicle is a collector's item!' George said in desperation. 'Please don't do that—' but Lieutenant Goodman effortlessly pushed him aside and inserted a crowbar under the lip to pry it open.

Overhead, a faint rumble intensified into a roar as a police helicopter hovered to a stationary position one hundred feet above the hospital complex. Seconds later, a powerful spotlight shone downwards as waves of turbulent air buffeted the crowd. Steadying himself against the downdraft, Captain Hall assessed his situation: the fugitive had slipped through his fingers and now Commander Visblat was here. Things had gone from bad to worse.

Lieutenant Goodman withdrew the crowbar and walked to his captain's side. Both of them had been in the briefing room earlier that evening to witness Commander Visblat's antics with Corporal Bishop. As a result, they were both suitably wary.

'What do you want me to do?' Goodman asked.

The helicopter was coming in to land.

Captain Hall cupped his hand to his mouth. 'Get the rest of these cars out of here as fast as you can. Secure the site. I'll give the commander an update.' He waved Lieutenant Goodman away.

As the chopper set down on the asphalt in a flurry of dust and debris, George did well just to hold on to his baseball cap. In the rear of the cabin he could see a tall redheaded man peering through the glass towards him. He was one of the most imposing men George had ever seen.

Lieutenant Goodman pushed George to his car. 'Get moving,' he ordered.

'Who is that?' George asked warily.

'That's Commander Visblat,' was the response—one that sounded very much like a threat.

The helicopter engine began to cycle down as the large man opened the Perspex door and stepped outside. Making momentary eye contact, George was filled with a sense of profound dread. The very same feeling he had when he stood in a tall building and looked out the window—he had a terrible fear of heights. Fumbling with his car keys, George turned the ignition and the engine came to life with a rattle. It was time to get out of here.

A CLOUD OF EXHAUST fumes wafted into the trunk and Wilson did his best to suppress a cough. Gazing through one of the rust holes in the side panelling of the boot, he saw a familiar figure standing outside: a large man with red hair—unmistakable. The same man he had seen the day he arrived.

'THAT'S ONE FREAKY-LOOKING dude,' George said to himself. 'Cops *are* getting uglier ... *definitely*.' The car picked up speed and jolted out onto the main road. Reaching over to close the glove box, George noticed his wad of cash was gone from inside.

Someone had stolen his money!

He threw his head back in disgust.

He'd stashed over two hundred dollars in there.

'What has the world come to?' he muttered, 'when cops are stealing from a poor luckless black man! It's criminal. I think I'll take the rest of the night off,' he decided. George lit another cigarette as MC Hammer throbbed out of the eight-track stereo at full volume: 'Can't touch this, der der der der—'

He sang along with the music, 'Can't touch this—' and shimmied his shoulders in perfect timing. '—Can't touch this!'

But things could have been worse, George decided. At least he didn't get arrested this time, and his haul of morphine was safe for the moment. And Jethro Nixon, well—it was time to get a partner with more brains, but not too much more; in his experience, when he had partners that were too smart, they were even more dangerous.

11

Houston, Texas
Richey Road, Bordersville
November 26th 2012
Local Time 2:35 a.m.

Mission of Isaiah—Day Two

WITH A SQUEAK of the brakes the white Ford Impala swung left. George negotiated the corner much faster than he wanted because the brake pedal went half way to the floor before it worked. He needed to replace the pads, and, like everything else that needed doing in his life, he had been putting it off for months.

The change in motion jarred Wilson out of his carbon-monoxide stupor. Trying to sit up, he slammed his forehead, hard, on the metal panel above him and almost knocked himself out.

At the sound of the thump, George decided his precious Ford was in need of some new rear shock absorbers, as well.

As he turned into his driveway a pair of fully grown Doberman Pinschers pranced about in the car headlights as if they were puppies. George smiled. 'How's my babies? Have y'all missed Daddy?' He was always happy to see them. With the car still moving, he turned off the ignition and the engine kicked a few extra beats before going silent.

'Stealth-fighter One, coming in to land,' he said to himself as his car rolled the full length of the driveway, stopping exactly at the front of the house.

George opened the driver's door. The two dogs frantically forced their heads into the car so they could lick their master's hands and face, which they did with unwavering enthusiasm. Using baby talk that he reserved only for his adoring pets, George began to fill them in on the evening's events.

'Daddy saw some strange fuckers tonight. Yep, strange fuckers.' A vision of Visblat's face was clearly in his mind. 'He was really ugly-wugly. Y'all wouldn't have liked him. I don't think so. No.' As George got out of the car the pair of Dobermans—one male, one bitch—bounded eagerly about him. The dogs were tall, slim and powerful, with sharp features and pointy ears. Both were black except for tan breastplates and narrow tan markings on each cheek.

George looked with trepidation towards the lime-green door of his trailer home. 'Where's Mama?' he breathed. 'Let's not wake her, whatever we do ...'

The dogs began growling, sensing a noise in the rear of the car.

George berated the pair under his breath, 'Shhhh! Do y'all want me to get in trouble?' The beasts persisted and he raised his voice a little louder, 'Quiet, both y'all!' At his harsh tone they obediently plonked down on their backsides in silence.

'Be quiet!' George reasserted. 'Not another sound.' It was unusual for his animals to react this way, but he was more worried about waking his wife, Thelma, than anything else.

'Maybe the bitch is still asleep,' he whispered as he tiptoed towards the front door.

A voice suddenly echoed from inside.

'Why the hell ain't you at work?'

George stood bolt upright, realising the game was up. *She lives!* His instinct was to sneak away, but the outside light flashed on and the door burst open before he had a chance to make a decision. A full-figured black woman appeared with hands on hips.

'I said, *why* ain't you at work?'

George smiled his sweetest smile in reply. 'Honey-pie-darling-thing. You ain't never going to believe what happened.' He attempted to tell her the whole story, but Thelma didn't believe any of it. Thelma Washington had a theory: if there was trouble, George T would find it. If there was work to be done—George T would break his arm to get out of it. If there was money—any amount—George T would try and steal it. With George T there was no truth: there were only lies. In her view, he was a lazy, thieving, arrogant, chauvinist pig.

They had an interesting relationship.

George couldn't win with Thelma, and he didn't try too hard. He knew the score. So after a number of heated exchanges their voices faded, as they always did. The uneasy truce at the Washington household reigned once again and the outside light was switched off.

The two Dobermans remained fixated on the rear of the car. One sniffed the edges of the trunk. But even though they were unsettled, the pair didn't dare make a sound. The male jumped up onto the roof of the vehicle, claws scratching the rusted paintwork as it stepped in circles before settling and placing its head between its paws. The other animal sat alertly, watching and listening.

Cocooned in his hiding place, Wilson could hear movement outside but he was too exhausted to care. His head was pounding and he felt a huge lump on his forehead where he had slammed it against the panelling. He shuffled his weary body among the cardboard boxes to get comfortable and plummeted into a fatigue-driven sleep.

A wave of mist silently rolled across the property and visibility faded to nothing. It was going to be a typical winter's night in Houston: cool and still. In the distance, the sound of aircraft landing—one after the other—could be heard at the nearby Intercontinental Airport.

12

Houston, Texas
Richey Road, Bordersville
November 26th 2012
Local Time 11:36 a.m.

Mission of Isaiah—Day Two

THE SUN WAS HIGH overhead before any blue sky appeared. It was becoming a beautiful day. A gentle breeze kicked up from the west and stirred the long wispy grass flanking the driveway. A silver aircraft thundered low overhead, leaving a trail of vapour across the sky.

The white Ford Impala sat in the clearing directly outside George's front door. The property was a shambles, overgrown with weeds and covered in garbage. Broken chairs, car parts, and the carcass of an old television set lay discarded with the rest of the junk piled around the yard. An old toilet seat hung from the limb of a tree—George was hoping that one day he would find another use for it. The Washington home itself was a large green caravan cemented into makeshift foundations. It sat next to a corrugated iron shed, which leant dangerously over to one side. The only thing stopping it from toppling was the concrete water tank it was butted up against.

George was rarely out of bed before eleven and this day was no exception. His wife left early for work every weekday morning—she worked in a fruit canning factory—which meant he had his days to himself; and that was just how he liked it. Wearing the same clothes as the night before, he appeared through the flyscreen door and immediately lit a cigarette. His dogs leapt from their positions and ran to him, howling with excitement.

George was confused as his dogs anxiously tugged at his clothes and drew him forward. He was still sleepy. 'Have y'all gone nuts?'

Both animals began scratching on the trunk of his car, trying to alert their master to the stowaway inside.

'It's just a stash of morphine,' George said drowsily.

Unexpectedly, a muffled voice called out from inside, 'Er, hello—'

In utter shock, George's cigarette fell from his lips.

'—Would you mind letting me out?' Wilson pleaded. '*Please* let me out.' He had been thinking about what to say, and how to say it, for hours.

'Well, I'll be a fuck-a-doodle-black-dude,' was George's response. Not the type to waste a cigarette, he bent down and inserted the smoke back into his mouth.

Inside the boot, Wilson pressed his hands together as if in prayer. 'Please let me out,' he said again. The air was stale and his head was pounding, probably a combination of the blow he took trying to sit up and severe dehydration. 'Please …' he groaned.

George looked under the car to make sure there was no way to escape. 'Y'all ain't that *serial killer* everybody's looking for, are ya?'

'I promise you,' Wilson responded. 'I'm not a serial killer.'

George rubbed his unshaven chin. 'Then what are y'all doing in the back of my ve-hicle?' There was silence. 'You ain't answering me— what y'all doing in my ve-hicle?'

'Let me out and I'll tell you everything,' Wilson said, trying to gather his thoughts. 'I promise.'

George rapped the trunk lid with his knuckles. 'What are y'all doing in my car?' he said, more forcefully.

The response was unexpected. 'Are you a drug dealer?'

George took a long drag of his cigarette and put two and two together. 'Oh—y'all mean the morphine. That's a little enterprise I got on the side. Totally legit. Yep, totally. To help make ends meet, ya understand.'

'So, you *are* a drug dealer.'

George circled his car, analysing the situation. 'I ain't no drug dealer, boy. And, by the way, it ain't cool for you to try and turn this situation around.'

Wilson's muffled voice continued, 'Well, seeing as you're not a drug dealer, and I'm not a serial killer—why don't you let me out and we can talk about it?'

'You're gonna have to do better than that!' George laughed.

'Look, I admit it,' Wilson replied, 'the police are after me, but I promise you, I'm not a serial killer.'

'Still nowhere near good enough! Know what I think? I think, I'll drive y'all to the nearest cop station and hand your ass over to them. Maybe there's a nice reward in it for me?' George's imagination ran away with itself: he was dreaming about being hailed as a hero, receiving a huge reward—thousands of dollars even. The mayor was giving him the keys to the city, that sort of thing.

Wilson's voice broke the silence. 'That's not what you want to do.'

George smiled. 'Sure it is.'

'No, it's not.'

'An' why is that?'

Wilson was quick in response, 'Because, I'll tell them about your little morphine problem.'

George's dreams vanished in a puff of smoke. 'They want *y'all* more than they want me,' he said. 'There were that many cops tracking your ass last night—they were like cockroaches at a cookout. Turned that hospital upside-down, they did.'

'But I'm *not* a serial killer. And when they figure that out they're going to be looking at *you* as a nice consolation prize.'

George brushed the dreadlocks away from his face. 'How 'bout I just leave yer butt in there for a couple a days? Till you starve? Then I can dump your ass at the police station an' leave them a note. Hell, I might just dig a hole out back and save myself the gas. Come to think of it, I could save m'self two week's worth o' dog meat if I store your body away right.'

'Are you sure you want me in here?' Wilson said. 'I could do a lot of damage in a couple of days.' He shook one of the medical boxes and the dozens of tiny morphine containers clinked inside. 'These look like they taste pretty good.'

A jetliner thundered low overhead and George waited for it to pass before he continued. 'How 'bout I go get me a gun and shoot y'all full of holes? That approach should only cost me a couple a vials. And I got me some rags here to wipe the blood away.'

Wilson's muffled voice replied, 'You could, I guess. But you shouldn't be shooting at me—you should be thanking me.'

'Thanking you ... *for what?*'

'It's because of me you're not in jail right now. I was the one who disconnected the trunk release. You'd be in real trouble if I wasn't in here. And anyway, you don't want to ruin this *fine* automobile by shooting a bunch of holes in it, do you? You said it yourself; this *vehicle* is a collector's item.' Wilson's imitation was perfect.

George laughed as he remembered the comment. 'I was bullshitting to try and save my skin! I'd lie about my grandma if I thought it was going to get me outta trouble.'

'Thanks to *me*, you're not *in* any trouble.'

'I can avoid those dumb cops without *your* help!'

'I figure you owe me at least one favour.'

George stamped down on his cigarette butt. 'I don't owe ya nothin'. Y'all ain't the reason I got away.' A vision of Visblat was clearly in his mind again. 'It wuz some freaky-looking monster what flew in on a police helicopter.' He grimaced. 'I mean, I'm no oil painting, but—*wow*! That guy had been beaten with the ugly stick ... seriously beaten.'

'The big guy, with the red hair?' Wilson said curiously.

'Yeah, Commander *something or other*.' George lit another cigarette. 'Ya know him?'

'If I tell you the truth, will you let me out?'

'Convince me why that freaky-looking monster is chasing after your ass, and you stand a chance of getting out, at least.'

Wilson knew he was going to have to conjure an elaborate yarn to get free—and conjure he did. 'The man with the red hair ... he's chasing after me because of a woman.' Wilson paused, deciding to draw the story out. 'I shouldn't be telling you any of this,' he said bashfully.

George's curiosity was sparked. 'Come on, tell me ...'

'I've said too much already.'

'Come on!'

'Let's just say that I've done some very bad things.'

George moved closer to the back of the car. 'What? Tell me!'

After a well-timed pause, Wilson answered, 'I slept with that guy's wife. That's why he's trying to catch me.'

'Yer shitting me?'

'It's true.'

George's mind filled with elaborate sexual images. 'Was it good?'

'Yeah, it was good!'

'What happened?'

In for a penny, in for a pound, Wilson decided. 'We were doing it on the kitchen table when her hubby caught us. I was right in the middle of it, too. Whipped cream and all. The works. I've been on the run ever since.'

'How fucked up does that guy look!' George said enthusiastically. He was just happy to have someone to discuss it with. 'I tell ya—you are one brave mother-fucker! Or should that be *wife-fucker*? Ha! Braver than me! I wouldn't go anywhere near that dude's woman.' He was imagining Visblat angry—really angry. 'You *must* be crazy!'

'Let me outta here,' Wilson moaned. 'Haven't I been through enough?'

The request was met with a stony silence.

Wilson peered through the rust holes in the side of the car. It seemed his conversation partner had disappeared. The sound of bending metal suddenly resonated inside the trunk and luckily Wilson had the clarity of mind to slap his newly acquired sunglasses over his eyes just in time. The boot lid swung open and fresh air and sunlight flooded inside. There was a moment of apprehension as he lay on his back with the silhouette of a man with dreadlocks leaning menacingly above him.

'I am so *glad* that you ain't no black man!' George grinned as he dragged Wilson to his feet. 'You look like total shit, boy. Are you hurt?'

'It's been a tough couple of days, that's all.'

'You can say that again,' George muttered, studying his guest. Blood was encrusted in Wilson's hair. His clothes were shredded and torn. There were no shoes on his feet.

'Screwin' bitches, then running for yer life. Oh maaan, you're dumb!'

Wilson was unsteady and George held him upright. 'A black man *always* knows how to stay out of trouble. Especially when it comes to bitches. Anyway, my name is George T Washington—no relation to the former president, in case you wuz wondering. Welcome to my home—*Vista Del George*.' He held out his hand in greeting.

Wilson reciprocated with a weak handshake. 'Nice to meet you—I'm Wilson, the idiot who got stuck in the back of your car.' His gaze shifted to the two large Dobermans skulking in the grass. They didn't look friendly at all.

George smiled at his pets. 'Don't go near them if y'all got any brains—which, under the circumstances, I seriously doubt.' He laughed. 'They don't like strangers much, 'specially white folks.'

When Wilson turned to face the animals, they froze, displaying their sharp white fangs with a snarl. 'I'll stay away from them, don't worry.'

'Let's just hope *they* stay away from *you*.' George brushed down Wilson's clothes with the back of his hand. 'Man. Looks like y'all have been to hell and back. How did you get that much crap all over you?'

Wilson gazed at what was left of his clothing. Dry blood was caked all over his skin, from head to toe. His chest and legs were still wrapped with bandages. How could he possibly explain his bizarre condition?

His mouth dry, he eventually replied, 'She wanted to pretend I was injured.' It was the only thing he could think of, that quickly anyway, to explain the scenario. Wilson knew it was a stupid response, but it was so stupid it might just work.

'She likes to play nurse,' he continued. 'Wanted to save me, you understand,' and he gave George a wink.

'She wrapped you in bandages!' George threw his arms upwards. 'That's one sick bitch y'all been messin' with!' He was grinning again—trying desperately to picture it. 'I thought I'd heard it all—but she covered y'all in dirt, an' blood, then pretends to save your ass.' He licked his top lip through his missing front tooth. 'She must be full-on twisted. I bet she's ugly, ain't she?'

'Actually, she's a real looker,' Wilson said, nodding. If he was going to make up a story about a woman he'd had a sordid encounter with, he'd at least make her beautiful. Little did Wilson realise, his flippant comment about her being 'a looker' would change George's destiny forever.

'No woman is worth having blood poured down your pants!' was the reply. 'Why would y'all want to put ya self in that sort'a situation?' George sniffed his hand and his expression immediately twisted. 'No offence man, but you *stink*!'

Wilson pulled his shirt to his face—the odour was just awful.

George held his hands as far from his nose as he could. 'Whoa, man! That's worse than my feet! My dogs'll eat your ass for sure, they got a taste for rotting meat. *Jesus!* Come round here.'

Wilson followed the skinny man to the rear of the property.

George was thinking out loud, 'That guy's wife must be one sick bitch. Her husband is, well ...' His walk slowed for a moment. 'It's hard to describe, but that guy is bizarre looking.' George knew the emotion was fear, but he didn't want to acknowledge it. 'Anyway, y'all is a braver man than me.'

Wilson was led towards a concrete structure separated from the main trailer home. The small shower cubicle looked like it hadn't been used in a very long time. Tall spindly weeds blocked the path, and George was forced to clear away a series of spiderwebs as he approached the entrance and kicked open the door.

'I'd let y'all clean up in the house, but frankly, y'all stink too much. And I don't need no more trouble with Thelma. Got more than I want already.' George pointed at the shower cubicle through the doorway. 'There's no hot water out here, but it should do ya.'

'I really appreciate your help,' Wilson replied.

'Y'all ain't from around here, that funny accent an' all.'

Wilson paused, then replied, 'I'm from Australia.' He wanted to say 'Pacifica' but that name was at least fifty years away from meaning anything to anyone.

A smile came to George's lips, 'G'day mate!'

Wilson replied, 'G'day.'

'You little ripper! Throw another shrimp on the *barbie*.'

Wilson appreciated the attempt but he was a little confused.

'Paul Hogan … *Crocodile Dundee!*'

'Of course,' Wilson responded. He knew that Paul Hogan had been an Australian actor, a comedian, but he'd never seen any of his movies.

'I love him too. He's great.'

George gave a broad smile, displaying his missing front tooth. 'Yeah—hilarious!' He then enthusiastically acted out a scene. 'When that guy tries to steal his money, in New York, and Crocodile Dundee pulls out that big-ass knife and says: "That's not a knife—*this* is a knife!" That sure was funny!' He laughed.

Even though Wilson was exhausted, he had to smile.

'Are all Australians funny like that?'

Wilson's response was absolutely deadpan, 'Yep. All of us.'

A serious thought suddenly popped into George's head. With a ruffled brow, he said, 'How'd y'all get in the back of my car, anyway?'

'The boot was open.'

'What *boot*?'

'I mean—the *trunk* was open.'

'Hold on a second!' George said accusingly. 'Did you take my money out of my glove compartment?'

Wilson held out his palms, pleading innocence, 'I didn't. I swear! The trunk lid was ajar and I crawled in the back, with the morphine. That's it!'

George studied Wilson's face—a thief always prided himself on recognising his own kind. There was a long pause. 'Those damn cops! Y'all can't trust 'em, can ya?'

George slapped Wilson on the back.

'The trunk pops open sometimes if I drive a little too fast. Do a bit of Mario Andretti an' the whole car starts comin' apart!' He laughed, then turned away. 'I'll get y'all a towel and somethin' to wear. Should be soap on the shelf.' There was always soap in the outside shower in case George got lucky and needed to wash away some evidence. As he walked back towards his trailer home he took another sniff of his hand. 'Whoa that's ripe! Covered y'all with blood. I can't believe it! Bitches is so *twisted* these days.'

The border of the property was surrounded with a barbwire fence. It had fallen in places and would be easy to climb over. But beyond it there was nothing but open grassland without any trees for cover. Wilson considered making a run for it, but he felt weak and the two Dobermans were menacingly near. Anyway, he thought to himself, a shower seemed like the correct priority. Wilson could think of nothing else but drinking straight from the showerhead and never stopping. He wanted water—as much as he could get. With every joint in his body aching, he gingerly removed his clothes and bandages, dumping them in a pile on the floor.

He looked down at his dirt-encrusted skin. All his body fat was gone. Wearing only his sunglasses—Wilson didn't want to take any chances—he waited as the water rattled through the pipes. When the spray hit him, the cold took his breath away. He gulped mouthful after mouthful, until he felt his stomach would explode.

A steady stream of brownish water circled down the plughole as Wilson scrubbed away at his skin until faint pink scars were the only indications of his recent injuries. For the second time, he reflected on how lucky he was to be alive. Seeing movement out of the corner of his eye, he flinched, then realised it was only some clothes and a fresh towel being slung over the wall. It seemed George Washington was a godsend.

Wilson took a deep breath and tried to relax. The soap smell was familiar, and unexpected memories came flooding back. Childhood memories of his time in Sydney. The long hot days ... endless days. He was always in trouble back then. He smiled to himself; life had been so simple.

Shivering so badly that he could barely stand, Wilson turned off the tap, removed his sunglasses and pressed the soft white towel to his face. The room suddenly began moving about, going in and out of focus.

He collapsed.

When the sensation of dizziness eventually faded, he opened his eyes. Crouched only inches away, nose to nose with him, was one of the Dobermans—the female.

The dog's ears were pinned back and she was ready to attack!

Wilson was naked, on all fours, facing the animal. His sunglasses were on the floor beside him. He looked the dog straight in the eye and tried not to move. Inexplicably, the Doberman licked him on the side of the face. Wilson's heart was thumping madly as he plonked himself on the ledge next to her.

'Ya mutt. You scared me half to death.' The dog just looked back at him. Wilson eventually stroked the animal. In reply she licked his face a second time. It seemed Wilson had a new friend. The whole situation was very odd. The reaction was the opposite of the security guard's— the complete opposite.

With the large dog happily looking on, Wilson inspected the contents of the wallet he'd stolen. There were three one-dollar bills, a U.S. driver's licence and a green American Express card. Wilson studied the name on the licence:

Jack Bolten

The picture looked nothing like him—a bald man in his fifties. He jammed the plastic identity card into a crack at the base of the wall. He gazed at the American Express card and flipped it over in his fingers, paying particular attention to the squiggly signature.

Wilson held the dollar bills out in front of him and something caught his eye: George Washington—President George Washington— was proudly emblazoned on the front of the note. A coincidence?

Wilson turned the dollar over and his heart skipped a beat. There were two images on the back—a pyramid and an eagle, both symbols of the *Great Seal of the United States*. The irony of what Wilson was seeing was not lost. The pyramid: the very structure that would play a central role in his mission here. And the eagle: the standard that symbolised the Legions of Rome in Judea during the First Jewish Revolt.

Barton's words echoed in Wilson's mind, 'Coincidence is merely the signpost of destiny. Take heed, Wilson. It will lead the way.'

'WHAT SIZE IS YOUR big white foot?' George called out.

Adjusting his sunglasses, Wilson approached from the shower cubicle wearing the clothes he had been given, his towel slung around his neck. The orange T-shirt he wore had 'Love Machine' printed across the front in fluorescent letters. And the blue tracksuit pants were entirely too small. He felt stupid to the core, but what choice was there? The clothes were clean, at least.

A commercial jetliner screamed directly over the property and Wilson couldn't believe how low it flew. After the sound dissipated he answered George's question, 'Um—about a size eleven, I think.'

George opened one of the four shoeboxes he had stacked on the table. 'We're less than a mile from the airport,' he explained. 'Depending on the wind direction those planes fly right over the top of us. No one wants to live around here.' He disappeared into his shed, but his voice continued, 'Just how I like it ... nice and private.'

One of the dogs shifted against Wilson's leg and he looked down to see the female wagging her stubby black tail.

George's voice suddenly screamed out, 'Don't go near them! They're killers!'

Wilson confidently stroked the animal's head. 'It's okay—'

George glared at his pet. 'Is this what I've taught y'all? To be nice and friendly to *white folks*?' He lifted his perplexed gaze to Wilson. 'What did you do to her?'

'I didn't do anything!'

George huffily tossed a pair of white runners at Wilson's feet. 'Y'all must a done somethin'! Ya must've!'

'She's just being friendly.'

'*Friendly?* My animals ain't *friendly!*'

Wilson shrugged his shoulders.

'Did you feed her somethin'?'

'No.'

'What happened then?'

'She licked my face, that's all.'

George grabbed the Doberman by the collar and tugged her away. 'Licked you? They *hate* white people!' He looked his dog in the eye. 'Y'all hate white people. *Don't ya?*'

'Would you have been happier if she'd attacked me?'

George thought for a moment. 'Yeah, I would.'

Wilson looked at the brand-new running shoes. 'Where did you get these from?'

George ordered his two dogs to sit at his feet and gave them each a light smack across the face. 'Wake up! Both of you.' He then answered Wilson's question, 'Off some dead guy. I got dozens of pairs.'

'I probably don't want to know this—but what dead guy?'

'When people die at the hospital—in the morgue—if they have new stuff, I take it. I figure they won't need it. What good are Nikes if you ain't running no more?'

'Not much, I guess,' and Wilson began to put the shoes on.

George just couldn't understand it. 'What did y'all do to these dogs?' he asked again. 'They're killers!'

'I didn't do anything. I told you, she came up to me and licked my face.' Wilson stood up and checked his new shoes—they were a perfect fit. But even so, he hoped, deep inside, that they would be luckier for him than they had been for their last owner.

George suddenly erupted with laughter. '*Love machine!* It's perfect!' Wilson's pants were too tight and his T-shirt barely covered his midriff.

'You think this is funny, don't you,' Wilson said drily.

'Yes, I do,' George sniggered.

Wilson watched George's smiling face, missing tooth and all. In a world where it was difficult to know who to trust, this dreadlocked character was certainly a welcome surprise.

'I actually think this stuff looks really good on me,' Wilson said.

George laughed even harder. 'Yer right, you are funny!' He was grinning from ear to ear. 'How 'bout some food, Aussie?'

Just the thought of it made Wilson's mouth water.

'Come in the house. That Thelma might be a bitch of a wife, but she sure can cook.'

George re-heated some leftovers and the pair talked and laughed as Wilson devoured everything put in front of him. They discussed all sorts of things, from politics to sport. Wilson was trying to learn as much as he could about George's world—a world where the Schumann Frequency was certainly out of control.

'Tell me about living here,' Wilson said. 'What's it like?'

'Houston?'

'Is it a good place to live?'

'It's a hellhole! Ain't y'all figured that out yet?'

'Tell me. I'm interested.'

George lit a cigarette. 'It's not like where *y'all* come from—with happy little kangaroos, an' all. There's crime everywhere in Houston. You can't trust no one. If you turn your back, if y'aint careful, they'll take yer for everything you got.'

'Then why do you stay here?'

'Man, I don't know about Australia, but here in America that's how it is. Everybody hates each other. The rich is getting richer, and the poor is getting poorer. The blacks hate the whites. The Hispanics hate the blacks. The Hicks hate the Spicks. The Muslims hate the Christians. I lose track—' He paused as he counted on his fingers. 'Let me think. The poor hate the rich. The rich hate the poor. Did I say that? Anyway, everybody hates somebody and we all hate each other. I'll let y'all in on a little secret.' George leant closer. 'The only way to stay ahead of the rat race is to be more creative—an' by that, I mean more *deceitful*—than the next guy. That's how y'all stop yourself from getting swallowed up by this stinkin' place.'

'Is there anything good about living here?'

George thought for a moment. 'The cigarettes are good. But they're killing me. Know what? There is somethin'. The days go so fast … it's like they blend into each other, which is good. I don't have too much time to think about nothin'.'

Wilson saw the irony of the situation—that was *exactly* what he was here to change. 'Time gets faster as you get older, doesn't it?' Wilson said.

George's eyes lit up. 'I say that all the time! I say: "no point worrying about tomorrow, 'cause it'll be here before y'all know it—and then, you will just have to worry about the day after that!" That's what I say.' George's eyebrows lifted as if he'd said the most profound words ever.

Wilson smiled. 'Well, I'm glad you're here, George Washington. You've really helped me out.'

George took a long drag of his cigarette. 'I know you will find this hard to believe—me being so charming an' all—but I don't have many white folks for friends.'

'Is that right?'

George seemed thoughtful. 'Yeah.'

'Well, George Washington, it looks like you do now.'

Flicking back his dreadlocks, George gave Wilson a cool look. 'Don't get too cocky, Love Machine. I never said we wuz friends.'

13

Houston, Texas
Memorial Towers, Level 14
November 26th 2012
Local Time 1:26 p.m.

Mission of Isaiah—Day Two

NOW IT WAS OFFICIAL, Helena decided—her medication was utterly useless. The previous night she had taken two tranquillisers, at Julia's insistence, and not only did they fail to stop her hallucinations but now she had a migraine. She was fuming. Two months this had been going on. *Two months!*

Helena paced in front of a wall of glass with a cordless telephone pressed to her ear. She had been on the phone for more than twenty minutes, being transferred from one department to another. Eventually she found Detective Olsen—her father's contact—and he was being more than accommodating.

Her voice was like syrup, 'Thanks Detective, I appreciate the favour. Like I said, it was only a small accident and I want to get the details for my insurance company, if I can.' She had fabricated the entire incident to get the information she wanted.

'Really, I don't mind waiting.' Helena switched the telephone from one ear to the other. 'Come on,' she muttered. Glancing at her watch again, she realised Doctor Bennetswood would be arriving at any moment.

The images were sketchy in her mind, but Helena definitely remembered seeing a white Ford—an old one. For some reason, the licence plate number 'DRO-735' was one of the few details she could visualise clearly. The medication made her recollections vague and she worried that forcing things might distort the facts in some way. But knowing a little about cars, her educated guess was that it was a Ford Impala, probably a late 70s model.

From what Helena had seen during the night, the man from her visions had survived the car accident, somehow. That was the only explanation. He was alive, seemingly injured—and she was still connected to him.

Minutes ticked by.

Helena bit her lip and listened to the music on hold. The monotonous tunes made the wait even more excruciating. Then he was back.

'Yes, I'm here,' she said. 'I have a pen.' Helena carefully repeated the information. 'Registered to a George Washington—23 Richey Road, Bordersville.' The licence plate number matched the car she had seen, perfectly.

'You're sure this is correct?' she said, as if doubting the strength of the coincidence. 'Thank you *so much* for your help. I will tell my father, I promise.' Helena was ready to end the conversation, but Detective Olsen was insisting on doing more. 'No Detective, I don't want you to send someone. I'm sure my insurance company will take care of it. Like I said, it was only a fender-bender.'

He wanted to despatch a patrol car to Bordersville to check out the situation. It seemed Mr Washington's registration had expired some years ago and he had thousands of dollars in unpaid parking tickets.

'Detective,' Helena said firmly. 'There's no need to do any more, thank you. This is not a matter for the police. *Detective*—'

He wouldn't take no for an answer.

'I *don't care* if my father would want you to help!' She was getting angrier by the second. 'Don't *do* anything, do you understand? You've done enough. Thank you!' Without saying goodbye she hung up the phone. 'Damn that guy!' In her experience, whenever you wanted a cop, there was never one around—and this was just the opposite.

Helena gazed out the window towards the city. If the police went to Bordersville, things would certainly be more complicated. Then the doorbell rang. Helena swore.

JULIA SHOWED DOCTOR Bennetswood in and he ambled towards the lounge. He was a balding man in his mid-forties with a barrel chest and short legs. A black leather medical bag was clasped in his right hand. At first glance he looked obscenely rich, with his solid-gold Rolex and chunky solitaire ring, which had to be at least three carats. His suit was olive in colour, with a matching olive tie. Very trendy. Not the suit for someone who didn't want to draw attention to himself. 'Armani,' he'd proudly tell you, if you asked.

Well known throughout the upper class of Houston, Doctor Bennetswood was regarded as a psychiatrist who could get results. He had a loyal following and recently business had been better than ever. Mental illness was on the rise, which meant things were going from good to great, for him.

Helena didn't acknowledge his arrival; she was looking out the window and thinking: stay or go? She needed to be cautious, she realised. Doctor Bennetswood's evaluation of her would be the difference between a trip to Conroe—the clinic—and having more time to figure out what was actually going on. The doctor sat down on the sofa and crossed his legs. He would say nothing, just observe, waiting for her to speak first. His techniques had become familiar to her.

Helena smiled gracefully. 'How are you, Doctor?'

'Hello, Helena. I'm quite well. More importantly, how are you?' He gestured for her to be seated.

Helena decided to co-operate; it was easier that way. In an effort to sound positive, she replied, 'Under the circumstances, I'm quite well.'

'Hmm.' There was a long silence. 'Work with me. You're thinking of a number between one and ten. Can you tell me what that number is?'

'Ten,' Helena said quickly.

'Why ten?'

'Because I like things to be perfect.'

'But, why ten?'

'Why not?'

There was another long period of silence. 'How do you feel?' he asked.

'I feel stronger.'

'Stronger?'

'Yes.'

He raised one eyebrow slightly as if he was challenging her ability to tell the truth. 'You look tired. A little dark around the eyes, maybe.'

Helena hated it when people told her that. That sort of comment makes you feel tired, she thought—he should know that! 'Yes. Maybe I am a little tired,' she replied, biting her tongue.

He pointed his gold Mont Blanc pen. 'How are you sleeping?'

'Not that well.'

'You're taking your medication?'

'Absolutely.'

'Are you dreaming?'

'Yes, Doctor, I am. The medication hasn't actually worked that well.'

'Really?' He seemed surprised and made a note on his pad.

Helena was already feeling frustrated, there were investigations at Bordersville to be conducted and she questioned her capacity to put up with this for the next hour.

'How many tablets and when?' Doctor Bennetswood asked.

'I had two tablets last night.'

He grimaced. 'That should have worked.'

The session continued for more than twenty minutes and Helena tried her best to remain positive. But the more he talked to her, and the more questions he asked, the more anxious she became to leave.

'Your father tells me you had some visions yesterday, while you were awake.' Doctor Bennetswood twirled the diamond ring on his finger. 'Why don't you tell me about that?'

Helena was convinced he would merely judge that she was imagining the events as a result of her past trauma.

'Don't you want to talk about it?'

'I'm sorry, Doctor. Maybe we could meet again tomorrow?'

'Tell me what you're feeling? It might help.'

The last thing she wanted to admit was that she was experiencing a psychic connection with a man she had never met—who she thought was dead, at first, but apparently not. She eventually replied, 'I'm sorry, Doctor, I don't know what to tell you.'

'Try, Helena. It may be useful.'

'I'm sorry, Doctor,' she sighed. 'I'm exhausted. Please, can we reschedule for tomorrow.' She stood up from her seat in an effort to end the session.

He appeared sympathetic. 'I think we should continue. You know, I'm on leave in two weeks. Then I'll be off work for at least a month. We should be taking the opportunity to talk. It would be much better if we persisted.' He crossed his arms, settling in for the long haul. 'I think it's time we discussed your mother again.'

Helena rolled her eyes—she couldn't stop herself.

'We need to talk about it, Helena. It's time for you to confront what happened.'

Helena turned away. She wanted Doctor Bennetswood to leave, so she could go to Bordersville and find a man called George Washington. She faked a yawn.

'Doctor, I know how important this is. Honestly. But I'm just not up to this conversation right now. Please forgive me.' She headed for her bedroom.

'Before you go—' He reached into his medical bag and produced an orange plastic container filled with tablets and placed it on the coffee table. 'These are a little stronger than the last ones I gave you. They will certainly help you sleep.' He gave a detailed explanation of what they were and how they worked. 'After you take them, you can't drive or swim for at least forty-eight hours. And it says here, you shouldn't operate heavy machinery.' He grinned up at her, like that was really funny. 'But there won't be much chance of that, I'd say.'

Helena thanked him graciously, at the same time determined she would never put a single one of those tablets in her mouth.

The doctor looked at his Rolex. 'I'll just wait here if that's all right. Your father will be here soon, I think. I said I would have a quick catch-up with him.'

The mere thought of them both talking about her future made her angry, but she managed a cordial reply. 'Make yourself comfortable.'

Helena gazed at the container of tranquillisers and time slowed to a crawl. *I have to take control of my life*, she thought, as if it were a major revelation. She begrudgingly snatched the pills from the table. If her father arrived, he certainly wouldn't let her leave the building—and the only way out of her apartment was through the lounge. She would have to be quick, as Laurence was often early.

'I'll talk to Julia and reschedule another time for tomorrow,' Dr Bennetswood said. 'Any particular hour suit you?'

'The afternoon would be better,' she said.

'And don't worry,' he added. 'Together we'll find out why you're not sleeping.'

Helena left the room, threw the container of pills on the bed and donned a black three-quarter-length jacket. Unlocking her gun cabinet, she selected a handgun, spun the weapon skilfully on her index finger, then clipped it into the holster sewn into the lining of her jacket.

It was time to find out the truth.

Helena took a deep breath, then strode back through the lounge room. Her re-entry caused the doctor to sit up in his seat. He was obviously surprised to see her leaving.

'I thought you were tired?'

'I'm going for a quick walk. I need to clear my head.'

Before he could respond, she was out the front door and into the elevator.

HELENA'S MERCEDES SPED out from the building car park and roared along the concrete parkway. With her foot pressed hard on the accelerator and windows wound down, she keyed the street address into the navigation computer and put on a pair of dark glasses.

Within seconds she was travelling at high speed, weaving in and out of the traffic. The downtown office buildings of Houston grew larger as she approached, the early afternoon sun flickering off the tall glass walls. Helena looked quickly left, then right, and sped through a red light. The wind swirled inside her car. Her blonde hair whipped about her head.

'I'm going to find out what the hell is going on,' she told herself.

Helena's visions had become much clearer in the last two days. Previously, when she slept, her mind was inundated with strange symbols and a constant rumbling, like thunder in the distance. That damn noise almost sent her mad—but miraculously it was now gone. In the last two days everything had changed and she was certain she'd *actually* seen through someone else's eyes, with a telltale red haze surrounding everything. It had to be a psychic connection of some kind. Although she couldn't comprehend why, at least now it all seemed tangible in some way, even if it was no less bizarre. If she could just track down the man from her visions she would surely understand more. And most importantly, she could confirm that she was not going crazy.

The Mercedes cornered at high speed and descended into a tunnel before shooting out into the bright sunlight once again. Did the man in her visions hold any specific significance for her? She pondered the question and concluded there was no special feeling. It was clinical. The only emotion she could be sure of was her own doubt as to the reality of it all. Could this George Washington be the man? Could he be the reason her life had fallen apart, all the therapy and the medication she had endured just to get through those long torturous nights? Just the thought of it made her feel sick.

The wind continued to swirl in through the windows as a favourite song began playing on the radio. Singing aloud, Helena tried to relax, but soon the same thoughts took over again. She was angry. That was it. She wanted to know why this had happened to her. Did she need someone to blame? Was that it? Yes, she concluded, she needed to identify an enemy. We Capriartys know just how to deal with enemies, she thought.

Taking a deep breath she realised it was unwise to jump to conclusions. There was still a chance this was indeed post-traumatic stress as Doctor Bennetswood had always said. First, she had to prove whether or not the man from her visions really existed. Then she would be closer to the truth.

The car began to vibrate as it thundered along the empty freeway at top speed. Bordersville was just north of the Intercontinental Airport and the anticipation of finding out more spurred Helena to test the Mercedes' limits. She shot off the exit ramp and jumped on the brakes, causing the car to squirm as it decelerated. 'Richey Road,' she said quietly as she drove down the narrow street.

There was only one house on this section of the road and it was number twenty-three, just as Detective Olsen had said. The car came to a halt on the side of the road and Helena looked towards the property. Tall weeds and shrubs obstructed her view. All she could see was the outline of a green trailer home in the distance. She stepped out of her car and discreetly looked both ways. There were no vehicles or people in either direction. Gripping her handgun, she flicked off the safety and walked down the driveway.

Overhanging trees stencilled shadows on the ground. There were two hand-painted signs hanging in the bushes:

Beware of the Dogs!
Intruders will be shot on sight!

As Helena stepped deeper into the property her senses became more acute, and her grip on her gun even tighter. Suddenly, a commercial jetliner roared over the top of the trees, not more than two hundred feet off the ground. The ear-shattering noise bellowed around her. Everything shook. She hastily turned full circle, to be certain she was not set upon during the clamour. Eventually, the sound faded into the distance and she took a moment to settle her racing heart.

She edged her way to the front door and rapped on the wood.

'Is anybody home?' she yelled. 'Is anybody here?' Her gun was by her right thigh. Except for the breeze whispering through the tall grass, silence reigned on the ramshackle estate.

Standing on tiptoes, Helena attempted to look through the grimy front window, but the blinds were drawn. She opened the torn fly-screen door and turned the raggedy handle. It was locked.

She looked around the perimeter of the property, searching for clues that might jog her memory. Nothing was familiar. Nothing. Her frustration grew like a tumour of doubt. Maybe she had taken one tranquilliser too many and everything had been blocked out. As she walked from side to side across the clearing her eyes flicked from one thing to another. Eventually she stopped in her tracks. 'What am I doing here?'

Maybe I am going crazy, she thought.

Leaning against a concrete water tank, the sunlight warm on her jacket, she was swamped by a feeling of uncertainty. To end up with nothing after so much anticipation was infuriating. She stood there, stunned by the lack of an outcome. The shadow of another jetliner thundered directly overhead and she gazed at the aircraft as it streaked away into the distance. Suddenly a memory was triggered—Helena had seen that same image before! Springing into action, she strode to the rear of the property. The first pieces of the puzzle were beginning to fall into place.

Sighting along the barrel of her pistol, she eased her way determinedly to the concrete shower cubicle and glanced in through the doorway. The floor was wet. A round garbage can caught her eye. Flipping off the lid with the handle of her gun, she found a bundle of black clothing stuffed inside. Helena poked at the garments, then backed away because of the putrid smell.

'What is it?' she mumbled to herself. There was something she was trying to remember. Helena dropped to one knee and peered into a thin crack at the base of the wall. There was something jammed inside. This was the moment when she would know beyond any doubt that she wasn't crazy. Clawing a driver's licence from its hiding place in the wall, she read the name:

Jack Bolten

Exactly the name she expected.

This meant that everything she had seen was real—the driver's licence was proof of that. She zipped the card into her jacket pocket, realising it might just be the thing that would keep her out of a mental institution. Helena wanted to laugh out loud in celebration, but she just stared at the clothing stuffed into the garbage bin. The man from her visions—Jack Bolten, maybe?—had survived the accident on the 610 freeway, his shredded clothing the proof. How was that possible? How could he have survived something so devastating? And even more importantly, where was he now? If previous events were any guide, her visions would tell her soon enough—most certainly if she stopped taking her medication altogether.

Feeling more relaxed, she made her way up the driveway towards her car. It was difficult to contain a smile as another airliner flew low overhead.

As the roar of the engines faded into the distance it was replaced by a growling in the nearby grass. Helena was trying to place the sound when two Dobermans leapt from the bushes in attack. As they sprang towards her, Helena tracked her gun from one snarling animal to the other. Just as she was about to shoot, a voice called out.

'Stop!'

The two animals stutter-stepped to a halt and Helen's finger eased off the trigger. Her gaze shifted to a skinny black man with dreadlocks, holding a double-barrel shotgun across his chest. He pulled back both triggers as if staking his claim.

'Who are you, woman?'

Her aim still on the fidgeting animals, Helena flashed a glance at the man, then the shotgun he was holding—it was in a poor state of repair and the barrel was badly rusted.

'I said—what y'all doing on my property? Answer me, woman!'

'I've seen you before,' Helena said softly. She lifted her sunglasses to get a better look at him.

At that exact moment, both Dobermans stopped growling and

wandered back towards their master, flopping down at his feet in the tall grass.

'*Not again!*' George moaned.

'Your name is George Washington, isn't it?'

'Get off my property!' he replied, trying to hide his shock.

Helena could see a white Ford now parked on the street behind her car. It was the vehicle she had seen in her visions. 'A man took a ride in the trunk of your car, Mr Washington. You let him clean up—*there*.' She pointed to the shower cubicle behind her.

'Get off my property!' he roared.

'Not until you tell me what I want to know.'

'Don't make me use this gun!'

'I wouldn't fire that if I were you,' she said calmly. 'From here, it looks like it has more chance of blowing up in your face than anything else.'

George gazed at the weapon in dismay. 'What's wrong with it?'

Helena lowered her gun. 'I mean you no harm, Mr Washington. Just tell me what happened to the man in the back of your car?'

'What man?'

'You had to pry open the trunk with a crowbar.'

'Crowbar? I don't know nothing about no crowbar.'

'Your car has boxes of morphine in it, doesn't it?' It was all coming back to her.

'You've been watching me!' he bellowed, pointing to the bushes in the distance.

Knowing for certain, at last, that everything she had seen in her visions was real, Helena felt strangely deflated, exhausted somehow. 'My name is Helena Capriarty,' she announced. 'And I assure you, I'm as confused about this as you are.'

George's dogs silently milled around at his feet, enjoying the sunshine. He turned his frustrated attention towards them. 'Twice in one day! What in hell's the matter with you two? I'm getting me some new dogs. *That's it! Real dogs* to guard me and my home! I've had it with the two of you!' The animals tilted their heads as if trying to comprehend what he was saying.

'The man who was with you today, where did he go?' Helena said.

'You tell me.'

'Is his name Jack Bolten?'

Perplexed by the question, George screwed his face up in wonder. 'What the hell are you talking about, woman? The only Jack Bolten I know works in radiology.'

The driver's licence must have been stolen; Helena had a sketchy vision of something similar. That's why it was jammed into the shower wall!

'You work at the hospital, don't you?' she said.

'You can't prove that.'

'That's where the morphine came from.'

'Like I said, y'all can't prove that!'

'I *don't care* about the morphine, I assure you. Just tell me where the man went. The man covered in blood. That's why I'm here. Where is he?'

'I ain't telling you nothin'.'

George suddenly gaped at the young woman in front of him.

'*Wait a minute!*' he said accusingly. 'You're the one! You have a husband with red hair, don't ya? Yeah, you're the twisted bitch!'

The comment made no sense to Helena at all.

He pointed. 'It's *you*, ain't it?' Elaborate images of Helena naked on her kitchen table flashed through his mind—whipped cream and all. 'You're the one Wilson told me about.'

'*Wilson*—is that his name?'

'Don't play games, woman. You know that's his name!'

'Where is he?' she asked again.

George looked at his watch. 'Y'all are too late, thank God! Wilson's not here, you coppo princess!' George shook his finger condescendingly. 'He told me *all about you*—the bitch who poured blood all over his ass. I've seen your husband, too! That man is seriously ugly. Are you *blind* or somethin'?'

Helena raised her gun. 'Tell me where Wilson is?'

'*Attack!*' George screamed. '*Attack!*'

Helena braced herself for the canine assault—

But nothing happened.

The two animals were obviously on edge. But the focus of their nervous scanning was on everything other than Helena and the gun she was pointing directly at their master.

'Attack, you stupid mutts!'

But strangely, the dogs didn't react.

With a lunge, Helena took the opportunity and wrenched the shotgun from George's grasp then threw it to the ground. 'You're making me very angry, Mr Washington.' She raised her gun to point it directly at his forehead. 'You're going to tell me everything I need to know. Is that clear? I want answers, and I want them now!'

George reluctantly raised his hands in the air. 'Wilson was right,' he muttered. 'You *are* a crazy bitch.'

14

Houston, Texas
Central Railway Station
November 26th 2012
Local Time 2:59 p.m.

Mission of Isaiah—Day Two

ABSORBED IN HIS thoughts, Wilson was barely conscious of his surroundings as he shuffled up the broad flight of steps leading to the side entrance. He was cold and tired. His clothes were odd fitting and ridiculously colourful. And he was definitely *not* a love machine. He felt stupid—*very stupid*. This wasn't quite the glamorous mission he had envisaged. As his grandfather always used to say: 'Things are rarely what you expect when you spend too much time thinking about them beforehand.'

A clear blue sky framed the high walls of the railway station. From a distance it seemed a peaceful place—grand and opulent, larger than life. But the high walls sheltered a congregation of human despair that was impossible to describe, and dangerous for the unwary traveller.

All the while, Wilson's thoughts were in overdrive. Why were the police tracking him the night before? Why did they appear in such great force? And the Doberman, her reaction was so unexpected. On a lighter note, George Washington was quite a character. An unusual find in this strange world, indeed. Honest, in a deceitful sort of way—a curious combination.

The unmistakable smell of human excrement shocked Wilson's nostrils as he approached the top of the landing.

He focused.

Dreary, granite walls bordered three sides of the square, but it was the sight of the people before him that took his breath away. There were hundreds of them, huddled in meagre shelters in a ramshackle cardboard city. Some were wrapped in sheets of newspaper for warmth; others lay under dirty blankets. There was garbage all over the place, piles of it, bisected by narrow pathways. Old shopping trolleys, many filled to the brim with obscure items, were everywhere.

A cold wind whistled overhead as Wilson watched the sea of dirty, unkempt faces studying his approach. Yes, they were carefully studying him. The future Wilson knew was nothing like this. He was dumbstruck. There were women and children amongst the cardboard. Their eyes were blank, empty, as if no life was left in them. It was the most depressing thing Wilson had ever seen. What kind of world was it when so many people were left with so little? A profound sadness filled his gut. Then his mood changed. He remembered the power that was at his disposal. By rectifying the Schumann Frequency, he was hopeful that *this* would not be part of their future.

A tooting horn resonated nearby—probably a train—and the sound jolted Wilson back to the present. Having stayed in one place for only a moment, he was now surrounded by a group of men. They had approached him in his stupor, their hands outstretched, clutching at him. They smelt terrible.

One of them spoke—his voice raspy, 'Money, Mister. Gimme a few bucks for food.'

Then another, 'Give me money. Give me money.'

'I need money, jus' a dolla' or two.'

They grabbed at Wilson's clothes, jostling him. He did his best to hold on to what was in his pockets—three dollar bills and an American Express card—but the fever of their actions was intensifying. As a priority, Wilson was trying to keep his sunglasses over his eyes while at the same time making a retreat. But the more he tried to back away, the tighter the gridlock around him became. He felt like a piece of meat being pulled apart by a group of hungry wolves. Unavoidably, Wilson's sunglasses were bumped from his nose. He just managed to catch them before they fell out of reach, and he quickly slapped them back into place.

But eye contact had been made.

An old man with a matted grey beard was now under the spell of a trackenoid response.

Everything went into slow motion as a glare of frightening intensity began radiating from the old man's eyes. The scuffle of the crowd grew fiercer as Wilson attempted to back up. In the distance a high-pitched noise, like whistling, could be heard. Wilson couldn't place the sound. Losing his sense of direction in the entangled throng, he suddenly felt a sharp blow to the side of the head. Then another. As he turned to identify his assailant—a fist slammed him square in the face. Stars twinkled before his eyes. The old man with the grey beard was punching away at him.

Greybeard's pupils had shrunk just as the security guard's had done the morning before. Wilson took another blow to the side of the head. It was impossible to defend himself and hold his glasses over his eyes at the same time. Thinking quickly, he pulled what cash he had from his pocket—three dollar bills—and stuffed them down the front of his attacker's shirt.

As if on cue, the crowd swung its ravenous attention towards the money.

Wilson backed away, Greybeard straining toward him, driven by the irresistible impulse to attack. Despite the other beggars reaching down his shirt—material tearing and buttons popping off—Greybeard was focused on only one thing—getting to Wilson at any cost.

A single dollar slipped through the fabric of Greybeard's shirt and slowly drifted, end over end, to the ground. In an instant, a group of men dived towards the money like gridiron players scrimmaging for the ball.

It was Wilson's only chance. He ran forward at best speed and launched himself off the back of two men, catapulting himself though the air and clearing Greybeard's outstretched hands.

The high-pitched whistle continued in the background.

Wilson landed on his feet and broke free. Sprinting over cardboard boxes towards the doors of the railway station, he knocked down at least three people who got in his way. With one desperate lunge, he dived into the revolving door, lost his balance and tumbled into the empty terminal, sliding on his chest.

He squeaked to a halt on the shiny marble.

Wilson was wheezing with exhaustion, his face still pressed to the floor. Through the dirty glass behind him, he could see four burly, well-dressed security guards carrying long black batons. In their mouths were shiny silver whistles, which they blew upon madly. Any vagabond that approached the revolving door was mercilessly struck down.

Wilson searched the courtyard for Greybeard, but he was nowhere in sight.

Unexpectedly, a voice asked, 'Are you okay?'

In the reflection of the glass, Wilson could see two policemen in black uniforms standing directly behind him, their guns drawn. Doing his best to subdue his heavy breathing, Wilson carefully adjusted his sunglasses to make sure they were in place and turned towards the pair. At the same time—from behind his tinted lenses—he eyed the nearest exit.

'Are you okay?' the sergeant asked again.

Wilson rubbed the back of his head. 'They wanted my money.'

'The main entrance is much safer,' the sergeant said, and pointed in the other direction. 'Better you come in that way from now on.' Little did Wilson realise that in the sergeant's breast pocket was an identikit picture of the fugitive they were chasing—Wilson's exact likeness.

Outside in the courtyard, everything appeared to be back to normal, and Greybeard had disappeared from sight. Security guards stood at the doors. The crowd had dispersed to their cardboard homes three dollars the richer.

Wilson gingerly climbed to his feet and one of the police helped steady him.

The officer said with a snigger, 'They didn't like your outfit very much did they, Love Machine?'

Wilson looked curiously at his own attire. 'It was a gift.'

'They can be a little sensitive to fashion around here,' the officer said.

The sergeant holstered his weapon, then pointed to the side of Wilson's mouth. 'You have a little blood there.'

Wilson wiped his face, a gooey red streak drawing a line across his palm. He pressed his lip to his sleeve in an attempt to stop the flow.

'You need to come in via the main entrance from now on,' the sergeant said again.

Wilson did his best to respond calmly, 'Absolutely, I will … I mean, I won't come *that* way again.' Sweat streaming from his face, he skulked away towards the ticketing hall. Once around the corner, his breath again quickened; his nerves felt distinctly shattered.

The ticketing counter was empty and he impatiently rapped his knuckles on the glass, causing a heavy-set black woman to lift herself from her desk and waddle towards him. He flicked the American Express card into the tray between them.

'A one-way ticket to Mexico City,' he said, and nervously glanced at the clock on the wall.

'Mexico City?' She said in a low voice, then proceeded to eyeball Wilson with a gaze that he interpreted as doubt. He wiped the mixture of blood and sweat from his chin and stared right back at her with the cool gaze of a television newsreader.

'Is there a problem?' he said.

She turned her attention to her fingernails. 'No—no problem,' and began softly tapping away on her computer, taking great care not to press too hard on the keys.

'Make that a first-class ticket, won't you, dear.' It seemed wholly appropriate to display a little confidence to disguise his entirely pathetic situation.

'The next train departs at 3:30 p.m.,' she said. 'You change trains in San Antonio.' The woman lethargically grabbed the credit card from the tray. 'You have a passport?'

At that moment, a voice blared over the public address system, 'Ladies and gentlemen—'

The sound caused Wilson to duck for cover like a child expecting a beating.

'—the 3:15 service for Dallas is departing from platform twenty-one. Last call.' It echoed around the building, then faded away.

The woman leaned toward the glass. 'I said—do you have a passport?'

Wilson anxiously scanned the foyer for Greybeard, but he was nowhere in sight. And just as thankfully, there were no police, either. Standing tall once again, Wilson composed himself as best he could and replied, 'Yes, I have a passport.'

'Can I see it, please?'

He patted his pockets. 'Err—my wife has it. She's coming any minute.'

'You want a ticket for her also?'

Wilson forced out a bloodied smile. 'No, *Judy*—my wife's not coming with me.' He had read the woman's name tag: 'Judy—Ticketing Agent'.

The woman did not appear impressed by his familiarity and abruptly inserted the credit card into a manual swipe machine, *Click—Click*, then slid the docket and a pen under the glass.

'That'll be $210.'

Wilson autographed the signature panel and immediately passed it back. The woman compared the two signatures with a critical gaze—they looked similar enough—then reached for the telephone. 'I'll have to authorise this.'

'Your nails are beautiful,' Wilson responded.

The compliment caused her to immediately study her fingers like she was trying to decide for herself. Her nails were bright red, very long, and contrasted sharply with her dark-brown skin.

She looked up. 'Really?'

'Yes, very classy.'

'They're porcelain.'

At that moment Judy remembered where she had seen the tall white man's face—the television! He was wanted for murder, or something like that! Her grip tightened around the credit card. She carefully clicked the phone back into the receiver and slid the ticket and the card back under the glass. There was a slight waver in her voice now. 'Platform thirty-eight is that way.' With a toothy smile she pointed to the left. Her hands were visibly shaking.

'Thank you,' Wilson said cautiously. 'You've been very helpful.' He sensed her sudden apprehension, the quivering fingers a distinct give-away.

Waiting until her fugitive customer had rounded the corner, out of sight, Judy snatched the telephone from its cradle and held it to her ear. 'Get me the police,' she said under her breath. 'This is an emergency.'

WILSON SCANNED THE lobby. There were a few well-dressed people milling around and everything looked relatively quiet. Even so, he felt like a cat in a doghouse. Something wasn't right. Judy had become nervous all of a sudden, but why? He wiped the accumulated blood from the corner of his mouth again. Maybe it was his injuries.

Crisp afternoon light was pouring into the foyer through high-set windows, flooding the expanse of the station with shafts of warm light. At that moment, Wilson drifted back into his memories. So much had happened in the last few weeks ...

THE SCHUMANN FREQUENCY

California, The Americas
Enterprise Corporation, Mercury Building, Level 3
May 10th 2081
Local Time 7:45 p.m.

13 Days before Transport Test

THE SETTING SUN made sharp rectangular images on the wall of the boardroom and the scent of fresh flowers filled the air. In the centre of the enormous space stood a polished oak table surrounded by twenty high-backed executive chairs. An amazing collection of well-known paintings by Rembrandt, Van Gogh, Picasso and Renoir hung upon the vast white walls.

These people have got way too much money, Wilson thought. He had been waiting for more than ten minutes, and, enjoyable though looking at the art was, it had done nothing to alleviate his concerns. This room was certainly designed to make visitors feel intimidated—and it was working.

He paced another circuit of the room, trying to predict what bizarre event was going to happen next. On the table in front of each chair was a platinum coaster. Etched on the surface was a map of the world, overlaid with a latitude and longitude grid. The company name was written across the top as if *they* were the owners of the entire globe. 'Enterprise Corporation,' Wilson recited. They were so arrogant. At that moment the large double doors swung open and a man in a white coat entered. Reaching forward, he grabbed Wilson's hand and shook it firmly—it was a good handshake.

Barton was the first to speak, 'So you're the man Karin has told me so much about.'

Wilson didn't respond.

'My name is Barton Ingerson. I'm very glad to meet you, Mr Dowling. Did you have a good trip?'

Wilson studied the middle-aged man in front of him. His silver hair was shiny and abundant, his tanned face symmetrical. He had clear eyes, hazel—the colour of a fox's pelt—and a disarming smile. He wore a white three-quarter-length jacket, tailored to perfection. His physique was slim and well proportioned. Wilson's first impression of Barton was that he was a good guy, but he cautioned himself; Enterprise Corporation would be too cunning to use any other type of person. Big corporations weren't to be trusted—that's what Professor Author always said.

Wilson read the banner on Barton's security badge:

Mercury Team

How appropriate, Wilson thought. Mercury was the Roman god of eloquence, skill and thieving.

'I said—did you have a good trip?'

'Yes—I mean, no!' Wilson replied, taking a step back as if the world had violently tilted away towards the windows. 'This morning I was in Sydney, having a nice old time. That's in Pacifica, in case you don't know. And now, as you can see, I've been transported halfway around the world to Enterprise Corporation—of all places!' Wilson pointed his finger at the floor. 'And to make matters worse, the woman you sent to bring me here wouldn't tell me why. She threatened to take away my scholarship!' Wilson touched his index finger to his temple. 'Tell me, what would you think if that happened to you?'

'Karin wasn't allowed to tell you why I wanted you here.'

'Well then,' Wilson's voice trailed off, 'she's doing a great job.'

'I can understand why you're upset, Mr Dowling. But all will be clear to you in time.'

Wilson rested his hands on the shoulder of a boardroom chair, as if using the high back as a shield. 'I want you to tell me why I'm here. I want to know the reason. And please, call me Wilson,' he said, mocking Barton's exaggerated charm.

'There is no need to be alarmed,' Barton said. 'I only want to talk.'

'You didn't fly me all the way here to get to know me. Of that, I'm certain. Tell me what you want.'

'In time—in time,' Barton replied. For a moment an uncomfortable silence hung in the air. 'First, let me ask you something. Are you religious?'

'What does *that* have to do with anything?'

'Please, Mr Dowling—'

Wilson leant forward. 'I told you, it's *Wilson*.'

'Are you religious, *Wilson*?'

'Why don't *you* tell *me*?' Wilson stared at Barton's palm device. He was trying to figure how religion could possibly relate to his being here. There was no reasonable connection that he could see.

Barton sat down across the table and gestured for Wilson to sit also. 'Look, Wilson, humour me. Are you religious?'

'I'm a religious fanatic,' Wilson said, easing himself into one of the comfortable chairs. 'I'm thinking about opening my own church. That sounds like a good idea. Yeah, my own church. The church of Wilson. The world needs *Wilsonism*.' Judging by Barton's expression, it was obvious he was not used to Wilson's special brand of humour. 'Why are you asking me a stupid question like that, anyway?'

Barton's expression was unruffled. 'I understand you are studying law at the University of Sydney. How is that going?'

'It's going well.'

Barton didn't look up. 'Your thesis is taking a long time.'

'I'm a perfectionist. I like to do things properly.'

There was a long pause. 'You fly vintage aircraft, I understand. The ones with propellers.'

'*Come on, Barton!*' Wilson blurted. 'Against my better judgment, I'd say you look like a pretty good bloke. So what the hell am I doing here? You've obviously got all that information in your computer.'

Barton looked up from his palm device. 'So you're telling me you're not religious?'

'*What* in hell does that have to do with anything?'

'Just answer me. Are you religious? I'm serious this time.'

'No—I'm *not* religious,' Wilson conceded.

'Do you believe in God?'

'Do I believe in God? That's a little personal, don't you think?'

Barton sat there, his face emotionless, waiting for an answer.

'To tell you the truth, I'm not exactly certain what *God* is. There's too much conflict when it comes to religion for my liking. Everyone has a different opinion—and they can't *all* be right. But, yes, I believe in God—I guess.'

'That's very interesting.' Barton tapped away on his keypad once again.

'Are you going to tell me what this is all about?'

The only plausible explanation as to why Wilson was in the boardroom of the most powerful company in the world was Professor Author's omega programming. That was definitely what they were after. And where was the professor now? Probably, back home in Sydney with his feet up.

'Well ...' Barton stared into the distance, deep in thought, refocused, then said, 'Your body is made up of a type of building block, called a Gen-EP. This is unique, because unlike other carbon-based building blocks, a Gen-EP can be separated into a simple molecular form, then reconstructed.'

'Which means what?'

'Your body can be taken apart, then put back together,' Barton explained.

'And all that means what?' Wilson said again. It was definitely Professor Author's omega programming they wanted. This is how they were going to trick him into doing some tests.

'Molecularly speaking,' Barton said, 'it's very straightforward. We need to conduct an experiment to see if it's possible to take you apart—then put you back together again.'

Wilson began laughing, wondering why Barton was going to so much trouble with his diversion. 'Why would you want to do something like that?'

'I need to prove that time travel is possible.' Barton didn't scratch his nose, twitch, even blink. He remained utterly composed.

'You can't be serious?' Wilson said.

'I am absolutely serious.'

'But, time travel is *impossible*.'

'Who told you that?'

'The Theory of Relativity states that matter can't exceed the speed of light. Therefore what you are saying can't be done. Tell me why I'm *really* here?'

'How do you know about time travel and its relationship to the speed of light?'

Wilson smiled inwardly. Professor Author was constantly trumpeting Albert Einstein's theories—but now was certainly not the time to bring *him* up.

'I have no idea how I became so intelligent,' Wilson said. 'Maybe it's genetic.'

'It *is* possible for matter to exceed the speed of light,' Barton said. 'Forget what you already know and assume that what I'm saying is true.' He paused long enough for Wilson's curiosity to build. 'It sounds amazing, doesn't it?'

Barton was mirroring Wilson's body language and Wilson moved in his seat to see if the mercury scientist would do the same. Sure enough, he did. So Wilson stood up and marched towards the window. 'This all sounds ridiculous, actually,' he said. If Barton Ingerson produced a *fate coin*, Wilson decided, it was time to jump through the plate glass, screaming like a fool.

'It would be worth your while to co-operate,' Barton said.

Wilson pressed his palms to his chest. 'Why me?'

'I told you. Your body is made of a rare building block that I can't replicate at the moment.' Barton spent the next ten minutes explaining how the time-travel process worked, about the time dilation formula, and how it had been proven that space could be stretched in order to get matter to exceed the speed of light. 'It's all simple quantum physics,' he concluded.

Wilson's internal sarcasm screamed at fever pitch: *Oh yes, that sounds so-o-o simple!* But on a more serious level, it was hard to know if he was hearing the truth. Barton sounded convincing enough. And the Rembrandt on the wall—seemingly genuine—forced Wilson to consider that the idea might not be as crazy as it initially seemed. He pointed at the painting. 'Is that real?'

Barton looked behind him at the work of art: a baby in its crib, her mother checking to see that she was asleep. Overhead, half a dozen angels hovered in the darkness, watching over them.

'Absolutely,' Barton said. 'It's called "The Holy Family". Rembrandt painted it in Holland in 1635. It's new here at Enterprise Corporation. We purchased it from the Hermitage Museum in St Petersburg.'

'Why me?' Wilson whispered to himself.

'What did you say?' Barton asked.

'Just talking to myself. That *is allowed*, isn't it?' There was a lengthy silence. 'So, you want to prove that you can send a human through time?'

Barton pointed at his watch. 'Yes. And the irony is—I don't have any time left.'

I'll play along, Wilson thought. 'Have you done this sort of thing before?'

'No. It's never been done.'

Wilson paced up and down by the window. It seemed he was everybody's favourite guinea pig when it came to mysterious experiments.

'We can structure a financial arrangement beyond your wildest imagination,' Barton said. 'You'll probably never have to work again. You certainly won't need that scholarship.'

Wilson knew that nothing valuable ever came without a price.

'What's the point in having money if you're not alive to use it?'

'We'll take every precaution.'

'Can you guarantee my safety?'

Barton took a deep breath, then exhaled. 'No, I can't.'

He was honest, at least. Wilson stared out the window. The sun was glowing like a massive orange ball as it dipped towards the horizon. Around it, the sky was a mixed palette of colours. 'Barton, I'm sorry, I like you—I have no idea why—but there's no way in hell I'm going to co-operate. Nothing you can do will convince me otherwise. I know my rights. I want to be escorted out of here.'

Barton walked towards the door, his perfect posture suggesting a certain nobility. 'Let's make a deal, Wilson. Give me twenty minutes. Either I can give you a compelling reason to co-operate, or you can leave of your own free will. Your scholarship will not be affected. Is that a deal?'

It was a perfect deal. In twenty minutes Wilson would be on his way home and this whole crazy situation would be behind him. There was no way there could be any other result.

'Barton, you drive a hard bargain,' Wilson said. 'But luckily, those are terms I am willing to accept.'

15

California, The Americas
Enterprise Corporation, Mercury Building
May 10th 2081
Local Time 8:21 p.m.

13 Days before Transport Test

WILSON TRAILED BARTON INGERSON through a maze of corridors and staircases, past various checkpoints, deep into the bowels of the building. They trudged along for a full five minutes. Barton hadn't said a word since leaving the boardroom—it appeared he wasn't trying to be nice just for the sake of it any more. And the silent treatment was somehow unnerving.

Eventually, the scientist stopped and pressed his hand against a rectangular security panel. A green light flashed, authorising entry, and a metal door lifted from the floor. The pair stepped into a small empty room and Wilson was not sure what to expect as the door closed behind them with a hiss. Sensing something unusual, he rubbed his fingers together. The air had become incredibly dry.

Barton approached a similar door on the opposite wall. 'We're in a dehumidification cubicle.'

That would explain it—but why? As the metal door lifted, a strange energy, something Wilson could sense in the air, came from inside the next room. He felt a fibrillation in his chest—a quivering in his heart. Gazing into the brightness, Wilson was drawn forward into a large, well-lit domed chamber. Rows of glass-topped tables—consoles—

some incredibly long, were carefully assembled in lines across the room, like a set of perfectly toppled dominoes.

Within the consoles were hundreds of tan-coloured documents of parchment and leather, pressed flat by the glass. Many of them were oddly shaped, a number of them badly damaged. Every square centimetre of their brittle surface was covered with ancient characters, written in black. The script was Hebrew and Aramaic.

Barton's voice cut the silence. 'The Dead Sea scrolls. The thirty-nine books of the Old Testament. That's the reason we're both here.'

Wilson placed his hands on one of the glass-topped tables.

'These scrolls were written more than 2300 years ago,' Barton said. They are arguably the greatest documents in the history of the world.'

Wilson knew exactly what the scrolls were, and their significance in history. He had read about them many times. 'I thought the Dead Sea scrolls were in Jerusalem, at the Rockefeller Museum.'

'That's correct,' Barton nodded. 'And there are also parchments at the Shrine of the Book.' It was a building in Jerusalem made specifically for the purpose of housing portions of the sacred scripture. 'Both those institutions have copies—temporarily, anyway. These are the *original* documents.'

Wilson peered down at a section of Hebrew text. 'How is that possible?'

'Enterprise Corporation owns the Rockefeller Museum,' he replied. 'And the remaining scrolls are on loan from the Shrine of the Book— we are their most prolific benefactors. In fact, this is the first time a complete scroll collection has been outside the Middle East since it was discovered in 1947, in the Dead Sea caves themselves.'

Wilson was unwittingly looking at the Book of Isaiah. The scroll was eight metres across and yet only twenty-five centimetres high, laid out in a single glass cabinet. Knowing that Hebrew was written from right to left, he walked to the far right, to the beginning, and carefully eyed the lettering. The workmanship was incredible. Wilson took a deep breath; he could feel an energy coming from them, as though they were humming in his mind. They had to be authentic. They just had to be.

'The scrolls were discovered by a Bedouin shepherd,' Barton said, 'a boy named Mohammad. He was searching for a stray goat near his home in Jericho, northwest of the Dead Sea, in Israel. The area is known as the Wilderness of Judea. The boy tossed a stone deep into a cave in one of the tall cliffs. To his surprise, he heard the sound of shattering pottery coming from inside. Upon investigation, the boy found several large jars containing leather scrolls wrapped in linen cloth. The jars were hermetically sealed and the contents preserved in excellent condition for more than 1900 years. That cave is now called "Dead Sea Cave, Number One". There were eleven caves discovered in total, containing more than 40,000 fragments—in varying condition—making up more than 500 individual copies of the thirty-nine books of the Old Testament.'[3]

Wilson was imagining it. The rugged desert of Israel, the young boy dressed in traditional Bedouin clothing. The elongated terracotta pots filled with ancient scrolls. He wondered what the boy, Mohammad, must have been thinking as he made his way deep underground into the narrow crevasses.

Barton continued, 'The Scrolls were written by a group of Holy Men, known as the Khirbet Qumran Brotherhood, between 200 BC and 68 AD. Legend has it they were saints, set down on this earth to chronicle the teachings of God, scholarly men of incalculable wisdom, committed to chastity and poverty and the teaching of the Holy One. They worked fourteen hours per day, seven days per week.' Barton paused. 'It was said their reward would be delivered in the afterlife.' He gestured across the room. 'Their lives are chronicled in the *Zadokite Documents* and the *Manual of Discipline*—scrolls also contained here.'

Wilson imagined these highly educated men and what they looked like—their shaved heads and pale skin, sitting at their easels in white flowing robes, chronicling the Word of God.

'What is so amazing about these scrolls,' Barton said, 'is that they are the oldest copies of the Bible known to exist.' He paused. 'In 68 AD the holy city of Qumran, where the scrolls were written, was invaded by the Roman army. This was as a direct result of the First Jewish Revolt, in 66 AD, when the Judean armies, led by Josephus, overthrew the Roman Twelfth Legion—the Garrison of Jerusalem. It was a humiliating defeat for Rome. Every soldier was slaughtered and the standard of the Twelfth

---

[3] *New Evidence Demands a Verdict*, Josh McDowell, Thomas Nelson, Nashville, 1999, page 78.

Legion, a solid gold eagle, was stolen. Emperor Nero, enraged by the Jewish reprisal, threw the might of Rome into gaining his own revenge. He sent his best commander, General Vespasian, and the Fifth, Tenth and Fifteenth Legions—over 16,500 professional soldiers—to overrun Judea and return Roman control to the region.

'That is the complex series of events that led to the scrolls being hidden in the Dead Sea caves. And they remained there, untouched, for nearly two thousand years.'

Roman legions, on a mission to reclaim Judea, destroying everything in their path—including the Holy City of Qumran, the home of the scrolls. Wilson stared at the symbols on the parchment in front of him, and without explanation the words began to make sense.

What was happening should have frightened him, but it felt natural somehow.

He read some of the names out loud, 'Tobit ...' Wilson walked to another cabinet. 'Levi ...' Then another, 'Psalms ...' He could read the ancient Hebrew characters without effort.

'You just named three of the scrolls,' Barton said in surprise. 'How did you do that?'

No one was more surprised than Wilson himself.

Barton approached the cabinets with a questioning stare. 'How did you do that?' he repeated.

Wilson stood in silence, looking confused. 'I'm not sure what just happened,' he replied.

'That was more than a lucky guess.' The cabinets were not labelled and Barton knew Wilson had identified each scroll correctly.

'I'm not sure,' Wilson said, rubbing his eyes. 'It must be a coincidence.'

'In my experience, there is no such thing,' Barton replied seriously. '*Coincidence* is merely a signpost of destiny.' Unexpectedly, he gave a warm smile.

Wilson slowly walked the full length of the Isaiah cabinet and stopped at the last page of text. He wanted to distance himself from Barton. Focusing on the characters, he effortlessly translated the words: 'As the new heavens and the new earth that I make will endure before me, declares the Lord, so will your name and descendants endure. From one New Moon to another ...' He could read it!

Wilson spun towards Barton. 'What do the Dead Sea scrolls have to do with time travel? Or are you just trying to impress me with how much money you have?'

Barton pointed to the other side of the room. 'The answer is *there*—in the Book of Esther.'

In the last row, a very well preserved scroll lay inside its cabinet; probably the most pristine in the room.

Wilson approached the parchment. 'I thought the Book of Esther was missing from the Dead Sea scrolls.[4] Wasn't it the only book of the Old Testament that wasn't located with the others?'

'I must say—you are full of surprises, Wilson.' Barton seemed impressed. 'You are absolutely correct. Common belief has it that the Book of Esther, the seventeenth book of the Bible, was found in Jerusalem. But that is not the case. It's a well-kept secret, but a copy was also found in the Dead Sea caves along with the others.'

'Why would anyone want to keep that a secret?'

'Because *Esther* is the most controversial of the scrolls—and in many ways the most important.'

Wilson pressed his hands on the glass and studied the perfectly preserved Hebrew script. He could read the characters without effort—it *was* the Book of Esther, just as Barton had said. 'And *why* is this the most important scroll?' Wilson asked.

'Because the secret of time travel is contained within the script. Coded within the text are detailed blueprints for how to assemble and drive a time portal using the magnetic field of the earth.'

Wilson glanced towards Barton, a stunned expression unavoidably gripping his face. At that moment, standing above the legendary Dead Sea scrolls, above the Book of Esther—the scroll that was not even meant to have existed—Wilson knew for sure this wasn't about his omega programming. This was something else—something infinitely more important.

Barton looked more serious than ever, then glanced at his watch. 'By the way, Wilson, your twenty minutes are up.'

---

4 *New Evidence Demands a Verdict*, Josh McDowell, Thomas Nelson, Nashville, 1999, page 80.

Houston, Texas
Central Railway Station
November 26th 2012
Local Time 3:13 p.m.

Mission of Isaiah—Day Two

A MESSAGE BLARED over the public address system and Wilson was jolted out of his daydream. Even now he felt a strange sense of awe when he remembered seeing the Dead Sea scrolls for the first time. The fact that he could read them that day—just over two weeks before, and seventy years into the future—was still astonishing to him. Mind-boggling. It was a moment that had changed his life forever.

As he limped towards platform thirty-eight, his stomach rumbled. The meal he'd eaten with George had hardly dented his hunger. Hopefully there would be something to eat on the train.

Emerging from the unlit gangway, he slowly scaled the stairs. The walls were covered with graffiti and a pungent smell was thick in the air. Flashes of sunlight beamed off the railway tracks as an orange commuter train rumbled into a distant platform. It came to a stop and its doors opened to reveal empty carriages.

The doors closed, and the train rumbled away again.

A discarded newspaper caught Wilson's eye as it gently fluttered in the breeze. There was a familiar face on the front page.

Very familiar.

Wilson was looking at his own picture—a sketch of his own face!

'What the hell?' he whispered.

Written across the front page of the *Houston Chronicle* was the headline: 'Police Chase Serial Killer', and below it:

> A man responsible for the deaths of more than fourteen people in the southwest United States is confirmed to be prowling Houston. The killer, believed to be seriously wounded, has already slain once since his arrival. In his most recent strike, Officer Tolle of the Houston Police Department was killed when he was run down in a pre-meditated attack.

Fourteen people? Pre-meditated attack? Wilson nervously scanned the surrounding platforms. Thankfully no one was looking in his direction. *They think I'm injured*, he realised. *That's why they didn't stop me coming in here.* He continued reading: 'Commander Visblat of the Houston Police is quoted as saying: "This man is the vilest type of killer. We will track him down at all costs."'

There was another picture.

Wilson realised he had seen that same unforgettable face before—twice. It was the redheaded man.

Staring at the photograph, Wilson wondered why a high-ranking officer—Commander Visblat—would fabricate such a deception?

Then he remembered the ticketing agent's hands, shaking with fear. Something was wrong—he'd walked into a trap! He limped to the edge of the train platform, jumped down onto the tracks and disappeared into the darkness of the railway tunnel.

16

Houston, Texas
HPD Headquarters
November 26th 2012
Local Time 3:24 p.m.

Mission of Isaiah—Day Two

COMMANDER VISBLAT SAT alone in his office. The venetian blinds were drawn and the air was dark and hazy. The wood-veneer desk in front of him was heaped with disorganised stacks of newspapers and notepads, numerous coloured pens, many more than he could ever use in a year, water bottles and used food wrappers. Around the room, throughout the clutter, there was nothing personal of any kind except for a few reference books about the Egyptian pyramids stuffed into the overflowing bookshelf.

In a clearing on the centre of the tabletop sat a carefully written letter from the Mayor, detailing his disgust at the treatment of Corporal Jeremy Bishop: 'Pointing a weapon at a fellow officer is not acceptable under any circumstances. Let alone the discharging of a bullet into the roof of the police auditorium.'

Visblat scoffed—there were more important things to worry about than being sacked from the force. But this was his second reprimand in the last three months for 'conduct unbecoming an officer'. He was now officially on probation. One more diversion from the rules and he was out for good—no matter how valuable he was to the administration.

Visblat's gaze shifted to the afternoon edition of the *Houston Chronicle*: 'Police Chase Serial Killer'. He was furious that details of the manhunt had been leaked to the media, specifically against his orders. There was even a quote in the paper attributed to himself! His piercing eyes shifted to the black telephone in front of him. He was looking for some way to vent his accumulating rage. He vaulted from his seat, grabbed the phone and violently wrenched the cord out of the wall. Clutching the unit in his hand, he burst out the door with the cable trailing behind him. As expected, people scattered in different directions as he stomped along the hallway, a ferocious look of grim determination on his face.

Police headquarters was a bustling and overcrowded office building in the centre of the Houston business district. Over 1800 staff worked there, on rotating shifts, twenty-four hours a day. The furniture and fittings were from the mid-1950s—lots of wood—and there was very little natural light inside the maze of corridors and small offices. Even though it was a place of law enforcement, a sense of futility pervaded everyone and everything at HPD. For no matter how hard they tried to maintain control, the crime rate continued to rise.

Visblat stomped along, his eyes fixed straight ahead. The murmur of voices gently trickled into the hallway from behind the call centre doors. Thrusting them open, he hoisted his telephone into the air without regard. It flew the entire length of the crowded room, missing everyone, and smashed into a wall with a loud *crack*, shattering into a dozen pieces that ricocheted across the floor.

Conversations ended mid-sentence and there was silence.

At one end of the room, up three steps to a landing, was the 'Crimes in Progress' section—known as CIP. The walls were covered with battle charts listing the location of every police unit throughout the district. This was where the manhunt for Wilson Dowling was being co-ordinated and every lead was being gathered. Around the perimeter of the room were thirty or so telephone operators, all facing the front, handling the despatch and enquiry services for the city's hundreds of patrol vehicles. Normally busy, the call centre had been frantic for the last twenty-four hours.

'Who's responsible for giving me an update?' Visblat yelled.

There was silence.

'Right, then,' he said. 'Who's the duty officer?'

'I am, Commander.'

A stocky, capable-looking man with short brown hair stepped forward and saluted. Detective Craig Robinson was the next-highest ranking officer in the room. He was a career policeman with more than twenty years on the force. A proud Texan, Robinson considered himself tough and honest. His uncle and brother were also with the HPD. Detective Robinson had just been promoted in the past month—no more uniform; he was a suit now.

'Sir, I was about to give you an update,' Robinson explained.

Visblat trudged ponderously up the stairs to CIP, stopped directly in front of Robinson and pressed his index finger hard into his lapel. 'Do you know what keeping me informed is supposed to mean?' he whispered. 'It means that you have to tell me *what the fuck* is going on!'

'I'm sorry, Commander.' Robinson's eyes nervously scanned the room. Everyone was watching for his reaction. He fought to keep his voice steady. 'It won't happen again.'

'When I'm sitting in my office and the phone doesn't ring,' Visblat continued, 'I begin to wonder if you care about my orders. Do you care?'

Detective Robinson had just begun a twelve-hour shift and for the last fifteen minutes he had been studying the evidence so as to make an informed report. 'It won't happen again, Commander,' he said vehemently. He was not a man who blamed others or made excuses.

Visblat swung his gaze away from his subordinate and scanned the charts. 'Tell me what you've got,' he said in a gruff voice. At the same time, the room began to hum again with the sound of people working.

Robinson's promotion to senior detective meant he would have to deal with Visblat on a more regular basis—a daunting prospect. But he was pragmatic about it: he didn't have to *like* his commander, he just had to report to him. Anyway, what choice did he have? It went with the territory. Visblat's response was to be expected—he was always going to react fiercely when he found out that details of the manhunt had been leaked to the media.

'We've thoroughly searched the train station,' Robinson replied professionally. 'We still have 125 men deployed in the immediate area—so far, nothing. The tip-off we received from the ticketing agent appears to be genuine. A man fitting the fugitive's description used the credit card stolen from the hospital.' Detective Robinson pointed at the details written on the whiteboard. 'A green American Express card belonging to a Jack Bolten—the employee at Harris County whose car was broken into.'

He paused. 'But, sir, what I can't understand is—the police officers on duty, and the ticketing agent, reported the suspect being in good health—except for a bleeding lip. Apparently, he sustained that injury in an altercation just outside the station. He was wearing a T-shirt with "Love Machine" written on the front.' He paused again. 'Hardly a low-key disguise, either. Therefore we need to consider the prospect that *this man* is not the one we want. A decoy, perhaps?'

'Impossible,' Visblat replied. 'He's working alone.'

'Sir, look at the facts.' Robinson pointed towards the red circle on the largest map on the wall—the red zone, as they called it. 'Our reports confirm that, yesterday morning, the fugitive was badly hurt in a car accident—on the 610 freeway, under the Westheimer Overpass. Severely hurt, in fact. I've read the hospital reports.'

'I know all that.'

Robinson took a deep breath. 'His injuries—the broken legs—would naturally rule out his escape on foot. Nonetheless, we conducted a thorough search of the hospital complex to a radius of one mile. As you know, we found nothing—which means the injured man must have been the fugitive, otherwise *why* would he have disappeared the way he did. Therefore, the fugitive is unquestionably injured. I've concluded, sir, that he must have an accomplice of some kind.'

'He doesn't have an accomplice,' Visblat said.

'The man at the train station was in good health—so something is wrong. In my view, the fugitive escaped from the hospital by car. Based on his injuries, that is the only possibility. He *must* have an accomplice.'

'I seriously doubt that,' Visblat said. 'He's doing all this on his own.'

Robinson rubbed the accumulated sweat from his forehead. The pressure of dealing with his commander was more than he could have imagined. 'One thing's for certain,' he said. 'The fugitive is quite inventive. The way he cut the electrical power at the hospital was ingenious. There are two electrical grids in that section of the building. He managed to short them both out simultaneously, dropping power to the lights and the security systems.'

'I agree, that *was* unexpected,' Visblat said. 'But what I want to know is—how did he get out of the building past the twenty SWAT officers we sent in to detain him? Especially considering his poor physical condition?'

Robinson rubbed his temples. 'Either the reports of the fugitive's injuries are *incorrect* or they are deliberately falsified. Or, as I said before, this man has an accomplice of some kind. Maybe even someone within the hospital system. That's likely.' He pointed at a map of the Harris County complex. 'The fugitive certainly exited via the eastern parking lot.' He pointed to another map on the wall. 'This is where we found the bandages. This is where the car was broken into and the credit card stolen.' On the desk to one side, a small television was running continuous taped footage. 'We checked the surveillance video. It went blank when the power was cut and didn't restart, but we've determined that *these* were the only cars that went in and out last night.' Robinson pointed to the whiteboard where sixty or so names and addresses were written in blue ink.

Visblat studied the names of the hospital employees. 'I see what you mean. All right,' he said reluctantly, 'get *all* these vehicles searched again. If your theory is correct, someone must have helped this man escape. And it's your job to find out who it was.'

'Yes, Commander.'

'Get Captain Hall back up here. He must have overlooked something important. Yes—that makes sense. Let's have another word with him.'

'Yes, Commander.'

Visblat pinched his bottom lip between his fingers. 'We *also* need to consider that the fugitive is not as seriously injured as we first thought.' He pointed at a map of the Houston area. 'I want double security at all the airports and aerodromes within two hundred miles of here. That's how he'll make his next move.'

'How can you be certain, Commander?'

Visblat's muscles tensed. 'Just do as I say! I want extra men deployed at all the airports, even the small ones. He may try to steal a light plane. Put everyone on alert. I want extra sentries posted *there*, *there* and *there*.' The commander stabbed the map in three places. 'Stop anyone who looks even remotely like him.' He paused. 'Detective, if this man manages to escape this time, it'll be your fault, no one else's.'

Even though Robinson thought it was ridiculous to assume the fugitive was uninjured, he turned to his staff. 'You heard the commander. I want teams doubled at all these airports. Detain everyone who looks even remotely—'

Without warning, Visblat spun towards a telephone operator sitting behind him.

'What did you say?' he snapped. Visblat stalked menacingly towards a tall blonde woman sitting in the front row. 'What did you say?' he roared impatiently. But the woman remained mute, frozen in terror. 'What did you say? Tell me!'

Seeing the commander's eyes, Annie McDonald's instinct was to run away, but the mere sight of him so close somehow paralysed her.

Visblat turned to Detective Robinson. 'Get her to talk—*now*. Before I lose my temper.'

Robinson ran to the young woman and stood between her and their commander. 'Tell him what you said, Annie. What did you say?' She just kept staring, dumbstruck with fear. 'Annie, you *must* speak.'

'It was just a registration check,' she whimpered.

'More information,' Visblat growled from the background.

'A white Ford,' she added hesitantly.

Robinson couldn't understand why Visblat's reaction had been so brusque. But it seemed rational behaviour was to be expected less and less from him.

'It belongs to a George Washington,' the young woman eventually forced out. 'From Bordersville. It was just a registration check,' she said nervously. 'Detective Olsen called it in. Said the car was involved in an accident this morning.'

The edges of Visblat's lips curled upwards into a smile as he approached the CIP whiteboard and thumped the flat of his palm on the list of hospital employees. 'What a coincidence,' he said. 'George Washington from Bordersville.' The name was written in blue ink. 'The fugitive is certainly involved,' he declared, happily. 'Where there's smoke, there's fire.'

Detective Robinson mustered his energy. 'I want any squad cars we've got in sector four directed to Bordersville, immediately. We'll provide more details in transit.' He pointed at his assistant. 'Inform SWAT that we want them deployed immediately—code red, everyone!'

'Disregard that order!' Visblat countered. 'Get my helicopter ready.' He poked Detective Robinson's chest with his finger for the second time. 'If I hadn't of come down here, this man would certainly have escaped. Hold everyone back—I'll do this myself.'

17

Houston, Texas
Richey Road, Bordersville
November 26th 2012
Local Time 3:36 p.m.

Mission of Isaiah—Day Two

BOTH HANDS GRIPPING the stock, Helena pointed her gun at the skinny black man in front of her—but he just smiled back. George was sitting on a wooden bench outside the front door of his trailer home with his arms crossed, legs apart. He didn't look worried—not even a little bit. Helena had threatened him countless times, pleaded with him, even tried being nice to him, but as yet she had been unable to get any additional information.

The two Dobermans were casually sitting in the long grass as if they were at a winter picnic. Helena was careful not to alarm them more than necessary, but they appeared completely unaffected by what was taking place.

'For God's sake,' Helena pleaded, for what seemed like the tenth time. 'Stop making this so difficult.'

'You are one *sick bitch*,' George replied. 'No doubt about it.'

'Why do you think that? Tell me *something*!'

George's expression was that of a man catching a whiff of rotten fish. 'Next thing I know, you are gonna wanna play nurse with *me!*' He shivered for effect. 'No sir! You ain't gonna be playing that sick little game here, woman. I work in a hospital, *kapeesh*? I know just how twisted that blood-fetish thing actually is.'

'I told you! I don't know what you're talking about.' Helena groaned in frustration. 'Why won't you believe me?'

'Cause you ain't trustworthy, that's why.'

'Not trustworthy! Are you serious?'

'I'm *always* serious. I'm a Washington!'

'You must have mistaken me for somebody else. Can't you see that?'

'I've seen ya husband! OH … MY … GOD!' George made another twisted expression. 'That dude is *King Kong* ugly!'

'I'm not even married!'

'I'd be lying too, if I were you,' George said. 'I know y'kind. My wife denies hitchin' up with me also. And *she says* I ain't trustworthy! That's a laff! It's y'all women that are the liars.'

Helena didn't want to hear any more stories about George's marital situation. He had drifted onto the subject numerous times already. 'Look, Mr Washington, I'm telling the truth. You must believe me.'

George unashamedly picked his nose with his little finger. 'How can I trust y'all when yer cannon is pointing at me like that?'

Helena took a deep breath. 'Money, is that what you want?' She reached into her pocket and pulled out a wad of twenty-dollar bills. 'This'll loosen your tongue, I'll bet,' and she threw it in his lap.

George gazed at the handful of cash. 'What do I look like—some sort'a snitch?' He threw the money back at her. 'I don't need no cash from no *twisted coppo wife*. No sir!'

'You must be kidding?'

'No sir-eee!'

Helena concluded he was delusional, and most certainly on drugs.

'I don't kid around when there's a wad of *Andrew Jacksons* involved,' George said seriously. 'I'm pleading the Fifth. That's it. I'm pleading the Fifth Amendment. That's what President Andrew Jackson would do.'

'All I want is to *find* the man who was in the back of your car.'

'Sure ya do.'

'I'm not trying to hurt him.'

George shook his head. 'Y'all could be an angel from heaven and I still wouldn't tell ya nothin'.' A jetliner flew low overhead, then roared into the distance—the sixth one in the last ten minutes. George watched the plane disappear, then casually asked, 'Mind if I smoke? It helps me relax … unlike y'all.'

In resignation, Helena shrugged her shoulders. 'Why the hell not.' Backing up a little, she lowered her weapon and crouched down in front of him. 'I give up, Mr Washington. But for the life of me I can't understand why you're acting this way. You don't even know who I am.'

'I'd never betray a friend,' George stated. That was it, he realised; Wilson was his friend and he would do what he could to protect him—even if it cost him a wad of Jacksons.

'But you'd never even met this Wilson guy before today. Why would you try so hard to keep information about him a secret?'

George took a long drag and smiled back at her. 'That's between me, an' him.'

One of the Dobermans wandered towards Helena and sat at her feet. She instinctively reached down and stroked the animal's head.

George was bemused as he watched his guard dog revel in the attention. Inhaling on his cigarette again, he blew the smoke out through the gap in his teeth. 'Her name is Esther,' he said.

A sloppy lick was bestowed on the back of Helena's hand.

'The big one is Tyson.'

'They're fine-looking animals,' she replied.

'You know what? I can't understand it. These two wuz the meanest critters in the world; particularly with white folks.' He paused. 'Now look at 'em. It don't make no sense.'

'Dogs are a good judge of character, Mr Washington. Maybe they know more about people than you do.'

George inhaled another puff. 'I seriously doubt it.'

'This man—*Wilson*—has information that I need,' Helena stated. 'That's why I'm here.' She gestured towards the trailer home. 'I saw this house, and I saw you—through *his* eyes. I saw him take a shower, back there. I saw him patting *this* dog.'

George watched Helena with great intrigue. He wanted to believe her, but his logic told him not to. She *was* the beautiful white woman Wilson had told him about. She had to be.

'This, *Wilson*, he isn't an ordinary man,' she continued. 'He's done things I can't even begin to explain ...' Realising there was no point in continuing, her voice suddenly tapered off. 'I will find him,' she reaffirmed—more for her own benefit than anything else.

'I told y'all,' George said. 'I don't know nothing.'

Helena stood up. 'Would it help if I threatened you again?'

Cigarette smoke poured from George's nostrils as he chuckled.

'I guess not.' Helena holstered her weapon. 'I know you're only trying to protect Wilson from something, but you're wrong to protect him from me.' It seemed Helena's excursion to Bordersville had reached a dead end. 'Goodbye, Mr Washington. Have a nice life.'

George crossed his legs and saluted her. 'Nice meeting y'all. Come again some time.' In his estimation, white women were always trouble.

Helena backed away, keeping a concerned eye on George at all times. Eventually she turned and made for her car with the female Doberman, Esther, trotting amiably by her side.

Helena was satisfied on some level; she now had Wilson's name, the mere fact of which was undeniable proof that the man she saw existed. But she would now have to wait for her visions to begin again—if they ever did—to find out more.

AN UNFAMILIAR DRONING approached from the west. It wasn't a plane this time, and Helena turned to face the ever-increasing rumble. A black helicopter, with the word *Police* in white letters on the fuselage, appeared over the trees.

It seemed that Detective Olsen had sent a chopper.

Thinking the worst, George's mouth gaped and the cigarette fell from his lips. The blonde woman's husband was here! The sophisticated black machine banked steeply and bled off speed. It was coming in to land in the open area just beyond the boundary of the property.

Under the roar of the rotor blades, the muscular aircraft descended quickly and touched down in a cloud of flying debris. The rear doors sprang open and four men appeared. They all had guns.

Helena shied away as a wall of dust billowed towards her.

George eyed his shotgun in the grass, but it was already too late. Tyson surged towards the intruders. George tried to hold onto him, but the large dog slipped easily from his grasp.

Rubbing the dust from her eyes, Helena recognised one of the men immediately—she had seen him in the media many times—his distinctive red hair and imposing height were unmistakable. It was Commander Visblat of the HPD, flanked by three tactical officers. This was not exactly the type of response she expected from Detective Olsen.

Tyson sprinted forward, growling in attack.

Visblat calmly raised his handgun and a muffled shot echoed over the whine of the helicopter turbines. The canine convulsed in mid-air and tumbled into the swirling grass.

'No-o-o!' George screamed. Running forward, arms outstretched, he dived beside his wounded pet. Blood was pouring from Tyson's chest—the animal wasn't breathing any more.

Out of the spinning dust, Visblat approached. 'Where's Wilson Dowling?' he yelled.

George's vision blurred with tears. 'Go to hell!' he screamed, but even so he found it difficult to stare into the police commander's eyes.

'I'll ask you one more time.' Visblat pointed his gun at the man kneeling before him. 'Where is Wilson Dowling?'

'You shot my dog!' Fury brimming, George glanced over his shoulder towards Helena. She was kneeling down, holding Esther by the collar. This is *her* fault, he thought. She was yelling something, but the whirr of the helicopter rotors made it impossible for him to hear.

Visblat's eyes locked on her also. 'A friend of yours?'

The police commander gestured abruptly in Helena's direction and as a result, the three troopers, weapons raised, moved cautiously after her. George felt a shiver quake through him. At that moment, he realised Visblat didn't know Helena—they were not husband and wife as he suspected. She had been telling the truth all along.

'I will ask you one last time!' Visblat yelled. 'Where is Wilson Dowling?'

George braced himself and stared into Commander Visblat's eyes—he was even bigger and uglier than George remembered. 'I've got a message for you,' he said with a smirk.

Visblat leant closer, intrigued by the comment.

'Wilson said to tell y'all something. He said to tell you—' George raised his voice to a yell '—you will *never* catch him alive, you ASSHOLE!' George began laughing manically. 'He enjoyed screwin' your bitch wife, he did!'

Visblat clubbed George mercilessly across the face with his gun. The solid blow split George's head open and he fell back, unconscious, in a spray of blood.

Helena was now locked eye to eye with Commander Visblat in the distance. Houston's most senior policeman looked consumed and twisted with anger. There was something in the commander's expression that made Helena panic. Esther began growling and tried to pull towards him, but Helena held on tight.

Was it best just to surrender? she wondered.

Then Helena remembered the promise she had made to herself long ago, that she would *never* allow herself to be at the mercy of anyone; no matter who it was. Not even the police.

'I want that woman alive!' Visblat yelled.

The three troopers, rifles in hand, sprinted forward.

Helena lifted her handgun and fired a warning shot in the air. The men dived into the tall grass for cover. Suddenly, dust and debris began flying in all directions as the police helicopter went to full power and hovered just above the ground. Helena knew it was now or never. Turning for her car, she ran as fast as she could, Esther bounding by her side.

THE CHOPPER TOUCHED down again and Commander Visblat vaulted inside. 'Get airborne,' he said and pointed upwards. 'I want that woman in custody!'

The pilot appeared edgy. 'What about him?' and he pointed at George's unconscious body, lying in the grass.

With the blonde woman already beside her car, Visblat slapped the pilot on the back of the helmet. 'Forget him! That bitch just took a shot at us! Get airborne!'

The pilot pressed a switch and spoke calmly into his helmet microphone, 'P-27 requesting emergency takeoff clearance. P-27 requesting—'

Visblat grabbed the pilot's helmet and twisted his head towards him. 'I said, take off!'

'Sir, we're in controlled airspace! The wind direction is—'

Visblat tore the cable out of the radio. 'Get this thing off the ground *now*! That's an order!'

HELENA COULD HEAR the roar of the helicopter as she jumped into her car. Looking back she saw the three troopers running through the scrub towards her. In reply, she squeezed off another round, high and through the trees.

Esther unexpectedly jumped over Helena's lap into the passenger seat. It seemed the Doberman was coming along for the ride. With no time to argue, Helena slammed the gearshift into reverse and stomped on the accelerator. The engine screamed as the black Mercedes sprinted backwards in a plume of tyre smoke. Spinning the wheel, Helena flung her car in the other direction and pulled the lever into drive, zigzagging the Mercedes away at maximum acceleration.

In her rear-vision mirror the three troopers shrank from view.

Breathing for what felt like the first time in the last two minutes, she decided she needed to get to her father as fast as possible—he would know what to do. She turned on her mobile phone and waited for it to come on-line.

'GIVE ME A BETTER angle!' Visblat yelled. He was leaning precariously out the back door of the helicopter as they chased the sports car towards the freeway. 'Closer!' he yelled into the cabin. 'She's not to get away!'

The pilot levelled out just above the treetops.

The black Mercedes appeared in Visblat's gun sights.

He fired.

Suddenly, a massive shadow streaked across the sky above the police chopper. The accompanying roar was deafening. For a moment the bright sunlight disappeared as a commercial jetliner—a Boeing 767, landing gear down, flaps open to their maximum position—flew directly overhead and scampered for the horizon.

In reaction, the helicopter pilot went to full power. He yanked the control lever back in a vain attempt to gain as much altitude as possible. The police chopper shot upwards, causing Visblat to tumble from his position into the rear seats. The cabin swung violently to one side, then yawed to the other. The vortices generated by the airliner's wings were having a catastrophic effect.

The nose dipped.

The engines flamed out.

HELENA STOMPED ON the brake pedal as hard as she could—the car squirmed as it decelerated, her seatbelt pressing firmly across her chest. Through the windscreen, she watched aghast as the police helicopter plummeted earthwards, the glass canopy slamming into the pavement with unbelievable force. The rotor blades shattered into thousands of particles, which shot in all directions as the remnants of the cabin slid to an inelegant halt in the middle of the road.

For a few seconds, a bombardment of large steel chunks continued to drop from the sky.

'Holy Jesus.' Helena gazed in horror at what was left of the multi-million-dollar machine. Her focus shifted to a bullet hole in the top right-hand corner of her windscreen. She turned to the Doberman beside her. 'They were trying to kill us,' she said.

The dog looked back at her with a stare of comprehension written on her face.

Unexpectedly, there was movement inside the helicopter cabin.

The rear door suddenly flung open and Visblat appeared from the crumpled hulk. A river of blood poured from a deep cut on his forehead, down his face, soaking into his shirt. He raised his weapon, stumbling forward at the same time. He was limping and clearly disoriented.

Helena sucked in a frightened breath. It was the sight of Visblat's eyes that made her skin crawl—his piercing blue eyes. Pressing the accelerator flat, she sped towards him at break-neck speed.

At the last second she swerved.

Taking aim, Visblat pulled the trigger, but his bullet ricocheted off the road, low and away to the left.

18

Houston, Texas
George Bush Intercontinental Airport
November 27th 2012
Local Time 6:11 a.m.

Mission of Isaiah—Day Three

THE SKY WAS VERY dark and there was no moon. Thin layers of mist hung in the heavy air.

Across an expanse of empty tarmac, the George Bush Intercontinental Airport glowed like a display of jewels in the blackness. The well-lit terminal building was surrounded by countless aircraft—from various airlines—that were arriving and departing every few minutes. It was one of the busiest airports in the southern United States. Above the row of buildings, a powerful red beacon on the traffic-control tower pulsed monotonously into the gloom.

The airfield too was speckled with brightly lit beacons—half of them blue, the other half orange—that marked the runways. Beyond the perimeter fence there was nothing but the murky night.

Outside the airfield, a lone figure shuffled across the dark, his warm breath turning to mist. It was Wilson, his attention focused on a yellow security vehicle patrolling the inside of the airport boundary. Hiding in the scrub, the van rolled past only metres away and trundled off into the distance.

Wilson strained to pull himself over the tall wire fence, then fell heavily into the grass on the other side. Having adjusted his sunglasses after the graceless landing, he set out across the acres of flat concrete towards the terminal building. His legs hurt and his migraine was worse than ever, but he plodded on regardless. The small van was completing its counter-clockwise patrol of the airport every ten minutes or so, and time was of the essence.

The drone of a gliding airliner came in from the north as a passenger jet crossed the airport threshold—nose high, wing lights beaming. The landing gear squealed as the aircraft hit the ground and its turbines clicked into reverse. An immense mechanical roar thundered across the airfield as the jet eventually slowed and began a lethargic turn in Wilson's direction. His pace quickened, but unavoidably the wing-lights swept across the darkness and engulfed him.

FROM HIGH IN the cockpit, the captain of the TWA airliner spotted a man on the tarmac, his endless telltale shadow trailing behind him across the concrete.

The captain turned to his co-pilot. 'You'd better call it in.'

'TWA 437,' the co-pilot said, his voice a bland monotone. 'Reporting an intruder. A lone man, crossing Runway-26 Left. Do you copy?'

'Roger that, 437,' the tower responded. 'We'll check it out.'

Without giving it another thought, the pilots went back to their post-landing checks.

NO MATTER HOW fast Wilson ran, he couldn't evade the blinding white light—it was all around him. He had changed direction several times, to escape somehow, when the sanctuary of the darkness suddenly enveloped him once again. The large jet had swung away towards the other side of the airport.

Doing his best to ignore his aches and pains, Wilson jogged the remaining few hundred metres to a parked Boeing jetliner. It was shut down in a holding bay just off the main concourse. The interior lights were extinguished and parking blocks had been jammed under the large wheels. Wilson's pace slowed—a mixture of fatigue and awe. The massive silver wings of the airliner were suspended above him, the cylindrical turbines hanging below. It was the first time he had ever seen a Boeing 747 up close; aircraft like this had ceased flying well before he was born.

The smell of aviation fuel filled Wilson's nostrils—an unforgettable scent, pleasant almost, and it reminded him of happier times. Wilson's grandfather, William Dowling, was the one who had encouraged him to fly vintage aircraft. His grandfather paid for the tuition because it was his way of spending lots of time with his grandson; at least that was how Wilson remembered it.

'When you fly up in the sky, in the clouds, you are dancing with angels,' William used to say. He was a sentimental old bastard.

Wilson smiled as he remembered his first solo flight, in an old Piper Warrior—a real piece of crap; the engine had about 150,000 hours on it. He remembered how sweaty his palms were that day. It was windy, the four-cylinder engine vibrating menacingly through the cabin. The sky was clear. Closing his eyes, Wilson could still see his grandfather standing there on the tarmac—a proud smile on his face—giving a double thumbs-up as Wilson taxied towards the runway for the first time on his own. It seemed funny upon reflection: Wilson had been more worried about letting his grandfather down than crashing the plane and being killed.

Wilson refocused on the 747's landing gear. The rear bogies had eight giant wheels each. They were colossal. The tyres alone were taller than he was. An awesome machine like this made all the small planes and gliders Wilson had flown seem inconsequential—there was just no comparison.

A pair of car headlights suddenly flashed out of the darkness as the yellow patrol vehicle screeched to a halt only a few metres away. Wilson tried to duck for cover, but it was too late.

A man leapt from the driver's seat brandishing a revolver.

'You're under arrest!' the security guard yelled. 'Don't move!' The burble of his car engine reverberated into the quiet darkness. 'Raise your hands!' he yelled.

A film of sweat covered Wilson's face. His heart was pounding madly. From behind his sunglasses he glanced towards the shadows, trying to measure his path of escape.

'Drop the gun!' a woman's voice called out.

Wilson squinted into the car headlights, confused.

'I said, drop the gun!' the female voice repeated, this time more assertively. 'Are you fucking deaf?'

The security guard released his weapon and it landed on the tarmac, with a *clank*, between his feet. 'What are you doing?' the guard said, frantically. 'Everybody's looking for this guy! He's mine!'

'Shut up!' the female voice replied.

The figure of a young woman holding a handgun glided out of the shadows: of slim build, with blonde hair, she spoke with a southern accent. She moved quickly, smoothly. Holding her weapon with both hands, she trained her sights on the security guard. 'Don't move a muscle!' she warned him. The newcomer then flicked her eyes in Wilson's direction. 'What's your name?'

Wilson stared back at her—he was dumbstruck.

'What's your name?' she said again. 'Is it *Wilson*? Is that it?'

But he just stood there.

'Listen idiot!' she snapped. 'Are you Wilson, or not?'

'As far as I know,' he eventually replied.

Helena's visions had finally led her to him. Wilson existed. Unfortunately the security guard had beaten her to him. As she studied Wilson's appearance, Helena felt only disappointment. *So he thinks he's a 'Love Machine'*, she thought to herself. *Great!* Just her luck—he was a moron.

In that split second, the security guard lunged for his weapon. With a thunderous *bang*, a bullet sparked off the tarmac by Wilson's feet, causing him to spring into the air like a scared cat. Operating on pure instinct, he dived for cover and scrambled on his hands and knees behind the landing gear. He sought darkness but was unexpectedly confronted by the security guard who had doubled back the other way.

Time seemed to slow as Wilson stared into the barrel of the gun.

Suddenly a large black dog, moving at lightning speed, sprang from the shadows, latched onto the guard's pistol hand and wrenched him, screaming, to the ground. In less than a second, the blonde woman reappeared and clubbed the guard on the back of the head with her revolver.

'Esther, let him go!' she commanded, pulling on the dog's collar.

The Doberman immediately released her grip.

Esther?

Wilson had a clear view of this mystery woman for the first time. Her hair was the colour of pale honey. She was quite tall, even-featured, with high cheekbones—she had a beauty spot just above the left corner of her mouth. She was attractive if you ignored the scowl— the type of woman you would expect to find looking at you from the front of a glossy magazine, not down the sights of a gun on an airport tarmac. Wilson tried to ease himself discreetly into the darkness, to escape somehow, but she waved him back with her weapon.

'You, my friend, are in a lot of trouble,' she said.

'Thanks. I didn't realise.' Wilson scanned the airport, his hands held high.

'I hope you know just how *much* trouble.'

'I do—thanks very much. May I ask, how is it you know my name?'

'Are you a serial killer?' she asked.

'Why does everybody think that?' he snapped back. Wilson looked around nervously. This was not the time for idle banter. The Doberman—Esther—caught his attention; her tongue was hanging out. It looked like George Washington's dog. Wilson pointed at the animal. 'You haven't by any chance seen a black guy with dreadlocks, have you?'

'Mr Washington was knocked senseless by the police at his home yesterday afternoon. There was nothing I could do. They took him away and arrested him.'

'You *know* George Washington?'

'Not before yesterday,' she said. 'I was looking for *you*.'

It explained how she knew his name, at least. Wilson decided the mystery woman was not going to pull the trigger—she would have done so already if that was her intention. He lowered his hands and began walking.

'My name is Helena Capriarty,' she said. 'I need some answers.'

'I'm sorry, Helena.' Wilson stepped over the unconscious security guard. 'I'm not sure what you want, but you must leave me alone. The police are after me.'

'I'm in as much trouble as you!' She circled Wilson and blocked his path. 'I have questions.'

Wilson stepped around her a second time. 'Leave me alone. Can't you see, this is all a terrible mistake.'

Helena shadowed him through a group of empty baggage trolleys toward the main terminal building. 'Where are you going?' she asked.

'You don't listen, do you?'

'You *must* answer my questions. It's the only way I'll understand what the hell is happening!'

'What's to understand?' Wilson said dismissively.

'Why I'm seeing visions—visions through *your* eyes!'

His pace slowed. 'You're seeing *what?*'

'I can see *through your eyes!*' She momentarily pointed at her temple with the gun barrel. 'We have a telepathic connection of some kind. I don't know what it is. But I'll say this: you've been up to some really strange things, Wilson, or whatever your name is. I saw the accident on the freeway. I saw your escape from that hospital.' *Part of it anyway*, she thought. 'And your time with that imbecile George Washington.' She knew she had Wilson's attention now. 'There are things I need to understand. And I'm not leaving until I get some answers.'

Wilson began walking again. He didn't want to believe what he was hearing.

Reaching into her pocket, Helena produced the plastic driver's licence she had found hidden in the shower cubicle and held it under Wilson's nose. 'Remember Jack Bolten?'

In the distance, a group of police cars swarmed through the outer gate of the airport and fanned out. Blue and red roof lights blazed into the haze. The sight started Wilson running.

'*Wait—*' Helena called out.

Wilson was desperately searching for anything with propellers; he couldn't fly a turbine aircraft even if he wanted to.

Behind him, police cars were approaching.

To his left, the young blonde and the Doberman easily kept pace. As he turned the corner a small silver plane came into view—a Saab 340 turboprop. It was tiny compared with the other jets around the airport and had 'Texas Air' emblazoned on the tail. Wilson came to a standstill in the shadows and took a moment to observe the aircraft. The interior lights were on and metal passenger stairs were pushed against the fuselage. Wilson had never flown that particular model before, but he knew the basic configuration well enough to be sure to get it into the air. It was a small plane by commercial standards—a regional flyer, twin-engine turboprop, low wings, capable of carrying about twenty people, plus crew. Ground staff were unloading the last of the bags and closing the rear cargo doors. Wilson concluded that it had just landed and the passengers had already disembarked.

Esther casually plonked herself down between Wilson's legs as he waited in the darkness for the exact moment to make his move. Helena looked towards the aircraft also. She was uneasy.

'You want to hijack a plane?'

There was no response.

'Are you planning on flying it yourself?'

'I'm pretty sure I can,' he replied.

'Either you can, or you can't.'

'I can.'

'No offence, "Love Machine", but you don't look much like a pilot.'

A police car suddenly swung in their direction. Wilson grabbed Helena's sleeve and pulled her swiftly into the shadows next to him. The vehicle drove by only metres away, searchlights scanning the outside of the terminal building. All the while, Helena had her gun pressed into Wilson's crotch, her finger resting on the trigger.

'If you plan to shoot me,' he said calmly, 'aim a little higher,' and he eased the weapon upwards. Eventually, the police car disappeared around the corner and Helena shoved him back with the palm of her hand.

'Don't ever touch me again!' she seethed.

'Stay out of sight and I won't have to!' Wilson returned his attention to the Saab 340. He could see at least one person still inside the cockpit.

'Why are you wearing sunglasses?' Helena said. 'It's dark out here.'

Ignoring the question, he announced, 'That plane is the best way to escape.' He pointed at the aircraft.

'You hid that driver's licence,' Helena said, 'in the wall—and I found it! You don't even seem surprised!'

'Don't worry, I'm surprised enough. But as you can see, I have other things on my mind at the moment. Anyway, I have a deal for you. Help me to commandeer that plane and I'll tell you everything you want to know.' He paused. 'Is that a deal?'

'How do I know I can trust you?' she replied.

There was a pause. 'You don't. But help me steal that aircraft and I'll do my best to explain.'

'You're sure you can fly it?'

'Provided there's fuel.'

Helena bit her bottom lip. 'I'm probably going to regret this.'

With that, she ran towards the metal stairs and up inside.

Helena glanced into the empty passenger cabin, then the cockpit. A pilot was sitting alone at the controls. The lights on the instrument panel beamed brightly. She nonchalantly tapped her weapon on the pilot's shoulder. Four stripes.

'Captain,' she called out. 'I'm commandeering this aircraft.' He turned, expressionless, and stared into the barrel of her gun. 'You don't mind do you?'

'No, Ma'am,' he said, co-operatively, his eyes wide with fear.

'Is there anyone else on board?'

'No Ma'am.'

'If you do as I say, you won't be hurt.'

Wilson led Esther by the collar as Helena calmly escorted the pilot down the steps to the tarmac.

'Are you sure we don't need someone to fly this thing?' Helena asked.

'I'm sure,' Wilson replied.

Helena ordered the pilot to run and he sprinted towards the safety of the terminal building. Wilson simultaneously clambered up the metal stairs and stopped in the doorway, blocking the entrance.

'You should take your chances with the police,' he said, and prepared to swing the aircraft door closed in her face.

Memories of what she had been through in the last twenty-four hours flashed through Helena's mind—there was no way she would let Wilson leave her behind. She forced her way past him.

'I'm in a lot of trouble,' she said. 'Staying with you is the best option I have—God help me.' Pushing him aside, she swung the curved door shut. 'I'm staying!' The large red handle was turned counter-clockwise and the pressure door sealed.

'So I see,' Wilson said. He pointed to the back of the aircraft. 'Double-check to make sure no one else is on board.' Then he stepped into the cockpit.

The first thing Wilson checked was the fuel—both tanks were half full. It would have to do. He scanned the dials and switches. He recognised everything: navigation computers, artificial horizons, altimeters, speed controls. He jumped into the left seat and lingered there for a moment. It was not often that anyone had the chance to steal a plane, let alone had anywhere near a good enough reason to do it. Wilson gazed out the windscreen. People were running from everywhere, staring at him through the windows of the terminal building. It was time to get out of here.

Helena jumped into the co-pilot's seat just as the cabin pressure increased. 'There's no one else on board,' she said. Staring out the front windscreen, she noticed the hundreds of faces looking back at her. 'We've drawn a crowd, I see.'

Wilson's hands darted around the switches and levers. 'I expect that's what happens when you try to steal a plane right in front of the terminal building.'

Helena tightened her seatbelt. 'They probably think we're terrorists.' She thought for a moment about the consequences. 'We're in serious trouble.'

Wilson checked the battery power, then looked up to the overhead panel. A small blue light confirmed the sequence. Flicking a few more buttons, he hit the engine-one start switch.

There was a whine and a shuddering vibration took hold of the plane. The interior lights dimmed for a brief moment before the left engine roared to life. The large propeller was spinning just outside Wilson's window. He loved that feeling. It had been more than ten years since he had been in a pilot's seat. The bus-light flashed on—everything was working perfectly. It was time to start the second engine.

A group of anti-terrorist police, uniformed in black, stood calmly peering through the terminal window. Helena watched them as they planned their deployment then sprinted towards the exit doors. 'Armed men are on their way!' she said.

Wilson saw them as the second engine came to life. Flicking on the hydraulics and the anti-ice, he pressed both foot pedals at once and the auto-brake released. He clasped the steering tiller, turned it as far as possible to the right and forced the throttles forward. The General Electric turboprops cycled faster—but for some reason the aircraft was reluctant to budge.

'Wheel blocks!' Helena called out. She had seen them as she climbed the metal stairs. 'Give it more power!'

The police sprinted across the tarmac, automatic machine-guns cocked and ready.

Wilson eased the throttles further and further forward. The roar of the engines went from loud to deafening. The cabin shook violently. Then, with a distinct jump, the aircraft hopped the wheel blocks and accelerated towards the darkness.

Outside, the group of anti-terrorist police were knocked off their feet as the left wing hurtled past and hurricane-like winds blasted towards them.

A stern male voice crackled over the radio, 'To the pilot of Texas Air 6965. Return to the terminal immediately. Repeat. To the pilot of Texas Air 6965—'

Wilson flicked a switch and the voice was gone. 'Don't they know I'm trying to concentrate?' He increased flaps to maximum. 'Now ... where the hell is the runway?' The ground-lights seemed like a jumbled maze. In the distance, a gaggle of police cars raced through the darkness towards them. They would be here in seconds.

'There!' Helena pointed. 'Over there!'

Wilson altered his heading towards a cluster of orange and blue lights in the distance. Their speed was increasing. A black strip of tarmac stretched off into the distance. He pushed the heavy throttles forward as far as they could go and the thrust increased tenfold, forcing them back into their seats.

Police vehicles, at least four of them, began swerving dangerously close to the landing gear.

'STOP!' Helena shouted.

High outside the right window, a pair of white lights pierced down through the haze. Another aircraft was coming in to land on a perpendicular runway.

They were on a collision course!

Wilson glanced at the airspeed indicator—he hadn't reached his rotation speed yet.

'Why don't they see us?' Helena yelled, and she drew her seatbelt even tighter.

'Oops,' he muttered.

'What do you mean, "*Oops*"?'

Wilson flicked on the identification lights. The exterior beacons flashed and the approaching jetliner aborted its landing, shooting skywards at the last second.

But they were too close!

Forcing the control column forward, Wilson attempted to keep his craft against the tarmac and skittle his way under.

Warning lights illuminated.

Collision alerts blared.

Helena closed her eyes and hoped for a miracle.

With a roar, the approaching jetliner streaked directly overhead. The accompanying turbulence engulfed them moments later, hurling the Saab 340 sideways and flipping two of the police cars off the runway into the grass. Wilson pulled back on the control column as hard as he could and they shot skywards through the violently swirling air, wings straining under the force. The harsh velocity of the lift-off tumbled

Esther out the cockpit door into the main cabin and down the aisle.

It took a few moments for Wilson to realise that everything was okay as he watched the altitude indicator spin up. Straining against the force of gravity, the 340 climbed quickly. The cabin shuddered. Cockpit dials spun wildly round and round.

Out the side window, Wilson saw the lights of the airport shrinking behind him and he reduced throttle. The aircraft levelled out and he checked the gauges. Satisfied that everything was fine, he began playing with the controls, getting a feel for how they reacted. He couldn't help but smile. 'You don't see that sort of thing every day,' he said.

'I can't believe you're *happy*! You've just stolen a commercial aircraft!'

Wilson looked at the stranger beside him. She looked a little pale. '*We* just stole it together, remember?'

A PAIR OF POLICE cars stopped at the end of the runway, their red and blue roof lights flashing into the haze. Two officers stepped out and met in the glow of the headlights. In the distance the sound of the Texas Air turboprop faded into the night.

'Visblat is going to be very upset about this,' one of the officers said.

'I'd hate to be the one to tell him what just happened,' replied the other.

THE VIBRATING HUM of the engines droned through the cockpit as Wilson studied the instrument panel. The plane was set out much like the Aero Commander he used to fly as a boy. The question was: did they have enough fuel?

'Who *are* you?' Helena asked, glancing sideways towards him.

'I could ask *you* the same question,' Wilson observed, looking back. He was equally curious about her part in all this.

The coastline near Galveston was rapidly approaching.

'Tell me about these visions you mentioned?'

'I can see things.' Helena pressed her head against the backrest. She hesitated for a long while to gather her thoughts. 'Visions through *your* eyes. There's no doubt that's what they are.'

'Go on ...'

'I know it sounds crazy.'

Wilson forced a white lie from his lips: 'It doesn't sound crazy.'

'It feels like I'm inside you, in your head.' She took a deep breath. 'I see *through* your eyes. There's always a red haze surrounding everything. From what I've witnessed, it's amazing that you're even alive.'

'Keep going ...'

'The visions started about two months ago. Vague images, a weird rumbling noise, symbols. At first they appeared to have no meaning at all. Then, over the last couple of days, *you appeared*. And for the first time I've been able to make reasonable sense of what I saw—if what you've been up to can be called "reasonable".'

'These visions—when do you see them? Can you see them now?'

'I don't have any control over when it happens to me.' Helena closed her eyes and concentrated. 'But I had a fleeting glimpse, back there, when we were taking off.'

'You saw through me, then?'

'Just for a moment. Sometimes that's all I get. It's disorienting when it happens. I sort of lose my balance because the vision overlaps with what I'm seeing through my own eyes.' There was a long pause as she remembered what she'd witnessed over the last two days. 'It took me a while to figure out what was going on. You've had some strange things happening to you, Wilson.' She shook her head in dismay. 'I would have found you sooner, but my psychiatrist had me sedated. He thinks I'm certifiable.'

Wilson looked over at her. 'And you came to the airport to find me?'

'I went to George Washington's. That's where I ran into Commander Visblat, of all people. It seems the HPD's most senior policeman is chasing after you.' She looked at Wilson with a piercing gaze. 'Is it because you're sleeping with his wife?'

'George told you that, didn't he?'

'Is it true?'

'Of course not!'

'Is it because you're a serial killer?' She watched his face for a reaction.

'If you've been having visions through me,' Wilson said directly, 'you already know the answer to that.'

The Saab 340 sped over the coast above the ebony waters of the Gulf. In the distance, the sun was conjuring a beautiful orange glow just below the line of the horizon.

'I don't understand why this Visblat guy is chasing after me,' Wilson said. 'Nothing makes sense. He lied about me in the paper ... said I was a serial killer.' Wilson rubbed the side of his face and was about to go on, but he was distracted by the Doberman wandering into the cockpit. 'Where's the other dog, the big one?'

'His name was Tyson. Visblat shot him.'

'Dead?'

'Yes.'

'Is George okay?'

'He took a blow to the head, a bad one. But it didn't kill him. I phoned the police station and they would only say they have him in custody.' Helena watched Wilson's profile. 'Wearing sunglasses at night is a little odd, don't you think? Are they prescription?'

'The less you know about me the better.'

'You told me if I helped you, you'd tell me everything! I've done my part!'

'Yes, my glasses are prescription,' Wilson said. 'I can't see a thing without them.' He would say anything to stop her asking more questions. From the very beginning, he never had any intention of telling Helena the truth.

Forcing the control column forward, he speared the aircraft towards the surface of the water. The revs increased until the plane was shuddering—the airspeed indicator went into the red zone. A warning alert began sounding in the cockpit.

Air Traffic Control
Houston Intercontinental Airport
November 27th 2012
Local Time 6:45 a.m.

A TEAM OF SIX men and women stood around one of the many circular monitoring stations at Houston Air Traffic Control. The massive display detailed all the current flight movements across the continental United States. The screen was filled with small square blocks, most of them green, with a few lines of data attached—flight number, aircraft type, destination—and they were slowly shifting in all directions. But everyone was watching the progress of one aircraft—the Texas Air Saab 340, marked in red.

'They can't be terrorists,' the technical officer said. He had four pens in his breast pocket. 'They're heading straight out to sea.'

'Let's not rule anything out,' the traffic director announced. He was the most senior person in the room, the only one wearing a suit.

'His airspeed is increasing,' one of the flight co-ordinators said. 'He's losing altitude.'

'Something's wrong. I'm going to lose him,' said another.

'If he drops below five hundred feet, he'll be under our radar.'

The technical officer pointed at the designation code. 'It's all right. We still have his transponder signal. Everybody relax. He's heading north-northeast, but you're right, he's losing altitude fast.'

The red transponder image suddenly disappeared. The group of men and women looked at each other with blank expressions. The plane had vanished.

'They must have crashed!' said a voice.

'Inform the Coast Guard immediately.' The traffic director nervously wiped his mouth with his sleeve. 'Hurry!'

Somewhere over the Gulf of Mexico
Saab 340 Turboprop
November 27th 2012
Local Time 6:46 a.m.

WILSON UNCLIPPED THE transponder fuse and casually threw it over his shoulder. 'We won't be needing that.' He pulled back on the control column and the plane levelled out, flying southeast at maximum revs just above the glassy water. Wilson knew that, at this altitude, their top speed would be restricted and their range compromised, but that was the price they would have to pay to be radar-invisible.

The sun crested the horizon and a golden glow defused in all directions. Wilson looked at Helena who was in a due state of shock.

'I need you to do me a favour,' he said. 'I want you to take the flight controls for a little while.' At the same time, he was setting the autopilot so the aircraft would not descend below one hundred feet.

Helena glared back at him. 'You must be kidding!'

'Just keep them steady. If you think you're going to hit something, all you have to do is pull back. It's easy.'

'There's no way!'

'I'm asking you for a favour.'

'You're in no position to ask me for *anything*!' Wilson lifted his hands from the controls and Helena could feel the plane slowly dipping to the left. 'Take them!' she blurted, but Wilson just smiled back at her and didn't move a muscle. The wings dipped further. With no other choice, she slid her handgun under her left thigh and grabbed both handles, levelling the aircraft out.

'That's better, isn't it?' he said.

'Take the controls!' she yelled.

'No.'

'Take them! We'll crash!'

'You're doing just fine—'

'Take them!'

He unbuckled his seatbelt and stood up. 'It's been a hell of a day, hasn't it?'

'You're such an asshole!'

'If you say so.' Wilson explained to her what she needed to know, but omitted the detail of the autopilot, then pointed to the altitude indicator. 'Try and make sure we stay below 300 feet, otherwise we may pop up on a radar screen somewhere. And, you understand, we don't want that.'

'I don't know about this.'

'You're flying it already,' he said encouragingly. 'Trust yourself.'

Helena was at the controls of a Saab 340 turboprop, flying at 250 kph just above the surface of the ocean. At that moment, an arc of sunlight crested the horizon, spilling a carpet of bright gold across the water before them. In some strange way Helena was where she wanted to be; it was the first time in many months. Her searching was over and answers appeared to be at hand.

It was crazy, but she smiled.

Wilson pointed out the front window. 'Try and keep the sun where it is now. That will keep us flying southeast.' He could sense Helena's confidence growing by the second. 'Just one more thing,' he said. 'Don't fly into any oilrigs. They're all over the place out here.'

The smile duly vanished from Helena's face.

19

Houston, Texas
HDP Headquarters
November 27th 2012
Local Time 7:15 a.m.

Mission of Isaiah—Day Three

THERE WAS A KNOCK at the office door.

'Enter,' Visblat called out. He had been sitting in the same position since his discharge from hospital. A wide adhesive bandage was stuck to his forehead and his face was bruised. The helicopter crash had beaten him up quite badly. He had a fractured left wrist—in temporary plaster to his elbow—some broken ribs and a sprained left ankle. Under the circumstances, it was a miracle that he had managed to survive the accident with just minor injuries. The pilot had not been so lucky.

The door opened and Detective Robinson appeared. Visblat looked him up and down. 'What are you still doing here?' Robinson's shift was supposed to have ended at 3:30 in the morning.

'Wagner called in sick, sir. I'm standing in for him until his replacement arrives.' Detective Robinson was all too aware of the incident report from Richey Road and was suitably wary. Visblat had forced the pilot to take off without the proper clearance and, as a result, the helicopter had crashed. Rumour around the precinct was that the Mayor would be processing Visblat's termination notice as soon as he arrived at his chambers that morning. It was only a matter of hours before the commander would be officially relieved of duty.

However, until the papers were served, Detective Robinson would have to follow procedure.

'What do you want?' Visblat said.

'I'm here to give you an update, sir.'

'Well?' he said impatiently.

Robinson braced himself for a harsh reaction. 'Sir ... it appears the fugitive has escaped. You were right. He's hijacked a plane from the Intercontinental Airport. A Texas Air regional aircraft.'

'You told me he was badly injured!' Visblat said accusingly.

'Our reports were incorrect.'

'How is that possible?'

'He was obviously *not* the one who was in that car accident, Commander.'

Ignoring his aches and pains, Visblat stood from his chair, rage welling inside him. 'I told you he would escape this way, didn't I? I told you!'

Detective Robinson's heart was pounding. 'We think the aircraft may have crashed, sir,' he said hesitantly. 'After takeoff it was heading northeast, over the Gulf, when it dropped from radar coverage. Air Traffic Control lost the transponder signal moments later. They said that could only mean one thing—they think the plane has crashed into the sea.'

Visblat was suddenly calm. 'Do you have any eyewitness reports?' he said.

'I don't think so, Commander. Not as yet.' It seemed Visblat was taking the news extremely well. In fact, he looked almost happy now. The commander *must* be going crazy, Robinson concluded.

'Until you have confirmation,' Visblat said, 'that plane hasn't crashed ... has it? Do you understand? It's a trick. Wilson's heading south to Mexico; most probably flying low enough to avoid being spotted by radar.' He tapped his thumb on his bottom lip. 'That's what I'd do.'

There was a long pause.

The comment caught Detective Robinson's attention. 'Commander, is the fugitive called "Wilson"? You mentioned that name just before. Should I put that in my report?'

Visblat lifted his gaze, his creased brow suggesting that he was carefully processing the question. 'No, that's not necessary, Detective. It's just a name I've created for him.' The commander walked to the window and pulled open the venetian blinds—bright morning sunshine burst in through the dirty glass. It was the first time he had opened the blinds in many months. 'It's terrible that he got away,' he muttered.

'Commander, I have other news.' Robinson steadied himself. 'I've been sent here to tell you this manhunt is no longer under our jurisdiction.'

Visblat turned, his facial injuries looking far worse in the harsh morning light. 'Let me guess,' he said. 'It's a federal matter now?'

'Yes, sir. I received a call from the FBI. They've taken over the entire investigation. I had nothing to do with it. I was told just a few moments ago.'

'I understand.' Visblat forced a smile. 'Normal procedure for a hijacking.' He limped back to his desk. 'Tell me what happened at the airport.'

'He was with a woman. A blonde woman. An accomplice. They hijacked a plane off the tarmac at Intercontinental.'

'Were there any other passengers on board?'

'No, sir. No passengers. They are the only two.'

Visblat's focus narrowed. 'A propeller plane?'

'Yes, sir. One of them is certainly a pilot.'

Visblat laughed manically to himself, then suddenly a frown gripped his features. 'Out of curiosity,' he said, rubbing his temples. 'What do we know about the woman that's with him?'

Robinson felt even more uncomfortable than usual—Visblat's mixed reactions were making him extremely nervous. 'Sir,' he said, 'it appears to be the same woman you ran into at Richey Road.'

Visblat placed both hands on his desk and stared at the cluttered tabletop. 'It doesn't make any sense.' He laughed again, then stopped—the strain of confusion contorting his expression. 'Find out what information you can about her and bring it to me.'

'Sir, this is a federal matter now.'

Visblat slid open his drawer, pulled out his .44 Magnum, and placed it gently on the desk. 'Are you disobeying my order?' The sight of the shiny, high-powered gun made Robinson's heart beat even faster.

'No, sir, I wouldn't do that.'

'Then, do as I say.' Visblat searched his drawer for ammunition. When he looked up he was surprised to find Detective Robinson still in his office. 'Is there a problem?'

'I shouldn't be getting this information for you. It's not in our jurisdiction any more.'

'Until the FBI get here, it is,' Visblat said. 'I'll take full responsibility. Is that understood?'

'Yes, Commander. Understood.'

Visblat limped to the door and ushered Robinson into the corridor. 'I'm going to need the information as soon as possible. Meet me at the compound level in ten minutes with everything you have. Get a move on,' he said softly. 'That's an order.'

It was an unusual place to meet, but Robinson dismissed his concerns. For now, he was happy just to get away.

VISBLAT CLOSED THE door and stood alone in his small office, reflecting. It seemed that Wilson was alive, thank God. But nothing made sense. It just didn't fit the psychological profile he'd been given. Wilson was supposed to be ordinary, an easy catch. And yet that had proven to be far from the case. However, Visblat prided himself on being a quick learner and now that he knew more about his quarry, he could adapt. He would *not* underestimate the time traveller in the future. And it seemed Wilson had friends—accomplices. People like George Washington, who were willing to stay quiet to conceal the truth. It was impossible to understand how—the opposite should have been true—and yet people *were* helping him.

Opening his desk drawer yet again, Visblat rummaged around inside. The important thing was that Wilson was alive, he thought, his mind abuzz. No one else would steal a propeller plane and set a decoy to the northeast. Suddenly, Visblat was angry again. His mood shifts had been getting more erratic over the past few months. *I'm going to teach Mr Dowling a lesson when I get my hands on him*, he thought. *He's made me look like a stupid fool!*

Visblat emptied a full box of ammunition into his jacket pocket—the more the better. It was time to take matters into his own hands. He stood up straight, as much as his injuries would allow, and did up the buttons on his jacket. Looking around the small office, the tall man knew he would never sit inside this room again. *What a pity—I like chasing criminals*, he thought. It was something he had always excelled at. His gaze fell upon the warning letter from the Mayor. He slid it off the table, scrunched it up into a ball, and threw it on the floor.

I'm in charge for now, he thought—*and no one can stop me.*

Exactly ten minutes later, Detective Robinson stepped out onto the compound level. Commander Visblat was already standing in the empty corridor, swinging his car keys on a chain. Visblat looked tired, Robinson decided. His face was starting to discolour and the grazing on his chin had begun to scab. His left arm—the one in plaster—looked badly swollen.

Dropping the keys into his pocket, Visblat said, 'What have you got for me?'

The detective displayed a stack of papers. 'We found an abandoned car at the airport. A black Mercedes. The same vehicle you reported at Richey Road. It has a bullet hole in the windshield. I had the registration number checked and it belongs to a ... *Miss Helena Capriarty*. She just happens to be the daughter of Lawrence Capriarty, the multimillionaire. You might remember; he was the one whose wife was killed a few years ago. It was front-page news.'

Visblat nodded. 'Yeah, I remember.'

'Here's a copy of her driver's licence.' Visblat took the photo ID and carefully studied the picture. Detective Robinson handed Visblat another page. 'This is the type of plane they hijacked—a Saab 340. So far, there have been no reports of a crash site. You might be right, Commander, it may have been a decoy.'

Visblat gave the propeller-driven aircraft a quick glance.

'They were the only two on board. It seems the fugitive is a pilot. He started both the engines, the plane then jumped the wheel blocks, nearly killing the anti-terrorist police who were trying to stop them.'

Visblat didn't seem surprised at all. 'What about his injuries?'

'We have fifty eyewitness reports. The fugitive looked fine, completely healthy. That proves he wasn't the one involved in the car accident on the 610 freeway.'

Visblat looked at Helena's picture again. 'What else have you got?'

The detective held out yet another page. 'Here's something very interesting. It's a transcript from the airport security guard. He claims that Miss Capriarty called the fugitive "Wilson".' The detective pointed at the name on the page. 'That's what you called him.'

Visblat made eye contact. 'You're right. I did.'

'How did you know that was his name?'

'It's called research!' Visblat snapped, and he handed all the documents back. 'Detective,' he said more calmly. 'You've done a good job.

I'll be sure to remember this at your next appraisal. There might just be another promotion in it for you.'

Detective Robinson smiled to himself—Visblat would soon be off the force for good, and if Robinson was lucky, it was possible *he* would get the top job. 'Thank you, Commander,' he said.

Visblat pointed to the restricted area behind him. 'I need to check some evidence in the police compound. I'll need you to sign me in.' He walked purposefully towards the bullet-proof window.

Detective Robinson was suddenly apprehensive. The compound was located in the basement of police headquarters; it was the most heavily guarded section of the building. Two officers were permanently stationed inside and there was a camera in the corridor. The small warehouse contained all types of police evidence, including confiscated money, drugs and weapons. Access could only be gained by two senior officers escorting each other in. Not even Visblat could get in alone.

'Requesting authorisation to enter,' Visblat said into the security microphone. 'Detective Robinson is my number two.'

The guard filled out their names, then pressed the intercom switch. 'Sir, what evidence do you want to see?' His pen was poised over the entry documentation.

'Open the door!' Visblat snapped.

Robinson glanced towards the guard, then back at his commander. The last thing he wanted was a confrontation—especially on Visblat's last day. What harm could it do, anyway? It was probably safer in there than anywhere else.

'I want to show you how I knew the fugitive's name,' Visblat offered. 'I'm going to teach you something.'

Robinson was intrigued. Was it possible there was evidence in the compound that only Visblat knew about? He pressed the intercom. 'It's all right, Jeff. Open up. We'll fill in the details later.'

There was a buzz as the electronic latch released. Visblat pushed the heavy steel door open with his plastered forearm. As they entered, Detective Robinson saluted the two men stationed inside—he knew them both quite well. With a thud, the door automatically closed again. The air in the compound held a distinctive scent, and not a pleasant one either—the smell of money.

Visblat scanned the endless rows of shelving stacked high with confiscated items.

'What are you looking for, Commander?' Robinson asked, but Visblat had disappeared into one of the many aisles without answering. Robinson turned to one of the guards and shrugged his shoulders.

Visblat picked up a black leather suitcase with '$2.3 million U.S.' written on the tag next to the evidence number and limped towards the exit with it firmly in hand. 'Open the door,' he said.

Robinson was shocked by the request. He gestured at the black bag. 'You can't take that, Commander. You're not authorised.'

'This is how it has to be,' Visblat said firmly.

The air was thick with tension and doubt.

'I can't let you out of here with that,' one of the guards said, his voice wavering.

Visblat placed the suitcase on the floor, held the trio's gaze without blinking and drew out his handgun. All three men quickly raised their hands in surrender.

'Please don't do this,' Robinson said. But there was a look in his commander's eyes that made him unable to move a muscle—as if he had placed them all under some hideous spell. It was the worst nightmare Robinson could imagine. He knew he needed to act, to reach for his gun and defend himself, but Visblat's eyes held him frozen, as if his veins were set with concrete. He wanted to cry, but Robinson could not even do that.

'I'm sorry,' Visblat said sternly. 'I have no choice.'

With a thunderous explosion, he fired, splattering Detective Robinson's blood all over the inside of the steel door. Before the spent cartridge even hit the ground, he swivelled towards the two officers, who stood equally rigid. The clamour of two more gunshots echoed off the walls.

Visblat calmly holstered his weapon, then picked up the suitcase. Wisps of gun smoke dissipated as he nonchalantly stepped around the bloodied carcasses on the floor. He casually tore away the top page of the entry documentation, then grabbed the blood-covered door handle with the paper, to be sure there were no fingerprints. In the silence, a piece of Robinson's mutilated flesh unstuck itself from the wall and hit the floor with a *splat*.

The situation was regrettable, Visblat decided, but it could not be helped. There was no other way.

Approaching the elevators, he pressed the Up button.

In the hallway, the security camera was pointing directly at him. Visblat smiled into the lens. It was the perfect crime, he decided. There were no witnesses and, thanks to his ingenuity, no security video—Visblat had disconnected the power to the videotape machine just fifteen minutes earlier.

It was all too easy.

20

Somewhere over the Gulf of Mexico
Saab 340 Turboprop
November 27th 2012
Local Time 7:52 a.m.

Mission of Isaiah—Day Three

THE ROAR OF THE turboprops droned in the background. The cabin gently shuddered.

Standing inside the small lavatory, Wilson wiped the last remnants of the shaving cream from his face. Some colour had returned to his cheeks and he decided he looked better. Not a hundred per cent, but well on the way. He slicked his hair back with water. Wilson had found a travel suitcase in the main cabin, probably the pilot's, and he pulled on the clean white shirt from inside. It was a much better fit than the ridiculous garb George T had bestowed upon him, and a relief just to get that stupid 'Love Machine' T-shirt off.

Wilson gazed at his reflection in the mirror. Everything around him, since his arrival here, had the hallmarks of a dream; and yet a dream it was not. One thing was definite: without his omega programming, he would be dead now. That was a certainty. It seemed that spinning his fate coin that day in his apartment with Professor Author had turned out to be one of the smartest decisions of his life. It was ironic.

Wilson's thoughts intermittently wandered back to Helena at the controls of the aircraft, like a compass swinging towards north. The role she played in his adventure here had been unexpected. And yet the name *Esther*—the name of the Doberman—reassured him that everything was exactly as it should be.

Wilson's brow ruffled. Helena's claims of a psychic connection didn't entirely make sense. She said her visions began two months ago, but he had only been here for less than three days. Yet, despite the conflicting facts, he believed her—he couldn't help that either. Everything about Helena, especially the look in her eyes, told him she was telling the truth. A smile came to his face as he remembered how her jaw had dropped when he mentioned flying into an oilrig. But there was no danger; with the autopilot engaged, and still safely over water, the aircraft would be impossible to crash.

From Wilson's knowledge of her so far, Helena was certainly the most determined woman he had ever met; and that was saying something when he thought of the way Jenny Jones and Karin Turnberry conducted themselves. Infuriating was probably a better description for them all. And the way Helena carried that gun around, well, that was disconcerting at best.

Wilson considered how a psychic connection could possibly have come about. His molecular reconstruction may have made him more susceptible to a telepathic connection, or maybe it was his omega programming that had triggered something. They both sounded like feasible explanations. But in reality, he had no idea at all—he was just guessing. Could Barton have known all this was going to happen? Was it possible that everything here, in the world Wilson now found himself in, was preordained in the Dead Sea scrolls?

He searched his memories for answers ...

California, The Americas
Enterprise Corporation, Mercury Building, Level 2
May 11th 2081
Local Time 11:14 a.m.

12 Days before Transport Test

BARTON SAT AT HIS desk, the Enterprise Corporation logo boldly etched across the wall behind him. Everything in the room was a model of orderly perfection; digital worksheets were in precise stacks, his laser markers evenly spaced on the table. The carpeted area of the floor was vacuumed in even, straight lines; the windows and tabletops were shone to a high gloss, like Barton's shoes. Even the plants lining his office walls were identical in size and health. It was actually a little troubling, as if nothing should or could be touched for fear of disturbing the perfect balance.

'Tell me what you're thinking,' Barton said.

Wilson decided it was best not to respond with the truth. It was the pair's second meeting. The first had lasted a full six hours. As a result, Wilson had not slept for the rest of the night, worrying and second-guessing everything.

'As you can appreciate,' Wilson replied, looking a little tired, 'it's a lot of information to absorb.' His gaze shifted to a magnificent glassy sphere, half the size of a basketball, sitting on the sideboard. He knew he shouldn't touch it but, intrigued, he lifted the object—dismissing his inhibitions—and played with it as though it were a mere trinket.

'Please be careful with that,' Barton said, easing himself to the very edge of his chair, as though he was going to leap forward and catch the sphere if it fell.

Wilson studied the glassy object more closely, gripping it with both hands, and noticed thousands of tiny rainbows flickering within the crystal. It was amazing, as if it were possessed with some enchanted energy.

'It's the DuPont Prize. I won it for—'

Wilson finished the sentence: 'Inventing the Ozone Booster.'

'How do you know that?' Barton said abruptly.

Wilson had to smile. 'Nothing more than simple genius.'

'It's hardly common knowledge.'

Understanding that he had tortured Barton enough, Wilson gently placed the fragile sphere into its holder and pointed to the faint strands of ornate writing etched into the crystal. 'It's written here: "Ozone Booster". You're a little jumpy, aren't you?'

'Sorry.' Barton looked embarrassed. 'It's just that yesterday evening, when you read the Hebrew text ... well, it has had me wondering ...'

After some reflection, Wilson understood how it was possible he could have read the ancient writings. Three weeks before, he had scanned through a book called *Strong's Numbering System*—a concordance of the King James Bible. A concordance is a dictionary of sorts, used to translate ancient documents into English. It alphabetically lists all the unique words and individually numbers them: hence 'numbering system'. Most importantly, it provides exhaustive detail on the Hebrew, Aramaic and Greek texts from which the words are originally derived: including diagrams of the characters and symbols.[5] It seemed Wilson had unwittingly absorbed the information with a level of detail that was astonishing—and his omega programming was certainly responsible.

'How did you do it?' Barton asked.

'Do what?'

'Read the scrolls.'

'I told you before—I didn't read them. It's insane to think I can.'

Barton rubbed his chin. 'They were three amazing guesses.'

'When do I get my contract?' Wilson asked, changing the subject. Both he and Barton had negotiated a financial arrangement and Wilson wanted to see the paperwork to be sure the offer was real.

Barton looked at his watch. 'It will be ready this afternoon.'

The conversation continued for the next ten minutes as Barton unveiled what was about to happen. He sat back in his leather executive chair. 'You'll meet the leaders of the mercury team. The tacticians. They're the scientists who are going to send you through time.' A short bleep chimed from Barton's palm device. He sucked in a quick breath and immediately stood from his chair. Without expression, he raised his index finger to his lips, then gestured for Wilson to follow him to an adjacent doorway. The opening led to a stylish bathroom, all black marble and polished wood, with a large rectangular spa bath overlooking the forests outside.

Wilson followed, but he was dubious.

Barton silently closed the door. 'The chime you heard lets me know that my office is being monitored. Somebody is trying to listen to our conversation.'

'So, you're keeping secrets from everybody, are you?' Wilson said condescendingly.

'There are no surveillance systems in the bathrooms.'

'That's good.' Wilson gazed at the black porcelain toilet. 'Privacy can not be underrated, even at Enterprise Corporation.'

Barton leant against the washbasin. 'Wilson, I think it's important to be honest with each other from here on in.' He seemed stressed

---

5 *Strong's Exhaustive Concordance of the Bible*, James Strong, Hendricson 1993.

now; quite out of character. 'Actually, this is where the whole thing starts to get a little more complicated.'

'Is that possible?' Wilson said, laughing. He always laughed when he was nervous. 'What could be more bizarre than what you've already shown me? It's not every day you find out that the Dead Sea scrolls contain blueprints for time travel.'

Barton rubbed his chin. 'The team of scientists you are going to meet—the mercury team—they won't really know what's going on. They think I'm going to send you *forward* in time, by only a few minutes.'

Wilson was wary now. 'Uh, huh …'

'But that's not the plan, should we come to an agreement.'

Wilson sat down on the lid of the toilet seat. 'So, what is the plan, exactly?'

The immaculately dressed scientist looked him straight in the eye. He was again a picture of cool confidence. 'The plan is to send you *backwards* in time.'

Wilson smiled to himself. Barton's approach was much more appealing than Professor Author's drunken ramblings. 'You are sober, aren't you?' Wilson confirmed.

Barton pursed his lips. 'I don't think you understand the seriousness of what I am saying.'

'Stupid jokes aside,' Wilson said. 'I agree we should be honest with each other. Just tell me the truth … what is this *really* about?'

Barton rubbed his chin the way he always did when he was about to say something important. 'It is my intention to send you seventy-five years into the past.'

Wilson felt an involuntary shiver rifle through him but, hiding his nerves, he leant back on the toilet seat and clasped his hands behind his head. 'Let's pretend for a moment that you *can* send me back in time—which I seriously doubt. How, exactly, do you propose I'm going to get my money … if *you* haven't even been born yet?'

'You will eventually return to the *present*,' Barton said, equally calm. 'You will get your money, from me—half now, half later.' He paused. 'I don't expect you to agree, immediately. Conceptually, this is a very difficult thing to understand. I realise that. I have trouble with it myself.'

Wilson scratched the side of his face. 'Why seventy-five years into the past? You must have a good reason.'

'I do—a very good reason.' Barton thought for a long time before answering. 'The objective of all this is to complete a secret mission.'

Wilson's broad grin was back. 'Oh, a secret mission! Why didn't you say. Let me guess, you want to send me back in time to kill someone—like in the movies—someone's great-great-grandmother or something. Yeah ... and destroy their bloodline.'

Barton was not amused at all. 'It's nothing like that, Wilson. I suggest you just listen and keep your wisecracks to yourself.' There was a prolonged silence as both men looked at each other, neither wanting to be the first one to blink. Eventually Barton said, 'The mercury team doesn't know anything about the mission. They think I'm trying to prove the *theory* of time travel.' He paused. 'I know all this is very unusual.'

'Actually—this sort of thing happens to me every day.'

Ignoring the comment, Barton rubbed his chin again. 'It all has to do with the twenty-third book of the Old Testament, the Book of Isaiah.'

'I thought the time-travel blueprints were located in the Book of Esther. The seventeenth book.'

'Wilson—you don't build a time portal unless you have a very good reason to use it. You can understand that, can't you?'

'So ... what is the *good reason*?'

'There is a mission that must be completed. A mission detailed in the Book of Isaiah. That's the reason why all this is happening—that's why my world, and now your world, has been turned upside-down.'

A muffled voice unexpectedly called out from the next room.

'Excuse me—Hello!'

Barton yanked open the door to reveal a teenager wearing a brown tracksuit, searching the other end of the office. Although Barton remained outwardly composed, Wilson could sense he was shaken by the interruption.

'Andre ... what are you doing here?' Barton said.

The boy approached. 'I need to tell my mother when to pick me up.'

Wilson searched Andre's eyes for even the smallest hint that he had been eavesdropping on their conversation, but saw only innocence in his youthful face.

'Tell her we'll make sure you get home, okay?' Barton said. 'You might even stay here tonight. How does that sound?'

'Sure thing.'

'Andre, I want you to meet Wilson Dowling,' Barton announced.

Wilson forced a reply, 'Nice to meet you.' They shook hands and Wilson quickly withdrew—the boy's palm was sweaty, almost dripping. Did it mean he was hiding something? Or were his hands always clammy?

'I was hoping to meet you,' Andre said with a look of pride. 'It was my idea to find you. I was the one who thought of getting a natural Gen-EP.'

Wiping his hand, Wilson quipped, 'Don't expect me to thank you.'

'Andre is one of the smartest young people we have here at Enterprise Corporation,' Barton said, coming in over the top. 'He's a newly appointed tactician on the mercury team.'

'Where's your labcoat?' Wilson asked.

Andre stared up at him. 'I should have it tomorrow.'

There was an awkward silence as all three stood in a circle gazing at each other. Wilson didn't want to say anything in case it prolonged the conversation.

Barton eventually pointed to the door. 'Andre, we'll meet you at the briefing room in about an hour. How does that sound?'

'I'll find Davin,' Andre said. 'Nice to meet you, sir.'

Barton waited for Andre to disappear before directing Wilson back into the bathroom and closing the door again. The office was probably still being monitored. Barton stood next to the basin, his gaze fixed on the bushland outside the window. Wilson had already witnessed how analytical the mercury scientist was and assumed he was calculating the distance to the door, the thickness of the wood, how loud he was speaking, and how far Andre was from them when he first discovered his presence.

'Do you think the kid heard anything?' Wilson asked.

'I can't be certain.'

'Tell me more about the mission,' Wilson said, wanting to move on.

'Yes, the mission.' Barton glanced towards the door, then lowered his voice a little. 'The Book of *Esther* contains information on *how* to time-travel. The Book of *Isaiah* contains information on *why* to time-travel. When I first translated the Esther writings, I realised I had made a wonderful discovery. Then I uncovered the link to the Book of Isaiah and my life has not been the same since.' He opened the door to his office, looked outside to make sure no one was there, and closed it again. 'The Book of Isaiah is a very powerful document—very powerful. So, for more than two years I've been keeping it a secret from everyone, at the same time manually decoding the text as quickly as I could.'

'But you're telling *me* now?'

'One person is an exception. The Isaiah text describes him as "the Overseer".'

Wilson was puzzled. 'The overseer of what?'

Barton crossed his arms, mirroring Wilson's body language. 'The Mission of Isaiah tells of the appointment of a man who will restore balance.' His gaze narrowed as if he was looking for the mark of the Gen-EP in Wilson's eyes. 'There is a strong possibility the Overseer is you.'

Wilson grinned nervously. 'I'm not an overseer, I assure you.'

'It's a possibility.'

'I can't be ... I'm from *Sydney*!'

'I think maybe it's you.'

'No one from Sydney is an overseer. Surfer, maybe—but overseer, *no chance*.'

'You have the mark of the Gen-EP, which means that we can send you through time. And the Book of Isaiah talks of the Overseer being a man who has no religion.'

Wilson waited for more, but Barton said nothing.

'Is that it?' Wilson asked.

Barton nodded.

'That's the very best you've got? *That's it?*'

'I admit; I can't be absolutely certain it's you. But of the billions of people on this earth, *you* have the correct genetic pattern. That has to account for something. My feeling is, if we manage to send you back in time—you must be the one.'

Wilson couldn't help but chuckle. 'How appropriate—I'm standing next to a toilet! You know, I think *that* is a sign! You said it yourself: there is no such thing as coincidence.'

Wilson nervously paced up and down on the rectangular black tiles. Again, sleep would be difficult to come by tonight. 'This whole thing is very strange—you know that, don't you?' He paced some more. What was worrying him most was that he liked the sound of it all— the notion of being someone special. The adventure.

'Let's imagine you *can* actually send me back in time,' Wilson said. 'I take it I don't have to kill anyone when I get there—then what *do* I have to do?'

Barton massaged his temples. 'I haven't decoded all of the mission notes yet, but I can tell you this much. The Overseer is destined to travel back in time to activate three energy portals that regulate the flow of magnetic energy throughout the earth's atmosphere.'

Wilson was lost already. 'Which means what?'

'They're like giant clocks that regulate time itself.'

'You want me to travel back seventy-five years into the past to activate a couple of giant clocks?' He paused. 'This whole thing is ridiculous!'

'You can joke about it all you want, but what you are saying is technically correct. That *is* the Mission of Isaiah—a mission prophesied in the Dead Sea scrolls.'

Wilson sat on the toilet seat again, feeling like he was going to throw up. He said, 'Tell me: *why*, exactly, does the magnetic energy of the earth need to be regulated, or whatever it was you said? Give me the non-genius version.'

A glint came to Barton's eye. 'You'll like this. Have you ever wondered why every day seems shorter than the last? Why time moves faster and faster as you get older?'

'Yes …'

'So you understand what I'm talking about?'

'Yes. Everybody feels that way.'

'That's correct, they do. The reason is—the magnetic frequency inside the earth's atmosphere is increasing. And, as a result, *time* is actually getting faster.'

'The atomic clock theory states that time is *constant*.'

Barton scoffed. 'An atomic clock is affected in exactly the same way as everything else. Let me give you an example: we take two highly accurate atomic clocks, both set to precisely the same time; put one on the ground next to you there, and the other into an Airbus shuttle and fly it around the earth, at maximum speed, three times, and bring it back to this exact spot. When we compare the devices, we will find that the atomic clock that had been travelling around the earth will have run *more slowly* than the clock sitting here next to you. A few hundred nanoseconds slower—exactly the amount predicted by Einstein's time dilation formula.'[6]

---

[6] *How to Build a Time Machine*, Paul Davies, Allen Lane/Penguin, 2001, page 10. Practical airborne tests completed by Joe Hafele and Richard Keating in 1971.

'Which proves what?'

'It proves that *time is elastic*. It can be stretched and it can be shrunk.'

'I'll humour you, Barton. So what if time is moving faster?'

Barton rubbed his chin. 'If the pace of time exceeds a certain speed, the world and everybody in it will go crazy. The consequences are endless: both psychologically and biologically, and on a global scale. Believe it or not, the Mission of Isaiah is about *slowing* time down to what it should be, and protecting all of us.'

Wilson didn't want to think too hard about what he was hearing. There was just too much information to absorb. 'And I'm the *Overseer*?' he said, his tone hinting at the absurdity of the claim.

'Yes, Wilson, I think maybe you are.'

It was the 'maybe' that stuck in Wilson's mind. He carefully ran through his options. One: Barton was completely crazy. Two: Enterprise Corporation was still after the omega programming, but that seemed unlikely. Three: Professor Author had scrambled Wilson's brains and this was all a twisted, but interesting, illusion. And, lastly, four: everything Barton said was absolutely true. Wilson thought for a moment. The scariest scenario by far was option four.

'Let's renegotiate our contract,' Wilson announced. It was time to raise the stakes to see how Barton reacted. 'You know that Rembrandt in the boardroom on level three? The sleeping baby with its mother. I want it thrown in with everything else.'

Somewhere over the Gulf of Mexico
Saab 340 Turboprop
November 27th 2012
Local Time 7:55 a.m.

Mission of Isaiah—Day Three

A SUDDEN MOVEMENT jolted Wilson back to reality.

Donning his sunglasses, he stepped out of the lavatory and made for the cockpit. The turbulence seemed to be getting much worse. Stumbling against the movement of the aircraft, he patted Esther on the head as he approached the small doorway. The dog seemed happy enough under the circumstances, totally unfazed by what was going on.

Outside the front windows, the morning sun had completely disappeared from the horizon; towering cumulonimbus cloud formations taking its place. The weather had changed very quickly. Helena's knuckles were white with tension as she piloted the turboprop towards a giant storm. She was struggling to maintain control.

Wilson slipped past her and jumped into the left-hand seat.

'It's about time!' Helena yelled.

Wilson strapped himself in. 'This looks like fun.' The aircraft was jumping around the sky, dipping and increasing altitude one hundred feet in either direction.

'I thought you weren't coming back!'

At times, their altitude was so low that Wilson could see froth being swept off the top of the ever-increasing swell. 'Maybe I'd better take over,' he said dryly. 'You not being a licensed pilot and all.'

Releasing her grip from the controls, Helena gave Wilson a burning stare. 'The storm came from nowhere! It's been impossible to keep things steady. Then, you come in, making jokes.'

'You've scared the crap out of Esther. Look at her, the dog is a mess.' Wilson gently pulled back on the control column and the Saab 340 gained altitude rapidly.

Helena couldn't understand what Wilson was doing. She had been flying at less than 300 feet for more than forty minutes. 'What about the radar? Keeping below the radar?'

'We're miles away from anything now.' Wilson scanned the instrument panel. 'There's no radar out here, I assure you.'

'Do you know how stressful it's been—flying that low?'

'You did a great job.'

Helena lifted her gun and pressed the barrel against Wilson's right temple. 'It's time you answered my questions!' His head was forced over to one side.

'Don't you think there are better ways to go about this?' he replied.

'From now on, I'll ask the questions, and you'll provide the answers! *Like*—who the hell are you? And where are we going?'

Wilson gestured towards the bulbous, swirling cloud formation ahead. 'In case you hadn't guessed, that storm's dangerous, *very* dangerous. Weather like that can produce powerful downdrafts.' A bolt of lightning struck the surface of the ocean, as if on cue, and the brilliant flash flickered inside the cabin. 'I'm going to get us out of here, okay?'

'I'm not going to let you change the subject.'

With Helena's gun still pressed against his temple, Wilson banked the aircraft to the right—the turbulence slowly diminishing—west, towards clearer skies. Wilson knew the change of course would make their fuel situation critical.

'Look, I know how you must feel,' he said.

'I want answers! Don't make me do anything stupid!'

'Let me get this straight—you don't think holding a gun to my head is stupid?' Wilson already had enough troubles—he was more than a thousand kilometres from his destination, fuel was a problem, and he still hadn't worked out how to operate the navigation computer. Back in Houston, the police were after him for a reason he could not understand and he had been run over in a car pileup just two days before. Enough was enough and he angrily slapped the barrel away with the palm of his hand. 'If you shoot me, who's going to land this plane ... *you?*'

That simple thread of logic had Helena stewing in her own juices.

'You remind me of my ex-girlfriend,' he added.

Clenching her teeth to hold back a frustrated yell, Helena said, 'Where are we going?'

Wilson gestured to the weapon. 'Is that the way you normally deal with people?'

'Idiots like you, yes!'

'You must be a terrific negotiator! Is that the line of work you're in?'

'Are you going to tell me what I want, or not?'

'*Not*.'

For the next fifteen minutes Helena didn't say a word—or move a muscle. The only sound in the cockpit was the reassuring drone of the engines. Wilson took the opportunity to figure out how to use the nav computer. It took some time, but he eventually keyed in the co-ordinates and calculated the fuel. It was going to be tight, but if the weather stayed fine they should make it.

Happy that things were looking better, he turned to Helena and said, 'My name is Wilson Dowling. I'm from Australia. We are currently flying a Saab turboprop at 5000 feet above sea level, heading southwest towards Mexico.'

'Where in Mexico?'

'The Yucatan Peninsula.'

Helena turned towards him for the first time since having her gun slapped away and studied his profile. He'd shaved and was now wearing a white button-down shirt and black pants. They were a much better fit and he was probably even handsome, but at this moment she was more inclined to resent him for that.

'Why the Yucatan Peninsula?' she asked.

'That's all I'm telling you.'

She breathed out through her nose in annoyance. 'You were doing so well there for a moment.'

Seeing clouds ahead, Wilson hit a button on the flight computer and the aircraft automatically gained altitude, thereby increasing their flight range. There was now little chance he could land somewhere and drop Helena off beforehand. She would have to come with him the rest of the way. It was an unfortunate development.

'I'm going to a place called Chichén Itzá,' he answered.

'The ancient city?'

'No, the fried-chicken place.'

'It doesn't matter which airport we go to. The authorities are going to be all over us when we land. This might sound strange to you, because you're an idiot, but I'm pretty sure Texas Air want their plane back.'

'We won't be landing at any airport,' he replied. 'The ruins of the city have a grass plaza running down the centre. It should be long enough to land on.'

'Are you crazy?'

'I'm quite capable of landing this aircraft without killing us. Have a little faith.'

'*Have a little faith!*' She rolled her eyes and flopped back in her seat. 'What the hell am I doing here?'

Wilson turned towards her. 'I have no idea either.'

Helena sat, staring.

'And, for the record, I didn't appreciate you pointing your gun at me like that. Don't do it again,' he said firmly.

Helena's thoughts shifted to her father and what he would be thinking right now. His only daughter had been involved in an aircraft hijacking. He would be angry; cursing that she was taking her 'rebel without a cause' persona too far, or, more likely, worried sick that she was finally certifiable.

Helena turned to Wilson. 'While you were gone I saw a vision of you staring at yourself in the mirror, in the bathroom. What were you thinking about?'

Trying not to look surprised, Wilson said, 'I was thinking about the events that led me here.'

Something told Helena it was the truth; she sensed it. She took a deep breath. In some way it was like she knew Wilson, and although he irritated her intensely, there was a trust there that she could not explain. No foundation for it, but it was still trust. 'I'll make a deal with you,' she said. 'You tell me the truth and I'll help you.'

Wilson didn't want to make a deal. He just wanted Helena safely out of his life so he could concentrate on his mission.

Helena clipped her weapon inside her jacket and gazed about the cockpit. 'What you're doing must be important. It must be. You wouldn't have stolen this aircraft otherwise.'

'I stole this aircraft because the police were chasing after me.'

'Yes, but you stole it to *go* somewhere. You have a reason, I know you do.'

21

Chichén Itzá, Mexico
Saab 340 Turboprop
November 27th 2012
Local Time 10:55 a.m.

Mission of Isaiah—Day Three

MISTY RAIN FELL in blankets, wave after wave, across Chichén Itzá.

Surrounded by dense bushland, the ancient metropolis was a cluster of flat grassy plazas scattered with diverse stone buildings that had not been inhabited in over 950 years. In the centre of this eerie, once-living place stood a single grey pyramid, a marvel of engineering, a truly mountainous structure: *El Castillo*. The flat-roofed construction of limestone blocks dwarfed everything in sight as it towered menacingly over the forests of the Yucatan Peninsula.

However, the city was dead. The ancient kings and the warriors, the craftsmen and peasants, were long gone. Chichén Itzá, once the centre of the Mayan universe, was now relegated to the status of 'tourist attraction' in Mexico—and it was a popular one at that. Thousands of people came each year to marvel at the architecture and the intriguing story of this once-great and sometimes brutal culture.

A WHITE IBIS GLIDED peacefully through the humid rain. The bird abruptly changed direction as the roar of approaching engines cut the tranquillity of the morning. The bird, startled by the increasing thunder, plummeted down into the cover of the bushland.

A Texas Air Saab 340 swooped low over the deserted city, then carved back into the clouds. The sound of the turboprops rumbled overhead as it circled in a long sweeping turn, appeared beneath the mist and flashed across the city in the opposite direction. Vapour trails streamed off the wing tips as the plane powered up into the clouds once again. With a groan, the undercarriage opened and the landing gear locked into place. The wing flaps fanned to their most open position as the aircraft descended on its final approach.

'YOU'RE ABSOLUTELY MAD,' Helena announced. 'You know that, don't you?' She pulled the straps of her seatbelt as tight as they could go. 'This is a bad idea. Bad. Bad.' She was rambling now, 'You said you were going to do this, but you know what? Part of me didn't believe it.' She glanced at the Doberman sitting in the jump-seat behind her. Helena had just spent the last fifteen minutes figuring out how to secure the animal by overlapping two seatbelts across her chest.

Wilson tapped the fuel gauges. They both read empty. *Nothing.* Doing a second flyby of the city was risky, but it was better than going in blind. He ran through the landing procedure in his mind yet again: flaps, speed brake, flight spoilers, reduce throttle. He glanced again at the fuel gauges. This was going to require precision flying. And he knew he was going to have to stomp the brakes, hard, when they hit the ground.

There was increased turbulence inside the clouds.

The engines hummed. Visibility was down to nothing. Beads of water swept off the windscreen. Suddenly the fabled city appeared through the mist. It must have been raining for some time and standing water lay across the plaza, deep in some places. The irrigation canals were overflowing.

'This is *not* good,' Helena said.

'This is the best opportunity we're going to get,' Wilson replied. He reduced throttle again and the pitch of the engines lowered. 'But I must say, it looked bigger in the photographs.'

'What do you mean *it looked bigger*?'

In a show of confidence, he released one hand from the flight controls and pointed forward. 'Relax, I know what I'm doing. The plan is to set down just over the edge of those trees.' Sure enough, through the centre of the city a flat grass plaza lay ahead like a runway.

Helena shifted nervously in her seat. 'Just be careful. It's my life you're playing with also.'

'We're going to need as much landing distance as we can get. To tell you the truth, I wasn't expecting rain. It may be a bit of a problem.'

'If I die, I'm going to be *so* upset with you,' Helena groaned.

An alert echoed from the cockpit computer: 'Fuel Warning ... Fuel Warning—'

The engines spluttered.

An unsettling quiver—a death quiver, as pilots call it—shot through the cabin. One of the propellers then swung to a grinding halt. Wilson was just thinking they were lucky to have the other still working when it too went silent, starved of petrol, and rotated its last cycle. It seemed his decision to do a flyby of the city had turned out to be a very bad idea.

The airspeed quickly fell away and Wilson forced the control column forward; he had no choice but to steepen their approach. They were now heading for the tree line. Everything was happening so quickly. The plaza dipped out of sight below the trees.

'Terrific, Wilson. Just terrific!' Helena called out.

Rain beat furiously against the window.

The wind whistled over the wings.

With a grotesque scraping of steel, the aircraft disappeared into the high foliage, severing the treetops. Limbs bashed against the fuselage. The nose of the aircraft suddenly speared out into the open, followed by the landing gear striking the very edge of the clearing with tremendous force. Wilson and Helena were thrown forward against their seatbelts as the plane burst out of the trees, through broken branches, in an explosion of leaves and debris.

Pressing the foot pedals, Wilson attempted to keep the aircraft on line as it hurled across the soggy grass at an insane speed. They shot past the Pyramid of Castillo, past the Temple of the Warriors.

They were going too fast!

A massive rock wall at the end of the plaza loomed before them.

'Not good,' Helena repeated, but now her voice was just a whisper. 'This is not good.' On top of everything else, a view through Wilson's eyes—cloaked in a red haze—was filling her mind.

The cabin was rattling and bouncing all over the place.

Wilson called out, '*Come on!*' as if somehow challenging an unknown opponent.

The Saab 340 hit an irrigation ditch half-filled with water, severing the nose wheel, and the front of the aircraft dived into the saturated turf. Glass cracked. Mud sprayed across the windscreen. A furious shudder went through the crippled superstructure.

Wilson, merely a passenger now, watched the approaching rock face. It was solid stone.

They were slowing—but would they stop in time?

An ever-deepening rut was being gouged into the plaza. Dirty water continued to spray across the windshield. They hit a second embankment, the cabin jarred and jumped. Then, with only centimetres to spare, they skewed to a halt, the stone wall looming just outside the front window.

Everything was silent.

Turning to his passenger, Wilson beamed a broad grin. 'Perfect landing, eh?'

Helena pressed her hands to her face in shock. 'Oh, God.'

'Okay—almost perfect.'

THE FRONT DOOR of the mangled aircraft swung open and Wilson stuck his head outside. 'I told you it would be okay.' Another wave of misty rain was falling and he felt it on his skin.

'By all rights we should be dead,' Helena stated. She wasn't at all impressed—at least that's what she wanted Wilson to think. 'You're crazy. You must be.' Her telepathic connection had stopped again and she was beginning to understand that her mental link was triggered by life-threatening events—something Wilson was certainly having more than his fair share of.

An enthusiastic Esther bounded outside onto the wet grass. The dog was thrilled to be on solid ground again, as if she knew how lucky they had all been.

'We're alive, aren't we?' Wilson said.

'You *are* crazy!'

'To make an omelette, sometimes you have to break a few eggs.' It was a French proverb Professor Author used to loosely quote when he'd made a mess of something—Wilson had heard it many times.

'This is more than a few eggs.'

Wilson looked up at the dark sky, then towards the ancient city. 'Hopefully the weather will keep the tourists away.' There wasn't another soul in sight. Unusual for this time of year—nearing peak season. Wilson grabbed a torch off the wall and handed it to Helena. 'Hold this please.' Searching about inside the galley, he proceeded to stuff his pockets with packets of dry biscuits. Eventually he found what he was looking for and removed the long iron bar—about the length of his arm—used for securing the food trolley. It was quite heavy.

Helena handed the torch back. 'I'm not coming with you.'

Wilson thought for a moment. 'That's fine with me,' and he jumped out the door onto the grass.

'Christ, Wilson! What are we doing here? Tell me!' she demanded. With no answer forthcoming, she begrudgingly followed him outside. The smell of the jungle filled her nostrils and she realised she was a world away from the life she knew. It was hard for her to imagine why Wilson would want to come to this strange place. Helena gazed towards the deserted ruins as a ray of morning sunshine momentarily beamed through a rift in the clouds: a sun shower. For Helena, that meant good luck—her mother had always believed that.

Wilson pressed his hand against one of the deformed propellers; two of the four blades were bent right back. The undercarriage of the plane was covered in mud, the nose wheel was gone, panels were missing from the base of the wings. Foliage protruded from the air-intakes on the engines. He cringed—the damage was serious. The nose of the aircraft had ploughed a deep gully down the centre of the plaza as if a giant snake had slithered through the city.

'Texas Air are gonna be pissed,' Wilson said to himself.

Helena stood beside him, hands on hips. 'You can say that again.'

'You want me to say it—again?'

'I thought George Washington was the most irritating person I had ever met,' she replied. 'That was until I met *you*.'

'Texas Air are gonna have a hell of a time trying to get this thing out of here.'

Helena felt the light rain trickle down the back of her neck. 'Wilson, what are we doing here? Please tell me.' Her tone was almost pleasant for a change.

'I'm going to that pyramid over there,' he conceded. 'El Castillo—it means "the castle" in Spanish.'

Thick stratus clouds shifted quickly above the city as Helena looked towards the massive structure of the pyramid. There appeared to be a square stone building perched at the very top. 'Why would you want to do that, exactly?'

'Well, it's a little complicated to explain.'
'Try me.'
'Come along and see for yourself. That's the best I can do.'
'Why the iron bar?'
'Also difficult to explain.'

Helena gazed at the eerie deserted buildings around her. She was amazed that she was actually here, in Mexico. It felt like a dream. And the fact that she was alive made it a fairly good dream.

Wilson remembered the detailed information Barton had given him less than two weeks before: the Mayans had constructed Chichén Itzá without metal tools, beasts of burden or even the wheel, and they had done it with an incredible degree of precision and creativity. While Europe was still in the midst of the Dark Ages, the Mayans mapped the stars, evolved the only true writing system native to the Americas and became masters of mathematics. Their society consisted of many independent states, each with a rural farming community, and a large urban site built around a ceremonial centre—generally a pyramid. One King, living here at Chichén Itzá, ruled Mayan society, but there were many cities like this scattered across Eastern Mexico, like Tikal, Copan and Uxmal.

The chief god of the Mayans was the mighty Kukulkan—the feathered serpent. It was said he came from heaven twenty centuries before, half man and half god—the Quetzal Bird representing heaven, the serpent representing the earth. White-skinned and bearded, he was the god of life and divine wisdom.

'Chichén Itzá,' Wilson said, 'means "the mouth of the well of Itzá".' He pointed. 'The well of Itzá is a freshwater spring to the south side of the city.' As they passed each building, he briefly described what it was and its function in the community. The Nunnery Annex. The Temple of the Warriors. The Group of a Thousand Columns. They were incredible structures—all very different, all very elaborate.

Wilson pointed towards the Great Ball Court: a large open area of flat green grass, with high stone walls on each side. 'They competed in ballgames that went on for days. Hundreds of men on each side. The problem was: if your team lost, you were sacrificed to the gods.' The walls were adorned with images depicting the massacre of the losing team at the end of a game. An elaborate platform, for the winners, stood at one end, decorated with hundreds of carved skulls. 'That's what I call a cause for motivation.'

'They sound like barbarians,' Helena said.

'People with strange customs, yes. But not barbarians.'

The wind was gusting through the trees as Helena looked towards El Castillo. 'Is that pyramid as old as the Egyptian ones?'

Wilson shook his head. 'It was built a couple of thousand years after. The Egyptian pyramids are much, much older.' He turned full circle. There were no tourists. 'I can't believe there's no one here,' he said.

'Why is there so much open space?' Helena asked. It was as though they were strolling down a well-manicured golf course, flat green grass on either side of them.

Wilson jumped across the furrow the plane had ploughed through the turf. 'It was once a heavily populated city,' he said. 'More than twenty thousand people would have lived here. This plaza would have been covered with tents and markets—all kinds of dwellings. Over time, all the minor structures have rotted away to nothing.'

Esther trotted happily by Wilson's side as if they were out for a casual stroll.

'Where did all the people go?' Helena asked.

'About 950 years ago it was abandoned.'

'Did the Spanish drive them away?'

Wilson shook his head. 'You're thinking of the Aztecs. The Mayan culture had completely disappeared well before Hernando Cortez and the Conquistadores arrived. That was in the early 1500s. This city was deserted at least 400 years before that.'

'So what happened to them?'

'Nobody knows why the Mayans disappeared. There's plenty of fresh water here, and food. No evidence of disease. For some reason their civilisation just disappeared. Gone.'

Light rain began falling again.

Helena studied the dense forest surrounding the perimeter of the city. 'How strange,' she whispered to herself. The Pyramid of Castillo loomed larger as they approached and Helena tilted her head in awe. 'It's gigantic.'

'The Mayans built their pyramids tall, legend says, so they could be closer to their god, Kukulkan.' The Pyramid of Castillo was a classic Mayan design: ten distinctive stepped levels of regularly diminishing size. On each of the four sides was a grand stairway that led to a platform on the top level where a small square building stood. Each stairway had ninety-one steps, plus one giant step all around the top, making a total of 365 in all—one for each day of the solar year. Wilson walked to the main staircase on the northern side where two massive carved snakes ran down each side of the extremely steep stairs, their tails at the top, their large aggressive heads, mouths open, reaching all the way to the ground.

Wilson took a deep breath. 'This is Snake Mountain. That was what the Mayans used to call it.'

'Charming,' Helena said. 'What now?'

'We climb.'

Esther bounded upwards of her own accord.

With each metre the views of the city became more remarkable. Helena thought out loud, 'How are we going to get back to civilisation? We're in the middle of nowhere out here. And we're going to need food, sooner or later.' Green bushland stretched in every direction as far as the eye could see. 'After what you did to that plane, it's not like we can fly out.'

Wilson scratched his chin as he surveyed the city. The complete absence of tourists puzzled him. Maybe the roads were blocked—flooded probably. 'I have to say,' he said. 'I don't really know how we're going to get out of here. That's funny, isn't it?' The original plan had been to hitch a ride on a tourist bus.

'Are you ever serious?' Helena replied.

'Rarely.'

She waited for him to catch up. 'You know, someone is going to come looking for that plane sooner or later, and we are going to be in serious trouble.'

'That's probably true.'

She glanced over at him with a menacing stare. 'And I'm going to blame *you* for everything.'

'I expected nothing less.' The higher they went, the windier it became. Wilson wiped the raindrops from his sunglasses as the trio took one last stride to the top level—it was a bigger step than the rest, about double the height. Grey clouds were sweeping by just above their heads. The view of the city below was amazing, the disabled Saab 340 adding to the unusual sight.

Wilson conjured thoughts of this place a thousand years before. It would have been a feast of colour and movement—the plaza filled with tents and wooden buildings, people mingling, buying produce at the markets, warriors walking in pairs, tanned and bare-chested, wearing elaborate feathered headdresses. It would have been crowded with thousands of people. Domesticated animals, oxen, chickens and dogs all roaming free. The smell of cooking would have wafted across the city. In the distance there would have been cheering as teams of men practised inside the Great Ball Court; knowing one day their skills would be a matter of life and death. Up here on the pyramid—the sacred Pyramid of Castillo—only a select few, holy men and kings, would have been privileged to watch the proceedings and marvel at the society they had created ...

Helena's voice broke Wilson's concentration.

'And what's this place behind us?'

He turned to face an unassuming stone building with three doorways, perched on the centre of the highest plateau. 'The Temple of Castillo,' he announced.

Two giant stone columns separated the three doorways, each one carved into the form of a feathered serpent with teeth bared. 'This is Kukulkan,' Wilson said. 'The god of the Mayans.' He patted one of the serpents on the belly, then circled the building on the narrow plateau, trying to learn what he could from the outside. Most of the drawings on the walls had been eroded away by the ravages of weather and time.

Helena rested against a waist-high pedestal just outside the middle doorway and wrung the rainwater from her hair.

Wilson rounded the corner. 'I wouldn't sit there if I were you.'

'Why?'

'That's a sacrificial table.'

Helena leapt up, her gaze fixed on the pitted slab of rock, wondering how many people were slaughtered at that very spot. 'You could have told me that *before* I sat down!' It was as if she could now sense their last moments of terror.

'It's said the Mayans sacrificed their enemies, for all to see, and tossed their decapitated bodies down the staircase, between the giant snakes. That was their way of saying: this is our temple, and no one shall desecrate it.'

It made Helena's skin crawl just thinking about it. 'Is there anything else I should know?'

Wilson peered in through the middle doorway at the small, empty room. 'It's a little complicated,' he said distractedly.

Hazy sunlight was angling in through the entrance as Wilson

stepped into the confined space. Further inside, four neatly carved pillars held up two thick wooden lintels that supported the heavy stone roof. Each rectangular four-metre length of hardwood easily weighed many tonnes. On the back wall was an inconspicuous mould-covered brick wall.

Wilson's gaze was drawn to the top right-hand corner, and he began to count—nine bricks down, seven bricks across. At the intersecting point, he pressed his finger against the imperfect stone. Scratching away a line of mould with his fingernail, he clearly identified the brick. Then, using the end of the iron bar, he reached up and pounded the stone. Pieces of rock were chipping off as he continued to hammer away with all his might.

'What the hell are you doing?' Helena called out.

Seeing her shadow on the floor beside him, Wilson struck the wall even harder.

'Let me guess,' she said. 'Too complicated to explain! Or are you just a vandal?'

He hit the wall harder again and the brick appeared to shift. 'I was just warming up when I crashed the plane,' he said. After another solid impact, the stone fell back into the wall and disappeared. Wilson backed away. He would soon know if his journey to the past was all for nothing.

There was silence.

'Have you completely flipped out?' Helena blurted. 'What the hell are—' She stopped, mid-sentence, as the walls began to shudder with an ever-increasing intensity.

Wilson ran out the door without a word.

Standing there alone, Helena could feel tremors through the soles of her feet.

The stone floor was vibrating furiously.

An earthquake!

Nervously, she backed outside, as if walking on very thin ice. Finally taking stock, she realised that Wilson and Esther were already halfway down the northern staircase. 'Hey!' she yelled out. 'Wait for me!'

Wilson descended as fast as he could. Getting to the 'inner pyramid' by the most direct route was imperative. Barton had been very clear: once the trigger was activated there was no telling how long it would last. The Pyramid of Castillo was in fact the outer layer of a smaller pyramid. An entrance was located at the base of the northern staircase.

It was discovered in the late 1990s by archaeologists using sonar equipment. With incredible crudeness they jack-hammered a hole through the outer wall, at ground level, which exposed the staircase leading to the inner chamber.

Wilson jumped down the last two steps, the wet grass squelching under his feet as he approached the rudimentary entrance. It was pitch-black inside. He switched on his torch and peered into the hexagonal tunnel that led up at a forty-five degree angle. The steps were slippery under foot. The interior was dripping with moisture that had trickled its way in through a hundred hidden cracks and niches of the outer pyramid.

Esther stopped at the bottom of the steps on the grass plaza, fixated on the sky. Her ears twitched nervously. Helena knelt beside her.

'What is it, girl? Do you sense something?' Helena looked towards the forest, then to the doorway through which Wilson had disappeared.

Everything was vibrating as Wilson reached the top of the stairs and entered the twin chambers. It was hot and humid and he felt a sense of claustrophobia coming on. A musty smell like damp clothes hung in the air.

His torch cast a shaft of light in the darkness.

Ahead, a steel gate, like a prison door, blocked the way. On the other side there were two small rooms with low ceilings and featureless grey walls. The outer chamber contained a Chac-mool—a Toltec statue of a chubby naked man, reclining in the middle of the floor. The Mayans had used it as a sacrificial table. Coins, which tourists had tossed through the gate for luck, were scattered on its flat belly and all around the floor.

In the second room stood the Throne of the Red Jaguar. The animal's jade eyes and pyrite fangs glowed ominously in the torchlight.

A padlock secured the gate.

Wilson slid the iron bar between the chains and twisted. The metal groaned. He twisted again, then again, until there was a fierce crack and the gate squeaked open.

This is a question of belief, he told himself.

Wilson stepped around the Toltec statue and approached the Throne of the Red Jaguar. It was a waist-high red seat, its exterior the colour of arterial blood. The animal stood side-on, with jade eyes and large jade spots all over its body.

Everything continued to vibrate.

The light from Wilson's torch scanned the walls.

About three-quarters of the way up, two holes had appeared—exposed by the earthquake—each one about the size of a hand. He stepped on the back of the jaguar so that the two openings were now at chest height and gripped his torch between his knees.

Wilson knew what he had to do, but he was still uncertain. It was against his every instinct to put his hands inside the blackened holes. Barton's words echoed in his head: 'Turn it clockwise. Do it without thinking.' Wilson rubbed his hands together and fearlessly plunged them in.

Something cold and metallic began pulling on his fingertips! For a moment, Wilson wondered if this was where his life would end—pinned to a cursed wall in Mexico. His arms were being stretched and he could feel his chest compressing against the stone wall, making it difficult to breath. Maybe his hands would be pulled clean off! This is a question of belief, he counselled himself again, fighting his instinct to panic.

With all his might, he twisted in a clockwise direction.

Nothing budged.

Wilson twisted clockwise, again—harder. With a grinding of rock, the seals finally cracked and his arms released. Losing his balance, he tumbled backwards, landing heavily, and his torch bounced across the dusty floor.

Shards of rock fell away from the wall as a large circle of stone, about a metre across, began to rotate above the red jaguar like a money wheel at a casino. Faster and faster it turned. With a flicker of energy, the round disk illuminated. There wasn't even time to appreciate how amazing it was. Everything suddenly went into slow motion. Cracks slowly opened up across the ceiling and dust sluggishly billowed into the air.

Wilson ran towards the Toltec statue and jumped, as if in a leisurely dive, just as the lintels let go behind him. The enormous rock ceiling hit the floor with a ear-splitting *thump*. The inner chamber was sealed, plunging everything into darkness.

As he blindly made his way down the flight of stairs, time surged faster once again. Another reverberating thud. The ceiling of the outer chamber had collapsed also, the gust of wind it generated blustering past him. In the commotion, Wilson lost his footing on the wet stairs and fell head first into the blackness.

About two hundred metres away, Helena, with Esther by her side, knelt inside a stone doorway looking back towards the Pyramid of Castillo. She had been looking through Wilson's eyes, through a red haze, just moments before. The overlapping images were disorienting, but it had happened to her many times now and she was learning to deal with it.

A thick cloud of dust flared from the side of the pyramid as Wilson tumbled outside onto the short grass. The sight of him, safe, was a relief for Helena.

In the distance, Wilson could see Helena crouched in the doorway of the *Caracol*—he recognised the distinctive dome-shaped building. His fall in the stairwell had been a heavy one and he was sore all over. His head throbbed. Above him the sky grew darker. Clouds swirled around the city. Ominous clouds. He had never seen anything like them.

A flock of screeching white ibises, hundreds of them, took to the air above the forest, just as heavy rain began to fall. The air was suddenly so thick with water, it was difficult to breathe. Everything went grey in a second and the sound of the falling rain was deafening. With visibility reduced to only a few metres, Wilson ran north through the downpour towards Helena.

The Caracol was an ancient Mayan observatory set on a raised stone plateau. The Mayans had constructed it to chart the path of Venus on its 584-day cycle around the sun. Much like a modern-day observatory, it was equipped with a viewing platform around the outside and square windows were cut in the dome-shaped roof to align with specific points on the lunar and celestial horizon.

Shielding his face from the downpour, Wilson could just make out the shadow of the Caracol as he approached. He sloshed through water that was already ankle deep and rising by the second.

Flickers of light began to illuminate the black sky.

Thunder clamoured overhead.

A bolt of lightning surged out of the clouds and Wilson felt the burning flash of electricity behind him.

For a moment his shadow was branded on the water.

Then another flash.

Discharges of intense energy thumped into the pyramid, over and over. The sky was ablaze. Wilson sprinted across the plaza and made a frantic dive towards the doorway of the observatory. Forks of electricity, like spiderwebs, arced and crackled between the buildings and across the water. He landed heavily on the stone floor, tumbling safely to dry ground. Helena pulled him away from the entrance just as the water outside energised with a deadly sizzle.

Lightning continued to flash across the sky.

Thunder boomed.

Bolts of heavenly fire struck with terrifying intensity. All the while, Wilson stared at Helena as she watched the storm through the doorway, the flicker of lightning illuminating her face. She was a beautiful woman, he realised. Yes—*very* beautiful. It was an odd moment for a revelation of that kind.

She turned towards him, her tone accusing, 'Did you do this? What you did inside the pyramid—did it make this storm happen?'

For a moment Wilson was off guard, then he insisted, 'Absolutely not. How could I?'

'You made the pyramid vibrate! The lightning is attracted to the pyramid!' A relative quiet followed her remark, for the storm was gone as quickly as it had begun and a ghostly calm descended. The pair stood frozen for a moment, listening, waiting for something else to happen. But there was only silence, save for the rain that continued to fall gently.

'I have never seen anything like that before in my life,' Helena said.

Wilson wiped the water from his glasses. 'Did you feel the electricity in the air?' The hairs on his arms were standing on end.

Helena looked at Wilson's face and saw that he had a purple bruise on his forehead. 'You hit your head.'

He felt the bump. 'I fell down some stairs.'

'I know you did,' she said. 'I saw you inside the pyramid. The locked gate ... the statue of the jaguar. I saw the wall light up! That spinning disk! The roof caving in! So don't give me any garbage about how the storm is not related!'

Wilson climbed to his feet, his clothes dripping wet.

'Aren't you going to answer me?'

He gave her a blank look. 'You won't like my answer.'

'Try me.'

'Too complicated to—'

She finished the sentence, '—explain. *Great!*'

Wilson walked outside. The clouds were already lifting. The plaza was flooded, completely covered with water at least a foot deep, and the gusting wind was generating rippling patterns across the surface.

The Pyramid of Castillo was covered with dozens of black scorch marks from the lightning. It was an eerie sight. A revelation suddenly struck Wilson: the portal had activated. His relief was enormous. The system appeared to work and it gave him confidence that he would one day make it back home to his own time.

The sound of a vehicle echoed across the city and a smile came to Wilson's face. In the distance a green four-wheel drive was emerging from the trees. 'You asked how we were going to get out of here ...' He looked around, but Helena had ducked back into the doorway. She had Esther by the collar. 'Our lift has arrived,' he said.

Helena nervously drew out her handgun. 'You don't know who they are.'

'They'll be tourists. We can get a ride out of here.'

'We should find out who they are first,' she said cautiously.

'Nonsense.' He raised his hands and waved the vehicle towards him. In the distance, the four-wheel drive rolled slowly across the plaza, water splashing off the wheels. Eventually, it turned in his direction.

Helena felt uneasy. 'You don't know who they are,' she repeated. Her eyes followed a carved stone staircase that circled high inside the dome of the Caracol. She jogged up the brittle stone stairs with some haste, to the outside balcony, taking great care to stay out of sight and keep Esther close by her side.

A SATELLITE TELEPHONE began to ring.

The driver of the four-wheel drive handed the phone to his front-seat passenger. Outside, a lone man was standing on the other side of the plaza, waving his hands in the air.

The driver carefully negotiated his way across the flooded grass.

There were four men inside the car, two in front, two in the back, all in their late twenties, clean-cut, tanned. The two in the back seat checked their military-issue handguns, then concealed them under their shirts.

Lieutenant Diaz waited before answering the telephone. 'Drive straight towards him,' he said. 'Everybody get ready. Let's round him up without any fuss.'

He answered the call, 'Hello.'

'Do you have him?' A deep voice replied. There was a constant whirring in the background.

'We've just arrived.' Diaz studied his surroundings. 'There was a bad storm. It slowed us down a little.' He couldn't explain the scorch marks on the pyramid. Didn't even try. 'I have good news. We can see a man just ahead, waving us towards him. He fits your description.' The four-wheel drive motored slowly across the flooded plaza. 'He appears to be alone.'

COMMANDER VISBLAT WAS sitting in the back seat of a helicopter, a satellite telephone pressed to his ear. Dark storm clouds brooded in the distance. 'Lieutenant Diaz,' he said. 'There may be a woman with him. She's dangerous and probably armed. Keep your eyes open.' The black leather suitcase from the police compound sat between Visblat's legs, the evidence tag removed.

'Yes, sir,' Diaz replied.

'And remember,' Visblat said firmly, 'I want him unharmed. What you do with the woman is up to you.'

THE FOUR-WHEEL DRIVE rounded the Pyramid of Castillo and the disabled Saab 340 came into view, but Diaz didn't say a word about it; he just took it all in. 'We'll have him in custody by the time you get here.' He paused. 'Don't forget to bring the money.'

The phone crackled, 'I have the money. Just make sure you detain him. And remember what I told you—his sunglasses are not to be removed under any circumstances. Do you understand?'

'Yes sir, I understand.' Wilson was now less than fifty metres away. 'We will have him in custody in a few moments. I'll call you back.'

'Be cautious,' Visblat replied. 'He can be tricky.'

'Yes, sir.'

The Army Rangers were a confident crew, particularly Diaz. He hung up the phone and tossed it to one of the men in the back seat. Speaking quickly, he said, 'All we have to do is catch this moron and we'll be set up for life.'

'This is too good to be true,' the driver replied.

'Remember, he's not to be killed,' Diaz said. 'And his sunglasses are not to be removed under any circumstances. Do you understand?'

The three men responded in unison, 'Yes, sir.'

'There could be a woman with him,' Diaz added. 'So keep a sharp lookout. She may be armed. Shoot her on sight if you have to.'

WILSON WATCHED AS the four-wheel drive came to a stop beside him and the passenger window wound down. A young man with nice white teeth smiled back at him. 'Thanks for stopping,' Wilson said.

'What can we do you for?'

Wilson glanced at the four men in the car, all young, wearing summer clothing—shorts and tennis shoes. They seemed nice enough. American. Wilson answered, 'I had a bit of engine trouble with my plane over there. Had to make an emergency landing.' The young man stepped out of the car and Wilson became suspicious when he didn't even think twice about standing in ankle-deep water.

'Yeah, I saw it. You okay?' Diaz said.

Wilson backed up on the stairs. 'Yeah, I'm fine. Bit of a rough landing though.'

Diaz smiled. 'You on your own?'

An alarm bell began to ring in Wilson's head. 'Yeah. I'm alone.'

Diaz nodded. 'You had to crash-land the plane, huh?'

'Engine trouble,' Wilson repeated. 'You boys on holidays?' He watched the young man's eyes as they searched the ruins. It was more than just curiosity.

Diaz waved the others out of the car. 'You could say that.' He momentarily studied the bruise on Wilson's forehead. 'You're injured.'

'It's nothing,' Wilson replied. 'You boys here on business or pleasure?'

'A bit of both,' Diaz replied as his men fanned out across the stairs.

'What sort of business?' Wilson asked.

Diaz wasn't smiling any more. 'Let's call it "acquisitions".'

Helena crouched on the viewing platform of the Caracol; she could hear every word.

One of the men briefly checked inside the doorway and Wilson didn't need to be a genius to realise that he was in trouble, and things were getting worse.

Producing a large pistol, another of the men said, 'Raise your hands. Now.' He was very calm. They all were.

Diaz rested his hand on Wilson's shoulder. 'Let me ask you again. Are you alone?'

Wilson pulled away. 'What's this all about?'

Producing a sizable handgun of his own, Diaz offered Wilson a view of the barrel. 'Are you alone?'

'I told you—yes. I'm alone.'

'Where's the woman?'

'I dropped her off at an airstrip in Texas,' Wilson said without hesitation. 'She was a real pain in the ass. I told her, "Get out of here." What's this all about, anyway?'

Diaz grinned a perfect smile. 'You, my friend, are the easiest money we have ever made.' The group of four unexpectedly broke into laughter. 'My name is Diaz, Army Rangers, Fort Bennington. And you, my unlucky friend, have a bounty on your head.' He rubbed his thumb and forefinger together. 'A large one.'

Wilson was praying they wouldn't remove his sunglasses. 'Boys, I'm sure we can come to an arrangement. I can pay you more.'

On the viewing platform, Helena was intrigued by the conversation.

'I doubt it,' Diaz replied. 'A million bucks is a lot of money.'

Abruptly pushing one of the men aside, Wilson made a run for it. He leapt off the plateau, three metres down into knee-deep water. All four men calmly walked to the edge of the landing as Wilson did his best to slosh away at speed, trying to make it around the corner.

'Bring him down,' Diaz said. '*Carefully.*'

A single gunshot echoed across the city and Wilson's thigh was torn apart by the impact.

Helena's grip tightened on the butt of her gun.

Lying half-submerged in water, Wilson pressed his hand against his mutilated quadricep. Blood was gushing in all directions. He was shivering in a mixture of shock and pain—the bullet had passed right through his flesh. Everything was going in and out of focus as two men dragged him back onto the steps of the Caracol, a trail of blood draining from the wound.

'I suggest you don't do that again,' Diaz warned.

Helena tiptoed back to ground level. Standing just inside the doorway, out of sight, she closed her eyes and took a deep breath. Flipping off the safety on her handgun, she leapt forward and yelled, 'Drop your weapons!' The four soldiers turned towards her, their expressions stern. Not one of them looked afraid. She yelled louder, 'I said drop the fucking guns!'

Diaz coolly gestured to the floor and his men released their weapons without hesitation. They didn't have a facial expression between them. They were professionals, Helena could tell. Approaching quickly, both hands on her pistol, she yelled, 'Raise your arms!' and kicked away the first gun. At that moment, one of the men swung his leg under her, a sweeping back kick, knocking Helena off her feet. He was so fast she didn't even see it coming. Helena somersaulted backwards, hitting the side of her face on the ground.

Lieutenant Diaz chuckled to himself, 'Stupid woman. She should know better than to get between us and a million dollars.'

The mercenaries roared with laughter.

Blood poured over Wilson's fingers. 'Leave her alone,' he groaned. Helena appeared to be unconscious. One of the men turned her on her back. Another took away her gun. 'Leave her alone,' Wilson pleaded. 'She has nothing to do with any of this.'

'Remove her clothes,' Diaz ordered. 'Tie her hands behind her back.'

Wilson sat up. 'I said—*leave her alone!*'

'We can have a little fun with her when she comes around,' Diaz said.

One of the men tore open the buttons on Helena's shirt.

'You are making a serious mistake!' Wilson said, trying his best to sound in control. 'Leave her alone!' One of the men approached and kicked Wilson in the chest, smashing the wind from his lungs.

'Shut up, you!' the soldier said angrily. 'She belongs to us now.'

Trying to catch his breath, Wilson crawled back to his knees. 'I have something I want to show you.' But no one looked in his direction; their attention was firmly fixed on Helena, who was just coming out of her stupor. Two of the men easily tore the shirt away from her body.

'Army Rangers are pussies!' Wilson yelled out. 'Everybody knows it!' In unison, the lieutenant and his men fixed a vengeful gaze on him—and that was all Wilson needed.

He removed his sunglasses and threw them to the ground.

Eye contact!

As expected, the four soldiers charged towards him like demented savages. Waiting until the last possible moment, Wilson called out the omega command: 'Activate Overload.' He smacked away the first man, then punched the second, knocking him to the ground with a single blow. But before Wilson had a chance to strike again, Diaz and the other man were on him, scratching and pounding at his face. With a primeval roar, Wilson swung the two of them together, but he was off balance and all three stumbled and fell in a tangle of bodies.

Wilson's attackers swarmed all over him. They were younger and stronger, and for some reason the effect to his omega command was weaker than usual.

The sound of an angry dog echoed off the walls as Esther leapt from the ruins and sank her fangs into Diaz's neck, dragging him backwards.

Frenzied screams cut the air.

Wilson managed to kick another of his attackers away, but every blow he absorbed took a little more of his energy. He tried to break free, but it was no use. With another heavy blow to the face, his vision blurred.

Two thunderous gunshots suddenly rang out.

Blang, blang.

Wilson looked up to see Helena, half naked, one hand covering her exposed breasts, slam the butt of her revolver into the back of Diaz's head. The four soldiers were now lying on the ground, a bloodied mess; only one of them was still moving—and he was writhing in pain. Helena climbed to her feet, pressed her palm to her bloodied cheek, then gave the soldier a swift merciless kick in the head. He went limp like the others.

'Esther, come here!' she called. The dog released her vice-like grip on Diaz's lacerated shoulder. At that moment, Wilson's eyes met Helena's. They had made eye contact!

An optical trackenoid response.

In a panic, Wilson tried to scramble away on his hands and knees. He should've taken precautions, he knew that, and now it was too late. Helena was almost on top of him! Her pupils were shrinking, her expression blank.

She flew towards him as if in slow motion.

There was no way Wilson wanted to hurt her. She had just saved his life. Her outstretched fingers reached for his face in attack.

But it was not what he expected.

'Try not to move,' she said, her voice soothing. 'Everything will be fine.' And she held him upright.

22

Mexican Coastline, near Merida
Bell 430 JetRanger
November 27th 2012
Local Time 11:56 a.m.

Mission of Isaiah—Day Three

A BLACK HELICOPTER thundered towards the Mexican coastline. In the distance, dark storm clouds moved steadily across the sky. The chopper crossed the white sandy beach at blistering speed and headed inland just above the treetops.

Commander Visblat slouched across the rear cabin, headset on, his face badly bruised. The helicopter was not designed to carry a man of his considerable height, and his legs were jammed awkwardly under the seat facing him. He tore the adhesive bandage from his forehead, revealing a wet fleshy wound. He didn't want any bandages on his face—they made him look weak, he decided. The cast on his arm was bad enough.

Visblat's eyes remained fixed on the thick forests that swept below the window. The sound of the turbine hummed in the cabin. He was running through scenarios in his mind. If things went well, Wilson Dowling would be in his custody at any moment. The large man was fidgeting, doing his best to suppress the urge to gloat. His heart rate increased with expectation. Soon he would have the opportunity to show how clever he had been.

Visblat looked at his watch. 'You said we were only twenty minutes away!' he erupted. 'That was half an hour ago!'

The navigator adjusted his headset, glanced at the pilot, then turned towards the cabin. 'We're approaching Chichén Itzá now. There was a sequence of electrical storms we couldn't pass through.'

They were an American crew that Visblat had commissioned from San Antonio. Both pilots were on edge; they had violated Mexican airspace without authority and everything was off the record, including the pay arrangements.

'I told you to fly straight there!' Visblat barked into his microphone. 'No deviations. I'm in a hurry.' The sound crackled in both pilots' ears.

'We had no choice,' the navigator said. 'The storm was too severe.'

Without pressing the intercom, Visblat swore out loud in the cabin. He grabbed his mobile telephone as if he was going to throw it, then restrained himself and placed it gently on the seat. *There's no need to be angry*, he told himself. Mr Dowling would soon be in his charge.

'Chichén Itzá is coming into view,' the navigator said.

Visblat sat up and surveyed the ancient city. The walls of the Pyramid of Castillo were covered with black scorch marks, hundreds of them, and the plaza was concealed under a shimmering layer of water. An aircraft, a Saab 340, sat at the edge of the clearing—it was badly damaged. Visblat's piercing blue eyes scanned the ruins looking for Wilson. Eventually, he looked towards the Caracol. People were standing on the plateau. He smiled to himself. This was his moment of victory. As the helicopter descended towards the ruins, his smile faded.

The pilot spoke into his microphone: 'Look at this place!' The mysterious black scars on the pyramid seemed inexplicable.

Visblat pointed towards the ground. 'Set us down. Over there.'

'We can't land in the water!' the pilot said.

'If you want your money,' Visblat replied, 'you'll land this aircraft. Just do it.' He threw his headset on the seat. 'Do it!' he yelled.

With a worried look, the pilot turned to his navigator, but the response from his co-worker was direct. 'Do as he says.'

The pilot eased the helicopter down as gently as he could and they landed in a plume of vapour. Visblat stepped out on the wet ground and looked back through the curved windscreen. 'Wait there!'

The pilot pressed his intercom. 'This job was your idea,' he said.

The navigator remained straight-faced. 'Shut your mouth and concentrate on what you're doing. We don't want to sink into the mud.'

SHOULDERS SLOUCHED, a dejected Visblat traipsed through ankle-deep water, through the misty rain, towards the men waiting for him on the steps of the Caracol. The Rangers had screwed up, he realised. Blood poured from the back of Lieutenant Diaz's neck. The man next to him pressed his hand against what appeared to be a gunshot wound. Another had blood trickling down the middle of his face.

Visblat shook the water from his leather shoes and climbed the stone staircase, making a particular effort to make eye contact as he approached.

'What happened?' he said.

'That *woman*,' Diaz replied. 'She gunned down two of my men, that's what *happened*!'

Visblat studied the fourth soldier, lying on his back, his eyes glazed with pain. It appeared he had been shot through the hip.

'We were ambushed. We had no way of defending ourselves.'

'Your overconfidence got the better of you,' Visblat grumbled. He stared intently into Diaz's eyes, causing him to eventually lower his gaze. 'I warned you this could happen.'

'We wouldn't be here if it wasn't for you!' Diaz had been on holidays in Mexico when Visblat called, offering him the freelance job of a lifetime. 'Two of my men have been shot for Christ's sake! Jeffries has a cracked skull. Everything is screwed.'

The chopper was rumbling on the plaza, water lapping away from it in ever-increasing circles. Visblat drew out an envelope and threw it in Diaz's direction. 'This'll help. There's your deposit, as promised. Twenty-five grand.'

Diaz picked it up. 'My men are wounded.' He felt the weight of the envelope. 'It's not enough.'

Visblat turned full circle. 'Twenty-five grand to show up—that was the arrangement. You didn't earn the million bucks—that's your problem. I *told* you to be careful.' He seemed distracted by his surroundings. 'You said you were ambushed. How did it happen, exactly?'

Diaz shifted nervously—he wasn't certain himself. 'The woman, she came from nowhere. She had a gun. Everything after that is a bit of a blur.'

Visblat pointed to a large pool of blood at the bottom of the stairs. 'What's this?' It didn't seem to tally with the kind of injuries suffered by Diaz or his men.

The lieutenant stepped forward to explain. 'The fugitive was shot during the gunfight. It was an accident,' he said defensively. 'Just an accident.'

'I told you he was not to be harmed!' Visblat erupted.

'The bullet went through his leg,' Diaz said without emotion. 'He'll survive, I assure you.'

'We agreed he wouldn't be harmed!'

'It was an accident!'

'Not good enough!' Visblat paused for a long while, trying to calm his ever-growing anger. 'You let a *woman* subdue the lot of you. *Christ!* I can't believe it.'

Diaz had no real recollection of what happened after Wilson took off his sunglasses. The entire episode was blocked out. He just remembered regaining consciousness and finding his men injured on the ground around him.

Visblat managed to get his emotions in check. 'They took your vehicle, did they?'

'A green four-wheel drive.'

'Which direction did they go in?'

'That way.' There was suddenly a hint of optimism in Diaz's voice. 'If we take your helicopter we can still catch them! They only left about half an hour ago. They can't be far away.'

'Forget it,' Visblat said, looking at the wounded quartet. 'They could be anywhere by now.' He scanned the ruins. The sacred waterhole of Chichén Itzá was bubbling, a thick tower of moisture evaporating into the air like smoke from a factory chimney. His eyes locked onto the Pyramid of Castillo, its exterior afflicted with a rash of scorch marks.

It seemed that Wilson had successfully opened the first portal.

'We can still get them!' Diaz said. 'It's worth a try! There aren't that many roads.'

Visblat was stony faced. 'You had your chance, Lieutenant.' He turned and made for the chopper. Wilson Dowling was turning out to be a difficult catch, and Helena Capriarty an unpredictable complication.

'You can't leave us here!' Diaz yelled. 'Our satellite phone was in the car. We have no way of calling for help!' With a wave of his index finger, Diaz spurred his men to attention. The able-bodied pair drew their automatic handguns and stood at either side of their lieutenant. 'We want our money,' Diaz called out. 'Visblat! We want all of it!'

Rage building, Visblat turned on the spot and strode menacingly towards them, his shoulders hunched, fists clenched by his side. It was all about eye contact, he told himself. With an unbroken stare fixed on each of his opponents in turn, he approached without hesitation. Visblat halted just a few metres away. 'Shoot me if you can!' he taunted. 'Do it!' He knew it would be impossible.

Diaz felt his pulse racing, a cold sweat flushing his brow. He was experiencing fear, primal fear. His legs had gone to water and somehow he was unable to move.

Visblat stood for a moment, relishing his overwhelming authority, ensuring the soldiers were riveted to their positions like stone statues. 'Drop your weapons,' he said with a growl.

As if under his absolute command, the three soldiers released their guns.

'That's better,' Visblat said, with a smirk. 'You men wait here. I'll radio for assistance.' But he had no intention of doing any such thing. Turning for the chopper, he stepped back into the ankle-deep water and made his way across the plaza.

VISBLAT HAULED HIMSELF into the cabin and latched the door behind him.

The navigator turned and faced his passenger. 'What now?'

'Take me to Mexico City,' was the reply.

'We'll have to book a flight plan.'

'Then book a flight plan!' Visblat snapped. 'I don't care what you have to do!'

'What about them?' The navigator pointed to the men outside on the plateau of the Caracol. 'They look in bad shape.'

'I'm not paying you to be a rescue service,' Visblat said. 'I told you from the very beginning—do your job and don't ask any questions.'

The navigator caught a glimpse of Visblat's eyes and abruptly turned forward; something about what he saw made his skin crawl. He gestured upwards with his hand. 'You heard him,' he said to the pilot. 'Mexico City, full throttle.' His voice wavered with unexpected fear. 'We'll have to re-enter—' he cleared his throat '—via US airspace. I'll call in a flight plan.'

The helicopter lifted into the air.

Visblat was clenching his fists open and shut in a vain effort to calm himself when his eyes fell upon the satellite telephone on the seat beside him. He reached over, pressed the redial button and held the unit to his ear. It was worth a try.

23

California, The Americas
Enterprise Corporation, Mercury Building, Level 2
May 14th 2081
Local Time 10:00 a.m.

9 Days before Transport Test

STARING QUIZZICALLY, BARTON placed the flat of each hand on his desk. He was trying to understand the request being made of him. Wilson was sitting in one of the visitors' chairs, arms crossed. '*Why* do you want to see the scrolls again?' Barton said. 'You're not going to be able to do anything with them.'

'I want to decide that for myself,' Wilson replied.

'I'll come with you, if you like.'

Wilson shook his head. 'If you don't mind, I'd like to go on my own.'

'Can you read Hebrew?' Barton said abruptly.

'I've already told you. *No* … I can't.'

'Then why do you want to see the scrolls again?'

'I don't know, exactly.'

Barton pointed towards the floor. 'I've been working on those translations for more than a year. I assure you, I've done everything I can.'

Wilson thought for a moment. 'They are part of the reason I'm here, Barton. I may never get the chance to see them again. Anyway, what harm can it do?'

'Drawing too much attention to the scrolls could be unwise at this point,' he replied.

Wilson closed his eyes for a second, then refocused. 'You said everyone knows about the blueprints for time travel and where they came from.'

'Everyone in the mercury team does.'

'Then what's the problem? They are going to understand that I'm curious about it.'

Put in those words, it seemed a reasonable enough request.

'Okay, Wilson, if you must,' Barton said. 'But it's against my better judgment. Complete the final tests we've prepared and I'll give you access. But please, be discreet. We don't need any more focus on the scrolls than we have already.'

'I understand.' Wilson stood from his chair.

Barton was momentarily worried that he'd told Wilson about the Mission of Isaiah too soon. It narrowed down the available options more than he would have liked. But it was done now and, he decided, there was no use thinking about it any further.

'Have you had much sleep?' he asked.

'What do you think?' Wilson retorted, rolling his eyes.

'Probably not.' Barton tapped the intercom on his lapel. 'Davin … Wilson is ready to take his physical. Do a psychological evaluation as well. Let's get everything out of the way.'

A reply echoed over the loudspeaker, 'No problem, Boss.'

'Psychological evaluation,' Wilson said. 'Are you trying to tell me something?'

'No. Just part of the procedure.'

Wilson's right eyebrow lifted. 'Which procedure is that? The one everybody knows about—or the other one, that only you and I know about?'

Barton's worried gaze swung towards his palm device—thankfully the green indicator light was on and he was not being monitored at that moment. 'I've told you to be careful about what you say, Wilson.' Barton scowled disapprovingly. 'Please try.'

Wilson warily scanned the room. 'You're right, I'm sorry.'

Barton studied his candidate. 'What do you think your psychological evaluation will tell me?'

'It won't be good,' Wilson said, still wary. 'I mean, who in their right mind would do something like this for money?'

It was an interesting response. 'What else will it tell me?'

'That I approach situations without being really prepared,' Wilson said. '*Obviously*. And that I'm a little disorganised.' He thought some more. 'Oh yeah, and I have a weakness for beautiful women—but who doesn't?' Wilson winked, trying to lighten the mood. 'I'm quite a comedian, too.'

'Will it reveal anything good about you?'

'They *were* the good things.'

'I see.' Barton cracked a rare smile. 'Well, I'll look forward to seeing the results.'

Wilson gazed at the Enterprise Corporation logo on the wall, a look of trepidation suddenly coming to his face. 'This whole situation is bizarre.'

'You're right about that, Wilson.' Barton glanced at his palm device again—it was time to leave. He was meeting with Magnus Kleinberg, the other Gen-EP candidate, in just twenty minutes. He was preparing both of them for the mission at the same time, trying to keep as many options available to him until the very last second.

24

California, The Americas
Enterprise Corporation, Mercury Building, Level 2
May 14th 2081
Local Time 7:59 p.m.

9 Days before Transport Test

THE SOUND OF CRASHING waves played in the background as Barton held a mug of steaming green tea to his lips. A holographic image shimmered above his desk. The grade-one security system was active. On the screen Wilson Dowling could be seen moving methodically between the glass consoles that contained the Dead Sea scrolls; he had completed the required tests and, in return, Barton had given him access to the scroll chamber.

Wilson stopped above another parchment—from the Book of Isaiah—and scanned it from right to left, top to bottom. Barton ticked off the corresponding scroll on his palm device. So far, his Gen-EP candidate had studied more than sixty parchments, every one of them either an Esther scroll or an Isaiah scroll; somehow he knew which ones were which.

Standing inside the domed chamber, Wilson glanced into the darkness. He paused for a moment, as if sensing something, then went back to what he was doing.

For more than thirty minutes Barton watched the screen. Wilson had to be reading the scrolls, but how was that possible? Hebrew is a very complex language, particularly when written in old verse, like the scrolls, without any punctuation or word spacing. Barton had checked with the University of Sydney—Wilson had never studied the language. Not for one moment, even that very first day, did Barton believe it was just a coincidence when Wilson read the unmarked text. There was no such thing as coincidence. Interestingly, the feat made it all the more likely that Wilson *was* the Overseer. On the other hand, it was a surprise, and Barton didn't like surprises.

Karin's voice came over the intercom, 'Davin and Andre are here. Will you see them?'

Barton tapped his lapel. 'Send them in.' Turning to his desk monitor, he whispered at the screen. 'System, shut down G-1-SS.' The security system image above his desk disappeared from sight.

The glass door swung open and Andre and Davin, both wearing mercury labcoats, hastily entered the room. Andre was biting his nails and at the same time reading information on his palm device.

'We have a problem,' Davin said, and he raised a stack of digital documents into the air. 'It's about Wilson's ECG results.'

'A *big* problem,' Andre added.

'His ECG is off the charts,' Davin continued. He handed Barton the readouts. 'Increased alpha and beta waves. Really unusual. Have a look.' As Barton scanned the worksheet, Davin said, 'I ran it through Data-Tran and couldn't find anything remotely like it. I thought it could be caused by a brain tumour, or an aneurism, but the MRI didn't show anything.'

Barton rubbed his chin. 'Interesting.'

'What do you want to do?' Davin said, adjusting his glasses.

Barton neatly placed the document on the table in front of him and lined it up with the others. 'Nothing,' he said.

Andre was taken aback. '*Nothing?*'

'How did he do on the other tests?' Barton asked.

Somewhat surprised by Barton's lack of concern, Davin looked at his handheld. 'Well ... his physiological makeup appears to be fine. No diseases or viruses. Bone density is good. Immune system, excellent. The guy is pretty fit. Dexterity is above average. Psychologically, he appears to be calm—in fact, this report says he's dealing with the pressure well.'

'We can't transport him if his alphas and betas are off the charts,' Andre said.

Barton smiled reassuringly. 'Don't worry. We'll check it again—I'll do it myself.'

Andre pursed his lips. 'I don't think we should use him.'

'I'll take that into consideration, Andre, thanks. If there's a biological reason not to proceed, I'll let you know.' Barton stood up. 'There isn't anyone at Enterprise Corporation who is more risk averse than I am.'

Andre's voice hinted at panic. 'This is more than a risk! His alphas and betas are off the charts!'

Barton stared at the pimply teenager. 'I understand *exactly* what you are saying. Thank you. But a strange waveform like this has to have a reason.'

'I'm not comfortable, Barton.' The comment seemed strange coming from a young boy. 'In my view,' Andre said, 'this precludes Wilson from the next phase of 81-07. He doesn't meet the criteria you yourself wrote for this transport test. We should shortlist down to Magnus Kleinberg. His results are all within limits. The implications are obvious.'

'Andre's right,' Davin said. 'There's something very strange about those results.'

Barton had seen an ECG waveform like that only once before, in a confidential Navy report. There was no doubt that Wilson *had* lied about his capabilities. 'You're right,' Barton said. 'A result like this does preclude Wilson from going to the next stage. Thank you for bringing it to my attention. Just to be sure, I'll redo his tests, personally. Let's keep our options open.'

He fixed Davin with an intense stare, long enough to be sure that his number two obeyed the instruction without question.

'Come on, Andre,' Davin said, taking the hint. 'We shouldn't be worrying about this sort of thing, anyway. Let's get back to the lab. I have an important project for you to work on.' The pair left the room with Davin talking the whole way.

The door closed and Barton was alone. The sound of waves breaking gently washed across the room again. The scientist sat down and stared at Wilson's ECG results. They explained a lot. He keyed in the high-level access code. 'System ... G-1-SS, Level B3, Scroll Chamber. Wilson Dowling.' The holographic image shimmered above his desk once again. As before, Wilson was carefully reading the Isaiah scrolls, line by line.

Wilson was now Barton's preferred choice for the transport test. Not because he was smarter or younger, or because he was more co-operative—nothing so rational. It was a combination of the ECG results, his strange actions with the scrolls, and a simple feeling that

Barton had in his gut: Wilson was the one—he was the Overseer. Convincing the mercury team of the decision, after this ECG setback, would be difficult but not impossible.

Wilson continued reading the scrolls; unbeknown to him, the final decision about his candidacy had just been made.

Barton studied Wilson's psychological report—it also held an interesting revelation. It appeared there was nothing at all that was ordinary about Mr Wilson Dowling. Which was a good thing, Barton concluded; only an extraordinary man should be sent on a mission like this.

25

Lowland Forest, Eastern Mexico
120 Kilometres West of Cancún
November 27th 2012
Local Time 12:13 p.m.

Mission of Isaiah—Day Three

WILSON'S WORLD CAME back into focus as if emerging from a mist. Everything was moving. Lush green vegetation flashed by the car window. Misty rain was falling outside. The windshield wipers were on. There was a woman he recognised at the steering wheel. Memories of Wilson's journey slowly began to assemble in his mind: he was in Mexico, lying across the back seat of a stolen four-wheel drive, and this was not a dream. His right leg ached—the gunshot wound—and a terrible migraine pounded inside his skull as if a percussion band had been playing in his head all week.

Helena drove down a muddy trail through the jungle. There was a livid bruise on her right cheek. Esther, the Doberman, sat with her head protruding out the passenger window, happily taking in the sights and smells of the bushland. Every now and then the animal licked the accumulated rainwater from her nose as she continued her happy vigil.

Wilson had received a tremendous beating. His jaw was lacerated and badly swollen on one side. His bottom teeth were loose. A makeshift bandage was wrapped around his right thigh—Helena had made the dressing by tearing strips out of some clothes found in the back of the car. Thankfully, the blood flow from the gunshot wound had all but stopped.

Wilson watched Helena for a moment. 'Thanks for saving me,' he said, eventually finding his voice. She glanced in his direction, her honey-blonde hair sweeping across her face.

'You're awake.' She winced at seeing the deep cut under his right eye. 'You and I, we *seriously* need to talk. A million-dollar bounty ... trained killers chasing after you. I think it's time you explained what's going on.' The vehicle slowed to a stop on the dirt road. 'Tell me ...'

Realising his sunglasses lay on the seat beside him, Wilson snatched them up and slid them over his face, despite what had happened on the steps of the Caracol. Helena should've attacked him when she saw his eyes, yet she appeared to be immune to a trackenoid response—something Barton had said was impossible.

'Why is everyone trying to kill you?' she said.

'*You* haven't tried to kill me yet.'

'Those men were all over you, trying to beat you to death. Why would they do that?'

Wilson reached into his pocket and retrieved four packets of dry biscuits—the contents were crushed almost beyond recognition. 'Just give me a minute to figure out what's going on.'

'You should be more open with me,' she huffed.

With a groan of discomfort, Wilson eased himself into a sitting position, opened one packet, and poured the contents into his mouth. It was painful to chew, but he needed food. With his mouth still half full, he pointed at the road ahead. 'I think you should keep driving.'

As a meagre form of compensation, he handed Helena the remaining packets and flopped back across the rear seat, saying, 'Esther must be hungry.' Wilson stared out the window, but it was not the dense jungle that filled his mind; he was drifting into his memories in an effort to find some answers ...

California, The Americas
Mercury Building, Level B3—Scroll Chamber
May 14th 2081
Local Time 8:50 p.m.

9 Days before Transport Test

WILSON STOOD UNDER the domed ceiling of the scroll chamber. The air was dry—zero humidity. He had been there for more than two hours and his head was pounding. He concluded there was a trio of possibilities. One ... he was dehydrated. Two ... he had absorbed too much information for one day. Three ... his brain was about to explode.

With the exception of a few words, Wilson could indeed read the Dead Sea scrolls, with almost no effort at all. There was now little doubt that it was due to *Strong's Numbering System*. Wilson could recall each and every numbered word—there were 12,858 unique symbols—and he remembered *all* the definitions. It was a testament to the power of Professor Author's omega programming—even though, technically, it was not meant to do this sort of thing.

Wilson had finished reading the Book of Esther. The story was about the deliverance of the Jews from Persia, and the betrayal of King Ahasuerus—Xerxes the First—by his trusted chief minister, Haman. Wilson stopped and contemplated what he had read. Betrayal was the worst crime he could imagine, because it was inflicted by someone in a position of trust. It's not always easy to recognise your enemies, he realised.

Wilson was now reading the Book of Isaiah and he moved two steps to the left and stood above another badly damaged parchment. At all times, he was conscious that hidden within the text was far more than the stories themselves. Imbedded there were the blueprints for creating a time portal and the details of a mission preordained more than two thousand years before.

A familiar voice suddenly pierced the silence. 'What are you doing, Wilson?' Barton eventually strolled out of the shadows. 'You said you couldn't read them,' he added accusingly.

Wilson gathered himself. 'I'm just looking at them, that's all.' It was such a bad lie—humiliating to even say it.

'You've read all the Esther scrolls and most of Isaiah.'

Wilson tried to look surprised. 'Really?'

'How did you know which scrolls were which?'

'Let's just say for a moment that I *can* read the scrolls. What does that mean to you?'

Barton rested against one of the glass cabinets. 'Besides the fact that you are a terrible liar?'

'Yeah, besides that.'

'It means there must be more to you than I'd imagined.' Barton slid one hand into the pocket of his mercury labcoat and retrieved his palm device. He stole a glance at the display to make sure no one was listening. 'The way I see it, that can only be a good thing. To be honest with you, I just need to know that we understand each other; that we are being frank. To me, that is *far* more important than anything else. Truly, I don't care whether you can read the scrolls or not. You obviously have your reasons for keeping your linguistic skills a secret; I'm prepared to let you keep it that way.'

'Maybe we *should* talk about it,' Wilson said.

Barton's hazel eyes were calm. 'Really, it's not important to me. But I will say this … whatever you've done to artificially increase your intelligence has had an effect on your brain scan. Your ECG revealed increased alpha and beta waves surrounding your temporal lobes. That's a problem for both of us. I have only seen that phenomenon on one occasion, and you and I both know that cerebral programming is illegal; so let's not discuss it further.'

Wilson just stood there, stunned.

Enterprise Corporation's number-one scientist cooly glanced at his handheld once more. 'If we're going to proceed to the next phase of this mission—which is what I would like—we're going to have to work together. From now on you can't wander around unsupervised reading ancient Hebrew texts. Someone might be watching you. So do me a favour, try to act a little stupider from now on. Can you do that for me?'

'I think I'm up to it,' Wilson replied sheepishly. It seemed Barton was always one step ahead.

'Are you finished here?' he asked.

Wilson scanned the remaining parchments of the Isaiah scroll. They would have to wait for another occasion. 'Yes, I'm finished.'

'Good.'

'Can I ask you a question?' Wilson said as they both headed for the exit.

'Certainly.'

'How did *you* decode the scrolls?'

Barton glanced at his handheld. 'What say we talk outside? It's a beautiful evening. Discussing this here is too risky.'

The pair stood in silence in the elevator.

As the doors opened, Barton gave a cursory wave to the security guard as they crossed the brightly lit marble foyer and stepped outside into the night air.

'I love this time of year,' Barton said. 'Nice and warm.' They continued to walk away from the main building down a pathway into the tiered gardens at the rear of the mercury building. There was not a breath of wind and the stars were shining brightly against the ebony sky. Barton eventually said, 'Have you ever heard of the Copper Scroll of Qumran?'

Wilson shook his head. 'Should I?'

Barton rubbed his chin. 'The Copper Scroll is integral to what is going on here. It was found in the Dead Sea Cave Number Three on March 20th 1952, along with a group of other parchments. The Copper Scroll is *actually* made of copper—the only scroll of its kind— very unusual. Initially, scholars thought it was a treasure map. The inscriptions in its surface detailed the locations of dozens of underground hiding places supposedly containing treasure from the Temple of Jerusalem. It was said the riches were amongst the most magnificent in the Hebrew world. There were manifests to thousands of pieces of gold, silver and jewels. The treasure was allegedly hidden away after Vespasian's Legions held the city of Jerusalem under siege in March 70 AD. You remember, I told you that the day we met.'

'I remember.'

'But interestingly, the Copper Scroll never led to any treasure. Not a thing. And it's been a mystery for the last hundred years. The reason is: the Copper Scroll is not a treasure map at all. It's where I found the algorithms—a gigabit encryption, no less—that unlocked the secrets in the Book of Esther and the Book of Isaiah.'

'No one knows?' Wilson said.

'No one. Everyone thinks it's merely a treasure map; a treasure map that never led to anything. And yet *it* alone is the source of the gigabit encryption. Everyone thinks I came up with the decoding algorithm myself. I'm smart, but not *that* smart. No one is.'

'Why were you looking at the Copper Scroll in the first place?'

'We leased the scroll,' Barton said, 'from the Archaeological Museum of Amman, as a temporary display item for our head-office foyer. It's a beautiful artefact. A highly polished tube of copper. Magnificent.' Barton looked up at the night sky, his gaze drawn to the North Star, Polaris, which was glowing brightly near the horizon. 'That's when I touched the scroll for the first time.' He extended his index finger like he was reaching for it now. 'That's when I knew.' Barton gazed at Wilson in the darkness. 'I just knew.'

'Can I see the scroll?' Wilson asked.

Barton shook his head. 'That's not a good idea.'

Wilson rested his hand on Barton's shoulder. 'For some reason, I feel I *have* to see it.'

Lowland Forest, Eastern Mexico
117 Kilometres West of Cancún
November 27th 2012
Local Time 12:20 p.m.

Mission of Isaiah—Day Three

THE SOUND OF A ringing telephone suddenly came from beneath the rear seat. Surprised, Wilson scanned the back of the four-wheel drive for its hiding place. A small rectangular satellite phone glowed at his feet as the piercing ring continued.

Helena lifted her foot off the accelerator.

Wilson looked at the display and his heart skipped a beat.

'What is it?' Helena asked.

'You're not going to believe who's calling.'

'Who?' The telephone continued to ring as Wilson turned the display towards her. Helena read:

VISBLAT (Mobile)

An image of the huge, redheaded man's face flashed into her mind. 'He must've been the one who sent those soldiers,' she concluded. Helena shivered as she pictured his eyes staring at her over George Washington's unconscious body.

Wilson was in turmoil. His instinct was to throw the phone out the open window into the jungle, but he stopped himself. He pressed the 'okay' button and held the telephone to his ear. Helena reached out to stop him, but it was too late.

A deep voice resonated on the other end of the line, 'You're full of surprises, aren't you, Mr Dowling?' In the background was a constant rumbling noise.

'Commander Visblat, I presume,' Wilson replied.

'I'd like to congratulate you,' Visblat said. 'You have succeeded at

Chichén Itzá.' He laughed sarcastically. 'You've done a terrific job ... of ruining everything.'

Wilson's mind buzzed with questions.

'But, Mr Dowling,' Visblat said, composing himself. 'I truly am sorry about the gunshot wound. That was a mistake. I told those idiots not to harm you. They disobeyed my direct order.'

Wilson looked at the blood-soaked bandage around his thigh. 'I agree—having me shot was incredibly unreasonable of them. My leg will take time to heal.'

Helena gave Wilson a long, hard stare. She whispered, 'Visblat is the one I was telling you about! He's crazy!' Wilson gestured for her to keep quiet and she begrudgingly obeyed.

'Pleasantries aside,' Visblat said, 'we need to talk.'

'I'm listening.'

'We should be working together. I know about the Mission of Isaiah.'

Wilson took in a quick breath, but he told himself it was barely noticeable.

Visblat's tone hardened, 'I need your help and I'm not ashamed to admit it.'

'Like I said, I'm listening.'

'The second energy portal, in Egypt, has been tampered with. If you open it—it will have the reverse effect. You should proceed directly to the third portal. Open *that* instead. The results will have some positive effect, at least. It's not perfect, but it's a step in the right direction. I've been trying to stop you, to tell you this, for three days.'

'A million dollar bounty,' Wilson replied, 'is a hell of a way to get my attention.'

Visblat laughed. 'I've been trying to protect you! Think about it—my men could have just killed you if they wanted.'

'I'm still listening,' Wilson said.

'We need to meet. To discuss things.'

'I'm willing to consider that.' Wilson paused, trying to buy some time to think. 'I have your number—it's on the phone here. I'll call you to arrange a meeting.' There was a long pause.

'Just in case you decide not to call,' Visblat replied, 'I need you to understand that I will use all my power to stop you from opening the second portal. I have no choice. I'm sorry. Call me when you're ready. I will be in Mexico for the next twelve hours. And, Mr Dowling, if you decide not to co-operate, I will take it that you and I are not on the same side.'

The receiver went dead in Wilson's hand.

Helena began ranting immediately, 'You didn't tell me you knew him!'

'Whoa, whoa—!' Wilson held both his hands in the air. 'Hold on for just a second. I have no idea what is going on. I was just playing along to try and find out more. I agree: this situation is totally bizarre.'

'You told him you were wounded! Are you a complete idiot?'

'He already knew!'

'Visblat was the one that knocked George Washington unconscious! I've seen him—the guy's a madman! I've seen it in his eyes. He sent those mercenaries to capture you, Wilson. A million dollars! Whatever he wants, don't give it to him. Believe me. Don't make a deal, no matter what it is.'

Wilson didn't know what to think.

'You're stupid if you do.'

'Please Helena. You're starting to get annoying.'

'From my perspective I have *no reason* to think you are anything *but* stupid. Stealing a plane. Crashing it. What you did inside that pyramid. I know it caused that storm! If it wasn't for me—'

Wilson held a palm towards her. 'Stop!'

She said even more forcefully, 'If it wasn't for me, you'd be dead!'

'Up until five minutes ago I was beginning to like you,' Wilson replied.

She gave him a steely glare. 'I'm yet to have that same problem with you.'

Wilson pointed towards the road. 'How about you just drive. Discussing this *logically* is getting us nowhere.' He motioned her forward once again.

She gestured wildly in the air. 'I don't even know where we're going!'

Wilson looked out the window towards the sun. 'Just keep driving. Sooner or later we'll hit a paved road. When we do, head towards Cancún. It's not more than a few hours away.'

'You want to go to Cancún?' she said in disbelief. Helena thought of the grand hotels and the white sandy beaches. 'How do you know Visblat won't be waiting for you there?' She slotted the car into gear.

'Because, he's expecting me to call. I heard it in his voice.' Wilson hadn't even had the chance to consider how Visblat could have known about the Mission of Isaiah.

'For all you know,' Helena huffed, 'he could be tracking us using the GPS on that mobile phone.'

She was right. In response, Wilson tossed the unit into the jungle. But as a precaution he had memorised Visblat's telephone number. Like Barton always said, there was no use ruling anything out.

26

California, The Americas
Mercury Building, Sub Level A5—Mercury Laboratory
May 15th 2081
Local Time 11:10 p.m.

8 Days before Transport Test

ANDRE FELT IMMENSELY proud wearing his new mercury labcoat. To him, it was an indication of his advanced intellect and now his career success. Alone in the laboratory, he stood facing a conductor bank—part of the Collider and Imploder mechanism. Davin had gone to bed hours before, leaving Andre with a list of twenty tasks that needed to be completed before morning.

The horseshoe-shaped conductor bank, making a constant humming sound, was a huge device, ten metres square and easily three metres tall. Dozens of white fibre-optic indicators flashed in perfect sequence across the front panel.

Andre had just finished fine-tuning the delivery mechanism—the critical point at which the conductors increased power to maximum so as to de-particalise anything inside the transport pod. It was now working perfectly. With a frown on his young face, he ticked off yet another completed task on his palm device.

The room was rectangular in shape, about half the size of an indoor football field. Its domed black ceiling was three storeys high around the outside and more than twice that height in the centre. In the event of a catastrophic failure—an explosion of some kind—the room would hydraulically collapse upon itself, thereby enabling the structure to absorb the force of a four megaton nuclear explosion. It was a marvel of engineering.

Independent of the rest of the building, the lab had its own reticulated airflow system and dedicated power grid. It was, without doubt, the most sophisticated testing area ever built. A thick glass wall ran the entire length of the western side of the room. Beyond the bombproof glass were various command areas and observation decks—all empty at this hour. An emergency exit was located at each point of the compass.

Scattered across the floor were all the components, according to the blueprints in the Dead Sea scrolls, which made up the time machine. Less than half of it had been installed.

Andre was away with his thoughts when, without warning, a hand reached out and grasped his shoulder. Startled by the contact, he jumped away, as if electrocuted.

'Relax, young man,' said Jasper Tredwell. 'It's only me.' He wore a grey pinstripe suit—Italian wool—with a red silk tie. A matching red carnation jutted from his lapel.

'You scared me half to death!' Andre panted. He nervously scanned the room for Jasper's escort, but he appeared to be alone. 'What are you doing in here, Mr Tredwell? You're not meant to be in the transport area.' Until the final test was completed, access was restricted to the members of the mercury team.

'Don't worry about me,' Jasper whispered. 'You're the one breaking the rules around here.' He gently scuffed his black leather shoes on the white false floor.

'I haven't done anything wrong,' Andre said defensively.

'That's not how I see it.'

Doubt crept into the boy's mind. 'Why, what have I done?'

'You're not keeping your end of the bargain.'

'But I've done everything you've asked? I have ...'

Jasper changed the subject. 'Is that the time machine?' He gazed towards a darkened area in the centre of the room. An egg-shaped structure twice the height of a man was covered with a large soft blanket.

Andre followed Jasper's line of sight. 'Yes, that's the Imploder Sphere. It's made of pure crystal. It took the mercury team over six months to construct it. An amazing design. There is *no way* we could have designed this without the blueprints from the Book of Esther.'

'What are these?' Circular titanium hoops lay on the floor.

'Inflator coils. They rotate around the outside of the Imploder Sphere. We pump a couple of petawatts of electricity into them and they form the low-level magnetic field that holds the electron matter inside the pod. Then we do a thing called *Z-pinching*.' Andre clenched his fists together. 'The matter inside the pod is violently compressed to make it reach *Planck* temperatures, forcing the nuclei to smash into each other and their protons and neutrons to be pulverised into fragments known as "quark-gluon plasma". As a result, the temperature soars to over ten trillion degrees. Incidentally, those are the same conditions that prevailed about a microsecond before the Big Bang.'

Jasper looked bored by the explanation. 'When will it all be finished?'

'In the next couple of days, I think. Mr Tredwell, what's this all about? You shouldn't be in here, you know.'

Jasper's gaze narrowed. 'I *am* in here.'

'You'll get us both into trouble.'

Jasper turned full circle, his expression blank. 'This lot must have cost a fortune.' He focused on the teenager again and came to the point, 'I need more information.'

'I've told you everything I know.'

Jasper moved closer. 'Why is Wilson Dowling in the scroll chamber?'

Andre thought for moment. 'I don't know.'

Jasper leant closer. 'I watched him reading the scrolls.'

'Wilson isn't capable of what you're suggesting,' Andre said flatly. 'No chance.'

'Why is he still even here?'

Andre was becoming a little nervous. 'I went to Barton and told him about the ECG waveforms, just like you told me to. I told Barton that Wilson Dowling should be excluded from the next phase. But he wouldn't listen to me.'

'You didn't try hard enough.'

'I think I tried *too* hard to convince him. We need to be careful, Mr Tredwell. Anyway, it makes no difference. Magnus Kleinberg checked out just fine. Barton has a Gen-EP candidate either way. We can't stall the process any more than we already have.' Then a thought came to the young boy. 'Out of interest, how did you see Wilson in the scroll chamber?'

'On the grade-one surveillance system.'

'You shouldn't be using that, Mr Tredwell,' Andre protested.

Jasper shrugged off the comment. 'I'm not worried at all.'

'Data-Tran keeps a hidden log of whoever's gained access. Anyone caught spying could face federal prosecution. Even *you* could be in trouble.'

The distinguished gentlemen replied, 'Not me. *You* should be the one that's worried.'

Andre was confused. 'What do you mean by that?'

'I used *your* security password.'

The boy's face went pale. 'Why would you do that?'

Jasper backed away a step. 'We have a deal, young man, and you're not keeping your end of the bargain.' Jasper's demeanour was totally untroubled. 'Don't worry, Andre, I'll make sure no one finds out about your little indiscretion with the security system. Remember, I used my considerable influence to get you *into* Enterprise Corporation in the first place. I have a vested interest in you. But in return, you're supposed to do your part for me.' Jasper fixed a piercing gaze on the young man. 'Barton's up to something—and I want to know what it is. It's *your* job to help me.'

'But why use my password?'

'Andre, we are being outsmarted here. Can't you see that?' Jasper moved closer again. 'Look, young man, I want you to be successful. I want you to make it to the top of your field. One day you could be the leader of the mercury team, if you play your cards right.'

Andre knew an opportunity when he saw one—it was time to play his ace. 'Barton did mention something the other day that surprised me,' he said innocently. 'Something about a *mission* of some kind ...'

KARIN SWIPED HER identification card through the reader and the door clicked open. She heard voices coming from the next room—and she froze. The lab was supposed to be empty. Taking great care not to be seen, she silently closed the door, rounded the corner to the observation deck and peered through the glass wall into the mercury lab. Jasper Tredwell was in there, talking to Andre Steinbeck.

What's he doing here? she wondered.

Karin knew that even the Tredwells were forbidden from entering the transport section, under Barton's strict orders. Unfortunately, the glass wall was more than a foot thick and she couldn't hear a word they were saying. But, not one to miss an opportunity, she concentrated on reading their body language.

'BARTON WAS STANDING in his bathroom,' Andre said, 'talking with Wilson Dowling. I know—I thought it was a strange place too. I took the risk to eavesdrop on their conversation. Barton was saying something about coded information in the Book of Isaiah.' The teenager scratched the back of his head. 'Maybe there *is* something going on here. Something strange. The Book of Isaiah has nothing to do with the blueprints for the time machine.'

'Why didn't you tell me this before?' Jasper said angrily.

On cue, tears pooled in Andre's eyes. 'I'm sorry, Mr Tredwell. Really, I am. I was afraid.' He sniffled. 'If Barton knew I told you this, he'd have me removed from the mercury team for sure.' The boy wiped his eyes, trying not to overdo it. 'I'd lose everything my mother and I have worked so hard for.'

Jasper could always spot a charade when he saw one; he was an expert at them himself. However, if playing along got him what he wanted, that was absolutely fine with him. He said, 'Andre, you need to remember that I'm the best friend you have around here.'

'I know that, sir. I do.'

'Now pull yourself together.' Jasper gazed at the silhouette of the transport pod. 'You've done the right thing by telling me. The Book of Isaiah, huh? There must be something important in there. Andre, I want you to find out what it is. There's not much time.'

'Only eight more days till the transport,' Andre said.

'Exactly. Report back to me as soon as you can.'

'But we have a problem. There's not enough time to do all the work I've been given already. Add in this … I just don't know.' It was Andre's way of asking 'What's in it for me?'

Jasper gave a sly smile. 'If Barton is caught out doing something that is not in the best interests of the company, he'll be off the mercury team for good. The team will be without a leader. You'd be well positioned,

Andre. And with my help—well, who knows?' It was the perfect political answer, committing to nothing and suggesting everything.

KARIN WATCHED AS Jasper made for the far exit. To her amazement, as soon as he was gone, Andre did a shuffle-dance across the floor, then threw his fists in the air as though he had just scored a goal in the World Cup.

Something strange was going on and Karin was determined to find out what it was.

27

Cancún, Mexico
Americana Hotel
November 27th 2012
Local Time 4:16 p.m.

Mission of Isaiah—Day Three

BRAKES SQUEAKING, THE mud-covered four-wheel drive came to a stop in very different surroundings to the tropical jungle and dirt roads it had just traversed. The pristine driveway of the Americana Hotel was lined with petunia and marigold plants—all in bloom, their colours rich and vibrant—forming intricate swirling patterns across the expansive garden beds.

A hotel porter wearing a white safari suit with gold buttons and pith helmet ran to open the driver's door. Helena climbed out and waved him back. 'There's a dog inside,' Helena said. 'Leave her alone. She bites.' Helena's face was bruised and her clothes were torn and dirty.

The porter spied the Doberman, teeth bared, staring at him through the glass and a look of terror came across his face. Helena handed him a twenty-dollar note as compensation.

'Don't open the door,' Helena said. 'I'll be back in a moment.'

A humid breeze blew in from the seaside, but the air was still uncomfortably warm. Helena had chosen the Americana Hotel because she had stayed there twice before—once with her father, and more recently on a secret rendezvous with Jensen Hemingway. She plodded up the familiar marble stairs towards the reception desk—

everything was exactly as she remembered. It felt good to be here. Wilson remained sleeping on the back seat of the car; his wounds, and the bumpy drive, had taken their toll. Helena hoped to secure a safe place to stay before rousing him.

The hotel was grand and majestic—tall white pillars supporting a broad peaked roof, crystal-clear swimming pools stretching in all directions. There were lush tropical palms everywhere. Afternoon sunlight beamed into the foyer, casting stretched shadows across the floors of polished parquetry. A dozen ceiling fans whipped up the air. Soft music played.

Helena strode forward with an elegant sway of her hips, hiding the fact that she felt self-conscious about her appearance. Her clothes were stained with blood that had turned dark brown and her shirt was tied at the front, with all the buttons missing.

Behind the reception desk stood two men wearing identical Hawaiian shirts of green and yellow. Helena recognised one of them immediately: Santos Rodriguez, the hotel manager. The olive-skinned, brown-eyed gentleman was distinguished-looking, even in the gaudy shirt, and his polished head gleamed in the afternoon sun, like a welcoming beacon. Helena had always thought him rather fun to be around—full of energy and style, and attractive. An openly gay fifty year old, he ran the Americana Hotel like a finely tuned machine. No one dared to cross him and everything was done precisely his way.

Helena stood before him and said, 'Santos, am I glad to see you.'

He looked up at her, not recognising her immediately. 'How can I be of help to you, madam?' Although he was Mexican by descent, he had been educated in England and his accent was one hundred per cent *Oxford*.

Helena eased her hair behind her right ear, exposing more of her face, and tried to smile. 'It's me—Helena Capriarty.'

Santos did a double take, recognising the characteristic way she rearranged her hair. '*Madam Helena!* Whatever has happened to you, my dear?' He was around the counter in a flash. 'Please, sit down,' and he ushered her to a group of lounge chairs. 'What can I get you? Anything!' He turned to his assistant at the reception desk. 'Get madam a glass of water. And some ice for that bruise. Quickly!'

Helena slumped into her seat. 'Santos, I need your help.'

He seemed very concerned. 'Anything, of course. What has happened?'

'I've had a very bad couple of days,' she sighed.

'That is plainly obvious, my dear.' Santos yelled to his assistant again. 'Get Doctor Wells down here, immediately.' He looked back at her. 'Are you hurt?'

She paused a moment to get her story straight. 'We were ambushed by bandits near Chichén Itzá. Armed men attacked us. We were lucky to get away with our lives.'

'Oh my goodness!' Santos snatched the glass of water away from the waiter's silver tray and handed it to her. 'Here, drink this.' He took the ice and placed it in a clean handkerchief. 'Is Mr Jensen with you?'

She held the ice compress to her face. 'No, he's not here. But I have a friend in the car outside. He's injured.'

Santos looked more concerned than ever. 'Do you want me to call the police?'

Helena shook her head. 'Santos, sit down. It's a complicated situation.' She gazed around the foyer. There wasn't another guest in sight. 'I need to call my father, immediately.' She cringed at the mere thought of it. 'Can I have a telephone, please?'

Santos snapped his fingers. 'A telephone. Quickly!' His assistant hustled into the back room. 'What about your friend?' He pointed towards the driveway.

'In a moment, Santos. First, I'll need a place to stay.' Helena had only a few hundred dollars with her and she didn't want to use her credit cards. That was the reason why she needed to call her father.

'We will give you the best villa we have.'

'Thank you. And my friend will need treatment from your doctor. He's been badly beaten.' She said nothing of the gunshot wound. Helena paused again, thinking. 'Santos, the car outside is not mine. We took it from the bandits who attacked us. I need you to get rid of it for me, quietly. It's a hire car, I think. Can you do that?'

'Are you certain you don't want me to call the police?'

Helena's mind reeled. What was she involved in? Who was Wilson, really? What uncanny destiny was behind the events that circled him? Her normal instinct would have been to run from a situation like this—yet she found herself trying to hold on.

Santos asked again, 'Do you want me to call the police?'

Helena came back to her senses. Again she shook her head. 'No, I don't.'

'I can arrange the disposal of your car,' he said thoughtfully.

'I'll make it worth your while.'

'There is no need, Helena. I'm just glad you chose to come here. We can abandon the vehicle, *quietly*, on the side of the road. Far from the hotel. There will be no connection.' He added, 'I was once a policeman in England, you know. Two years.'

Helena imagined Santos Rodriguez, one of the most elegant men she knew, wearing a blue constable's uniform and helmet. 'I didn't know that,' she said.

'Yes—after I left university. Not the career for me, fortunately. Very *blood and guts*. But I will say this, I saw a thing or two that prepared me for the real world.'

'Things like this?'

'Exactly. But let me add—those Bobbies looked terrific in uniform.' He gave her a wink. One of the hotel staff appeared with a cordless phone and handed it to him. In turn, Santos handed it to Helena, asking, 'How long is it since we last saw you here?'

She dialled the number. 'A year, I think. About that.'

'It feels like just yesterday, my dear.'

A voice immediately answered on the other end of the phone. 'Helena, is that you?'

She was quick to respond, 'Before you say anything—I'm fine.'

Santos stood up and backed away—he could see Helena needed her privacy.

'I've been worried sick about you, Helena!' Lawrence blurted in her ear. 'The police told me you hijacked a plane. Tell me it isn't true!'

'I wish I could tell you that, Dad.'

'It's true?'

'Please, Dad, I need your help. I don't have much money and I'm stuck in Mexico.'

'Mexico?'

'It's a long story.'

'I'm coming to get you! Where are you?'

'No, Dad. I got myself into this—I can get myself out.'

Lawrence's tone was severely condescending. 'And *how* do you propose to do that?'

'I know it looks bad, but you have to trust me. I know what I'm doing.' Helena knew her father would be there in a second to get her, given a chance. That was something she couldn't risk. Wilson was a fugitive and she needed to understand more before she introduced anyone else into the equation. Especially a control addict like her father.

'Tell me where you are,' Lawrence said. 'Now, Helena!'

'I don't need that sort of help, Dad. Just a bank transfer. Twenty thousand dollars.' There was silence on the other end of the phone. 'You've got to do this for me.' She tried to reassure him, 'I know what I'm doing. You've got to believe me. I'll explain everything when I see you.'

'Tell me what sort of trouble you're in.'

'I'm not in any danger. Not any more.'

'Julia's worried sick about you!'

'Please, Dad, just send the money and everything will be okay.' She held her hand over the receiver. 'Santos. I need your bank account number.' He quickly wrote it down on a piece of paper and handed it to her. Helena gave her father the details, then added, 'Send it from an account that can't be traced.' She knew Lawrence could easily arrange such things—he moved money under the table on big business deals all the time.

The request worried him even more. 'Helena, *please* let me come and get you.'

She was firm. 'I'm fine, Dad.' They argued back and forth about whether he should come to Mexico. Eventually, Helena said, 'If you come looking for me, I'll disappear. I will. I don't need that sort of help.'

'It appears I have no choice,' Lawrence said in a resigned voice.

'Thanks, Dad. Really.'

A man with glasses—middle-aged, tanned—approached the reception desk with some haste. He wore shorts and carried a small black bag. Santos mouthed the word *doctor* and Helena nodded in acknowledgement.

She said to her father, 'I'm sorry if I worried you. I'm safe. Everything will be explained very soon. I'll call you no later than tomorrow. It'll be fine. You'll see.'

'Just tell me the truth,' Lawrence said. 'Is everything okay?'

Helena thought of Wilson in the back of the four-wheel drive. She replied, 'It's nothing I can't handle,' and pressed OFF.

Houston, Texas
Capriarty Tower, Level 22
November 27th 2012
Local Time 4:31 p.m.

T‍ALL, BLUE-TINTED windows, at least twenty metres across, framed the view of the Houston CBD. It was a sunny afternoon without a cloud in the sky. Lawrence's office was on the top floor of his own building, twenty-two floors up. He leant back in his executive chair and gazed at the bank details neatly written on a square of yellow paper. It wasn't ransom money, he decided. It wasn't enough. Certainly not. Helena sounded in control—the call was not made under duress, he could at least tell that. It was her sense of reality that was his primary concern. Had she lost her mind?

'Stella, get in here!' Lawrence yelled.

A slim, attractive woman in a red business suit immediately appeared as if she was waiting for him to call. Stella—Lawrence's personal assistant—was in her early forties. Her thick brown hair was shoulder length, her features well-proportioned. She was cunning and quick, and when it came to getting something done, the woman was a magician. She could make the impossible happen.

Stella had a pen and notepad in her hand. 'Sir?'

Lawrence held out the yellow piece of paper. 'Find out the name of the business that operates this bank account number.'

She looked carefully at the document. 'No problem.'

'It's in Mexico, I think.'

She nodded. 'How soon do you want the details?'

Lawrence looked directly into her eyes for a moment. '*Yesterday.* Then get on the phone to Warren Lewis—tell him I want my plane ready to take off within the hour. This is important, Stella. It's got to do with Helena. I'm going to find her and bring her home where she belongs.'

'Anything else?' she said alertly.

'That's all.'

Before Lawrence could look up, Stella was already gone.

28

California, The Americas
Enterprise Corporation, Storage Section G2
May 16th 2081
Local Time 9:25 a.m.

7 Days before Transport Test

THE CRAMPED STOREROOM smelt of dust. The only illumination came from a bare light globe hanging from the ceiling. Hundreds of cardboard boxes were stacked high against the walls, their barcode labels faded. The tape holding many of the boxes together was brittle and dog-eared. Barton rummaged through the back of the room and eventually lifted a rectangular wooden case from the floor, propped it up and unlocked the lid with a small key.

Inside was the Copper Scroll of Qumran.

A rich, golden light reflected from the artefact. The sight made Wilson's stomach go into freefall. It resembled a relay baton—a solid tube of metal about twenty centimetres long.

'Amazing, isn't it?' Barton said.

'Can I pick it up?' Wilson asked. At a nod from Barton, he carefully lifted the gleaming object from its velvet-lined box. It was quite heavy, much heavier than it looked.

'A magnificent piece of craftsmanship,' Barton said. The pair pored over the artefact like two women admiring a newborn baby. 'If you look closely you'll see there's not a single weld or seam on the surface. It was forged in one solid unit. A team of archaeologists from Harvard found it buried under a metre of dirt, encased in a crude clay pottery shell. But there were two parts to what they found: a copper outer shield, and this, which was safely housed inside. The outer shield was made of three sheets of 99 per cent pure copper, 30 centimetres by 80 centimetres, which were wrapped around the scroll like Christmas paper. Unfortunately, the three sheets were so badly oxidised that the process of opening the scroll was debated for a full year before anything happened. After much discussion, measurements, X-rays, debates, it was decided to cut the outer shield away into twenty-three strips. It was taken to Manchester College, in England, where the copper sheets were removed with a small circular saw.' Barton touched the scroll with his index finger.

'*This* is what they ultimately found inside. The team who opened the outer shield were so surprised by their discovery that this inner scroll was kept a secret for more than sixty years, while they searched in vain for the treasure once housed in the Temple of Jerusalem. Interestingly, the text on the copper sheets is exactly the same as you see here, but it was unreadable, due to oxidisation, until it was cut apart and laid flat.'

Wilson spun the scroll in his hands and the tiny raised characters felt like Braille lettering beneath his fingertips. Feeling a strange sensation, Wilson held the scroll to his ear. 'Do you hear that sound?' He paused. 'I think it's vibrating!'

Barton smiled; he had been hoping Wilson would say that. 'Yes, the Copper Scroll is forged in such a way that it oscillates, like a crystal. It's actually an alloy rather than pure copper, with a small amount of titanium and some nickel blended into it—the result is a vibration of exactly 6.5 hertz. Interestingly, it was the vibration you are now feeling that made me pay attention to the scroll in the first place. I'm glad you noticed it also.'

Wilson held the scroll out in front of him, the harsh light from the bare globe doing nothing to diminish the scroll's beauty. The gigabit encryption that unlocked the secrets in the Book of Esther and the Book of Isaiah was located in the palm of his hand.

'Not everybody feels the vibration,' Barton said.

The harder Wilson gripped the scroll, the more noticeable it became.

'Can you read the script?' Barton asked.

Wilson squinted at the tiny characters. Clearing his mind of all other thoughts, he did his best to translate. '"In the fortress which is the Vale of the Achor. Forty ... *something*."' Wilson stopped. 'I can't read all these words.' There were some characters he had never seen before.

Barton rubbed his chin. 'Keep trying.'

Wilson concentrated even harder. '"Under the steps." I think that's what it says. "Entering the east. A money chest ..."' Another word he couldn't read. '"Be discovered?" I think that's it. "The contents are—seventeen talents."'

'That's very good, Wilson. I'm impressed.'

Wilson scanned more of the text. 'I can't read a lot of these symbols.'

'I would have been amazed if you could,' Barton admitted. 'This is not standard Hebrew. Most Hebrew texts—ancient ones—are religious in nature. But the Copper Scroll is something else again. Some of the vocabulary is simply not found in other ancient documents. You see, we now realise that the Copper Scroll was made *after* the other parchments in the Dead Sea scrolls. This makes perfect sense in a way. But the mystery is, if that's true, *how* did it end up in the Dead Sea caves? That is one of the many reasons everyone thinks it's a fake.'

'I don't understand.'

Barton explained, 'The Dead Sea parchments were hidden in the caves by the Khirbet Qumran Brotherhood in 68 AD, to protect them from the invading Romans. At first we believed that the Copper Scroll was hidden away at the same time. But carbon dating of the clay pottery the Copper Scroll was sealed inside suggests otherwise. We now realise that the Copper Scroll was hidden away more than 500 years later.'

'Then,' Wilson said, trying to process what he was hearing, 'whoever put the Copper Scroll into the caves knew the location of the Dead Sea scrolls.'

'Exactly. The parchments were locked away for almost two thousand years in total. The mystery is *why* add the Copper Scroll to the horde some 500 years after the others were originally hidden? What I realised was, the Copper Scroll was somehow linked to the books of the Old Testament. I later found the link to be the gigabit encryption it held. If the Copper Scroll had not been in the Dead Sea caves, I would never have made the connection.'

'Five hundred years, that's many, many lifetimes,' Wilson said.

'I can only deduce the Copper Scroll was added by the Khirbet

Qumran Brotherhood—they were the only ones who knew of the Dead Sea caves. This is interesting, because my research indicates they were believed to be disbanded, or killed, in 68 AD. But it seems the sect continued on long after the invasion of Vespasian.'

'Does the brotherhood exist today?'

'I'm not sure.'

'Were they the ones who made this scroll?'

'Again, I'm not sure.'

Wilson looked around the small storeroom. 'Why do you keep it in here?' There wasn't even a guard at the door.

'Nobody thinks this is the *actual* Copper Scroll. I had a duplicate made and replaced the scroll in the main foyer of the Enterprise Corporation building with a replica.'

Wilson felt the vibration of the copper alloy radiate through his palms once again. The sensation made him feel at peace, somehow.

Barton discussed the Copper Scroll for the next ten minutes. He was obsessed by its place in history. The intense conversation was brought to an abrupt halt by a knocking on the storeroom door.

Wilson had the presence of mind to whip the scroll behind his back as the door swung open to reveal a tall, thin man wearing a three-piece suit. He had bushy eyebrows, gaunt cheeks and a knowing smirk that reeked of unmistakable authority.

'*Jasper*,' Barton said. 'What a surprise!'

'You know me,' he said dryly. 'I'm everywhere.'

Barton began introductions. 'Wilson Dowling, I'd like you to meet Jasper Tredwell.' Wilson reached out to shake in greeting, but Jasper never lifted his hand.

'This is an interesting place to have a meeting,' Jasper said, an odd tone in his voice. 'Typically unconventional, Barton, as always.'

'I do try.'

Wilson took note of the white carnation blooming in Jasper's lapel. His nails were carefully manicured, his hands soft and supple. The suit was an immaculate example of European tailoring. His shoes were buffed to a high gloss. And his tie was magnificent—a glossy white with a herringbone weave through it.

'Won't you come in?' Barton said.

Jasper stared down his nose as if he was offended by the invitation. 'I came to tell you something, that's all. I won't stay.'

'Please join us,' Barton said, coaxing him inside. 'We were having an interesting conversation about the scrolls.'

The comment made Wilson uneasy, but he figured Barton knew what he was doing.

Jasper eventually entered the storeroom after a short, sharp breath of reluctance. The three men were now standing in an uncomfortably tight circle. To Wilson's surprise, the other two were seemingly going out of their way to ignore him, so he took the opportunity to study the pair without reservation. Even so, Wilson found it difficult to determine the relationship between the men: most importantly, who was in charge? Barton was uncomfortable—Wilson could sense that, at least—it was nothing obvious, but he sensed it.

'What can I do for you?' Barton said.

Jasper lowered his voice to a whisper, 'I came here to warn you.' His voice then resumed its normal volume. 'Someone's been using the grade-one security system without authorisation. I think we should lock it down. I wanted to check with you first.'

Barton looked surprised. 'You think someone's been using it?'

'I have a preliminary report. At least sixteen unauthorised incidents.'

'Sixteen! Who's behind it?' Barton asked.

'We're not certain. That's why we must conduct an investigation, immediately. Whoever it is, they've been successfully cloaking their identity.' There was another lengthy silence. 'Enterprise Corporation's security is at stake.'

'I agree,' Barton said with great conviction. 'We must launch a full investigation. I suggest we call in the police as well.'

Jasper shook his head. 'That's not necessary. We can handle it on our own. I think it's important we minimise any government interference. It's easier that way.' Jasper's eyes scanned the room, momentarily stopping on the empty wooden box that normally held the Copper Scroll.

'I trust your judgment,' Barton replied.

'Well—that was all I wanted to tell you.' Jasper seemed awkward now. 'I knew you would be interested, considering how secretive you have been about Project 81-07.' Jasper backed away towards the door, then stopped. 'Just out of curiosity—what *are* you doing in here?'

Barton didn't miss a beat. 'Looking for some research notes.'

'You keep them here?'

He crossed his arms. 'My older material.'

Jasper held his gaze, as if he sensed Barton was lying, and said, 'Fair enough. I just wanted to let you know about the security violations, that's all. You know me ... security first. I suggest you be careful—someone could be watching.'

'You only need to be careful if you have something to hide,' Barton replied.

'That's a ridiculous comment,' Jasper scoffed.

Barton smiled. 'Just testing you, Jasper.'

'This is not a time for jokes,' he replied. 'Definitely not.'

'The sooner you get to the bottom of these security concerns,' Barton said seriously, 'the better it will be for all of us. You're doing the right thing.'

Wilson chimed in, 'It was great to meet you.'

Jasper gave Wilson a short, hard stare, then turned to Barton again. 'Do you want the door left open?'

'Closed would be fine.'

It clicked shut and there was a stony silence.

Wilson eventually said, 'No doubt about it, there's an interesting chemistry between the two of you. Possibly toxic, if I'm not mistaken.'

Barton sat down on one of the storage boxes. 'This is bad.'

'Who was that guy, anyway?'

'He's the president of Enterprise Corporation. Second in charge here. To make matters worse, his grandfather is the chairman.'

'Is he always so friendly?'

'Be happy—Jasper treated you better than most. He doesn't like strangers much.' Barton paused. 'I think he knows why we were in here.'

'I had the scroll behind my back the whole time,' Wilson said. 'But he did see the empty wooden box.'

Barton stole a glance at his palm device. 'Yes, I noticed that also.' He thought a moment. 'You know, I think Jasper told me about the grade-one security system to spook me.'

'Why would he do that?'

'Either he's the one watching me—or he knows I've been using it myself.'

Wilson was surprised. 'You've been using it?'

'Yes. To watch you while you were in the scroll chamber.'

'You spied on me?'

'Yes, I did,' he said unashamedly. Barton reached out and carefully took the Copper Scroll. 'Things are getting more difficult to anticipate. Remember that chime you heard in my office the other day, before we went into my bathroom to talk? I wrote that computer program to let me know when I was being monitored by an external source. I will now lose that advantage.'

'I don't understand.'

'Jasper's going to lock down all the systems. Surveillance will be impossible.'

'That's a good thing, isn't it?'

Barton rubbed his chin. 'No. That's a bad thing. Knowing when someone has been watching me has been my greatest advantage.'

'But, *who* was watching you?'

'I'm not sure. And I couldn't risk drawing too much attention to myself trying to find out. The Data-Tran surveillance system is very secure and requires a court order to gain access to the information logs. That's what Jasper will do now. And when that happens, a lot of people get involved—that's not what we need. This is not the time for an enquiry.'

'But Jasper said he would keep it in-house.'

'There'll still be a lot of people involved.'

'At least you'll find out who's been spying on you.'

'True.'

Wilson felt he understood only a snippet of the pressure Barton was under. There was so much at stake. 'What happens when they find out *you* were using it also?'

Barton smiled. 'I'll blame it on you, Wilson. I'll tell them I thought you were a security risk.'

'Will that do it?'

'It will certainly get their attention.' Barton placed the Copper Scroll into the wooden case and locked the lid. 'As I said before, things are getting increasingly complicated. From now on, we need to be more careful. It's important that we stay at least one step ahead.'

29

Cancún, Mexico
Americana Hotel
November 27th 2012
Local Time 9:37 p.m.

Mission of Isaiah—Day Three

SUITE THIRTY-NINE WAS a freestanding two-bedroom villa with its own private garden, outdoor gazebo and deep-blue swimming pool. Every room had ceiling fans and the floors were polished wood. The décor had a Mexican theme, the colours yellow and ochre. Windows in the lounge and main bedroom offered panoramic views, north towards the hotel marina. It was roughly what you would expect for US$1,300 per night.

Sitting on the bed beside Wilson, Helena looked away as he began to open his eyes. *Why has he come into my life?* she thought. That single question had been running over and over in her head for the past ten minutes. Watching him sleep, she had been intently studying his face, the texture of his hair, and his hands—in an effort to understand.

Stunned out of his drowsiness, Wilson tried to sit up, but a sharp pain in his right leg halted his progress. He grabbed his thigh in momentary anguish.

'Take it easy,' Helena said gently. 'You're okay.'

'Christ,' he groaned. 'That really *hurts*.'

Helena dried her hair with a towel. 'I had a doctor clean up your leg and change your bandages; he's prescribed you some antibiotics. They're on the table, over there. Apparently the bullet passed right through you.' She was wearing a white flannel dressing gown. 'I was worried about you when we brought you inside. Your face ...' Helena winced as she looked at him. 'We need to put ice on that again.' She pressed the back of her fingers against his swollen cheek.

Wilson pulled away in discomfort. 'I'm fine.'

'The doctor said you were lucky the bullet didn't hit any bones.'

The bandage strapped around Wilson's thigh was tight and his lower leg felt a little numb, but the smell of food was in the air, which quickly took his mind off it.

'Are you hungry?' she asked.

Wilson smiled. 'You *can* read my mind.'

'Wait there. I'll be right back.' Helena disappeared outside.

The villa was spacious, the king-size bed warm and comfortable. Through a wall of tall glass, red and green lights glowed against the ebony blackness—boats bobbing around at an adjacent marina. It was the nicest hotel room Wilson had ever seen.

Helena returned wheeling a large trolley stacked high with all manner of dishes—everything from lasagne to nasi goreng. As soon as the food was within easy reach, Wilson shovelled a piece of chicken into his mouth, chewing only once, then followed up with a bite of a bread roll.

'You were unconscious when we pulled you out of the car,' she said.

Wilson noticed the dusky bruise across Helena's cheek. He gestured towards her with a half-eaten roll. 'Are you okay? Your face?'

She gently touched the injury. 'Yeah, I'm fine.'

'We got ourselves into big trouble, didn't we?'

'Yeah, *about that*,' she said. 'Are you going to tell me what's going on, or what?'

Wilson forced a comment through the food in his mouth, 'It's very complicated ...'

'I think we both agree, *that's* plainly obvious.'

The handle of Helena's revolver was sticking out of her dressing-gown pocket, weighing down the material and pulling the garment open at the front. A good part of her left breast was exposed. She had beautiful skin, something Wilson had noticed the day he first met her. He pointed, then swallowed. 'You might want to adjust that robe, not that I'm complaining.'

Suddenly self-conscious, she turned away and pulled the dressing gown across her and tied the belt more securely.

'Do you always carry that gun with you?' he asked.

She gave him a burning glare. 'If you don't take care of yourself, who will?'

'That's an interesting way of looking at it.'

'Stop changing the subject!' she erupted. 'I demand to know what's going on!'

It took a moment for Wilson to swallow. 'Look, I told you,' he said seriously. 'I don't know *how* to explain what's happening.'

'You're going to have to do better than that,' she said with a huff.

Wilson's thoughts wandered to his satellite-phone conversation with the mysterious Commander Visblat. Was it possible the second portal had been tampered with? Worried for a moment, Barton's advice echoed in his ears: 'Don't let anyone stop you from completing your mission.'

The longer Wilson stayed silent, the more Helena's irritation grew. Finally she burst out, 'There's a one-million-dollar bounty on your head, Wilson! You *have* to tell me what the hell is going on!' Her cheeks flushed the colour of ripe watermelon flesh. 'Christ! We could have been killed today. At least let me understand why! I saw what you did inside that pyramid. I saw you!'

Wilson took a long drink of water. He'd heard it all before. 'You have a bad temper, do you know that?'

'I deserve the truth!'

'Where's Esther?' Wilson asked, looking around for the dog.

Closing her eyes, Helena suppressed another outburst. 'I locked her in the other room,' she said, suddenly deflated. 'She nearly attacked one of the room-service boys. George was right: she doesn't like white folks, much.'

'Look ...' Wilson felt a pang of guilt. 'Thank you for saving me,' he said sincerely. 'I mean it. I would have been in serious trouble without you. The way you handled those soldiers was amazing.'

A pained expression suddenly gripped Helena's face. 'That's how we deal with our mistakes,' she said. 'We evolve.'

Wilson was confused. 'What do you mean by that?'

Helena stared into space. 'Nothing,' she said curtly, then dropped her gaze to the floor. 'But I will say this, if I knew *back then* what I know now, things would be different.'

'What would be different?'

'My mother ... she'd be alive if it wasn't for me.' Her gaze lifted to meet Wilson's. She was expressionless, frozen like granite—beautiful in her sadness—barely breathing.

Defying his curiosity, Wilson decided not to ask any more questions. If she wanted to talk about it, she would, and he began eating again.

Helena couldn't understand why she had opened up the way she did. The only person she had ever spoken to about her mother was Dr Bennetswood. And that was because she had to, more than anything else.

At that moment, Wilson realised he wasn't wearing his sunglasses. A splash of panic shot through him. 'Where are my sunglasses?' he said, rustling the sheets. 'I need them.'

'Why do you always change the subject?' Helena pounded the bed with a closed fist. 'I was being honest with you!'

Wilson grabbed her wrist, holding her arm steady. 'You don't understand—this is important.'

'You are *very, very* screwed up!' Wrenching her hand free, Helena left the room and appeared moments later with his sunglasses dangling from her fingertips. Wilson reached out to take them, but she pulled back. 'Not so fast! Tell me why you need to wear these all the time? They're not prescription … and you don't strike me as being even *remotely* fashionable.' She held them out, almost taunting him. 'In case you haven't noticed, it's dark outside.'

'Give them to me—'

'*No!* Tell me why you need them.'

'Why don't you try pointing your gun at me again?'

'I just might!' Helena threw the glasses on the bed and stormed into the bathroom.

Relieved, Wilson slid them over his eyes and flopped back on the sheets. A hairdryer switched on in the other room and he found himself feeling bad about the way he had reacted. The hum of the dryer eventually stopped and Helena reappeared, her hair shiny and golden.

Before she could say anything, Wilson said, 'If I tell you what this is all about, you're not going to believe me.'

'After what I've seen you do,' she said seriously, 'I'll believe just about anything.' Helena stood at the end of the bed, hands on hips, unmoving.

Wilson cleared his throat. 'I need to wear sunglasses because I'm vulnerable if people look into my eyes.' He was matter-of-fact. 'I have a weakness that makes people want to attack me. I know it's hard to believe.' Rubbing his bruised and battered face, he said, 'Why do you think I've had the crap kicked out of me so many times in the last couple of days?'

'I can think of lots of reasons.'

'That's funny.' Wilson gave an exaggerated smile, then continued, even more serious than before. 'Those men at Chichén Itzá attacked me because they looked into my eyes.'

A feeling of sickness suddenly filled Helena's stomach as she remembered the gruesome beating he had taken. It was unlike anything she had ever seen. 'How is that possible?' she said. 'You're deliberately being stupid to confuse me.'

Wilson stared her in the eye. 'People attack me—that's how it is.'

'Why take your glasses off, then?'

'There was no other choice,' he said sincerely. 'They were all over you.'

'But ... if that's true, then why haven't I attacked you?' she asked.

'I'm not certain.'

'That doesn't make any sense.'

'I agree with you.'

'Why is this happening to you? Why now?'

Wilson took a deep breath. 'What I'm about to say is the truth ...' he lifted his glasses. 'I was part of an experiment that went wrong.' He paused, seemingly choking on his words.

Helena encouraged him, 'An experiment for what?'

'A time-travel experiment.'

She laughed despite herself.

'It's true.' Wilson had expected her to be dubious. 'When I was sent back in time, a small part of me was lost in the transportation process. That's why I'm vulnerable. It stripped an element out of me and my eyes have a weakness. When people look directly into them, they're compelled to attack me. It's called a "trackenoid response". Humans are genetically programmed to destroy weakness. Those men at Chichén Itzá were no exception.'

'Then *why* don't I attack you?' she said again.

'I'm not sure.' He shrugged his shoulders. 'I don't know enough about it.'

Helena took a moment to absorb what Wilson had told her. Yes, it was the most ridiculous explanation she had ever heard. And yet she believed him.

'I'm telling you the truth, Helena. And you know what? I don't even care if you believe me. I've tried.' Wilson began eating again.

Helena sat down on the bed next to him, stunned. 'No one in their right mind would make up a story like that.' Seconds ticked by. 'I believe you,' she said earnestly, looking over at him. 'Wilson, I'm sorry about how I've acted. It's just that I get anxious if I don't know what's going on.'

'None of this is simple,' he said.

'How does Commander Visblat fit into the equation?'

'I'm not sure.'

'You're definitely not sleeping with his wife?' she confirmed.

Wilson forced a chuckle. 'No, I'm not.'

'That's good news, at least.'

In truth, Wilson was already having second thoughts about having told Helena the truth. 'I know this,' he said with obvious determination. 'I've already exposed you to more than I should. You said you wanted to know what's going on. Now you do. And if you're lucky, soon I'll be gone and you can get back to leading a normal life.'

'I can help you,' she offered.

'I've imposed on you enough.'

'You *need* my help,' she said resolutely. 'We have a connection for a reason. Have you thought about that?'

Wilson didn't want to—it was just too indulgent. Gingerly, he climbed out of bed and approached a pile of clothes neatly folded on the chair. His leg began to throb more insistently. 'There are forces at work here that are beyond my control.' He pulled on a shirt with 'Americana Hotel' written across the breast pocket. 'I have to go.'

Outside the window, across the hotel grounds, a glimmer of torchlight caught his eye. One moment it was there, the next it was gone. Turning off the bedside lamp, Wilson plunged the room into darkness. 'We've got company!' he said hurriedly, and knelt down to stare out the window.

Helena sprang to his side and searched the darkness, but could see nothing.

'Activate Possum,' Wilson whispered. Everything lit up in greyscale—and the secrets hidden in the darkness were revealed. Across the perfectly manicured gardens a group of men rapidly approached, five of them in a tight huddle, wearing suits.

'They have guns!' Wilson said. 'Come on, we're getting out of here!'

Helena squinted into the gloom. 'I can't see anything.'

'Five men are coming. You have to believe me …'

Helena hastily pulled on her pants under her dressing gown and tucked the barrel of her gun inside the waist strap.

Wilson silently slid open the glass door to the patio. 'This way,' he whispered as he watched the men hustled around the corner towards the front entrance. 'Quickly, Helena!'

A muffled voice suddenly called from outside: 'Helena! Open this door!'

She spun round. 'Dad?'

'Open this door, immediately!'

Helena turned towards Wilson. 'It's all right,' she said, trying to stop him from running. 'It's my father. Wait there!'

The door suddenly flew open and the foyer light flashed on. Wilson was blinded by the illumination as a group of armed men burst inside.

Helena yelled, 'Wait, Dad! WAIT!'

In the background, Esther went into a frenzy of barking.

It seemed as if everything had gone into slow motion as Helena focused on one of the men running through the door—the full head of black hair, short-trimmed dark beard and piercing brown eyes were all too familiar: *Jensen Hemingway.*

Helena yelled at the top of her voice, 'Everybody stop! STOP!'

'You've got a lot of explaining to do,' Lawrence growled. His daughter was half-dressed, her gown barely covering her. She had only one shoe on. Catching sight of a man—a stranger—out on the patio, Lawrence yelled, 'There he is … get him! Hurry! Get him!'

Helena attempted to block the group's approach, but Jensen moved too swiftly, wrapping his arms around her and wrenching her aside.

'He's a friend!' Helena yelled.

Three bodyguards sprinted past and Helena realised Wilson was in trouble. They would remove his glasses when they caught him!

'RUN!' she screamed.

Half-blinded by the light, Wilson heard the warning and stumbled around the swimming pool onto the grass.

Jensen's grip was strong on his former girlfriend.

'You've got a lot of nerve,' Helena seethed. 'Let me go, or I'll tell my father everything!' Suddenly free, she broke away, drew her gun, and aimed it out the open doorway into the night sky. With a squeeze of the trigger, there was a single blinding flash, accompanied by a sound so intense it felt like her eardrums would rupture.

'Everybody stop!' Helena bellowed.

With the bodyguards frozen, Wilson disappeared into the darkness. Esther's barking was even more furious.

Lawrence pressed his hand on his daughter's shoulder. 'What are you doing?' He snatched the gun from her hand and pulled her dressing gown closed at the front. 'You're coming back to Houston with me, young lady. No arguments!' Lawrence turned to his men. 'Well ... find him!' He gestured for the group to continue their pursuit.

Helena gave her father a hard stare. 'That man has done nothing wrong ...'

'He's wanted by the police!'

'He's innocent!'

'You hijacked a plane last night, Helena! You're in a lot of trouble.'

'There's more to this than you realise.'

Lawrence's face was a mask of worry. 'Helena, sit down! Over there, where I can see you.'

'Like hell I will!' and she stormed into the bathroom and slammed the door shut. She needed time to piece everything together.

Lawrence turned to Jensen. 'Watch *that* damn door,' he said with an agitated tone. 'She's not to go anywhere!'

WILSON LIMPED ACROSS the sand and waded into the warm waters of the Gulf of Mexico. His thigh began hurting even more, the saltwater biting at the wound. A sleek sailing boat was moored at one of the far anchorages. It seemed like his best option of escape, if he could swim that far.

Behind him, torchlight scanned the landscape. There was no choice and he dived into the choppy swell.

HOW COULD WILSON be a time traveller?

Helena gazed at herself in the mirror. How was that possible? Studying her own face, she decided she looked tired. So much had happened in such a short time ... and now Wilson was gone. She put on a hotel shirt and tucked it into her pants. He was gone! The mere thought made her heart heavy. She felt protective of him, and the strength of her emotion took her by surprise. And now he was out of her life, just like that. The magnitude of her emptiness was difficult to comprehend.

Lawrence had arrived—trying to do the right thing, Helena realised—and everything had been turned upside-down. One moment she was opening the door of her understanding, the next, Lawrence had blundered onto the scene to slam it shut. And Jensen was here also. Helena knew he was going to be furious about her choice of hotels.

Jensen Hemingway was Lawrence's most trusted bodyguard. That was a laugh, Helena thought. But it was her own fault for getting involved with him in the first place. She should have known better. Yet, for over two years they had been sleeping together, and her father knew nothing about it. Julia was privy to the truth but sworn to secrecy. Jensen and Helena had discussed it at length—if Lawrence ever found out about them, his reaction would be impossible to predict. It was something that used to amuse her, but now it seemed only a complication that she could do without. Somewhere along the way she had moved on, grown up.

Suddenly Helena gripped the marble washbasin—a familiar red haze filtering across her sight. She was seeing visions again. Wilson was in trouble!

The darkness was like daylight. How was that possible?

Wilson was swimming, struggling towards a large sailing boat. The waves were choppy. He was drowning! His head was going under! Then a boat appeared, just in time, and Wilson wearily hauled himself onto the rear deck. The boat was named *Number Twenty-Three*. A tall mast loomed above him, a glowing red beacon at the top. Wilson's eyes shifted in the direction of the resort.

Suddenly the vision was gone.

Helena tried to force herself to see more, but it was no use.

Wilson was on a yacht in the marina!

Helena tried to run out the door, but Jensen blocked her path, his chest in her face.

'Move!' she said, trying to push him out of the way.

'You didn't have to threaten me, back there,' he whispered, clearly angry. 'What if Lawrence heard what you said?'

'Out of my way, Jensen!'

'What is your problem?' He grabbed her arms, holding her still.

'*You* are my problem. Now get the hell out of my way!'

'Why haven't you called me?'

'I told you—it's over between us.' Helena wrenched herself from Jensen's grasp and strode towards the patio. Her father was out there, talking on his mobile phone. When he saw her approaching, he ended the conversation and reached into his pocket, producing a small orange bottle of tranquillisers.

'These are for you.'

Helena pointed at the bottle. '*They* are not the answer.'

'We need to get you better.'

Her stomach was in knots. 'Drugs are not the answer.'

Lawrence gazed at his daughter. 'Dr Bennetswood said this medication ...'

She stopped him in mid-sentence, 'You have no idea what's going on here.' Their gaze locked together. 'I don't need drugs any more,' she said confidently. 'The dreams are over.'

They both stood in silence.

'Give me time,' Helena said, 'and you'll see that I know what I'm doing.'

Lawrence reluctantly slid the pills into his pocket. 'I'm only here because I was worried,' he said.

Helena watched the lights in the harbour. 'I told you not to come.'

His brow wrinkled. 'Helena, you *hijacked* a commercial aircraft this morning! That man you were with—well, he killed a policeman. He's a serial killer!'

Helena remembered her visions and shook her head. 'He didn't kill anyone.'

Lawrence rubbed his face in frustration. 'Where's the aircraft you took?'

Her gaze met his once again. 'We crash-landed at Chichén Itzá.'

'Crashed?'

'There was nothing I could do.'

Lawrence stared at his daughter. 'How bad?'

'It was bad. The plane ran out of fuel and we crashed.'

'Have you lost your—' he stopped himself just in time. 'Do you know how much this is going to cost me?' Tension hung in the air. 'I'm very disappointed, Helena. I expect more from you.'

Her reply was more calculating than sincere. 'I'm sorry, Dad. Everything was out of control. There was no time. The police were after us. Really—there was nothing I could do.'

'What do you mean, *us?*'

She pointed into the darkness. 'Me, and him.'

Lawrence gripped her upper arm. 'You will never say that, ever again! Understand? That makes you an accomplice! Christ, Helena!'

She removed his hand. 'Okay, okay. I understand.'

Lawrence turned away, at the same time pressing a number into his mobile phone. 'This is not good, Helena.' He swore under his breath, then made a concerted effort to be positive. 'But you're okay—that's what matters.' He thought a moment. 'I know Hanson Manning—the owner of Texas Air. This is really going to cost me. *Christ!*' Lawrence turned away; he was asking Stella for the direct number.

Helena sensed a familiar presence behind her.

Jensen said under his breath, 'Did he hurt you?'

'No.'

'That bruise on your face?'

'I told you, he didn't hurt me.' She continued to watch the water.

'You were half naked!'

Helena turned. 'Your job is to protect my father. I'm not your problem any more.'

'I can't believe you came here … to this hotel. This is *our* hotel.'

'God, Jensen! Since when were you *sentimental*?'

Lawrence ended his telephone conversation and approached the pair. 'What are you two whispering about?'

Ignoring his question, Helena spun towards the water and Lawrence followed her line of sight, scanning the marina also. Esther was constantly barking in the background—scratching at the door.

'That dog in there,' Lawrence said. 'Whose is it?'

'I'm taking her back to Houston with me,' Helena replied.

'Is that *his* dog?' Jensen said.

'It belongs to a man from Bordersville. A man called George Washington.'

'How did you end up with it?' Lawrence asked.

One of the bodyguards, puffing from exertion, ran towards the patio. 'We searched everywhere,' he said. 'He's disappeared.'

Jensen warily scanned the darkness. 'Get everyone back here. I want a perimeter around this place. Get Stevens to the front door. You two, out here. No one is to come near this place, understand?'

The junior bodyguard nodded in reply.

Jensen turned to Lawrence. 'I recommend that we leave, now.'

'No. We wait until morning,' Lawrence replied firmly. 'We have to work things out with the police before we go anywhere. We're staying the night.' He turned to his daughter. 'Helena, you have to answer my questions ... all of them.'

'I'll talk to the hotel manager about extra security,' Jensen said. 'That lunatic is still wandering around out there somewhere.' He deliberately caught Helena's eye. 'Who knows what he's going to do next.'

But Helena already knew the answer.

In the distance, a red light began to move steadily across the water.

THE LARGE SAILS began to ripple, then, with a soft thud, they filled and the boat eased towards deep water. Wilson was just beginning to get his breath back as he watched the sparkling lights of the Americana Hotel shift across the darkness.

It was then that he saw the name of the sailing boat: *Number Twenty-Three*. It certainly meant he had chosen the correct means of escape. The Book of Isaiah was the twenty-third book of the Old Testament. It was yet another signpost.

Barton's voice rung in Wilson's ears: 'There is no such thing as coincidence ...'

30

Cancún Airport, Mexico
Capriarty Private Jet
November 28th 2012
Local Time 9:00 a.m.

Mission of Isaiah—Day Four

WITH A FROWN, Helena clipped her seatbelt into its buckle. She had not had a vision from Wilson since late last evening and she worried that she never would again.

Being the last person to board the plane, Jensen secured the door. Lawrence and the other three bodyguards were already in their seats. The familiar cabin of the Bombardier executive jet was narrow. The windows were round. Polished wood-veneer lined the walls. Half the leather seats, sixteen in all, faced forward, the other half towards the back in three separate lounge sections. An aisle ran down the centre. Esther was crouched between Helena's legs in the middle grouping, a new leather muzzle clipped to her jaw. The animal looked unsure about proceedings, but Helena stroked her reassuringly until she settled.

Lawrence smiled at the pretty young hostess. 'Tomato juice, thanks.' He turned to Helena, 'Do you want one?' She shook her head in reply. 'There's no use being upset any more,' he said assertively. 'It's done. We're going home. And you can take that stupid dog back to its owner.'

Helena hadn't said a word all morning.

'You'll thank me one day,' he added.

Jensen sat down towards the front of the plane, his back to Helena, trying his best to ignore her. But unable to help himself, he turned and said, 'And to think, I used to like Mexico.'

A prolonged sigh whispered from Helena's lips as she turned towards the window and stared at the flat, dry airstrip. If the last two minutes were any indication, this was going to be a long and painful journey. Outside, a strong steady wind fanned a towering wall of dust high into the air.

Captain Lewis emerged from the cockpit and walked down the centre aisle. In his early forties, he was wearing black slacks and a white short-sleeved shirt—four bars on each epaulette. He shook hands with Lawrence warmly, knelt down beside his chair as he always did, and gave a detailed briefing before they took off.

Helena knew her father's chief pilot well. Originally from Canada, he had moved his family to Houston from their home in Toronto, six years before, to take what he called 'his dream job' flying a Bombardier Global Express. The aircraft was the pinnacle of corporate jets, with the longest range and highest top speed. Anyone who knew anything about executive aircraft knew exactly what it was.

Helena listened to Captain Lewis's first few words then zoned out, her thoughts drifting back to Wilson again. She had reflected on the events of the last three days many times through the night. There were so many unanswered questions, so many complicated feelings that she found difficult to understand.

The engines purred as the small jet rolled to the end of the runway and turned on the dusty tarmac. Then, with a surge of power, it shot effortlessly into the clear, pale sky. There was not a cloud in sight as they banked over the Gulf of Mexico and streaked northeast towards the rising sun. As far as the eye could see, the rich-blue ocean was covered with whitecaps, the gusty wind mercilessly carving the tops off the short swell.

Helena sat back in her seat. She'd soon be in Houston and the FBI would be waiting for her. Not to arrest her, but to ask her questions about what had happened and why. Her father had taken care of everything; he was amazing like that. Lawrence had done a deal with Texas Air's owner, Hanson Manning, who had agreed—under duress, apparently—that Helena was an unwilling participant in the hijacking. Texas Air would claim the full insurance but, as a sweetener, cash was changing hands under the table—a sizable amount. A hard negotiator, Manning would come out of this scenario a certain winner. The surprising development was that Commander Visblat had gone missing, and the charges against Helena at Bordersville had been dropped.

Helena had been briefed by her father, again and again, not to admit to doing anything illegal. She was to fiercely deny that she pointed her gun at the Texas Air pilot's head and escorted him out of the cockpit. They would assert there was no gun with her at the time—that Wilson had seized it from her.

The plane reached cruising altitude and the hostess began taking breakfast orders. Helena was preoccupying herself with the ocean and the patterns of wind gusting against the water.

Time slipped away.

Suddenly, Helena's eyesight became blurry and the sensation of seeing something telepathically filled her mind. All night she had hoped this would happen again. But things were different this time: there was a blue haze surrounding her visions, not red.

Wilson was braced at the wheel of a Beneteau sailing boat—a single-masted cruiser with black Kevlar sails. The seas around the yacht were enormous. As the vessel crashed down into the dark-turquoise swell, the mast stays strained against the wind whipping across the deck with hurricane-like force. Ocean spray plumed high into the air as the bow speared a wave and came out the other side, in a relentless cycle, over and over.

WILSON FELT THE fury of the wind shuddering through the helm. Saltwater stung his face. It was exhilarating and frightening at the same time. He had always loved the ocean but had never seen it like this. Water flooded across the deck then spilled out the drainage vents. The height of the swell was growing minute by minute and the wind gauge read forty knots. The sails creaked; the boat was heeling severely to one side.

HELENA'S BODY TENSED as she watched the scene before her. If Wilson reduced sail, the tall seas would be easier to handle, but there was no way of conveying her message. The Beneteau crested the top of a wave and she saw an island outcrop in the distance. It disappeared from sight as the boat dived into the swell, only to reappear moments later as the yacht crested the steep swell once again.

Wilson was holding to a steady course.

Pressing her fingers into the armrest, Helena felt the sensation of being slammed up and down by the force of the ocean. Then, as quickly as it appeared, her visions were gone. Opening her eyes, she glanced anxiously around the cabin—luckily everyone was occupied with their meals. She jumped from her seat and ran to the opposite window. Wilson was close—she could feel it. There, in the distance, was the island outcrop he had been heading for. She scanned the water; there was no sailing boat in sight. He had to be right below them.

'Dad,' Helena said sweetly. She gently pressed her hand on his shoulder. 'There's an island down there I'd like to have a look at. Do you mind if we fly a little lower?' Lawrence seemed uneasy, but Helena turned on her daughterly charm before he could deny her. '*Please, Dad*—it would mean so much to me.' Her voice was like syrup. 'We're not in any rush. Just five minutes? That's all.'

Lawrence pointed his butter knife. 'Only a quick look, young lady!'

HELENA CLOSED THE cockpit door, put on a headset and sat behind the two pilots. 'Warren, there's an island down there.' She gestured out the window to the right. 'I've spoken with Dad, we'd like to take a closer look.'

Captain Lewis was very accommodating. 'Certainly, Helena,' and he promptly flicked off the autopilot.

'I saw a beautiful sailing boat down there,' she said. 'Maybe you could do a flyby. You don't mind, do you?'

Turning towards her, he said cheerfully, 'No, I don't mind. In fact, it'll be fun.' He took the controls and reduced power. 'I hear you had a bit of an adventure getting down to Mexico.'

'You could say that,' she said evasively.

'Well ... I'm glad you're safe.' He gave her a fleeting smile.

The executive aircraft gently spiralled downwards and the ocean grew larger and bluer in the window. As they swung east in yet another descending turn, a black Kevlar sail suddenly came into view.

'That's it!' Helena said excitedly. The Beneteau was ploughing hard through the swell, keeled well over. There was a man alone on the deck. Helena pressed her hand against the side window, trying to reach out, somehow.

WILSON DIDN'T HEAR the jet until it was almost beside him. Wiping the mist from his eyes, he watched the aircraft streak by, very low, and only a few hundred metres away. There were thousands of things to look at as the sleek machine shot past, but Wilson's gaze fixed on the hand pressed against the cockpit window.

He had no doubt who it was.

An odd sense of security filled him, knowing that Helena could find him, even out here in the middle of the ocean. At that moment, a rogue wave—an enormous wall of water—broke over the bow of *Number Twenty-Three*. The unusually huge swell engulfed Wilson, threatening to wash him overboard, the impact of the water knocking the wind from his lungs. Yet, somehow, the smile never left his face.

HELENA FELT THE icy temperature of the glass radiate through the palm of her hand—she was both happy and sad. The connection between her and Wilson was undeniable; that was reassuring. She yearned to be near him. It was ludicrous, but that was where she wanted to be.

The cockpit door swung open and Lawrence loomed in the entrance. 'That's enough, Warren,' he said authoritatively. 'People are waiting for us.'

'No, wait!' Helena replied, trying to hang on for another second.

'I said, that's enough!' Lawrence snapped. 'Back to Houston.'

WILSON WATCHED THE aircraft increase altitude, with a thundering roar, and race away towards the horizon. *Number Twenty-Three* dived to the bottom of yet another wave. A frothy wall of blue water spread over the bow and raced across the deck towards him, dousing his already soaked and weary body. Helena was gone again and so too was Wilson's smile.

31

California, The Americas
Mount Whitney, Sierra Nevada Ranges
May 17th 2081
Local Time 11:12 a.m.

6 Days before Transport Test

A FOREST OF GIANT sequoias crowded the hillside, their short, stubby limbs thick with green foliage. It was dark in their shadow. Some of the trees were more than fifty metres tall, with trunks five metres in circumference. Barton said they were more than two thousand years old—the oldest and largest organisms on the planet. As with everything, Barton had turned their hike into another lesson.

The leader of the mercury team bounded up the gravel path with little effort. Every few minutes he would stop, press his hiking stick into the ground and look back to Wilson.

'It's not far now,' he said again. 'It'll be worth it.'

They both wore climbing outfits: white overalls, backpack, bright-yellow survival vest, Raichle hiking boots. Although Wilson looked the part, he was sweating. The altitude—more than eight thousand feet now—was beginning to affect his breathing. By contrast, Barton appeared crisp and unruffled.

'You could've told me it was going to be this difficult,' Wilson puffed. 'Then I wouldn't have come.'

Unclipping his water bottle from his belt, Barton took a sip. 'You need to be prepared for the unexpected. It's all about having the discipline to continue,' he said, and walked on.

'We have only six more days to prepare,' Wilson moaned, studying the forest yet again. 'I can't believe you dragged me out here.'

Barton doubled back, grabbed Wilson's sleeve and led him forward. 'It's not far now.' He glanced at the navigation aid around his neck. 'Less than two kilometres.'

'This doesn't seem like a good use of our time.'

Barton released his grip. 'This is an *ideal* use of our time.'

As they walked on, they emerged from the shadow of the tree line and the landscape transformed to grassy tundra, the trail levelling out and continuing across a rather narrow and desolate plateau that cascaded towards a distant mountain peak. Wilson's breathing eased, as if coming out into the open had freed him somehow. The sun's warmth on his back felt good.

The pair continued without talking for the next thirty minutes.

Striding up the steepening incline, Barton was first to arrive at the summit. Mountain ranges surrounded them on every side, like majestic temples reaching for the heavens. Wilson's legs ached as he trudged up the last few steps and took in the full view for the first time. His mind instantly expanded—it was nature at its finest. This was indeed a beautiful place. There wasn't a cloud in sight, the sky was pale blue. Wide, free-flowing rivers cut through the valleys below. The forests all around them were lush and green. The air was chilly. A bald eagle swooped high on the thermal currents above.

It was divine.

Barton took a deep breath. 'These mountain ranges are formed by the San Andreas Fault, which passes right under us, here—where the Pacific tectonic plate butts up against the North American tectonic plate.' He gestured off to the left. 'The Pacific plate is over there—slowly shifting in a northward direction.' He gestured to the right. 'The North American plate is over here; its relative motion is in a southerly direction. As a result, you get all this.' His expression was filled with delight. 'What a wonderful world we live in.'

There was silence, then Barton said, 'Wilson, I've brought you here to tell you about the most valuable lesson I've ever learned.'

Wilson turned towards the mercury leader.

'Always stay focused on the positive. That's essential. I cannot stress this enough.' Barton wasn't even breathing hard. 'Your mind is not designed to defend itself from what is *inside* you. Negativity is by far your greatest enemy. Try to remain in the moment if you can.' He looked out at the scenery. 'You must do this if you want to be successful.'

'You brought me all the way out here to tell me that?' Wilson said.

Barton wouldn't be distracted. 'There is no use preparing for a mission like this if your head is not in the right place. Training is nothing if your attitude is wrong. You *must* remain positive at all times,' he reiterated. 'You *must* remain in the moment.'

Wilson bleated like a spoilt child, 'Tell me you didn't make me hike forty kilometres to tell me that …'

'You ignorant fool!' Barton had a rasping anger in his voice. 'I need you to pay attention to what I'm saying! I need you to understand how important this is! It's not what you've read or what you *think* you know that's important—it's how you act in the field. *That's* why we're here. If you approach your mission like you approached this hike, you will fail!'

Wilson was stunned. Barton had never spoken to him that way before.

'Wilson, you are rarely in the moment. You *always* look towards the future … and you have a tendency to become negative. If that is your attitude, you will *fail* your mission.' The steely look that had suddenly come into the scientist's eyes was gone and his voice was gentle again. 'Your mission will be difficult: physically, emotionally and intellectually. You will be travelling to another time. It is a concept *beyond* rational thinking. Nothing we do can prepare you for that element, except what I'm teaching you now: be positive, focused and in the moment, and you stand a chance.'

Something in Wilson's psyche altered in that split second. He shivered. It was unexplainable, as if he had been stabbed by a harsh reality that set solid inside him. Barton's words were branded in his mind. *Positive, focused, in the moment.*

Satisfied that he had made his point, Barton held his hand out towards the scenery. 'When you are under pressure, really feeling it, I want you to think of this place.' There was another long silence. 'Stop trying to predict how things are going to turn out. Learn all you can, of course—the facts. But leave your speculations about the future behind you. They will only get in the way.' The sound of his voice was soothing. 'This mountain range has been this way for thousands of years. Evolving, yes, but somehow always the same. That's very comforting to me, and I want you to remember that.'

They both sat down on the grass.

'This place will be here long after we are both gone,' Barton added.

Wilson tried to soak up what he saw around him. Mountain peaks. Forests. The colour of the sky. The way the river snaked through the valley. He tried to imagine the mighty Pacific and North American tectonic plates doing battle underground, beneath them. And yet this place felt utterly peaceful. It was like so many things in life: everything was more than it seemed—you just had to look closely enough.

'Remember this place,' Barton reiterated. 'It has always helped me.'

There was silence for the next five minutes. Wilson was trying to untangle so many thought processes that were rampant in his mind. He would think of this place when he was in trouble, he told himself. 'I will remember.' But there was an overwhelming feeling of dread in his chest, like a heavy stone upon his heart.

'It's a struggle to be positive,' Wilson said, 'when I can't understand why *I am the one* going on this mission.'

'It's your destiny.'

'But what does that mean? *Destiny?*'

Barton sat back and rested on his elbows. 'Let me tell you a story ... this also relates to the Dead Sea scrolls. Do you remember I told you about Flavius Vespasian, the Roman commander sent to reclaim Judea after the slaughter of the Twelfth Legion?'

'Of course ... when the scrolls were hidden in the Dead Sea caves.'

'AD 68 to be exact. The Roman Emperor, Nero, chose *General Vespasian* as commander of the Judean offensive because Vespasian had fallen asleep in Nero's presence while the emperor was reciting one of his poems. You see, many believed that the task to re-occupy Judea, and destroy the city of Jerusalem, was impossible. The Jews, led by Josephus, had proven their strength and cunning by destroying the Twelfth Legion and many in the Senate worried that Judea would supplant Rome as *master of the world*. Added to that, the walls of Jerusalem were tall and their defences strong.'

'So, Vespasian was sent on an impossible mission?' Wilson asked.

Barton smiled. 'Vespasian was a gifted commander and he gathered the Fifth and Tenth Legions and marched for Judea. His son, Titus, led the Fifteenth Legion overland from Egypt and they met at the walls of Jerusalem. Realising the city could not be breached without huge losses, or even the defeat of his army, Vespasian set about conquering the rest of Judea, one town at a time.'

'That's when the scrolls were hidden.'

'Exactly. Avoiding a direct assault on Jerusalem was Vespasian's master plan. He was able to do pretty much what he wanted in Judea because the bulk of the Jewish forces were holed up inside the walls of the city.'

Barton took a drink from his water bottle. 'Eventually, Vespasian captured the leader of the Jewish forces, Josephus, after a 47-day siege at Jotapata, and prepared to send him back to Rome as a prize for Nero.' There was a glint in Barton's eye. 'This is where it gets interesting. Josephus requested an audience with Vespasian, which he reluctantly accepted. At that meeting, Josephus proclaimed himself a "Messenger from the One God". He said to Vespasian, "You are to be Caesar, O Vespasian, and Emperor, you, and your son will be."' Barton held up a finger. 'But there were conditions. Josephus was not to be sent to Nero and he was not to be harmed.'

'So what happened?'

'Vespasian was not in line for the throne of Caesar,' Barton said. 'At a minimum, you had to be a senator for that. Even so, he was significantly moved by Josephus's prophecy that he did not send the Messenger of God to Rome. He kept Josephus in bondage, but safe, in Judea. Naturally, Emperor Nero was furious. This was in blatant disregard of his command. He desperately wanted Josephus paraded through the streets of Rome as a prize, then killed for all to see.'

Barton took another sip. 'Before the year was out, as predicted, the Roman Empire was in turmoil. Nero was dethroned and he subsequently committed suicide. And so began one of the most unstable times in Roman history. Galba succeeded Nero, who was killed by Otho, who was dethroned by Vitellius, who in the end committed suicide himself. During this two-year period and the instability that came with it, the loyal armies of Vespasian—in the middle of a war themselves, with the Jews—proclaimed Flavius Vespasian emperor in July, 69 AD.'

'The prophecy came true, then?'

'Not quite yet. The Senate refused to recognise Vespasian as leader and he was forced to send his loyal armies from Moesia, Pannonia and Illyricum to fight for the throne. The battleground was Rome itself, where his armies confronted the revered Praetorian Guard—the protectors of the imperial city—and the legions of Gaul and the Rhineland. After a furious battle, Vespasian's troops eventually took control, accidentally burning half of Rome to the ground in the process. With no other choice, the Senate endorsed Vespasian as emperor. At the same time, Vespasian and his southern armies defeated the Jews and burned Jerusalem to the ground—as he had previously been ordered.'

Wilson was astounded.

'And so began the reign of the Flavian Dynasty,' Barton continued. 'One of the most prosperous eras in Roman history. It saw the consolidation of Roman power in Britain, the building of the Colosseum and, most importantly, the foundation of the infant Church of Rome. In many ways, Josephus's prophecy allowed Christianity to take root in the modern world. And because of him, in a way, the Dead Sea scrolls are with us today, in one piece.'

'So what happened to Vespasian in the end?' Wilson asked.

'He lived until he was almost seventy and died of natural causes. And his son, Titus, went on to become Emperor after him—the first time the Purple had been passed from father to son.' Barton smiled. 'As a final odd footnote, Vespasian adopted Josephus into his own family, and the one-time enemy of Rome became Flavius Josephus and lived out his days as a Roman citizen.'

'Wow!' Wilson replied. 'Don't mess with a prophecy from God, whatever you do.'

Barton looked his Gen-EP in the eye. 'Exactly. *That's* destiny.'

For a brief moment, the heaviness in Wilson's chest was gone.

There was another long period of silence.

Barton gazed out at the scenery. 'You know, I've been coming here for more than thirty-five years. I found this place when I was scouting a trout river near here, called Angel Falls. Great fishing, by the way.'

'Your surname, Ingerson—that's a Norwegian name, isn't it?'

'That's right.'

'They were professional fisherman, weren't they?' Wilson had looked up the name on Data-Tran.

'At one time, the Ingersons controlled nearly all the commercial fishing in Norway.' Barton had a quiet chuckle. 'I argue that the need to fish is biologically programmed into me. Do you like fishing?'

Wilson nodded. 'Yeah, but I haven't spent much time doing it.'

'I'll take you to Angel Falls when you get back.'

It was a nice offer. One that assumed that Wilson *would* be back.

There was another long period of silence.

'Do you have any other words of wisdom for me?' Wilson said.

'I want you to focus on what I've told you already.'

Wilson admired the way Barton never wasted his words.

'Things are improving in my life. My mentors are anyway,' Wilson said in an upbeat tone. He lay back on the grass and looked up at the sky. 'Do you want to hear the definition of being positive? You'll like this.

'A man walks into a bar and approaches the most beautiful woman he can find, and says: "If you can guess what I have in my hands, I'll gladly sleep with you."' Wilson had a big smile on his face. 'The woman is obviously repulsed by the approach, and of course, she doesn't want to play. So he says: "Come on, just guess what's in my hands." To get rid of him the woman says: "A two-tonne elephant." The man peaks carefully between his hands and responds: "That's near enough—we have a winner!"'

'Is that what you mean by being positive?' Wilson said.

Barton was expressionless. 'God help us.' After a moment's thought he said, 'Look, maybe it is,' and a smile cracked his lips.

Wilson laughed. 'You see, I *was* listening when you were talking about being positive.'

'So it seems.' Barton lay back and put his hands behind his head. 'You know, when I first decoded the Book of Isaiah I was convinced it was a hoax. But as I continued translating I realised, in no uncertain terms, that it was genuine.' He ran his hands through his brittle white hair. 'I decoded something I knew was undeniably true—that *time itself* was speeding up. Every year going by, faster and faster.'

'Why *is* time speeding up?'

'Let me give you a quick physics lesson.' Barton sat up, happy to be giving another lecture. 'The earth is a giant rock spinning through space. Surrounding it is our atmosphere, and outside that, the ionosphere.' Barton clenched both fists and held them out in front of him. 'The earth is a *negatively* charged object.' He pointed his left thumb down. 'Space, and the energy that comes from the sun, is *positively* charged.' He gave a thumbs-up with the other hand. 'The problem is, our atmosphere—which is in between—is a very poor conductor of electricity.' He knocked both fists together and they bounced apart. 'Electricity moves from positive to negative. And, as a result, there's a continuous electrical noise inside our atmosphere. And it's *that* vibration that dictates many of the laws of nature.'

Wilson looked up at the sky. 'The electricity inside our atmosphere can alter the speed of time?'

'Almost. It's the magnetic frequency of the earth that can alter the speed of time. The reason why our atmosphere plays such a big part is because the magnetic frequency of the earth is calibrated by the electrical energy that comes from space. I did some research and that's when I ran into the Schumann Frequency.' Barton explained that a German scientist named W. O. Schumann had been measuring the earth's electromagnetic resonance (or electromagnetic frequency—EF) since the mid-1950s.

'You must have been disappointed,' Wilson said.

'By what?'

'That you didn't get a chance to call it the "Ingerson Frequency".'

'Again … not funny.' Barton explained how the resonance had been rising at an exponential rate for the past twenty-five years. 'You see, the Schumann Frequency has a direct relationship with the speed of time. According to the Book of Isaiah, the ideal frequency of the earth is 6.53 hertz.'

'The same frequency as the Copper Scroll.'

'You remembered, that's good.' Barton pressed his hand into the soil. 'If the magnetic frequency of the earth gets high enough, time speeds up. You've felt it yourself. Every day goes by more and more quickly. But there are additional indicators. Tangible ones. It's why the temperature of the atmosphere is rising. Why there are more earthquakes, tsunamis, volcanoes, storms, droughts. More lightning. It's all part of the way the earth tries to recalibrate itself. It's the reason whales ground themselves.' Barton had an unending list of symptoms. 'In humans, it causes lowered immune systems, miscarriages, chronic fatigue, increased levels of aggression and violence.'

'Violence?'

'That's right. Every living thing, plant or animal, has its own aura. The Schumann Frequency can *compromise* that aura. My understanding is, the more your aura becomes saturated with a significantly higher frequency, the more violent and paranoid you will become.'

'What is the Schumann Frequency reading seventy-five years ago?' Wilson asked.

'That's a very good question. According to the Book of Isaiah, things were at their worst at the turn of last century. When I went back to look at the data, I found that the Schumann Frequency was off the charts. My calculations indicate that a 24-hour day would feel something like a twelve-hour day does to us, here, now. Then, all of a sudden, the Schumann Frequency abruptly reduces to normal levels. The reason is that *this reality*—' Barton pointed at the ground '—is based on the portals being opened and the Schumann Frequency being restored.'

'What date does it drop?'

'I think it's important that we don't focus on dates.'

'Isn't that the date I'm supposed to open the portals?'

'It's actually the other way around. The date you open the portals will be the date on which the Schumann Frequency reduces. You see, we live in a holographic universe. All time exists simultaneously.'

'But you said the Schumann Frequency was already *reduced* seventy-odd years ago. So why worry about it?'

'Because *time* does not exist like a length of string—going from one end to the other. It exists all at once, and we have an obligation to play our part in the past. Let me give you an example. If you fail to complete your mission—if you were killed, say—theoretically, all time in this holographic universe would immediately cease to exist. In my estimation, an alternative universe would be created with a totally different history, and a different future.'

Wilson didn't want to think about it any more—it was too much.

'When Einstein was fifteen years old, he asked himself a question: "What would happen if one were to move at the speed of light and look into a mirror?" The answer is: you would see *nothing*, because the light from one's face would never reach the mirror. In my estimation, that's what will happen if *you* don't succeed. Everything will cease to exist.'

'No pressure,' Wilson replied. 'That's good.' His thoughts were in a spiral. 'Look, I understand about the electricity from space and its effect on the Schumann Frequency, but why does it need calibration?'

Barton rubbed his chin. 'It's affected by how many people there are on the planet.'

'You're saying that *people* can affect the Schumann Frequency?'

'Over six billion people can.'

'And the higher the Schumann Frequency gets, the more violent they become?' Wilson asked.

'So it appears. And the more violent and unstable they become, the worse the Schumann Frequency gets. It's a vicious circle.' Barton explained that the time portals allowed the resonance to be tweaked to allow the magnetic energy to be calibrated within certain levels. 'It effectively ensures the existence of *this* particular holographic universe.'

The pair talked for the next two hours, about the mission, the transport process and the energy portals. Barton reached into his pocket and drew out a hand-written note. 'This is a section I decoded from the Book of Isaiah. The scroll was written in 24 AD in the ancient city of Qumran. I think you should read this.'

Wilson took the piece of paper and opened it.

> To the pure, all things are pure, but to those who are corrupt and do not believe, nothing is pure. Mother Earth will be caught in a spiral, when time has lost proportion. It will be an era of rebellion and betrayal when the unjust prey upon the weary. Mother Earth will fight back with raging weather, bitter storms, oppressive heat, but it will no longer be enough.
>
> At this time, an Overseer will be appointed to strengthen what is weakened. The Overseer must be untarnished; not a follower, but rather, one who is pure of heart; one with no obvious religion. The Overseer must hold firmly to the challenge, so that with the guidance of sound doctrine, he may overcome the forces of opposition. As it is written, light will battle darkness.

With his hands shaking, Wilson folded up the paper and handed it back. There was suddenly more pressure than he could imagine.

Barton pocketed the document. 'You just need to follow the mission notes—sound doctrine—and you'll be okay.'

Caribbean Sea
130 Nautical Miles South of San Juan, Puerto Rico
December 2nd 2012
Local Time 3:23 p.m.

Mission of Isaiah—Day Eight

WILSON REMEMBERED THE dread he felt when he saw the decoded version of the Book of Isaiah for the first time; it made him feel sick to the stomach. There was just so much history behind what he was doing. Barton had stressed the importance of *destiny* in his journey; and while it was a difficult concept to accept, Wilson realised that destiny *was* very real—the life of Vespasian was a testament to that. Upon reflection, the story of his succession to Emperor *did* make Wilson feel better about his prospects of success.

A fizzing noise suddenly broke the silence.

Springing from his resting place, Wilson pulled back on the fishing rod hanging out the back of the boat. The reel was spinning madly. The seas around *Number Twenty-Three* were calm as a light breeze fanned the Kevlar sails fully open. In the distance, islands peeked over the horizon. Wilson pulled back on the rod again. The line tightened and a glistening silver tuna leapt from the cobalt-blue water, its streamlined tail thrashing from side to side.

Wearing only a pair of shorts and sunglasses, Wilson was over the worst of his wounds. He'd eaten well and regained some of the weight he'd lost using the Nightingale command. The weather was hot and his days had been spent fishing and lying in the sun as his body healed and favourable winds drove his craft steadily east.

The tuna felt powerful as Wilson, muscles straining, fought to bring it towards him. He bounded across the deck against the action of the line, fully understanding now why Barton liked fishing so much. After a good fight, Wilson hauled the tuna to the rear of the boat and flipped it on board. He took a knife, as he had done numerous times, and plunged it into the fish's head, killing it instantly. *Number Twenty-Three* had plenty of fresh water in the holding tanks but hardly any food left in the cabin. Fishing was imperative.

Wilson scanned the horizon. There were no other ships in sight and he checked the navigation computer one more time. Since leaving the Gulf of Mexico, he had sailed south of Cuba and was now just off the Lessor Antilles—a strip of coral islands that linked the Bahamas to South America.

This would be his last view of land until he reached the coast of Morocco. Satisfied that he was on track for the African continent, Wilson rested his head on a pillow and looked up at the mainsail as it gently flapped on the mast above him. The warm glow of the sun was like a healing balm for his body and soul.

Wilson wondered if Helena could be watching him at this very moment. It had been reassuring to see her fly past. Comforting, somehow. He wondered if her mental link to him was restricted by their proximity—but it was impossible to say.

The boat was barely moving.

Wilson's thoughts turned to Commander Visblat. He had entertained numerous theories about him over the last few days, many of them outrageous, but none of the pieces of the puzzle fitted together. Not yet. One thing was certain, though: Visblat knew why Wilson was here and what his destination was. He would be waiting.

Had the second portal been tampered with? There was no way of being certain. But for now, the plan was simple—sail across the Atlantic, through the Strait of Gibraltar and into the Mediterranean. From there, Wilson would turn into the Nile Delta and south to Cairo.

32

California, The Americas
Mercury Building, Sub Level A5—Mercury Laboratory
May 17th 2081
Local Time 9:12 p.m.

6 Days before Transport Test

IT WAS LATE EVENING before Wilson and Barton made it back to Enterprise Corporation. Still wearing their hiking clothes, they entered the high-security transportation laboratory. Barton looked well; the day spent walking in the fresh air had done him wonders.

'Here we are,' he said.

Wilson's eyes were immediately drawn towards a giant glassy bubble, under a spotlight, elevated just off the ground. The sphere was encircled by three polished rings of titanium, like thick silver hula-hoops, that appeared to rotate in some complex fashion around the exterior.

'That is the Imploder Sphere,' Barton announced. 'Or *transport pod*, as I like to call it.' The clear globe was surrounded by fifty-six laser guns—five-terawatt particle atomisers—mounted at a variety of angles, all pointing towards the centre.

It made Wilson nervous just to look at it. The entire laboratory was crowded with conductor banks, battery packs and computers. Thick cables ran everywhere. 'I suppose I get in there, you shoot those, and I disappear.'

'Correct.'

Wilson took a deep breath. Only an idiot would allow their molecules to be broken up and accelerated to 186,000 miles per second, he thought. 'Maybe I *am* the man for the job,' he said. Walking between the lasers, he pressed his hand on the smooth surface of the pod. It was warm to the touch. 'This thing is vibrating!'

Barton nodded. 'The transport pod is made of pure crystal. When it's heated to the right temperature, the carbon compound oscillates. That's a key element in the time-travel process. By varying the temperature of the pod we can change the frequency of the energy inside and thus alter the destination in time we send you to.' Barton rested his hand on one of the giant metallic hoops.

'What does the vibration of the pod have to do with it?'

'The higher the frequency, the further back in time you travel. Therefore, the hotter the transport pod, the further back you go.'

'Yeah, but how? Why?'

Barton cupped his hands together like he was holding a ball in his fingers. 'The earth is encased by an electromagnetic field. The time-travel process works by passing energy *through* that magnetic field. The transport pod allows us to convert matter into pure energy and inject that energy *into* the magnetic field encasing the earth, via that.' He indicated a diamond-shaped scaffold suspended in the air at the far end of the room. Dozens of thick power cables draped from it and led to a series of conductors. 'The four titanium shafts that make up that diamond are highly charged magnetic poles, set up in opposing directions. When we energise them with enough electricity—about twenty petawatts—the opposing forces open a chink in the magnetic field of the earth. That's called a Z-pinch. In theory, the result is a wormhole effect. Depending on the frequency of the energy that goes in—that's the date the energy gets recreated.'

Wilson felt panic coming on. It was only Barton's unquestioned confidence, and the calmness in his eyes, that stopped him from completely freaking out.

Barton said, 'Your unique chromosome structure allows us to take you apart, with these.' He pointed at the five-terawatt particle laser guns surrounding the transport pod. 'They'll convert your molecules into pure energy, known as "quark-gluon plasma". Then, with an encrypted frequency, you'll get sucked into the magnetic field of the earth.' He pointed to the diamond-shaped scaffolding again. 'That's called the Inflator.'

'You're sure this is going to work?' Wilson said, sounding dubious.

'I didn't invent it—I just built it,' Barton replied.

It was not what Wilson wanted to hear.

The mercury team leader smiled. 'I'm certain it will be okay.' For the first time it seemed as if Barton was unsure.

Wilson's confidence was suddenly in freefall. 'Don't bullshit me, Barton. Is this going to work, or not?'

Barton's expression was composed again. 'Nothing is certain, Wilson. But I will say this, from the deepest part of me: I believe this *will* work. I believe *we are* doing the right thing. This *is* destiny. I wouldn't say that if I didn't mean it.' This time his expression didn't waver.

Wilson gazed at the complexity of the time machine. Because he couldn't understand it fully, it frightened him. It was a natural reaction, but one that would not be impossible to overcome.

Sensing Wilson's fear, Barton said, 'I have a confession to make.' He stood tall and composed. 'There is a second Gen-EP candidate—someone with the same genetic building blocks as you. He was my contingency plan in case things didn't work out.' Barton rubbed his chin. 'I want you to know, I believe *you* are the Overseer.'

'I vote that we send the other guy anyway,' Wilson said dryly.

Barton shook his head. 'You *are* the Overseer, Wilson. I'm certain of it.'

Fear and curiosity were running parallel in Wilson's mind. 'What if it doesn't work? I mean … all this.'

Barton thought a moment and said, 'It will work. The Book of Esther was written by—' he struggled for exactly the right words, '—by *God himself*. You are never going to get a better insurance policy than that.'

'I still think we should consider sending the other guy.'

A THICK GLASS wall, with a green tinge, ran down one side of the laboratory. On the other side was the primary command centre. The mercury team were inside and Barton looked pleased to see them. 'It's been a very long day,' he whispered. 'So be careful what you say.' The pair walked down a narrow hallway and turned left twice. Barton gave Wilson a reassuring nod before he pushed open the door.

Numerous three-dimensional holographic images floated in mid-air. All twelve members of the mercury team were in attendance, some standing, others sitting down. Simulation programs were running on every screen. The atmosphere was dominated by a studious silence.

Davin looked up, obviously surprised. 'You're back!'

'How is everything?' Barton replied.

'Almost there.' Davin popped a chocolate biscuit into his mouth. A half-eaten packet sat on the table in front of him.

Vibrant as ever, Karin jumped up from her chair and proudly held forward her digital worksheet. Her chestnut hair was impeccable, her eyes bright. As Barton took the page, her hand touched his, ever so softly, and lingered there. It was only very subtle, but Wilson noticed that Barton made no attempt to pull away. Wilson scrutinised the lengthy gaze that passed between the pair. A long, fixed stare ... too long. Barton clapped his hands together, ending the moment between them.

'This is fantastic!' Barton addressed the group collectively. 'Thank you all for your efforts. I know this has been a very difficult project and I can appreciate the sacrifices you are all making.' He paused. 'I have good news!' Everyone was listening intently. 'I have selected Wilson Dowling as our transport subject. Please factor that into all your equations. In six days we will be sending him on a journey of discovery.'

There was brief applause.

Andre approached, grimfaced, and spoke quietly in Barton's ear. 'I need to talk to you, *in private*,' he said.

'What seems to be the problem?' Barton replied.

Davin appeared equally confused by the boy's actions.

'Certainly, Andre, step outside.' Barton opened the door and gestured into the hallway. 'You too, Wilson.'

'I want to talk to you alone!' Andre insisted.

Barton was firm. 'Step outside, please.' He ushered them both into the corridor and closed the door. 'Now, what seems to be the problem?'

'I can't talk in front of Wilson,' Andre said. 'This is about him.'

Barton was expressionless. 'Wilson, wait down there please.'

Wilson plodded away, the hushed conversation continuing behind him. It sounded calm at first, but the voices began to rise and a strained tone came into their speech. Andre began to whine and bleat, noticeably distressed. Wilson looked over his shoulder. Barton's arms were crossed and he didn't look happy at all. Andre pointed accusingly down the hall in Wilson's direction.

Kid, do me a favour, Wilson thought to himself. *Tell Barton to use the other Gen-EP candidate and I'll be forever in your debt.* Trying not to listen to what they were saying, Wilson leant against the wall—there were so many other things to think about. Time travel, for example; he wondered if it would hurt. When Wilson looked up again, Davin and Karin had joined the hallway congregation.

Barton appeared agitated. 'I'm sorry, Andre,' he said loudly, 'I won't discuss it any more! This is the way it has to be.' He called out, 'Wilson, come here!' Barton tugged the mercury badge from Andre's labcoat and turned to Karin. 'Get Andre's worksheet. *Now!*'

She hesitated for a moment, then scurried inside.

Wilson approached slowly. Things didn't look too good in idyllic ol' mercury land.

Andre had turned pale. 'You're making a mistake,' he said under his breath.

'Get him out of here,' Barton ordered.

Everyone was grim-faced as Davin led Andre away. The boy made eye contact with Wilson as he passed; his expression screamed unhappiness and anger.

'What's going on?' Wilson asked.

Barton looked flustered. 'It seems we have put too much pressure on that young lad.' Karin appeared moments later and handed Barton a digital worksheet. Barton carefully scanned the pages, then said, 'Karin, take care of Wilson. Make sure he gets back to his room.' With that, he wandered off down the hall in a daze.

Wilson turned to Karin. 'What was that all about?'

'Andre's off the mercury team,' she replied coolly. 'He was caught using the grade-one security system. What a foolish boy.'

Wilson couldn't understand why Barton hadn't told him about this—they had just spent the entire day together. Surely, he must have known.

'Andre was a valuable member of the team,' Karin said with some regret.

They both stood for a moment without speaking.

'Why is it that you and I are always left standing in a corridor?' Wilson said, trying to lighten the mood. He was referring to the first time they met, at Pacifica University.

'It seems to work out that way, doesn't it?' Karin replied. 'Is this your first time inside the transport lab?'

'Yes.' He focused on her. 'Apparently, that's where my molecules are going to be disassembled at the speed of light. By the way, thanks for bringing me to Enterprise Corporation.' His comment reeked of sarcasm. 'My life was so boring before I met you.'

She flashed a perfect smile. 'Come inside, I'll show you around.'

Karin gave Wilson a full tour and introduced him to the members of the mercury team he had not met before. She was a model of professional courtesy. It was interesting, but no one in the room appeared to be perturbed by Andre's sudden disappearance. Wilson stood next to the glass wall and stared into the mercury lab, the transport pod glowing ominously under a bank of spotlights. For some reason, nothing felt right.

'Are you nervous?' Karin asked.

Wilson stared at the bubble of crystal. 'Wouldn't you be?'

She kept her tone bright. 'The mercury team will get you through.' Flicking back her shiny dark hair, she was a picture of self-confidence. 'I think you are very brave to do this. I'm impressed.' She looked him up and down, studying him. 'Yes, brave.'

'I think *stupid* is the word you are looking for.' Wilson was privy to the truth about the Mission of Isaiah and travelling *backwards* in time; if Karin knew, she would certainly agree with him.

'No, definitely brave,' she reiterated, as if confirming the life-threatening danger he was soon to be in.

33

The Nile River, Egypt
Eight Kilometres North of Cairo
December 20th 2012
Local Time 4:40 p.m.

Mission of Isaiah—Day Twenty-Six

AN UNSEASONABLY WARM breeze blew from across the desert.

In the distance, a bright-orange sunset splashed its rich colours against the tall African sky, the mighty Nile reflecting the image off her windswept surface. The Nile, the longest river in the world, was the only source of life in these parts. A huge body of water, hundreds of metres wide and over six thousand kilometres long, it flowed through eight other countries—from its higher elevation tributaries in the south—before reaching Egypt, crossing the barren Sahara Desert and eventually emptying into the Mediterranean Sea.

Standing alone at the helm of *Number Twenty-Three*, Wilson might have been an advertisement for an adventure-travel magazine. He wore long pants, no shirt, a cap and sunglasses. The trip from Mexico had taken three weeks and his skin was tanned a deep brown, he was unshaven and his hair had grown longer, bleached slightly by the sun.

Lush crops of cotton flanked both sides of the broad river, their green-and-gold stalks shimmering in the breeze. Replacing the annual flood of the Nile, a complex irrigation system pumped water inland over the banks for miles in both directions. It would be easy to imagine there was no desert at all in Egypt, but every now and then the sandy dunes peaked over the greenery to give away their presence.

The river itself was crowded with boats—Egyptian feluccas: small rectangular-sailed vessels with a low, wide hull. Wilson smiled as he passed the expressionless, unfriendly-looking old men piloting the boats. With skin resembling battered leather, they gave the appearance of having sailed these waters all their lives. To a man, each of them had a rolled cigarette hanging precariously from his lips as they nonchalantly zigzagged their cargo up and down the river.

Wilson imagined what it would have been like here thousands of years before: giant Egyptian galleys, loaded with soldiers in battledress, relentlessly patrolling these waters. The Nile had required constant protection—from the Romans to the north, and the Nubians to the south. It was by far the easiest way to invade. But the pharaohs protected the river with great skill and no invading army had ever successfully arrived via that route.

Wilson continued to conjure up images of the past.

The Nile was used to transport pink granite, basalt and alabaster from the distant quarries to the south, near Aswan. The materials were used in conjunction with sandstone, quarried not far from here, to build the mighty pyramids. Men with ropes pulled enormous barges from the shore wearing only loincloths in the searing heat of the day. It would have been amazing here, Wilson thought; a cradle of modern civilisation. But it was a civilisation that had suffered much turmoil since the days of the pharaohs. The list of conquering armies that had marched across these lands was long, and the Egyptian people had suffered greatly—under the Persians, the Greeks, the Romans, Turks, Arabs, French and English. Forever this land would bear the scars of their occupations.

A rich crimson glow now painted the sky as the sun dipped behind the horizon, the serene waters of the Nile flickering crimson in sympathy. In the distance, the sound of a bustling metropolis gradually filled the air. Cairo, the largest city in Africa, was slowly coming into view.

A luxury sixty-foot motor cruiser sped in Wilson's direction—a British-built Sunseeker—the drone of its diesel engines somehow out of place here. From its stern, a tall wake fanned across the smooth river, causing feluccas to drastically alter direction to meet the wave head-on. This was already a land of great contrasts, Wilson realised, where the modern met the ancient and the desert met the Nile.

A silhouette of dozens of skyscrapers, lights glistening in the dusk, marked the city centre. And Wilson knew that, just across the valley, some ten kilometres away on the desert plateau, was the ancient Giza complex and the Pyramid of Khafre.

THE SCHUMANN FREQUENCY

California, The Americas
Mercury Building Gardens
May 18th 2081
Local Time 8:45 a.m.

5 Days before Transport Test

THE TABLE WAS neatly set for breakfast. As Barton had ordered, everything was low fat and healthy: muesli, fresh fruit, yoghurt, brown toast. There was even Vegemite—a token effort to make Wilson feel at home. The smell of fresh coffee hung in the air.

'Now,' Barton said, 'the second portal.' He touched his worksheet with his digital marker and a detailed diagram appeared. 'Egypt is much more complex.'

'How do I get from Mexico to Egypt?' Wilson asked.

'Getting from place to place should be relatively easy. We can talk about that later.' Barton pressed his marker on the document and it became three-dimensional, giving exceptional detail, like an interactive video. 'This is the Pyramid of Khafre, near Cairo. This 4500-year-old pyramid is the *second* portal as chronicled in the Mission of Isaiah. The one next to it is the Pyramid of Khufu; they're the two largest pyramids in the world. Khufu is 137 metres tall, Khafre is smaller by some few metres.' Barton pressed the worksheet with his digital marker again. 'You enter the portal *here*, via the Sphinx.'

Wilson had seen photographs of the ominous sandstone statue many times. A massive lion, on its belly, front paws extended, its head held high: the head of the Pharaoh Khafre. Additional details flashed up on the side of the page:

The Sphinx

Length: 57 metres
Width: 6 metres
Height: 20 metres
Commissioned by: Pharaoh Khafre, Fourth Dynasty
 born 2558 BC—died 2532 BC
Arabic Name: *Abu al-Hôl*
 (English Translation: Father of Terror)

Wilson asked, 'Why "Father of Terror"?'

'It is said,' Barton replied, 'that anyone who tampers with the Sphinx will be cursed for all eternity. Legend says the beast uproots itself at night and prowls the darkness, devouring the souls of those who threaten to desecrate it. And there's good reason, because *this* is the entry point to the second portal.'

Barton drew a direct line from the Sphinx to the Pyramid of Khafre. 'It's more than 500 metres between *here* and *here*. You enter via a secret doorway.'

It appeared on the screen in great detail.

'It's located between the front paws, through a stone breastplate known as the "Dream Stela". You are going to have to study some Egyptian hieroglyphs.' He fleetingly smiled in Wilson's direction. 'Based on your Hebrew, that shouldn't be too much of a problem.'

'Once you're inside,' Barton ran his marker under the causeway, 'a tunnel will lead you in the direction of the pyramid. This is where it starts to get complicated.' He took a brief sip of coffee. 'You enter the Labyrinth of Khafre, a series of staircases and tunnels. There are five decision chambers you must successfully negotiate to get inside the pyramid—choices you must make. You will have to study hard to be able to complete this section, and I can't help you with the questions, because I'm not certain what the riddles will be. According to the text, the riddles change every day.'

How is that possible? Wilson thought. He gazed at the table of food in front of him, but his appetite was gone. There were just too many scenarios to think about.

The Nile River
Cairo, Egypt
December 20th 2012
Local Time 5:20 p.m.

Mission of Isaiah—Day Twenty-Six

NEARING THE DARKENING shore, Wilson made sure his sunglasses were held firmly at the back with a rubber band. He lowered the sails down and *Number Twenty-Three* drifted between a group of feluccas and nudged gently against the sandbank. Wilson jumped ashore; he was standing on dry land for the first time in many weeks and his legs began to quiver.

The aluminium mast towered imposingly above him and he realised it was a sight he had truly grown to love. He would buy a sailing boat just like it one day, if he ever managed to get home alive. Affectionately tapping his hand on the bow, he knew he would probably never see *Number Twenty-Three* again and that meant having to find another means of transport when he was done here. If Chichén Itzá was any indication, utter chaos would reign when the second portal was activated.

CARS AND MOTOR scooters, headlights ablaze, sped chaotically through the streets of Cairo as if there were no road rules at all. People hurried along the footpath in both directions—mostly men in suits, but there was the occasional beggar wearing nothing more than rags. The buildings, too, were a mixture of modern well-lit offices interspersed with rundown dwellings that looked as if they had not been inhabited in a hundred years. In size and magnitude it seemed like any other city as Wilson strolled confidently towards the noisy street corner. It was just what he'd hoped for; busy and impersonal, somewhere he could move around unnoticed. He was on a mission prophesied through the ages, he told himself, and nothing would stop him.

Wilson hadn't walked more than five blocks when a stout man dressed in red and white striped robes approached. The accent was Arabic.

'You need guide, yes?'

Wilson shook his head. 'No guide.'

The little Egyptian grabbed Wilson's wrist. 'I show you sights, yes? Magnificent city. Yes ... magnificent! Ancient, beautiful, wondrous!' The dark-skinned local was less than five feet tall, with a well-groomed handlebar moustache. A scarlet fez with a ragged black tassel perched precariously on his head. It was clear the little man liked his food and drink—judging by his bulging waistline; equivalent to about seven months pregnant, Wilson decided.

'Please, master ... I show you sights,' the local said expectantly.

Wilson pulled himself free. 'No guide, thank you.'

'I am Farouk Nasser,' the man said proudly, his words a little slurred. 'Best guide in Cairo. I show you everything.'

The smell of alcohol wafting on his breath, Farouk was noticeably unsteady on his feet. He gestured in the direction of the river and made a boat shape with both hands. 'You get off sailing boat, yes? I take you to best hotels. Bars. *Women*.' He swayed his podgy little hips in a rotating motion. Seeing that Wilson was not to be seduced by this sensual display, he suggested something more cultural. 'Tour ancient city, yes? Pyramids. You want taxi? I take you where you want.'

'How do I get to Giza?' Wilson asked

Farouk smiled broadly; his crooked, irregular teeth were stained brown. 'I take you tomorrow. *First*, hotel. *Fine hotel!*'

Wilson shook his head. 'I want to go to the pyramids, now.'

'No good now. *Tomorrow!* First, hotel.'

People hurried past them on the footpath.

'Tell me how I get to the pyramids,' Wilson asked again.

'Not good now!' he said vehemently. '*Tomorrow!*'

Wilson started walking. 'If you don't want to give me directions, that's fine with me.'

Farouk scurried in front of him, his arms raised in the air. 'I have family, master. *Sick children!* They need food. Medicine. We go tomorrow, yes?'

'No.'

Farouk grabbed Wilson's wrist and held on tight.

'Not safe at night, master!' he pleaded.

Shocked by the firmness of the contact, Wilson ripped his arm free and Farouk stumbled. He lurched forwards and back, trying to regain his balance before landing heavily on his well-padded rear end. On impact, dozens of coins leapt from his pockets and tinkled across the pavement. Sitting on his backside he seemed a little confused about how he got there.

'Not safe, master,' Farouk repeated. A car sped by, momentarily flooding the street with light. 'Many soldiers at Giza. No tourists,' he added.

Soldiers at Giza? Wilson wondered.

Farouk crawled around on his hands and knees retrieving his scattered money.

'What soldiers?' Wilson asked, as he pulled the local to his feet again.

'Many soldiers,' Farouk said vaguely, dumping the handful of coins into the large pocket in the front of his robe. He brushed his clothing down, an optimistic grin still on his face. 'We go to Giza tomorrow, yes? Only go in daytime.'

'You take me now,' Wilson said. 'Which way?'

Farouk's expression took on a look of amusement. '*Ahhhhhh!*' He laughed. 'You Westerners are all the same. Not safe, I say, and you still have no caring!' He waved a chubby finger. 'No Giza at night, I say … many soldiers.' He began to back away, looking decidedly more inebriated, then turned and wandered in a less-than-straight line up the footpath.

A sparkle of brightness from the middle of the street, on the cobblestones, caught Wilson's attention. It appeared to be a silver coin, probably one of Farouk's. Wilson scanned the crowded streets for the small man's stumbling walk, then realised he was gone. Waiting until a gaggle of motor scooters had sped past, Wilson dashed out on the road and snatched the coin up.

It felt familiar. Very familiar.

It was an Egyptian pound.

The coin was in perfect condition, minted in the very same year as his fate coin: the Pyramids of Giza on one side, the Queen of England, undamaged, on the other. If coincidence counted for anything, Wilson thought, then he was exactly where he needed to be. He remembered his grandfather William's smiling face. It was a good omen and he slid the heavy coin into his breast pocket and buttoned down the opening.

34

Cairo, Egypt
Western Quarter
December 20th 2012
Local Time 11:17 p.m.

Mission of Isaiah—Day Twenty-Six

HAVING CHOSEN TO avoid the main roads, Wilson had been lost for much of the last few hours. The backstreets of Cairo were generally narrow, gloomy cobblestone laneways. He headed into yet another unnamed alley, where he stopped and studied the crude tourist map he had found on the footpath. Just keep heading east, he told himself. Wilson was looking for a Pizza Hut restaurant, of all things, located just near the outskirts of the pyramids. To his dismay, that was the best reference his map could provide.

The laneway snaked through a middle-class section of the city where most of the buildings were irregular-shaped terraces, two storeyed, very plain, with few if any windows looking onto the street. The majority had a deck on the roof—somewhere to sit in the cool of the evenings. Not many lights were on at this hour.

Wilson was thinking about getting to the Sphinx in one piece and entering unnoticed. Would there be soldiers stationed at Giza, waiting for him? He would use the cover of darkness and his omega program-ming to make his approach—things would be fine, he thought positively. No one would see him in the dark. Yet in the back of his mind, he was still questioning whether the second portal had been tampered with, as Visblat had said. Although Wilson had made a conscious decision to ignore the warning, it still weighed heavily on him.

Bright light suddenly flooded the narrow laneway, as curtains parted, revealing an old woman standing behind thick, steel security bars. She had to be at least ninety, Wilson thought. And thankfully, judging by her appearance, not too dangerous.

Even so, he was eager to avoid attention and ducked out of sight below the windowsill, holding his breath to maintain the silence. The old woman struck a match, her hands shaking with old age, and held the shivering flame to a long, thin pipe. Her gaunt face was spider-webbed with wrinkles, her hair a wispy mop of white strands. A purple wrap hugged her fleshless shoulders.

She looks like my Aunt Martha, Wilson thought.

Puffs of tobacco smoke gently drifted out into the laneway, a pleasant smell, and Wilson decided he had a better chance of avoiding detection if he held position rather than tried to sneak away.

When the old woman eventually finished smoking, she gently tapped her pipe on the bars and the glowing embers fell to the ground beside Wilson's crouching body. As she reached up to pull the curtains closed, she caught sight of him below her windowsill.

Wilson calmly pressed his index finger to his lips.

'*Shush* ...' he said quietly.

In response, the barrel of a shotgun slid out through the bars!

Wilson jumped to his feet and scampered from side to side, desperately trying to avoid the aim of the old woman's gun.

The weapon fired and a bright-red flame leapt towards him!

Wilson dived to the ground as the buckshot blasted a hole in the far wall, shattering pieces of rubble across the cobblestones.

Forced back by the recoil, the old woman clumsily pushed the barrel through the bars a second time. Seizing his opportunity, Wilson stepped forward, not back. He swiftly wrenched the weapon from her grasp and threw it to the ground.

Then he raised his finger to his lips again. 'I said ... *shuuuush!*'

For a moment they just stared at each other, blank-faced.

I never liked my Aunt Martha very much, Wilson remembered.

Suddenly a blood-curdling scream echoed from the old woman's throat—loud and high-pitched, like the final approach of a kamikaze pilot. It was even more terrifying than the sound of the shotgun.

Lights began turning on in the adjacent buildings.

Windows began to open.

Sprinting for the end of the laneway, Wilson turned right, by chance, and finally found the Pizza Hut restaurant he had been looking for. Its doors were padlocked and the inside lights were extinguished.

Behind him he could still hear the sound of Cairo Martha yelling her lungs out.

Wilson crossed the street at full pace and ran directly into the sand dunes. The city had expanded all the way to the foot of the Giza plateau, to within metres of the ancient burial sites. Up ahead, he unexpectedly saw the perfect outline of two giant pyramids, closer than he had imagined, silhouetted against the night sky. The location of the nearby Pizza Hut filled him with cynicism. It was hard to imagine that the pharaohs would have approved.

The Pyramid of Khufu was the largest structure and the closest to him. The next pyramid was Khafre's: the second portal. It was easily recognisable by the sharp pointed tip—the upper third was still covered with the original tura-limestone casing.

Wilson couldn't see the third great pyramid, Menkaure. Much smaller than its two larger companions, it was easily blocked from view. A hazy light from the city radiated into the night sky and there was no moon. The only star that was clearly visible was Polaris—the Northern Star—part of the Little Dipper.

Wilson slid down the face of a steep dune, further into the darkness. The sand was squeaking under foot as he crawled on all fours to the highest point of the next and gazed down into the blackness of the ruins.

'Activate Possum,' he whispered.

My God ...

The darkness revealed the colossal pyramids of Giza in all their angular magnificence. They were huge—the size of mountains—so much bigger than he had expected. These colossal structures had withstood the elements for over four and a half millennia. Wilson remembered the Arab proverb that Barton had shown him:

"Man fears time, yet time fears the pyramids."

At the foot of the two largest pyramids, bench-like tombs littered the flat desert floor. Hundreds of them. An ancient cemetery. They were *mastaba*s—small granite structures about two metres tall arranged in perpendicular rows. Each mastaba housed the body of a nobleman or noblewoman who had lived in the fourth or fifth dynasty, between 2600 and 2300 BC.

Three smaller pyramids—entombing Khufu's three favourite wives—flanked the western side of the mastabas. Each one was twenty-five metres tall, but they were like toys in comparison with the massive bulk of the great pyramid of Khufu.

That was the path Wilson would take, the darkness protecting him: between the three smaller pyramids and the mastabas.

Crawling across the sand, trying to stay quiet, Wilson could see the face of the Sphinx not more than four hundred metres away, peering at him over the sands. He felt proud of himself—he'd made it all the way to Egypt and was now in sight of the entrance to the second portal.

HIGH ON THE EASTERN face of the Pyramid of Khufu an Egyptian army officer adjusted the focus on his night-vision goggles. The high-tech device gave him perfect vision in the darkness, albeit with a green tinge.

The officer hastily pulled a walkie-talkie from his belt and whispered in Arabic, 'I have identified a target!' he said excitedly, as he peered down at Wilson crawling across the sand. 'He is 150 metres to the north. Coming your way. Move straight ahead. Keep each other in sight.' He flicked the channel on his walkie-talkie, and spoke in English, 'Sir, we have something.'

There was a gentle squawk as he released his finger from the talk button.

On the desert floor, two commandos, from the most elite unit of the Egyptian military—Unit 999, Direct Action and Reconnaissance—clad in desert-camouflage fatigues, ran through the rows of stone. Wearing night-vision goggles and headsets, they carried high-powered assault rifles. They moved swiftly and quietly.

On top of the pyramid, a gruff voice came over the walkie-talkie. 'Do you have him?'

The officer pressed the talk button. 'Yes, we have him in our sights. He is alone in the darkness.'

'That man is not to be harmed,' the deep voice replied. 'Do you understand?'

'Yes, sir.' The officer nodded. 'I understand you, sir.' He watched confidently as his men closed in on their target.

THE IMPOSING FIGURE of Commander Visblat hastily climbed into the back of a silver limousine. The windows were heavily tinted. 'I repeat: he is not to be harmed. Under no circumstances are his sunglasses to be removed. Do you understand?' The driver closed the door behind him. 'Just hold Mr Dowling until I get there.'

CHANGING THE CHANNEL on his walkie-talkie, the officer spoke in Arabic again, 'He is not to be harmed. Repeat. He is not to be harmed.'
The commandos from Unit 999, each in sight of the other, stopped and nodded in acknowledgement. Their target was only a few metres away. They were trained to act in perfect unison.

WILSON WAS TAKEN completely by surprise as two soldiers jumped into view. They were wearing night-vision goggles. It seemed Farouk Nasser had spoken the truth: soldiers were indeed guarding the ruins.
Wilson found himself staring into the barrels of two assault rifles.
'Raise hands in air!' one of the soldiers barked in broken English.
'We not hurt you!' said the other.
Wilson pretended to be blinded by the darkness—the soldiers weren't to know any better, he concluded—as the pair approached him at forty-five degree angles.
'Hands in air!' the soldier repeated.
In one swift action, Wilson lunged towards the nearest man and wrenched the night-scope from his face. In response, a sweeping volley of bullets flashed from the commando's gun.
Clasping the night-scope in his hand, Wilson ran as fast as he could into the cover of the mastabas. He turned left ... right ... and headed in the general direction of the Sphinx. In the distance, the sound of a two-stroke engine rumbled across the ruins, the approaching illumination affecting his vision.
They have motorbikes! Wilson realised.
He turned hard right ... then left, but somehow the bike was still tailing him. Everything was getting brighter, affecting his vision. There was no choice but to cancel the possum command.
Suddenly, he tripped and fell.

The roaring machine was right behind him now!

Leaping up, Wilson desperately sprinted again, his shadow jiggling on the ground in front of him. In a last-ditch effort, he dived between some narrower tombstones. The gaps between the mastabas were smaller and it would be difficult for the bike to follow.

But Wilson had turned into a dead end!

The motorbike slid to a halt, blocking the exit. The harsh brightness of the halogen headlight exposed him.

He was trapped.

35

California, The Americas
Mercury Building, Level 2
May 19th 2081
Local Time 7:12 p.m.

4 Days before Transport Test

BARTON WAS PREOCCUPIED with how he was going to reprogram the thermal inputs for the transport pod. As a consequence, he was barely listening to the conversation going on around him. Deceiving the mercury team would not be easy, he realised; each and every member was an expert in the science of measurement and effect. But it was imperative. Ensuring that the transport pod was seventeen degrees hotter than indicated was the only way Wilson would be sent seventy-five years into the past.

Karin, Barton and Davin were sitting on the blue sofas in Barton's 'discussion area' drinking green tea, the whisper of breaking waves echoing gently in the background. Their meeting had been going for more than two hours. Above them a holographic worksheet was suspended in mid-air. It was covered with data from the transport simulations in different compartmentalised sections.

Davin knew he didn't have Barton's full attention and said a second time, 'Listen to me Barton, if we send Wilson without modifying him, there's a real chance he'll be weakened by the process.'

Barton refocused. 'I'm sorry. What did you say?'

'Wilson may be weakened by the process,' Davin repeated.

'What will the side effects be?' Karin asked.

Davin cleaned the lenses of his spectacles with a small cloth. 'Well, that depends on how far Wilson is time travelling.'

The comment snared Barton's full attention. 'Why is that?' he asked.

Davin slid his glasses back on his face. 'My simulations indicate that *time* becomes like a filtering mechanism. It has to do with the magnetic frequency of the earth. Luckily we're only sending Wilson a short distance through time. Thirty minutes forward is almost nothing. Even so, my research indicates that he may be subject to attack without cause after the transport.' Davin stood behind the sofa and did a series of Tai Chi moves. His shirt was untucked, his mercury labcoat wrinkled. 'I've done the calculations.' Davin stopped after three manoeuvres, seemingly taxed by this minimal exertion, and rubbed his soft belly. 'There's a chance he may be vulnerable to an optical trackenoid response.'

It was the last thing Barton needed to hear.

'The military have completed comprehensive studies on the phenomenon,' Davin added.

Typing away on her handheld, Karin was already bringing up additional information on the screen. She said with some interest, 'Why does it happen?'

'The eyes are the most complex component of the chromosome table,' Davin responded. 'On a micro-level, sensory endings called optical trackenoids, which terminate in the eye, stop secreting chemicals on specific radials of the iris. Subconsciously, we interpret these missing radials as *fear*. All humans, and that includes the three of us, are biologically programmed to be hostile to anyone who shows a profound weakness in this way.'

Davin stared up at the display. 'It's a core instinct. The root of it is found in the carnivorous background of human evolution. When an animal is dying, its eyes have a zero optical trackenoid secretion. That, in turn, reinforces our need to kill. That's the reason why serial murderers often have a desire to continue taking life. They become addicted to seeing the optical trackenoid response just before the point of death. That's how it was discovered in the first place—research on serial killers.'

Pages of confidential information flashed up on the Data-Tran segment.

Barton listened with great interest, doing his best to conceal his intrigue.

'I've read about this,' Karin said. 'It's also the same reason why you can meet someone and, for no reason at all, dislike them.'

Davin gestured to the graph in the top left-hand corner of the screen. 'That's called a *minor* trackenoid response.' He pointed. 'That's at the lesser end of the scale. If there's an imbalance or mismatch in the radials of both eyes, it can cause a negative reaction. Things that can trigger a minor imbalance are ... illness, stress, having low energy. But that's nothing compared to what I'm talking about. I'm talking about the possibility of a *zero* trackenoid secretion.' He pointed at the upper end of the scale. 'The effects would be uncontrollable. Like I said, the military did a lot of research.'

Karin tapped away on her handheld. 'Why were the military so interested?' she asked.

'They were trying to figure out how to *amplify* the trackenoids,' Davin answered. 'You see, the process also works in reverse. With the right modifications they learned how to manufacture people who were scary to look at. The theory was, they could create soldiers who struck fear into anyone who looked into their eyes.'

'Super soldiers,' Karin whispered. She understood perfectly.

Barton studied the information. 'Are you saying that Wilson will be vulnerable?'

'No, I'm not saying that, categorically.' Davin pointed to the hologram above him. 'My simulations indicate a twenty-three per cent chance of a minor problem. Just be thankful we're not sending Wilson *backwards* in time. Otherwise the probability of a severe reaction accelerates all the way up to one hundred per cent. Depending, of course, on how far back you send him.'

'Twenty-three per cent is not that bad,' Barton replied. But he knew that one hundred per cent was the likely outcome of Wilson's imminent journey into the past.

'Why do the chances multiply as you go back?' Karin asked.

'From the simulations I ran—actually Andre and I did them together—the further back you go, the worse the problem gets. It's got to do with the magnetic frequency of the earth, a thing called the Schumann Frequency.'

Barton swallowed, trying desperately to control his surprise.

'The transport process,' Davin continued, 'which uses the magnetic field of the earth as a launching pad, strips a small element out of the recreation.'

Barton was astounded. The cause being described was the very thing Wilson was being sent back to rectify.

Karin said, 'It's a good thing we don't have to worry about sending him *backwards* in time.'

For the next ten minutes, the trio discussed how the optical trackenoids functioned and looked over the data they had obtained from the military.

'Just for interest's sake,' Barton said. 'How can we combat a trackenoid response?'

Davin slumped into his chair. 'There are two methods I would recommend. One. We could do a molecular reconstruction of Wilson's DNA—to amplify his trackenoids. But there's no time for that. Two. We give him a pair of specially designed contact lenses. That's the easy option, I think; they'd be simple enough to make. After the transport, we can check his trackenoid levels and amplify them if required, in a controlled environment. No risk. It should be pretty easy to re-calibrate them afterwards, if there is a problem.'

'If he covers his eyes he'll be safe?' Barton asked.

'Tinted sunglasses or anything like that will work just fine. Anything that covers his irises. Permanent contact lenses are a little more complicated, but they're worth the trouble, I think. Glasses are too cumbersome. They could fall off, and then we'd have a problem.' Davin pointed his finger at his own eye. 'It's only direct eye-to-eye contact that'll cause a reaction. Yes, my suggestion is to use tinted contact lenses. Let's not take any chances.'

A telephone began ringing and Karin sprang from her chair.

Barton nodded. 'Davin, you're right—there's no point taking any chances. Go ahead and make up the lenses.'

Karin pressed her hand over the mouthpiece. 'Barton. GM wants to see you.'

Barton wondered why, but was unruffled by the request. 'Tell him I'm on my way,' he said.

'He wants you to bring Wilson Dowling with you.'

Barton forced a smile—he didn't like the sound of that at all. 'Tell him we'll be there in thirty minutes.' It seemed that no sooner was one problem solved than another had arisen.

36

Cairo, Egypt
Giza Plateau
December 20th 2012
Local Time 11:57 p.m.

Mission of Isaiah—Day Twenty-Six

THE HAUNTING GROWL of the motorbike echoed off the walls of the mastabas. It was easy to imagine it was the voice of the Sphinx come to life. With it, the piercing brightness of the headlamp shone in Wilson's eyes. His arms were stretched into the air in abject surrender. There was nowhere to run. He fleetingly scanned the bare stone walls around him. If he tried to scale them, would he be shot?

'Get on!' a female voice yelled.

The headlight tilted slightly away to one side and the rider came into view. Helena raised her visor, at the same time impatiently smacking the seat behind her.

'Get on!' she yelled again. 'Hurry! There's not much time!'

Wilson was momentarily dumbstruck.

'Hurry!' she yelled.

Coming to his senses, Wilson leapt onto the pillion and grabbed Helena around the waist. She was dressed in a black military outfit: short-sleeved polo-neck top and cargo pants with large square pockets on the thighs, a helmet and riding boots. Two handguns were strapped against some type of Kevlar vest with numerous Velcro compartments on it.

'I've been looking for you everywhere,' she said.

'Towards the Sphinx!' Wilson yelled. 'We need to go towards the Sphinx!' Helena spun the dirt-bike around with great skill and zig-zagged into the open—in the wrong direction. 'The Sphinx!' Wilson said again. 'I have to go towards the Sphinx!'

'There are soldiers everywhere!' she called back.

Wilson hugged at her waist even more tightly. 'Turn around!'

Bright speckles of gunfire randomly lit up the sand dunes, the subsequent volley of bullets whizzing just over their heads. At the same time, the front wheel hit a semi-concealed ditch, launching the motorbike into the air and catapulting the pair over the handlebars. They both tumbled to a halt in the sand.

Instantly Helena leapt to her feet with great dexterity, drew her handgun, and fired three random shots into the darkness. Ducking behind the mastabas for cover, she wrenched the helmet from her head.

'They've been here for weeks!' she said angrily. The motorbike engine was still running as it lay on its side in the sand, the headlight illuminating the huge sandstone blocks of the eastern face of the Pyramid of Khafre.

A CONVOY OF THREE cars—a silver limousine and two black Ford Broncos—sped along a palm-lined boulevard towards the Giza plateau. There were no other vehicles on the road. As they crested the hill, a glitter of gunfire could be seen on the desert floor, adjacent to the pyramids.

Visblat growled into his walkie-talkie, 'What's going on?'

'We have them pinned down!' the officer's muffled voice responded. Gunshots could be heard in the background. 'They will not escape us!'

Visblat became agitated. 'Stop shooting! That's an order! He is not to be harmed!'

'There are two of them!'

'Stop shooting!' Visblat repeated.

A STEADY CLAMOUR of gunshots continued to ring out from the darkness, the odd tracer bullet streaking overhead. Putting the stolen night-vision goggles to good use, Wilson strapped the unit over Helena's eyes and switched it on.

Seeing clearly now, she glanced around the rectangular granite block in front of her.

'I'm not getting arrested,' she said determinedly. 'I'm telling you that much. I'll shoot my way out of here if I have to, but I'm not surrendering to them. No way.' At that moment an eerie silence reclaimed the plateau.

The shooting had mysteriously stopped.

'I have to get to the Sphinx,' Wilson insisted. 'It's vital.'

'In case you haven't noticed,' Helena seethed. 'We have a bit of a problem.' She briefly surveyed the men entrenched in the sand dunes. 'There are about thirty soldiers out there who might have a problem with your travel plans.'

'I'm going anyway!'

Helena stared at Wilson through the night-vision lenses.

'You go that way,' Wilson said, pointing to one side of the granite block. 'I'll go this way,' and he pointed to the other side.

Helena shook her head. 'No.' She had risked everything, travelling around the world against her father's wishes, to find Wilson. There were just too many dangers out there, and too many unanswered questions for her to let him go alone. Helena was involved in this—whatever *this* was—and she would do her part.

'*I have to go!*' Wilson insisted.

'We go together,' she said firmly.

'There's a secret doorway,' Wilson explained. 'Between the front paws of the Sphinx.' He extended both arms, fists clenched like that of the statue. 'There's a stone breastplate.' He touched his own chest. 'It's a secret doorway, and it's imperative that I get inside.'

She corrected him, 'You mean *we* get inside.' Ripping open a Velcro pocket, she produced a cylindrical tear-gas canister—a British made, Pains-Wessex, high-explosive crowd-control device. It was designed to stun, then immobilise. 'We'll get only one chance to escape from here,' she affirmed. 'Are you sure you know what you're doing?'

'I'm sure.'

'One chance!' she said again, and prepared to pull the pin.

Wilson never wavered. 'Just throw it!'

Helena gestured at her fallen motorbike. 'On three.' With a metallic click, the pin was pulled. 'One ... two ... *three!*'

The grenade was hurled in the direction of the soldiers, as far as Helena could throw it, and the device exploded in mid-air. An intense flash lit up the ancient ruins, accompanied by a disorienting *warp* of sound—a sonic charge—and the ruptured canister landed in the sand, an ever-growing cloud of toxic teargas pluming from its innards.

THE FLASH OF THE grenade illuminated the rear cabin of Visblat's limousine as it neared the Giza plateau. '*Christ!* I told you to stop firing!' he said. There was a squawk as he released his finger from the talk button.

His handset crackled, 'They are trying to escape!'

'It's that bitch, Helena Capriarty—it has to be.' Visblat nudged his driver on the shoulder and pointed ahead. 'Take me towards the Sphinx. Quickly!' He pulled his .44 Magnum from under his jacket and checked the magazine. Pressing the talk button again, he said, 'Send all your men to the Sphinx! Surround it! No shooting! Do you understand? They are trying to make it to the Dream Stela.'

HELENA PULLED HER motorbike upright, switched off the headlight and waited for what seemed like an eternity as Wilson leapt on behind her. With a twist of the throttle, the engine screamed, catapulting them through the noxious smoke towards the statue of the Sphinx. Helena's eyes burned from the chemicals and she held her breath to suppress any gagging.

Soldiers were everywhere—some doubled over in agony from the smoke, others blinded by the flash—and no one was shooting. They were all momentarily incapacitated. Helena's motorbike picked up speed, dipped into a small crevasse and jumped out the other side.

Emerging from the toxic haze, they raced past the roofless structure of the Valley Temple, zigzagging past two more soldiers. Still, no one was shooting. They leapt high into the air once again. Helena cornered quickly and they flew down a sandy embankment between the ruins, skidding to a halt in front of the Sphinx.

WILSON ENGAGED HIS night-vision command and ran between the outstretched paws. The stars in the night sky gleamed brightly. The statue of the Sphinx was massive, each giant paw being four metres tall—and, Wilson concluded, impossible to climb over. The only way to get to the Dream Stela was to approach it head-on through the paws.

Helena let the motorbike fall, produced two identical Colt pistols and backed nervously into the dead end. Wilson gazed at the sombre face of the Pharaoh Khafre silhouetted above him. The nose and beard of the statue had broken away many centuries before, and its remaining features were badly eroded. Even so, the large stone eyeballs gazed with menacing intensity, east towards Cairo.

'*Abu al-Hôl,*' Wilson whispered. The Father of Terror.

Helena was by his side, her guns pointing back towards the opening. 'I hope you know what you're doing.'

A rectangular four-metre-tall tablet, or stela, of red granite was mounted on the breastbone of the Sphinx. It had been erected in 1396 BC. The hieroglyphic script etched into the Dream Stela's surface told the story of Thutmosis IV, a prince of Egypt, who fell asleep in the shadow of the statue. At the time, the Sphinx was buried up to its neck in sand. According to the hieroglyphics, as the prince lay in its shadow, the Sphinx appeared before him in a dream and complained that its body was falling into ruin, taken over by the sands. The prince was promised he would one day become Pharaoh of Egypt, if he freed the creature and fixed its weathered body, returning the Sphinx to its former glory.

As was written on the stela, Thutmosis IV fulfilled his end of the bargain and, as promised, became Pharaoh of Egypt within less than one year.

Wilson studied the surface of the Dream Stela; it didn't appear to have been tampered with. He gently ran his fingers along the hundreds of Egyptian hieroglyphics adorning it. They were all different sizes and covered the tablet from top to bottom. Wilson calculated the date—taking into account that it was now after midnight—thereby determining which two characters to search for. He quickly found the first.

An Egyptian soldier ran across the entrance. Spotting him, Helena crouched down next to Wilson and tapped him gently on the shoulder. 'They're here,' she hissed warily.

After finding the second symbol, Wilson reached into his pocket and pulled out a broken pencil. 'That's not good.'

The remark caught Helena's attention. 'What's not good?'

He selected the longer of the two pieces and threw the other away. 'My pencil's broken.'

Another soldier ran across the opening.

'Whatever you're doing—do it fast!' Helena pleaded.

Wilson inserted the sharp end of his pencil into the indentation that marked the midpoint between the two characters. He pressed as hard as he could into the granite ... there was a faint *click*.

A heavily accented voice began yelling, 'Do not move! You will not be harmed!'

Wilson pounded his fist on the stela. Nothing was happening! Then, a trickle of pure white sand began to make its way lethargically down the surface of the stone.

VISBLAT STRODE TOWARDS a group of Egyptian soldiers gathered at the base of the Sphinx. Even though time was of the essence, he didn't want to run forward; that would make him look desperate and out of control, he decided. An officer approached, his eyes red and watery from the teargas explosion.

'They are trapped inside,' he said, pointing. 'They have guns.'

Visblat poked his head around the corner; all he could see was darkness. 'I told you idiots not to let him in there,' he said. 'Somebody give me a night-scope. Quickly!'

THROUGH HER NIGHT-VISION goggles, Helena saw the familiar face of Commander Visblat briefly staring towards her. Her heartbeat duly quickened. 'Visblat's here,' she said nervously. 'He's been here for at least two weeks.'

'You need to buy me more time,' Wilson replied.

'What do you want me to do?' Helena said sourly. 'Ask him to wait?'

'Do *something*!'

Helena took aim at the motorbike—the petrol tank—and pulled the trigger. With a mighty yellow flash and a thunderous blast, it exploded.

Blinded by the illumination, Wilson was forced to terminate his omega command.

'You have twenty *extra* seconds!' Helena said abrasively.

Petrol flames licked high into the air, the heat cradled within the outstretched paws of the Sphinx. Wilson refocused on the Dream Stela; the sand that had begun as a trickle from the seams now poured forth at a furious rate. Even so, he pounded the surface again, encouraging it to flow faster still.

Helena flicked up her night-vision goggles. Soldiers were gathering on the other side of the flames, preparing their assault. 'Ten seconds,' she said, aiming both her handguns. 'Then we're in big trouble.'

Sand was flooding out all four sides of the stone at the same time. Behind him, Wilson could feel the petrol fire dying out, its light dimming fast. Suddenly there was a *clunk* and the Dream Stela tumbled backwards.

A pitch-black doorway had appeared.

Without regard for what was on the other side, Wilson grabbed Helena's forearm and wrenched her through the opening.

Bouncing off the smooth stone walls, the pair fell into the blackness, down a vertical shaft. It was a seemingly endless drop. Stomachs in their mouths, they plummeted through a cool ebony world. Vertigo exerted its mysterious grip as wind ripped at their ears. Gradually the tunnel levelled out, their motion slowed and they tumbled to a halt in the darkness.

With a faint *pop*, a copper lantern ignited on the wall, a solitary flame licking upwards. Then, with another *pop*, a second lantern ignited further along. Lights continued to fire systematically as far as the eye could see, until a perfectly straight corridor led them in the direction of the pyramid.

The air was saturated with a powdery mist.

'Next time,' Helena snapped. '*You can say* ... "Hey, I'm gonna throw you down a bottomless hole in the ground!"—just as a warning. Then you won't scare the hell out of me quite so badly!'

'I thought you'd be grateful,' Wilson replied, as he picked himself up from the floor.

'If that's your idea of being funny, then—' Helena checked herself, holding back an insult. They were lucky to escape, and she knew it. She holstered one of her handguns and removed the night-vision goggles. Upon inspection, the unit proved to be smashed beyond repair and she tossed it aside. Suddenly, she caught a whiff of the air. 'It sure does smell funny down here.'

Wilson was already walking away. 'That's because we're the first people to set foot in this corridor in over 4500 years. And to think, the lanterns are still working. Amazing. You know, my landlord can't even get the elevators in my apartment building to work.'

THE SECRET DOORWAY was agape and Wilson was gone, Visblat realised. Waiting impatiently for the petrol flames to die down, he stepped around the burnt-out shell of the motorbike, trying to remain calm.

'Anchor one end of a long rope,' he said, gesturing around a fallen block of stone. '*Here*. And throw the rest of it down this shaft. Let no one else inside. I'll be back soon.' The soldier beside him looked worried.

'But master! You should not go in there. The curse of *Abu al-Hôl*.'

Visblat turned and glared into the officer's eyes. 'You superstitious fool,' he muttered. 'Just do as I say. Anchor off that rope, understand?'

The officer took a step backwards, his expression gripped with inexplicable fear; he had caught a glimpse of Visblat's eyes.

The commander turned and stared inside the body of the Sphinx; there was light shining up at him from deep underground. 'Do as I say.'

With that, Visblat dived through the opening.

THE PASSAGEWAY LEADING under the causeway between the Sphinx and the Pyramid of Khafre ran perfectly straight for at least four hundred metres. In the distance, the tunnel ended at a sizable chamber under the Mortuary Temple. Wilson and Helena had fallen quite some distance through the blackness and there was no telling how deep underground the passageway was.

'When we get to the end,' Wilson said, walking at a brisk pace, 'we'll find four doorways. The beginning of the Labyrinth of Khafre.'

'A labyrinth?'

'Yes, a labyrinth.'

'Here we are again, Wilson. Another pyramid ... another country.'

'How did you find me?'

'Oh, you're easy to find.'

'The visions?'

'Some old woman took a shot at you in one of those laneways,' she said.

'Yeah ... Cairo Martha, the old hag. She nearly killed me.'

Helena gripped the back of Wilson's arm, stopping him mid-stride. 'Why does a time traveller want to visit pyramids all over the world? Please tell me ...'

'The Pyramid of Khafre,' Wilson said, 'is built directly above a natural energy fissure.' He began walking again. 'A giant energy portal. And I'm here to activate it.'

'How many energy portals are there?'

'Three. This is the second.' Thinking a moment, Wilson asked, 'Where's Esther?'

'She's back with George,' Helena replied. 'He said to say *hello*, by the way.'

'How is he?'

'He's been busy suing the Houston Police Department for wrongful harm and wrongful detention. If he wins, he stands to make some money. If anyone could make a bad situation work in his favour, it's that guy.'

Wilson had to smile. 'You said you saw Visblat?' he asked, his smile promptly disappearing.

'The first time, about a week ago ... by chance, on the street, outside Cairo. Because of you, I assume, no one has been allowed near the Sphinx after dark.'

'The Dream Stela can only be opened at night,' Wilson said in explanation. 'It won't open during daylight hours.' It seemed Visblat really did know everything about his mission.

'Soldiers are stationed all across Giza,' Helena stated. 'The media reports are that it's because of a terrorist threat. You're not a terrorist, are you?'

'That depends on whose side you're on.'

'*Please* ... try not to confuse me any more than I already am.'

'Of course I'm not a terrorist.' Wilson didn't have the courage to admit he couldn't get Helena out of his mind these last three weeks. 'It's not safe being around me,' he added. 'You shouldn't have come.'

'You need me,' she said determinedly.

A faint scraping sound, increasing in volume, suddenly pierced the silence of the corridor. Moments later Commander Visblat tumbled into view, a hundred metres behind.

Wilson and Helena exchanged a worried glance.

'Maybe I do need you,' Wilson said, and they both ran as fast as they could.

The corridor eventually ended at a well-lit hexagonal chamber. The perfectly symmetrical construction had a high-peaked ceiling and walls made of rectangular blocks of sandstone. There were five doorways—the one they had just come through and four others. The remaining wall had painted hieroglyphs carved into it. The saffron-yellow characters were outlined with raven black and appeared to rotate on some sort of swivelling stone block. They were striking.

It was the riddle of the chamber, written in Egyptian hieroglyphs.[7]

Wilson's eyes flicked to the four stone doorways—a group of symbols painted above each one. The many hours of study were about to pay off as he effortlessly translated the question.

'Travel the morning sun,' he said.

He gazed at the four symbols, one above each door.

They were easy to recognise.

'North … South … East … and West,' he said.

North, the direction of the life-giving waters of the Nile. South, where the papyrus reeds grow. East, representing the city, life and food. West, the burial place of the dead—the tombs of Egypt were always on the western side of the Nile.

Fine sand was filtering through tiny cracks in the ceiling and running down the walls. Wilson knew what it meant—Barton's warning was accurate—in a matter of minutes the labyrinth would collapse upon itself, crushing everything inside.

Looking back into the corridor, Helena watched Visblat sprint through the mist of falling sand towards them. She whispered under her breath, 'Hurry, Wilson!'

---

[7] Egyptian hieroglyphs, circa 3000 BC, provided by Mr Y. Youssef, Senior Research Associate (Masters in Egyptology) Centre of Early Christian Studies, Melbourne, Australia.

'The sun rises in the east,' Wilson muttered. 'That means the *sunbeams* travel west. That's the answer … *West!*' Wilson pointed at the far left door and together they descended a seemingly endless flight of stairs as fast as they could. The corridor turned hard right and entered another chamber. As before, there were four doorways. Above each one was a new set of hieroglyphics. Another riddle was etched down the remaining wall.

'What does it say?' Helena demanded impatiently.
'The pathway to success,' Wilson translated.

'Wisdom … Intelligence … Faith … Power.'

VISBLAT SKIDDED INTO the first chamber and scanned the walls.
'Travel the morning sun,' he carefully recited. Without hesitation he ran into the doorway with the Egyptian symbol for 'West' above it.

THE PATHWAY TO SUCCESS. Wilson knew the answer immediately. It had been written in the text from the Book of Isaiah. The answer was *Faith*; it had to be.

The corridor went up an incalculable number of steps, then turned sharp right. Helena and Wilson were bounding upwards two stairs at a time. Wilson was gasping for air by the time he made it to the third decision chamber. Again, there were four doorways, but this time there were no symbols on the riddle wall. No symbols above any of the entrances. The only differentiating factor was that three of the passageways were lit, while one was pitch-black.

'This is a question of faith,' Wilson said knowingly. He grabbed Helena's hand and ran into the darkness. Without some kind of emission, no matter how small, his omega command was useless. The pair felt their way, metre by metre, around each corner and up the stairs.

'I hope you know what you're doing,' Helena said under her breath.

VISBLAT APPEARED IN the third decision chamber and without hesitation ran into the darkened passageway. Up ahead he could hear Helena's whisper and he yelled into the blackness.

'Mr Dowling, you must listen to me,' he called out. 'You've got to stop! The pyramid has been tampered with! You *must* stop! You're making a mistake!'

THE THROATY SOUND of Visblat's voice echoed down the hall.

'Don't listen to him,' Helena said quietly. 'He's lying. I can sense it.'

How was Visblat following them so easily? Wilson asked himself.

A light appeared in the distance, like a pinprick, and the pair ran towards it as fast as they could. With each step the corridor brightened. They eventually emerged into another well-lit chamber, identical to the others. All four doorways leading off it were dark inside.

Wilson read the hieroglyphs on the riddle wall.

'You entered. You've taken many steps,' he translated. 'Where are you now?' His eyes flashed towards each door.

'East ... West .... Above ... Below,' he said.

Helena checked her guns. 'Which is it?' she said. 'Pick one!'

Wilson knew that the Sphinx faced east. That meant when they entered the first chamber, they were facing west. From there, he attempted to reconstruct the journey, step by step.

Helena listened to the sound of Visblat's footsteps echoing through the silence towards them. He was getting closer, seemingly walking now, with long strides, at a steady pace. Pointing her gun down the blackened corridor, she nervously rested her finger on the trigger. A thin film of sweat covered her face. She was imagining Visblat appearing in front of her. It was his eyes she feared, she knew that, and she dreaded the idea of facing him again.

The labyrinth had changed direction many times and Wilson reconstructed the journey as best he could. In his estimation, they had circled back to where they began, but this time they were approximately thirty steps higher. The answer had to be *Above*.

Wilson grabbed Helena's hand and hastily led her into the darkness. He would have liked time to go through it all again, to be certain, but Visblat was sure to be right behind them. The pair hadn't taken more than twenty steps when the ground suddenly disappeared from under their feet—a concealed trap door—and they plummeted into the raven darkness!

'WE HAVE TO TALK!' Visblat yelled, doing his best to suppress his increasing frustration. 'You must listen to what I have to say!' He entered the fourth decision chamber, but there was no one inside. Hearing the scraping of Helena's Kevlar vest against the sandstone, he easily identified the doorway they had gone through. Not taking any chances, he stepped back and read the hieroglyphic script, then scanned the telltale footsteps on the sandy ground.

BOTH HELENA AND Wilson fell through the blackness, eventually shooting out a tubular duct into another well-lit chamber. All the way down, Helena had made a telepathic connection, the second one in the last five minutes. By now, she had become skilled at seeing through Wilson while maintaining the ability to see through her own eyes.

Wilson's heart was thumping as he read the symbols listed down the riddle wall.

'The destined will take the correct path,' he whispered. There were four unmarked doorways, each one pitch-black inside. A thin layer of sand covered the floor. Wilson suddenly realised that Visblat could see their footsteps on the ground. That was certainly the reason he could follow them so easily. Without a word, Wilson made an imprint with his shoe, and directed Helena's attention to it. She understood immediately and the pair ran in and out of the corridors, in a frenzy of motion, making a random mess of footprints, hopefully impossible to interpret.

Wilson gazed at the riddle once again: 'The destined will take the correct path.'

'Theoretically, I can't get this wrong,' he said and gingerly pointed at one of the gloomy entrances.

Helena seemed dubious. 'Are you sure?' she said.

'You're right, it's this one!' Wilson grabbed her hand and they both leapt into another doorway, their feet not striking the floor until they landed in the safety of the darkness.

AS SOON AS THE pair disappeared from view, Visblat tumbled into the empty chamber and slid across the floor. The large man's face twisted with annoyance as he took note of the mass of footsteps randomly scattered everywhere. Thin streams of sand continued falling from the ceiling, making Wilson's path even more difficult to decipher.

'I'm beginning to think you don't want to co-operate!' Visblat yelled out.

Stepping back, and with no other choice, he read the hieroglyphic script. The cryptic question made his mouth dry. He hated these stupid riddles. How was he supposed to answer a question like that?

Using the next-best option, he stood in silence and waited, listening intently. Eventually he honed in on a faint sound issuing from one of the four doorways and a smile of relief crossed his lips.

'My men could've killed you!' Visblat called out. 'The only reason you're alive is because of me! But either way, it makes no difference, Mr Dowling!'

VISBLAT'S BELLOWING VOICE bounced down the corridor—then, two seconds later, the echo came from the opposite direction.

How was that possible? Wilson wondered.

His question was immediately answered as he turned the corner to find an immense underground cavern before him. The gaping, rectangular burrow was easily ten times the width of the grass courtyard at Sydney University—and that was a square acre, in total. This had to be at least two hundred metres wide. All around, the glow of hundreds of oil lanterns cast ghostly shadows against the irregular walls and ceiling. Below him, the corridor had given way to a flat, stone bridge, seemingly sturdy, that spanned the darkness. There were two identical bridges to the left, and one to the right—all parallel—each one about five metres apart. There were no railings.

'Four doors ... four bridges,' Wilson concluded. It explained why he heard Visblat's voice coming from both directions. Making his way to the very edge of the walkway, Wilson nudged a loose pebble over the side, then waited. There was no sound at all; the fissure below them was seemingly bottomless.

All four bridges crossed the abyss and terminated at a carved wall, about fifty metres away. Judging by the size of the stone blocks, it was the base of the Pyramid of Khafre. Wilson realised there was no way to get from one bridge to the other without going back through the labyrinth—it was much too far to jump across.

Helena pulled Wilson back.

'Don't go out there,' she said.

'What choice do we have?' Releasing himself from her grip, Wilson ran across the void to the other side and pressed his hands against the enormous stones now impeding his progress. The length of the wall was roughly the same as the eastern face of the pyramid. *But how do I get inside?* There was nothing obvious that Wilson could see. No markings. No levers. Just rectangular blocks of stone.

He pushed at the wall with all his might, but nothing shifted.

Helena eased beside him and nervously panned her gun towards the doors to the labyrinth. Her fears were suddenly realised as Visblat's voice called out from nearby, yelling into the cavern through one of the doorways that led into the labyrinth.

'Why won't you listen to me, Mr Dowling? Why?'

Sighting along her gun, Helena tried to pinpoint where the voice was coming from. It was difficult, because the sound was bouncing off the irregular walls.

'I've tried to be reasonable!' Visblat yelled. 'I have! But you won't co-operate!'

Wilson turned on the spot and faced the doors. 'I'm willing to talk,' he yelled back.

Helena muttered under her breath, 'I don't like this.'

The commander's voice bellowed, 'Tell Ms Capriarty to lower her gun!'

Wilson spoke softly, 'Lower your weapon, Helena.'

She shook her head.

'Just do it,' Wilson said, and he pushed the barrel of her gun downwards.

Visblat calmly strolled out into the open—he was on the next walkway along, his gun also pointing to the ground. 'You can read Egyptian hieroglyphs, I see. Very impressive, Mr Dowling. You've learnt a lot in a very short time.'

Visblat looked a little thinner than the last time Wilson had seen him.

'You picked the wrong door,' Wilson said, with a confident grin.

Visblat smiled back. 'No, Mr Dowling, you did.'

Helena was almost frozen, paralysed by the sight of Visblat's eyes. Her pulse was racing, her hands sweating. There was a sinking feeling in her stomach, as though she was about to throw up.

'You've seen sand pouring from the ceiling,' Wilson said. 'The labyrinth is going to collapse upon itself. If you're not careful, you'll still be inside.'

'There's plenty of time,' Visblat replied.

Both men stared at each other across the void that separated the two bridges, Wilson's eyes protected by his sunglasses.

'You're making a big mistake,' Visblat added, waving a huge finger. 'You should trust me.'

'Don't listen to him,' Helena whispered, forcing herself to speak.

'Tell me what you want,' Wilson called out, ignoring the warning.

'The second portal has been tampered with,' Visblat stated, 'as I've already told you.' There was an unusual calm in his voice now, as if he was playing his part with Academy-Award poise. 'Don't open it. Go straight to the third.'

'How do I know I can trust you?'

'You don't.'

'Why *should* I trust you?'

Visblat smirked. 'Because I could have killed you if I wanted.'

The comment didn't make Wilson feel any more co-operative. 'Your negotiation skills *seriously* need some work.'

'The portal *has* been tampered with,' Visblat said, restraining a sudden outburst.

'How can you be certain?'

There was a long pause. 'I just know—'

'Tell me *how* you know?'

'What does it matter, you fool?' An agitated tone had taken over, as if all Visblat's restraint was already exhausted. His right eye was now twitching, as were his hands and fingers. 'Barton Ingerson is the reason I'm here, you fool!'

Wilson was stunned.

'Yes! He was the one who sent me to stop you. Ha!' The large man was acting like he'd just laid down a royal flush at a poker tournament. 'There is no other justification required, Mr Dowling. Barton Ingerson was the one who told me the second portal had been tampered with.'

'You *are* from the future,' Wilson muttered.

Another manic laugh was the response. 'Where else would I be from—?'

Wilson's gaze narrowed behind his glasses. 'Prove it.'

And Visblat did.

'You are a Gen-EP candidate, Mr Dowling.' Visblat was calm again, as though he had expected the question. 'There were only fourteen days to prepare you for your mission. Barton Ingerson was the only one who knew you were being sent *backwards* in time. Everyone else in the mercury team thought you were going forwards, by just thirty minutes.' Visblat was enjoying this, Wilson could tell. 'You did very well to learn everything in just fourteen days.'

'Who *really* sent you?' Wilson asked, a deliberate hint of doubt in his voice.

'I told you. Barton Ingerson sent me.'

'And you became a police commander?'

'I had to amuse myself somehow. You've kept me waiting for six years, Mr Dowling.'

'Don't trust him,' Helena whispered, a bead of sweat dripping from the end of her nose.

'You, shut up!' Visblat erupted.

Wilson said, 'Barton and I had a code word for just this scenario. A way of aborting the Mission of Isaiah. Give me the code word and I'll do as you ask.'

Visblat was expressionless.

'Well?' Wilson said, impatiently.

'There is no such code,' Visblat replied, his right eye twitching again. 'And, I'm warning you, Mr Dowling—I don't like games.' Another wave of hostility was building. 'If you activate the second portal, Barton will die. Yes, you fool! He will! His life depends on it staying open.'

Just the suggestion of something so bizarre had Wilson in a spin.

'He's lying,' Helena whispered.

Suddenly, Wilson's mind was clear again. As if Helena's words had freed him of the erratic thoughts hindering his ability to think. She was right; Visblat was lying.

'Do you believe,' Wilson said, 'that *coincidence* is a signpost for something?'

Visblat seemed confused. 'What sort of a stupid question is that?'

'I bet you don't even know Barton's favourite fishing spot.'

Visblat rubbed the barrel of his gun as if it were an affectionate cat. 'I told you ... if you don't do as I say, Barton will never fish again!'

'Have you ever been to Mount Whitney?'

Visblat began pacing from side to side, trying to calculate how long it would take for him to re-enter the labyrinth, find the doorway Wilson had gone through, and get to the bridge Wilson was on—then smash some sense into him.

Wilson studied the black void separating the two walkways. 'Do you mind if I show you something?' Peeling back his sunglasses, he stared directly into Commander Visblat's eyes.

But the reaction was unexpected.

Wilson's legs immediately went to water. His chest constricted as if he was trapped in a vice. It was fear that Wilson felt. Paralysing fear. Certain confirmation that Visblat's optical trackenoids had been over-amplified.

'You make me furious, Mr Dowling,' Visblat said, standing there, motionless—the flicker of oil lanterns illuminating his angry gaze.

'Did you think I would be susceptible to something as pathetic as a trackenoid response! I'm better than you will ever be!' Visblat measured the distance between the two walkways and, realising he could not make the jump, he took a step backwards and raised his gun.

Helena pushed through a mental pain barrier and raised her gun in response, avoiding direct eye contact—targeting Visblat using only her peripheral vision. As if sensing her ploy, the large man turned his fearsome gaze on her.

'Try and shoot me!' he taunted. 'I dare you!'

Helena continued to avert her eyes, to protect herself, not staring directly down the barrel of her gun. She wanted to pull the trigger, but something was stopping her. Then she realised it was the visions she was getting from Wilson. 'Put your sunglasses back on,' Helena whispered. 'Do it!'

'We can make a deal, Visblat,' Wilson offered, the sound of his voice feathered with uncontrollable anxiety.

In a fit of rage, Visblat waved his .44 Magnum in the air and prowled back and forth along the walkway. 'The time for deals is over!' he said. 'From now on, we do it my way!'

'You need me,' Wilson replied. 'Otherwise, you wouldn't be here.'

'The second portal has been tampered with!' Visblat screamed. 'I told you! We must go directly to the third! I'll take you there myself!' He paused. 'But there's no room for three of us ...'

For Wilson, everything suddenly went into slow motion. Visblat's eyes. The gun. Helena standing by his side. The cool, stale air. The hundreds of small, oily flames licking into the darkness of the cavern. Somehow, Wilson knew what was going to happen next. Without a thought for his own safety, he stepped into Visblat's line of sight.

The gun fired.

Wilson could see the projectile coming towards him.

THE BULLET SLAMMED into Wilson's chest, just below the heart, catapulting him into Helena. Together, they tumbled to the very edge of the walkway. Wilson's shattered body slipped over the side towards the abyss. Helena's hand immediately snaked out and grasped hold, gripping him with grim determination as his weight dragged them both towards the drop.

'No! Not him!' Visblat cried, his eyes wide with terror. 'Oh my God!'

With a sound like grinding rock, the walls of the cavern began shaking, an earthquake rumbling and shuddering through Giza—a prelude to the labyrinth collapsing upon itself. Visblat had no choice but to retreat, his emotions swarming with limitless regret. He had killed his guaranteed ticket out of here. In a moment of madness, he had inadvertently destroyed the only man who could save him. He was now stuck in this nightmare forever.

'My God, what have I done?' he muttered as he staggered from the collapsing cavern.

HELENA PULLED WILSON upwards from the darkness, her muscles quivering with exertion. She didn't know where she'd got the strength to drag him back onto the walkway, but she did. All around, the walls were shaking. The bridge below her danced about. Fragments of rock were falling from the ceiling. She gazed at Wilson's lifeless body. His face was pale, his chest covered with blood. So much blood.

The bullet had been meant for her, she knew that.

An unbridled scream escaped her lips, echoing around the empty void in chorus with the quake. She turned and scanned the next walkway for Commander Visblat. But he was gone. Raising her weapon, she fired into the empty doorway of the labyrinth—shot after shot—trying to vent her anguish.

Why did I hesitate? she asked herself. *Why?*

The gun eventually jammed open—empty.

The painful memories of twelve years before came flooding back in stunning detail. Helena's worst fears had materialised. History was repeating itself in a slightly different form. Helena had failed. She had failed, yet again.

Meanwhile, the cavern shook and larger pieces of rock let go from the ceiling, smashing down onto the bridge. All the while the frightening tremors increased in magnitude.

37

California, The Americas
Enterprise Corporation, Head Office Tower
May 19th 2081
Local Time 8:05 p.m.

4 Days before Transport Test

'I'LL DO ALL THE TALKING,' Barton said. He stepped into the elevator with Wilson following and pressed the twelfth-floor button. 'Don't be lulled into a false sense of security. Keep your wits about you at all times.' The elevator began moving upwards. 'By being anywhere near the Tredwells we only put the transport test at risk. I warn you Wilson: you can't be too careful about what you say. These men are highly perceptive. They are experts in analysing people, with instincts that are rarely incorrect.'

Though Wilson had got the warning message perfectly the first ten times Barton had told him, he kept his reply cordial, 'I understand.'

'And no jokes. They don't have a sense of humour, like I do.' Barton raised an eyebrow as he checked his hair in the mirror, then fastidiously adjusted his mercury jacket. 'GM won't offer to shake your hand. He doesn't like unnecessary human contact. So don't offer to shake his. Same with Jasper.'

Wilson remembered that Jasper had avoided shaking hands in the storeroom that day.

Barton checked himself in the mirror one last time. 'Are you ready?'
'As ready as I'll ever be.'
The elevator doors opened and a beautiful blonde woman was

standing just outside. In her early twenties, she was about six feet tall, with broad shoulders and tanned skin. An Amazon princess, no doubt. Wilson had come to expect nothing less from Enterprise Corporation, but, even so, it was an effort for him to refrain from looking stunned.

'Barton, welcome back,' she said cordially. 'Mr Dowling, welcome to the executive level. My name is Cynthia. I am here to be of assistance, if you need anything.' She turned and glided towards the tall oak doors of the boardroom through an atrium-style foyer with a circular, peaked glass ceiling at least ten metres high. 'GM has allocated fifteen minutes to meet with you both.' She had on a dark pleated skirt and a tailored business shirt that outlined her perfect body. 'Please be brief with your discussions. Attempt to answer GM's questions as directly as possible.' She was all business—Cynthia the Amazon—with not a hint of emotion coursing through those genetically superior veins.

Barton smiled at her. 'No problem.'

The tabletops in the foyer held enormous displays of cut flowers. The walls were adorned with more famous paintings. Wilson immediately recognised a Van Gogh and a Picasso. They looked incredible, beggaring the photographs he'd studied in books. *The Rockefeller Museum must be bloody empty!* Wilson decided. Scanning the room, his attention was drawn to the half a dozen women working around the office, all young, all gorgeous. His eyes drifted towards Cynthia's perfect backside as it swayed from side to side in front of him. He bit his lip. This was the type of office he wanted to work in, one day.

Cynthia drew back the heavy oak doors with ease, flashed a bright smile and pointed inside.

'Thank you,' Wilson said. 'I like your outfit.' It was the most charming comment he could think of saying. She smiled in a way that suggested he was a lamb-to-the-slaughter in the most polite fashion one could imagine.

Two men sat silhouetted at the boardroom table, floor-to-ceiling glass behind them. In the distance, the setting sun was a bundle of gold, flooding warm summer sunshine across the room. The office was similar in layout to Barton's, but larger and more opulent. The Enterprise Corporation logo was again emblazoned across the wall behind a large desk. A separate lounge area with golden upholstered chairs stretched away to one side. What appeared to be a medical unit, with oxygen and a blood transfusion machine, was at the other end.

GM pressed down on his ivory cane and lifted himself from his seat. 'Come in Barton. You too, Mr Dowling.' He was immaculately dressed in a grey three-piece suit with a bright silver tie. At first glance, he was older and smaller than Wilson expected. His skin was pale and translucent, his fine hands laced with veins. And yet there was a youthful energy about him, as bright as the white carnation in his lapel. 'So this is the most powerful man in the world?' Wilson said to himself. He clearly had a liking for beautiful women—judging by his support staff—but that was merely a sign of power, which he obviously had in abundance. Wilson was keen to study GM's manner, and intellect, to find out what set him apart from everyone else. This was a rare opportunity.

'Good to see you, GM,' Barton said.

The response was warm. 'It's good to see you too, Barton.' Gesturing to his left, he said, 'Mr Dowling, this is my grandson, Jasper. Oh, that's right, you've already met.' Jasper stood beside his grandfather, looking like a slightly fresher clone of the old man, wearing exactly the same outfit, even down to the carnation.

'How are you, Jasper?' Barton said.

There was little sincerity to the reply. 'Never been better, thanks.'

Wilson just smiled at everyone.

With the setting sun behind the Tredwells, it was difficult to see them clearly. GM sat down and rested his white cane against the table. 'Please, everyone, be seated.' He made himself comfortable, then said, 'I suppose you are wondering why I called you here?' The old man took a sip of water. His hands were steady. 'Barton, we've known each other a long time.' He carefully placed the glass back on the table. 'You've been my top scientist for many years. One of the strengths of our relationship has always been the trust and honesty we have shared. Would you agree?'

Barton mirrored GM's body language. 'Yes, I would.'

'So tell me, Barton, what is it about *this* mercury project that would cause you to act differently?'

There was a pause, then he replied, 'There is no reason I can think of.'

'None?'

Barton waited a moment then said, 'None that I can see.'

'Let me rephrase my question. If the Dead Sea scrolls in some way told you to betray Enterprise Corporation, would you do it?'

Barton stayed outwardly calm. 'The Dead Sea scrolls were written thousands of years ago, GM. I don't see how they could possibly affect us here.' The logic was not at all consistent with what Barton had been preaching to Wilson—that all time existed simultaneously—but now was not the moment for Wilson to raise the issue.

GM sat back in his chair. 'Tell me, my old friend. What if coded messages in the Dead Sea scrolls in some way asked you to keep information to yourself? Would you do it?'

Barton thought a moment. 'If I was convinced there was no danger to Enterprise Corporation,' he said, 'or any of the mercury team members, I might keep the information a secret. Yes.' Jasper leant towards his grandfather and whispered in his ear. Barton continued, 'In *every* mercury experiment there is a level of risk that must be managed. That has always been the case. Certainly in my experience.'

'So you're telling me you have secrets?'

'If keeping from you information that you don't absolutley need to know is a secret—then yes, I do have secrets. Mercury projects are *always* complex. I can't tell you everything that happens; otherwise nothing would get done.'

'How do you decide what I *should* or *shouldn't* know?'

Barton took a short breath. 'You give me the objective, GM—I *always* give you the outcome. Remember, we built this company together. That's the way it has always been, and the way it always will be—for me at least. It's one of the reasons we've been so successful. You pay me to find solutions. And that's what I do. In the past you've never asked me how … only *when*.'

GM held his gaze. 'Today I start asking *how*. Are you comfortable with that?'

Barton didn't even blink. 'If that's what you want.'

GM pressed the intercom on his lapel. 'Bring it in now, thanks.'

All four men sat in silence again, studying each other. Moments later Cynthia appeared in the doorway with a rectangular wooden box in her hands. Wilson was always happy to see a woman as beautiful as her, but this time it was the box she held that sent his pulse racing. She gently placed it on the table, opened the lid, and extracted the Copper Scroll of Qumran.

'So tell me,' GM said. 'What does *this* have to do with time travel?'

Staring at the tube of copper, Barton was silent for a moment. Eventually he said, 'Wilson wanted to see it.'

GM shifted his gaze to Wilson. 'Why would you want to see this?'

Barton replied, 'He was concerned—' but GM stopped him mid-sentence.

'Not you, Barton. Mr Dowling can answer.'

'I asked Barton to show it to me,' Wilson said cautiously.

'Why is that? When *this*,' he held up the scroll, 'is supposed to be just a copy?'

Wilson could sense that the Tredwells knew it was the *genuine* Copper Scroll. It was the only reason the question would be asked the way it was. Against Barton's instructions, Wilson gambled with the truth. 'I think you will find that is the *real* Copper Scroll of Qumran,' he said confidently.

The old man's face showed no surprise as he shifted his gaze back to Barton. 'You told me this was a copy,' he said.

'Wilson's right,' Barton continued. 'If that scroll came from the G2 storage room, you are indeed holding the *genuine* Copper Scroll of Qumran. I had a duplicate made and swapped it for the original, in the foyer, so I could have access to it when I needed it.'

'Why would you do that?'

'Because, at one time, I believed the Copper Scroll of Qumran was important.'

'What do you believe now?' GM said slyly.

'The Copper Scroll you are holding is inconsequential.'

GM's eyes drilled into Wilson. 'Then, why did you want to see this?'

'Because,' Wilson answered. '*That* scroll doesn't lead to any treasure.'

'Please explain,' GM said.

Barton respectfully offered to answer and GM agreed. The mercury scientist went into great detail about the Roman invasion led by Vespasian and the priceless treasures of the Temple of Jerusalem.

'And *this* scroll never led to any treasure?' GM said.

'No, it did not,' Barton answered.

'What does it lead to then?'

'I'm not certain, GM. It may not lead to anything,' Barton said.

Light flickered off the shiny copper as the old man turned it over in his frail hands. Seeing it again confirmed for Wilson that it was one of the most extraordinary objects he had ever seen. He would never forget the sensation of holding it—the subtle vibration it emitted. Cynthia carefully took the scroll from GM and placed it on the table.

'Why would you want to see this if you know it's a fake?' GM asked.

Wilson answered thoughtfully, 'That's simple. If the Copper Scroll is a fake, then the Book of Esther might just be a fake as well.'

'That means what, exactly?'

'If the Book of Esther is a fake, then this whole transport thing might get a little messy. That means *more* danger. And to me, that means *more* compensation.' Wilson looked up at Cynthia—from the blank expression on her face she considered him merely an opportunist. But under the circumstances, greed was his most secure backup position.

Barton covered Wilson's tracks perfectly. 'The mercury team are fully satisfied that the Book of Esther and the blueprints contained within them are real, Wilson.'

'*You* were satisfied—I was not.'

GM thought a while. 'Are you satisfied now?'

Wilson rubbed his chin the way Barton always did. 'As much as I can be, I guess.'

GM placed one hand on his ivory walking stick. 'I feel much the same way, Mr Dowling. Experimenting with time travel is of great concern to me. And yet I know that we must proceed. I *too* am not fully satisfied with all this, and yet I am going along with it, also.'

Wilson said, 'Would you climb inside that crystal transport pod and allow your molecules to be disassembled at the speed of light?'

GM smiled. 'No, I would not.'

'Just out of curiosity, do you think I'm crazy?'

'Not at all. I think you have made a commercial transaction that suits you. I understand that. I have done it many times in my life.' GM paused. 'There are risks here. There is no question about that.' He paused again. 'As a result, Jasper and I are extremely nervous about the transport test. For the record, we have considered putting a stop to it, immediately.' The old man's gaze shifted to his mercury scientist. 'Have you got anything you want to say to that?'

'Simply this,' Barton replied. 'There will be no danger to Enterprise Corporation because of this transport test. Trust me.' His gaze was steady. 'The information was put into the scrolls, two thousand years ago, for a reason. By an intellect far greater than our own.'

'That's what I'm worried about,' GM said.

'It's funny, but that *very* thing is comforting to me,' Barton countered.

GM tilted his head ever so slightly to one side. He was unwittingly deciding the fate of the Mission of Isaiah at that very moment. 'Your judgment has always been good enough for me, Barton. I'll let you proceed.'

Jasper interjected, 'We have more questions, Grandfather.'

'I haven't forgotten, Jasper.' At GM's command, Cynthia replaced the Copper Scroll in the wooden box and closed the lid. 'So tell me, Barton, what have you got to say about Wilson's brain scan? Apparently his alpha and beta waves were unusually high. Why is that?'

'I redid Wilson's medicals myself,' Barton said calmly. 'The ECG machine we used the first time was malfunctioning. The original results were completely ridiculous—I knew that the moment I saw them. Wilson here is completely normal.' Barton continued to give more details of the ECG fault and what he did to fix it.

'Okay,' GM said. 'That's enough. I'm happy. Let's talk about something a little more serious. Jasper's investigation revealed that *you* were one of the people illegally using the grade-one security system. You should know better, my friend.'

Barton took on a disarming pose, both palms held upwards. 'I knew you were going to bring that up,' he said. 'I was trying to protect Enterprise Corporation, GM—as I'm sure you already know. I only used the system to spy on Wilson, here. Nothing else. I would expect you to forgive me for that indiscretion.'

GM locked his gaze on Jasper. 'Is this true?'

'Yes, Grandfather, that appears to be the case.'

GM adjusted his seating position. 'Well, that seems reasonable enough to me.' He drummed his fingers on the tabletop, thinking. 'As a favour to you, Barton, we'll keep this under wraps. Out of interest, why have you chosen Mr Dowling over the other gentleman from Europe?'

Jasper said, 'Are you aware, Mr Dowling, there is another candidate?'

Wilson nodded. 'Yes, I am. I've been encouraging Barton to use him since the very beginning.' The flippant comment was met with a stony silence.

Barton cleared his throat. 'He's only joking, GM.'

GM asked the same question again, even more seriously. 'Besides Mr Dowling's obvious sense of humour, which must be very entertaining for you ... why did you select him?'

'Because he is clearly the best choice.'

'Is he the choice you would make if you had more time?'

'Are you offering me more time?'

'No, I'm not. Just answer the question, please.'

Barton looked over in Wilson's direction. 'He would be my number one choice even if time was unlimited.'

'Good,' GM said. 'That's what I want to hear. Now give me a quick update and then you can get back to work. I'm sure you have plenty to do. Time is ticking.'

Barton rubbed his hands together. 'The mercury team are on track to conduct the final transport test in four days, at midday. The experiment will send Wilson into the future by thirty minutes. He will disappear from inside the Imploder Sphere—de-atomised by particle lasers—then get sucked into the magnetic field of the earth via the Inflator diamond. Exactly thirty minutes later, his quark-gluon energy will reappear from the magnetic-field portal and he will be reconstructed, as he is now, right where he began.'

Wilson rubbed his temples, the stress clearly evident.

'That sounds easy enough,' GM said, seemingly amused by Wilson's reaction. Jasper whispered in his grandfather's ear again and the old man's eyebrows lifted. 'That's right, thank you, Jasper. There's one more thing ... we want Andre Steinbeck reinstated.'

Barton's cool demeanour was suddenly compromised. 'He used the grade-one security system to spy on me! I found that out myself.'

GM shook his head. 'Our investigation indicates he was not the one using it. Someone else had control of his authorisation password. It appears that Andre is innocent.'

Barton stared into space. 'Who was watching me then?'

'We are not certain.'

'I'm not comfortable bringing Andre back on the team,' Barton stated. 'We are at a sensitive stage in the transport process. Even the most minor miscalculation could cause a problem beyond imagination. I need a team of people I can trust.'

'This is not a point for discussion,' Jasper interrupted.

'You're undermining my authority,' Barton replied.

'It's a small price to pay, my old friend.' GM pressed down on his walking stick and stood from his chair. 'You're lucky I'm not stopping the test altogether.' It seemed the discussion was over. 'You are to reinstate Andre, immediately. See to it.' He gave Wilson a fleeting smile. 'I wish you both good luck, gentlemen. Especially you, Mr Dowling.'

The tall oak doors to the foyer swung open and Cynthia gestured towards the elevators.

'This way gentlemen,' she said.

THE DOORS EVENTUALLY closed and Jasper crossed his arms. 'I'm uncomfortable, Grandfather.'

GM steadied himself with his cane and gingerly sat down again. 'Interesting, wasn't it?'

'We should put a stop to the test. This is too risky.'

'If Barton succeeds,' he replied, 'we will have an awesome weapon at our disposal. Imagine having the power to travel time? It's mind-boggling.'

Jasper stared out the window, blank-faced. The sun had dipped well below the horizon and the sky was a pallet of purples washing upwards into the darkness. 'I can see the benefits also, Grandfather. I just question how much control we really have over what's going on here. It worries me.' He tapped his bottom lip with his index finger. 'Barton's telling Wilson everything. It's obvious. Clearly, they already knew we'd figured out the Copper Scroll was genuine.'

GM concurred, 'And the young man didn't even flinch when he found out Barton had been spying on him.'

'Or when you mentioned the second Gen-EP candidate,' Jasper added. 'I question their relationship, Grandfather, and their motives.'

'Yes, I agree. They have become quite close in a rather short time. It's surprising. Very un-Barton like. He's generally much more discerning about people.' GM took another sip of water. 'It was a very controlled display from them both.' He thought a moment. 'Wilson is interesting, isn't he? Confident to a fault. Unusual … especially under the circumstances. We need to get an angle on him; something other than money.'

'I'll have him checked out again.'

GM stared at the wooden box on the table. 'There must be a reason why Barton wanted the Copper Scroll under his control. That charade about it being a fake seems absurd, on reflection. Barton's gone to a lot of trouble, and he doesn't do anything without a very good reason. The Copper Scroll is important … it must be.' The old man held out his white cane. 'You were right to bring this to my attention, Jasper. Start by finding out why the Copper Scroll of Qumran is so important.

Get someone to look at it again. We're obviously missing something.'

GM was unaware that Jasper had Andre researching the matter already.

'Are you sure you want to continue with the transport test?' Jasper asked.

The old man nodded thoughtfully. 'For now, we let Barton proceed. But as a precaution, put him and Mr Dowling under constant surveillance. If they're up to something, I want to know about it before it happens.'

38

Giza Plateau, Egypt
Under the Pyramid of Khafre
December 21st 2012
Local Time 0:51 a.m.

Mission of Isaiah—Day Twenty-Seven

THE UNDERGROUND EARTHQUAKE intensified. Gaping cracks splintered across the ceiling. Dust filled the rattling air. Oil lanterns dropped from the walls, one by one, to be swallowed by the darkness, a faint echo of their destruction rising from the chasm below.

The entire world seemed to have become unstable and shivering.

Helena hovered over Wilson's blood-soaked body. The bullet had struck the left side of his chest, tearing his flesh to shreds. She searched for a pulse, but felt nothing. At the same time she was trying to protect him from the debris raining down upon them. One of the four bridges, the furthest away, suddenly sheared from its foundations. The stone structure groaned as gravity dragged its enormous mass downwards into the abyss. With a thunderous bang, the four doors to the labyrinth slammed shut, simultaneously.

Helena drew Wilson's limp body closer to hers. There was nowhere to run. No means of escape. Everything around her was possessed by a relentless fit of shuddering. To the deafening roar of crumbling rock, the bridges on either side vanished from sight. Helena was so terrified she had to concentrate just to keep breathing. The bridge she was perched upon was certainly next to fall.

A veil of stillness suddenly descended.

Even the dust floating in the cavern appeared to hang motionless in the air. The earthquake seemed to be over.

Clasping Wilson's body tight, Helena searched for any sign of life. She had spent the last month chasing after him, and now he was dead in her arms. In many ways she hardly knew him, but there was an undeniable connection between them that would now be lost forever.

Desperate to find help or a means of escape, she scanned her surroundings. Nothing remained in the gloomy underground cavern except for the lone bridge she and Wilson were on, and the few oil lanterns still clinging valiantly to the walls. In a way, Helena's resolve to find Wilson had been like this bridge, she thought; it had held up against the odds, while all else around her had crumbled.

She stared at Wilson's face. 'You chose the correct door, Wilson,' she said comfortingly. 'You chose the correct path.'

Helena reeled in utter disbelief as Wilson's eyes peeled open.

He was breathing—gazing back at her with a distressed comprehension in his eyes. How was this possible? The front of his shirt, just below his heart, was saturated with blood, rags of flesh jutting through the ripped material.

'Activate Nightingale,' Wilson said, wincing in agony.

His expression immediately relaxed. In a trance-like daze, he sat up in robotic fashion, yanked open his shirt and thrust his fingers deep into the fleshy wound, as though trying to extract something wedged between his ribs.

Helena cringed as she watched the blood pour relentlessly out of the open wound. 'Activate *what*? How can you be alive?' she said, backing away as if she was looking at a ghost.

With the lamplight flickering over him, Wilson used both hands to try to dislodge something jammed between his ribs. Finally it came free. Not showing any pain, he wiped the bloodied object clean and held it up for them both to see.

It was a large silver coin.

Helena leaned closer again, trying to understand what was happening.

Wilson carefully tucked the folds of skin back into his wound. From his brief inspection, it felt like his ribs were definitely broken. Gazing at the bloodied coin a second time, he saw the indentation where the bullet had struck the surface.

'What the hell is going on?' Helena whispered. 'How did you ... *how?*'

Wilson held the coin in his fingertips. An Egyptian pound—the very coin his grandfather had given him in the future; his *fate coin*. The question of how it had been damaged—a secret Wilson had wondered about many times—had now been answered.

'You shouldn't be alive!' Helena said.

'The bullet hit Farouk's coin,' Wilson announced. 'It was in my breast-pocket.' Although groggy from the healing command, he was still able to remember the little Egyptian's face.

Helena's mouth hung open in an expression of disbelief.

'Hit a coin in your pocket?' She was dumbstruck. 'Don't you feel anything?' At that moment some of her visions made more sense. Wilson had a way to manage pain; that was how he was able to escape from the hospital that night. She sat cross-legged on the walkway in front of him, unable to move for fear that everything she was seeing was merely a dream.

Gingerly removing his shirt, Wilson wiped his body clean of excess blood. He looked down and saw that the flow from the gunshot wound was now just a trickle.

'Don't you *feel* anything?' Helena asked again.

Wilson tore a strip off his shirt and folded the coin into the material. The Egyptian pound was an object that had been with him all his life, and here it was—the indentation on its surface made by a bullet that otherwise would have taken his life. It was so complicated it was almost frustrating to think about. He stuffed the coin into his pants pocket.

'I need to lie down,' Wilson whispered, his body exhausted. 'Just for a little while.' His skin was pale as ivory and he felt he could faint at any second.

Helena grabbed Wilson's hand and steadied him. Up to this moment, her own shock had made it difficult to think clearly. She half-carried him to the end of the walkway, cleared away some fallen pieces of rock, and laid him safely by the wall of the pyramid. Sitting next to him, she gently placed his head in her lap.

'I'm right here with you,' she said soothingly. 'I can't believe it. I'm so happy you're still alive.' She was overwhelmed with gratitude that this second chance had been given her.

Wilson smiled, his voice barely audible, 'I just need some time to rest,' and he drifted into unconsciousness.

FIVE HOURS LATER, Wilson emerged from his self-induced coma. He was lying in the same position, with Helena bent over him, her eyes closed. She was breathing on his forehead and he took a moment to enjoy the warmth of her being so close.

Helena was momentarily startled as he cancelled his omega command.

'You're awake,' she said drowsily. Her gaze settled on her wristwatch. 'We've been here for hours. I wanted to let you sleep.'

Under the circumstances, Wilson felt amazingly well. He slowly lifted his head and gazed about him. Though the air in the cavern had cleared of dust, it had also grown gloomier—more than ninety per cent of the lanterns were extinguished, or gone.

Helena pressed her fingers against Wilson's chest. 'Your wound?' The torn skin had healed over and was now just a red welt. 'You're not going to believe this ...'

'I used a healing command,' he said.

She tried her best not to look surprised. 'Can everyone do that in the future?'

He sat up. 'Not everyone.'

'That was how you survived the car accident, wasn't it?'

Wilson nodded. 'It's a cerebral command. It helps speed up my natural healing systems.'

'That's how you see in the dark, right? Another command.'

'Yes.'

Wilson looked around the empty cavern. The other three bridges spanning the abyss had disappeared and a thick layer of rubble covered the last remaining walkway. The four doors to the labyrinth were gone, closed over by huge blocks of stone. The roof had shut down upon itself, just as the prophecy said it would.

'There was an earthquake,' she said. 'Right after you were shot.'

'And Visblat?'

She pointed. 'He went back inside. I'm not sure if he made it.'

Wilson probed his ribs, feeling the sharp indentations where the coin had been wedged. 'I can't believe Visblat shot me.'

'He's possessed in some way.' Helena said. 'It's in his eyes.'

'Visblat needed me for something. I know it. Otherwise he wouldn't have gone to so much trouble to chase us the way he did. It just doesn't make any sense.'

'He was shooting at *me*,' Helena replied. She ran her hands through her hair in obvious frustration. 'I couldn't pull the trigger.' Visblat's fearsome gaze momentarily entered her mind and she felt a cold sweat flush her body. 'I don't know what happened.' Helena's breathing became shallow as the face of her mother, Camilla, flashed before her. 'I was utterly helpless,' she muttered.

Rising to a crouched position, Wilson said, 'It's not your fault. His eyes have been modified. You couldn't shoot him even if you wanted to.'

'He's just a man!' Helena said wrathfully. 'I should have been able to protect you.' Every muscle in her body was rigid. 'I knew he was going to fire, yet I couldn't do anything!' Helena could feel the sensation of the trigger against her finger, the cold hard steel. It was the very same situation she had promised herself she would *never* let happen again.

Wilson did his best to explain about Visblat's optical trackenoids and the work the military had done to refine the process. 'There wasn't anything you could have done,' he reiterated. But the explanation did nothing to mollify her.

'It makes no difference. I never should have let it happen.' Helena's tone suddenly became accusing, 'Visblat's from the *future*, and you say you've never seen him before! He seems to know you! How many time travellers are there, anyway?'

'Obviously, lots of them,' Wilson replied sarcastically. 'And, by the way, I'm quite certain I'd remember if I'd seen *that* guy's face ... *hell!* He ain't no oil painting.'

Wilson's attention diverted to the wall behind him. 'Have you seen this?' he asked. A smooth black disc, a ceramic of some kind, was now exposed at chest height on the wall of the pyramid. Over the next minute Wilson took great care to check the rest of the stone blocks to make sure he hadn't missed anything.

Meanwhile, Helena continued to seethe. 'What was the code word?' she said. 'The code word Barton told you?'

'I made that part up.'

She looked confused. 'You made it up?'

'Yep.'

'There was *no* code word?'

'Correct.'

'Then, how did you know Visblat was lying?'

'I can guarantee you one thing: Barton never sent him here. If he did, Visblat would've known that *coincidence is the signpost of destiny*. I heard that bloody comment ten times a day for two weeks. Anyway ... Visblat claimed that Barton's life depended on the second portal staying open. That didn't make any sense ... still doesn't.'

Watching Wilson standing there, Helena suddenly wanted to pinch herself. He was alive, in front of her, shirt off, strutting about as if nothing had happened. The left side of his pants was stained with blood, but otherwise he looked fine. It was remarkable.

'Let's see what happens, eh?' Wilson fearlessly jabbed the black ceramic disc on the wall. There was suddenly a loud crunching sound like two pieces of rock sliding together.

'Why did you do that?' Helena said frantically, her eyes scanning left and right. 'Every time you touch something there's an earth-quake!' She gazed apprehensively at the jagged ceiling, waiting for something bad to happen.

Instead, only streams of harmless-looking white sand poured from two vertical gaps, about two metres tall, cut into the wall of the pyramid. In moments, the rock split under its own weight and dropped apart in a series of thuds. A V-shaped doorway cantilevered open, a cool gust of wind equalising the pressure inside.

'You worry too much,' Wilson said.

'Just promise me you won't touch anything else, *please*.' With a popping sound, another bank of lanterns ignited, revealing a steep, narrow staircase that continued upwards into the pyramid.

'I guess I won't tell you about the portal room, then,' he replied. Without waiting for her to respond, he grabbed Helena's hand and led her up the V-shaped staircase. It ascended high into the bowels of the structure, at least a hundred steps, then turned left, an intense white light shining ahead.

Approaching the triangular entrance, Wilson squinted inside. The chamber itself was pyramid-shaped, about ten metres square at the base, with triangular walls that tilted in towards the peaked roof. The inside of the room was almost phosphorescent in colour—the radiant glow just short of overpowering. On each of the four walls was a single hieroglyph. Wilson knew the images well. 'North, South, East and West,' he said. In the centre of the chamber stood a large stone pedestal, cylindrical in shape, with a flat top. A crystal statuette of a pyramid gleamed in the middle of its surface.

'The task,' Wilson said, 'is to take the *little pyramid* and drop it into one of those.' He gestured to the numerous square indentions on the circular surface. There were more than eighty in total, like a giant chessboard cut into the stone.

'How do you know which square?' Helena asked.

Wilson leapt up on the tabletop and prepared to lift the fist-sized pyramid from its holder. *'Release the Morning Sun'* he recited to himself; which meant it had to be one of the twenty or so slots on the eastern quadrant—because the sun rises in the east. Placing the crystal pyramid towards the rising sun would reduce the earth's magnetic field by *lowering* the Schumann Frequency. Placing it towards the west would have the opposite effect.

'There are dozens of positions,' Helena said.

Rubbing his thumb and forefinger together in preparation, Wilson lifted the highly polished statuette from its holder. The walls of the portal room immediately turned a glowing scarlet.

'There won't be any storms this time, will there?' Helena said dubiously. 'Lightning, that sort of thing?'

'Not a chance,' Wilson replied. The crystal pyramid vibrated in his hand. The sensation was very similar to the one created by the Copper Scroll, only with a higher pitch.

'Can you hear that?' he said. When he moved the statuette from side to side, the frequency altered. Waving it over the numerous squares on the eastern quadrant, within seconds, Wilson detected the spot where the crystal was chiming at a similar pitch to that of the Copper Scroll. It was his best guess of 6.53 hertz.

Instinctively, he dropped the statuette into place.

The red walls became jet-black and a shaft of startling white light shot from the crystal towards the apex of the ceiling. Stunned by the brightness, he tumbled backwards off the tabletop, landing heavily at Helena's feet. The entire pedestal sheered at the base and began rotating in an anti-clockwise direction, faster and faster—the steady beam of white brilliance cutting through the air in sweeping arcs, like a miniature searchlight. As the podium picked up speed, the whistling sound it generated grew steadily louder.

Suddenly, everything went into slow motion.

The events at Chichén Itzá still fresh in his mind, Wilson grabbed Helena's arm and pushed her towards the northern exit, but as they approached the doorway it disappeared from view.

Helena pointed across the chamber. 'There!'

A new entrance had cantilevered open on the eastern wall. The swirling beam of light from the podium provided a strobe-like illumination as the pair, disoriented by the slowness of time, ran into the blackened corridor. No sooner had they stepped outside than a massive block of granite thumped unhesitatingly into the floor behind them.

The portal room was sealed off.

Silence.

The ground tilted away ever so slightly.

In the distance, Wilson could see a faint arc of golden light. He squinted, trying to identify what it was. Then another block of stone dropped from the ceiling with a thud, missing the back of Wilson's heels by only centimetres.

The corridor was collapsing!

The pair broke into a sprint. The slowness of time was so profound, it felt like they were hardly moving. With every step the corridor brightened. Something was peppering against their faces as they ran. They were breathing it in, also. The increasing light revealed thin streams of sand trickling through the cracks of the ceiling.

'Hurry!' Wilson yelled.

'It's the rising sun!' Helena called out, pointing towards the golden glow ahead. Her voice was reduced to a deep drone.

The corridor was leading them east, outside the pyramid.

The roof systematically slammed closed, from the inside out—stone blocks falling faster and faster.

Thud … Thud …Thud … Thud …

Wilson shouted as he ran, Helena just in front of him, 'Run, Helena! Run!'

Gusts of wind blustered past them as they dived outside, full stretch, onto a narrow rock ledge just as the last section of the corridor slammed closed with a mighty crunch, behind them.

They found themselves three-quarters of the way up the eastern face of the Pyramid of Khafre, just under the limestone casing.

Time swiftly surged back to its normal speed.

In the distance, the sun was creeping over the horizon into a clear Egyptian sky. There was no breeze. The bustling city of Cairo lay sprawled out before them. Green croplands were clearly visible against the desert, flanking the Nile on both sides, as it snaked its way through the barren wilderness.

'Did you feel the way everything went into slow motion?' Helena said. 'It was just like Chichén Itzá.'

'Yeah, I felt it,' Wilson replied. Both his elbows were grazed and bleeding from the heavy landing. He looked up at the sky to see a group of dark clouds magically forming above them. 'We need to get off here, I think.'

The temperature suddenly plummeted and the atmosphere became moist. Thunder rumbled overhead.

'You said there wouldn't be any storms,' Helena called out over the clamour.

Wilson gazed down the stepped face of the Pyramid of Khafre, assessing the best path to ground level. 'I lied. Now get moving!'

Within twenty seconds a torrential downpour covered the landscape, repainting the world with a misty palette of greys. It was difficult just to breathe with so much rainwater in the air. Wilson and Helena crawled down the pyramid, block by block. Swelling streams cascaded after them, hastily pushing them forward.

'It hasn't rained like this on the Giza plateau for over ten centuries!' Wilson yelled. 'Around here, the average rainfall is less than one inch per year!' The Giza plateau had just received one inch of rain in the last five seconds.

Thunder continued to rumble deafeningly overhead.

Wind swirled and blustered.

The storm clouds crackled like an overcharged battery.

Everything grew darker.

With a flash of intense brightness, a huge lightning bolt—millions of volts of electricity—struck the pyramid with a deafening *crack*. The rainwater cascading down the stones energised.

The sudden charge caused Wilson and Helena's bodies to convulse, flinging them into the air, end-over-end, off the pyramid into the wet sand.

39

Cairo, Egypt
Ritz Carlton Hotel
December 21st 2012
Local Time 7:00 a.m.

Mission of Isaiah—Day Twenty-Seven

ON THE OTHER SIDE of Cairo, Visblat sat in his second-floor hotel suite. The room was a mess. Pieces of overturned furniture, including lamps, chairs and a flat-panel TV, lay in pieces on the floor.

Visblat stood up, fists clenched in fury, and paced to the other side of the room, where he kicked another hole in the plaster wall. He then turned his livid gaze back to his .44 Magnum on the side table. He was reliving the exact moment when he had pulled the trigger.

Regret speared through him, the same way his bullet had pierced Wilson's chest.

Why did he shield that bitch? he asked himself. *She's ruined everything!*

He poured another glass of scotch and slammed it back.

Killing Wilson Dowling was a mistake he would have to live with for the rest of his life. Visblat glanced at his weapon, assessing his options. Maybe it was time to end things right now, he thought. At this moment, his depression easily overwhelmed his desire to live.

It was certainly the only way to escape this nightmare.

He poured yet another scotch and sculled it to fortify his courage. The bottle was now three-quarters empty. Wiping his mouth with his sleeve, he eyed his gun yet again, loaded and ready, and reached over to pick it up. At that moment, an unexpected sound tapped against the window as if telling him to stop.

It was a shower of rain.

Visblat took a moment to realise what was happening. He walked to the balcony, his legs a little wobbly, and stared west towards the Giza plateau. Thick grey veils of rain swept over the city towards him. He felt his pulse increasing. In just seconds he couldn't see more than ten metres in any direction. The deluge was so heavy that the gardens and streets outside the Ritz Carlton disappeared under a torrent of muddy water.

Had the second portal been opened? It was the only explanation.

Visblat recalled the medical report he had read in Houston, and the pieces began to fall into place. The injuries Wilson sustained from the car accident on the 610 freeway were reported as 'severe'. Was this more of the same?

That bastard has tricked me!

Wilson should never have been able to walk away from that car accident, Visblat realised. He nodded to himself. It seemed his rival had a way of cheating death. *That's it!* Barton must have done something—taught Wilson something. There must be information in the scrolls that Andre hadn't seen. *The fool!*

A stroke of lightning surged from the clouds over Giza, the dazzling flash lighting up the hotel room. Visblat stepped out onto the balcony, dizzy from so much alcohol, and felt the sobering rain against his face. In a complete change of mood he raised his arms towards the heavens as if in supplication. It seemed that Wilson was still alive.

In just seconds, Visblat was soaked to the skin by the deluge, an unashamed smile plastered across his face. There was reason to live again.

40

Giza Plateau, Egypt
The Base of the Pyramid of Khufu
December 21st 2012
Local Time 7:02 a.m.

Mission of Isaiah—Day Twenty-Seven

HEAVY RAIN FILLED the air. Thunder clapped and groaned with ear-shattering intensity. Gusts of wind swirled erratically backwards and forwards in no particular direction. Lightning flashed, thick bolts cracking into the Pyramid of Khafre, making an outline of the structure leap out of the haze with every strike.

Wilson felt himself being lifted to his feet by Helena. He was groggy and wasn't sure what had just happened.

'Get up!' she yelled, frantically. 'We have to go!'

Wilson steadied himself in the downpour, torrents of water now swirling around his ankles. The desert sands were being overwhelmed by the sheer amount of rain falling from the sky. The water levels were rising by the second.

With Helena taking the lead, Wilson was dragged through the deluge as lightning continued to flash behind them. His joints ached and his muscles were sore, as if he had been beaten all over. He had been struck by lightning, he eventually concluded. The last thing he remembered was climbing down the last few blocks of the pyramid—then nothing. Blackness and silence, until Helena's yelling drew him back into consciousness and she pulled him to his feet out of the rising water.

Wilson cupped his hand over his nose and mouth, the same way Helena did, to form an umbrella against the driving rain. They sloshed forward, the seemingly endless stone wall of another pyramid—Khufu—beside them, waterfalls gushing down the stepped surface.

The outline of a modern building came into view through the downpour. It was exactly the place Helena had been looking for. She ran towards the entrance and rattled the glass doors. They were padlocked together with a heavy steel chain. A wall of frothy water spewed and swelled towards them, like a rising point break at a surf beach, getting deeper with each passing moment. Taking aim, she fired a shot through the plate-glass window and the panel shattered. She kicked it free, then dived inside just as the wave engulfed the doorway. Seconds later Wilson was washed into the silence of the stairwell and struggled up the concrete steps beside her. The swirling torrent continued to stream in through the opening as they moved towards higher ground.

'This is a museum,' she said. 'It's the only modern building around here. It houses a royal sailing boat, or something like that.'

Every muscle in Wilson's body was still aching.

The pair emerged from the staircase into a huge free-span building that housed a single perfectly preserved sailing ship. The slender vessel was suspended on pylons. Made entirely of cedar, it was more than forty-three metres long, with a tall sweeping bow and a deck that tapered elegantly at both ends. Five enormous oars jutted from each side. A long trailing rudder projected from the stern.

Rain continued to hammer the angled roof of the museum.

Lightning flashed in through the windows.

Water dripping from her clothes and hair, Helena began reading a copper plaque mounted on a pedestal, as if to distract herself. 'It belonged to the Pharaoh Khufu,' she said. 'It says here, this ship carried him into the "next life". It was buried with him as part of his treasure in 2566 BC.'

The Royal Ship of Khufu was hermetically sealed in a thirty metre rock pit just outside the Great Pyramid—it had been dismantled into 650 parts. After its discovery, and five years of careful restoration, it was returned to its former glory to reside in its brand-new viewing museum above the very spot where it had laid underground for so long.

Thunder rumbled outside, lightning flashed.

Thoughts were conjured in Wilson's mind of the great ship gently drifting down the Nile more than 4500 years before, its sails flapping in the breeze, slaves manning the oars. Wilson imagined Khufu wearing his elaborate headdress and loincloth. His four wives lounging on the deck. Young children—including his second-eldest son, Khafre—playing in the sun around him.

Helena slicked back her hair. 'How long do you think this storm will last?'

Wilson had no idea, but replied, 'Not long.' He struggled up the stairs to the next level, muscles burning, to a concourse that went the full length of the enclosure. The sailing ship was magnificent. The timber was still dark, like a ripe plum, and each joint was precise and tight fitting. On the deck, towards the rear, was a single square state-cabin. Stepping aboard, Wilson peered inside. The cabin had chiffon drapes, pink and light blue, hanging loosely from the ceiling. A low bed, inlaid with gold, was covered with dozens of soft cushions.

At various points around the large museum, streams of liquid poured from the ceiling, splashing into ever-growing puddles on the floor.

'If this storm gets any worse,' Wilson said, 'we're definitely going to hope this thing still floats.'

Helena remembered the grief she had endured when Wilson was lying in her arms and she had thought he was dead. The emotion was overpowering—even now. She watched him carefully, the gait of his walk, the muscles of his bare chest and stomach, the smile he gave her that somehow oozed a total self-confidence in what he was doing. He was handsome to her now, not annoying as she had sometimes found him to be. Backing Wilson into the state-cabin, she unclipped her Kevlar jacket and let it fall to the floor. Her wet clothes clung to every curve of her flesh.

She held his gaze.

Just seeing her look at him that way made Wilson self-conscious.

'There's no way out of here until the storm clears,' she said softly. 'Is there?'

'I guess not.'

'We're stuck here, then?' she confirmed.

Wilson glanced towards the glass windows on the eastern wall of the museum. The storm seemed to be raging even more wildly, the roof of the building groaning and squeaking like it was about to be torn off.

'I think you're right,' he said, but before he could finish his sentence, her lips pressed against his and her tongue slipped passionately into his mouth. Then she pulled back, and pushed him away.

Was it just an experiment to see if he would kiss her back? Wilson wondered.

Helena stood silent, as if she was thinking.

A bead of rainwater rolled down her face and she licked it away as it settled above her top lip. She raised her hands to her shirt buttons and began to undo them, one by one. The storm continued to pound the walls of the museum as she stripped off the military garment, leaving her naked from the waist up, as Wilson was.

The sight caused him to back up, aching muscles forgotten, and he fell backwards on the bed. Helena crawled slowly across the silk sheets towards him and pressed her flesh against his. Their lips met again in a gentle kiss that quickly became more urgent. Wind and rain whistled through the walls of the museum, but the air inside the state-cabin of the royal ship was utterly motionless. Wet clothes were removed piece by piece, hitting the wooden floor with a slap, the combined heat of their bodies fast drying their skin.

While Wilson was sailing aboard *Number Twenty-Three* he had fantasised about this moment—and now he was here. Everything was so natural, so uncomplicated in a way, as they pressed skin against skin and explored each other's lips with abandon.

Helena probed with her tongue, her kisses moving to his neck and chest. Wilson watched her, the way she moved, the curves of her flesh. For a moment he wondered if the Pharaoh Khufu had made love with any of his wives on this very spot. In Wilson's opinion, nothing the King of Egypt had experienced could possibly compare with this.

Helena felt the strength in Wilson's body and it fuelled her need for him. Who was this man she was with? She was unlikely to ever know the real answer, but she was certain of her attraction to him; and the more they touched, the greater her need became.

Wilson pulled back for just a moment, entranced by Helena's beauty. The misty blueness of her eyes took his breath away. He pulled her on top of him and she sat astride his body, kissing more deeply and fiercely than she had ever kissed another. Whatever she felt for him, there was no denying her hunger at this moment. She wanted him now, to hell with the consequences; she would wait no longer.

Helena eased herself back, and he slid effortlessly inside her.

She moved now, rocking gently with a power that overwhelmed Wilson's senses. Each thrust was pure ecstasy as they joined so perfectly, so closely. It was as if the chaos outside would wait until their passion had taken its full course.

Helena moaned, gently clawing Wilson's skin. So deep, all the way to her soul, so passionate. Feeling an orgasm welling in her, she threw herself to the sheets and brought Wilson on top of her, to watch him loving her, adoring her, devouring her with his gaze. The minutes felt like seconds as the tide of their union advanced and receded as inevitably as the ocean under a full moon. The tempo increased with their passion, till they reached a world beyond any that either of them had known before. Then it happened: an explosion of emotion and love, their eyes locked on each other, as wave after wave shuddered through them.

It was as if every ounce of passion Wilson had ever felt was condensed into that single moment. Part of it was the unexpected nature of their coupling. Partly, that he had flirted with death so many times in the last few days. His emotions for Helena had been compressed, and the intensity scared him. Breathing heavily, he lay down beside her and held her tight.

Wilson suddenly felt exposed, not wanting Helena to know his feelings. But little did he realise that, at that moment, through a blue haze, she could see clearly through his eyes. His tears were no secret to her.

The visual connection slowly faded from Helena's mind as bright sunlight beamed across the bow of the Pharaoh's sailing boat. The storm had ended abruptly and they hadn't even noticed.

'Maybe you are a Love Machine, after all,' Helena said softly.

Wilson wanted to laugh, but he just couldn't force it out, so he studied Helena's hand on his skin. He wanted to remember this moment forever.

Then something snapped in him—the realisation that he had crossed the line, that he had made a serious mistake by making love with her. One moment he was so content and self-indulgent, the next moment he was utterly regretful.

'Why are you here?' Helena said, as if in response to his thoughts. 'You have to tell me.'

He kissed her gently on the forehead, trying desperately to hold on to the moment, but part of him was already backing away.

'Have you ever wondered,' he said, 'why it feels as though every year goes by faster and faster? Why, as you get older, time moves more quickly?'

'Yes,' she said. 'I have.'

'It's caused by a thing called the Schumann Frequency. Time itself—right now—is moving faster than it should. And I've been sent from the future to slow time down again.'

'The pyramids can slow time down?'

'They were created to regulate the flow of time through the universe. They can make it go faster, or slower.' Wilson lay beside Helena—their naked bodies entwined—and told her about the Book of Isaiah and the blueprints for time travel. He attempted to tell her everything in only a few minutes; about the mercury team, the Khirbet Qumran brotherhood and Vespasian's invasion of Judea. After everything they had been through together, she had a right to know why he was here. The only detail Wilson left out was the existence of the Copper Scroll—the key to unlocking the secret algorithms. That was a piece of information too valuable and dangerous to mention.

'That's why the world has become such a violent place,' he said. 'The Schumann Frequency. When it gets too high, like it is now—it can drive people mad.'

The image of Helena's mother, Camilla, flashed into her mind. And there was no alternative but to agree. The world was an extremely violent place; Helena knew that with great certainty—she had seen it with her own eyes.

'So what's next?' she said, as if this was her mission also.

'The third portal?' Wilson replied. 'It's in England. At an ancient druidical site on Salisbury Plain.'

'Stonehenge?'

'Yes.'

'I've always wondered what that was built for.' For the first time since Helena's visions had begun, everything made sense. And while she was numbed by the knowledge she now possessed, she was happy that she had achieved her goal to find out the truth.

'My father's plane is at the airport just outside Cairo,' she offered.

'When I open the third portal,' Wilson said matter-of-factly, 'I'll be transported back to *my time* ... to the future. Your life will be back to normal,' he said, as if he was doing her a favour.

Wilson had already begun burying his emotions—something he was very good at. This beautiful interlude on the Pharaoh's sailing boat was over. From now on there was no place for confusion or sentiment—absolutely no room at all. He pulled himself away from her, his muscles and joints aching again, and began to dress.

'Come on,' he said. 'We have to go.'

41

California, The Americas
Mercury Building, Sub Level A5—Mercury Laboratory
May 23rd 2081
Local Time 11:44 a.m.

Transport Test

UNAWARE THAT IT WAS exactly one year to the day since he had spun his fate coin with Professor Author, Wilson was now following another scientist, Barton Ingerson, along a stark white corridor towards the mercury lab. Wearing black pants and a black three-quarter-length jacket, Wilson was filled with uncertainty as the security door opened and he stepped inside. His eyes were immediately drawn towards the Imploder Sphere glowing ominously under a bank of spotlights. A curved transparent door at the bottom hung open. As they approached, he could hear the crystal softly humming.

Barton halted with a few steps to go. 'I want to take this opportunity to tell you what a terrific job you've done. I'm confident you have all the information you need to complete the Mission of Isaiah.'

'Should you be saying that, here?' Wilson said warily.

'There aren't any surveillance systems in the mercury lab,' Barton replied. 'This is a confidential workspace. You can say what you want in here.' He winked—an uncharacteristic gesture for him. 'Just make sure no one reads your lips.'

Through the observation wall, Wilson could see the mercury team checking the transport systems. Karin glanced over her holographic computer and their eyes met for a moment, before she quickly looked away. Wilson turned and studied the Imploder Sphere once more. In some way he just couldn't bring himself to face his transport just yet—he had to find some way to stall his departure.

'I'm curious, Barton,' Wilson said. 'What's going on between you and Karin?'

'What do you mean?'

'You said we should be honest with each other.'

'What are you implying?' he said, obviously defensive about the subject.

'I know what I saw.'

'I assure you. It's a purely professional relationship.'

'There's something going on between you two,' Wilson said. 'And *before* I get in that Imploder Sphere, I demand to know what's happening.'

'What *are* you talking about?'

'*Come on* ... you're just about to vaporise my molecules for Christ's sake! You said we should be honest with each other, about everything. I've done my part—humour me and do yours.'

'This subject is irrelevant to what you are doing.'

'Not to me, it isn't.'

Barton moved closer. 'Why do you think there's something going on?'

'I know there is!' Wilson said confidently.

'Oh God,' he sighed.

'It's so obvious, Barton.' Wilson studied Karin's face in the distance. 'And I don't blame you. Anyway, it's good to know you're not so perfect. It gives someone like me a little hope for the future.'

'Do you think anyone else notices?' Barton said quietly.

Wilson watched the mercury team through the bomb-proof glass. 'Those people are incredibly smart, but lucky for you, they don't appear to be very perceptive when it comes to human interaction.'

Barton rubbed his chin. 'IQ versus EQ,' he said, as if it all made sense. 'You did extremely well on the emotional quotient test, Wilson. I shouldn't be surprised by your perceptiveness.'

'So tell me, how long has it been going on?'

'This is really not the time to discuss it. Keep your mind on what you have to do. Stay focused.'

'Barton, my good man. Right now, anything that stops me from getting inside that Imploder Sphere seems like a wonderful subject. I could happily talk about this for hours.'

Barton glanced at the clock on the wall. 'Wilson, I'm sorry. It's time to leave.'

Suddenly such a simple thing as breathing seemed difficult. Wilson gazed in trepidation at the Imploder Sphere humming softly behind him. 'Do me a favour,' he said. 'Tell me again that everything will be okay.'

The mercury leader, one of the smartest men in the world, studied the transport pod with a look of sincere affection. 'I know what I'm doing.'

Wilson scrutinised the high-powered collider lasers encircling him. 'That's what General Custer said at Little Big Horn.'

'It'll be fine.'

'I hope you're right, Barton. 'Cause if this all goes to hell I don't think I'm going to be in much of a position to tell you how disappointed I am. I mean, are you certain you've done everything? I'd hate for you and your girlfriend there to forget something simple and accidentally send half my molecules to Pakistan, or something like that.'

'Stay positive, Wilson. Keep focused on what you have to achieve. I'll take care of getting you there. Trust me.'

Trust me. That's what Barton had said to GM, that day in the executive boardroom, Wilson remembered. And he was lying to him!

'Do you have your contact lenses in?' Barton asked.

'For the fourth time ... *yes*,' Wilson snapped back.

'Without those contact lenses you are vulnerable.' Barton was again distracted by the countdown display on the wall. 'You have to climb inside, Wilson. It's time to meet your destiny.'

Destiny. The word rumbled around in Wilson's head. He pictured Barton saying: 'Wilson was destined to die in that Imploder Sphere.' Suddenly he wanted to talk some more—about anything. 'Aren't you even a little bit curious about my ECG readout? You never asked me exactly why the readings were so high.'

'It would only worry me,' Barton said.

For the first time, Wilson was concerned that his omega programming could cause the transport process to malfunction, somehow. He was surprised he hadn't thought of it before.

'Anyway,' Barton said confidently, 'I'm certain you are the Overseer. Not only do you have the correct genetic pattern to be transported, but you have all the attributes you require to be successful. Some more extraordinary than others. In the boardroom, when I told GM I would choose you anyway—I wasn't lying. You would be my primary choice no matter what the circumstances. So let's make a deal. When you get back you can tell me about your ECG results, and the powers you must have. That'll be something for me to look forward to. But now, it's time to leave.' He motioned towards the sphere.

'And—when I get back,' Wilson said in return. 'You can tell me about you and Karin; all the gory details. Okay?'

Barton smiled. 'That's a deal.' He paused, rubbing his chin. 'By the way ... don't use cerebral commands while you're transporting. It could be a problem.'

Wilson began to feel profoundly sick in the stomach. 'We should've discussed this before!' he said frantically. 'I knew this would be a problem. We should call the whole thing off! Delay things for a day or two. Yes, that's what we should do ...' Barton pressed his hand on Wilson's shoulder, stopping his rant mid-sentence.

'It will be fine, Wilson!' he said firmly. 'Just remember one thing: don't let anyone stop you from completing your mission, no matter what. Stay focused.' Barton's steady gaze was reassuring. 'Watch your step as you get inside.' He gestured under the sphere. 'It's a little tricky.'

Wilson gazed at the floor. 'You know, it's funny isn't it,' he said sincerely. 'We've got a time machine here, and yet I don't have any time left. Don't you think that's ironic?'

'I said a similar thing to you when we first met.'

'I know you did.'

Barton tried to smile, but his face just wouldn't co-operate. He removed his hand from Wilson's shoulder and looked at him like a long-lost son. 'You know what ... I'm envious. You are about to go on an incredible adventure.'

'Just make sure you and your girlfriend get me through this,' Wilson quipped. Stepping forward, he gave Barton a heartfelt hug.

'Don't worry,' Barton said, holding him firmly. 'Everything will be fine.'

Wilson knew the comment was supposed to make him feel better, but it had no such effect. Part of him didn't want to go. Seconds ticked by. Eventually he took a deep breath and stood back. Don't think; just get inside, he told himself. With a quickening breath, he climbed between the titanium rings, through the narrow porthole, up inside the radiant warmth of the Imploder Sphere.

Barton secured the door and gave a double thumbs-up. His outward expression was calm, but in reality, he was running on overdrive.

The countdown display read:

5 minutes 17 seconds

Barton was less than six minutes away from achieving everything he had laboured towards for more than two years. A combination of relief and anticipation filled him. Soon he would have done his part in the incredible mission that had dominated every facet of his life.

Wilson stood alone inside the Imploder Sphere. He wanted to laugh. *What the hell am I doing in here?* he asked himself. It was like being inside a giant fishbowl. He adjusted one of his contact lenses. It was hard to believe that wearing them would be the difference between life and death. He smiled—he was about to *willingly* be disassembled by lasers. It was almost funny. Almost.

STRIDING PURPOSEFULLY INTO the command centre, Barton called out, 'Are all stations ready?'

There was a flurry of activity as the twelve members of the mercury team checked their designated systems. All eyes eventually swung towards their leader.

'Looks good here,' Davin said.

Barton approached the master console and stood next to Karin.

'A hug?' she whispered. 'That's not like you.'

'Wilson was nervous,' Barton said back to her. 'He thinks we might screw this up.'

'I wouldn't be nervous, if I was him.' She raised her voice to a normal pitch and said, 'Everything looks fine here.' With her gaze locked on the holographic image in front of her, she said, 'This transport test will make history.'

You have no idea how true that is, Barton thought.

The temperature readout was, in actual fact, 17.5 degrees hotter than indicated. Barton had reprogrammed the diagnostic sensors—such a stunningly simple solution to his problem. His finger hovered over the red ignition switch. The temperature was perfect and, at last, it was time to proceed. He glanced towards Davin one more time.

'Are we *go* for the transport test?' Barton said.

'All systems are go,' Davin replied.

'That's affirmative,' Andre chimed in. 'All systems are *go*.'

One by one, every scientist in the command centre gave their approval. Barton gazed at Wilson through the observation wall. *This is it, my friend,* Barton thought. *There's no turning back now.* An epiphany suddenly struck him: I'm looking at the Overseer, he realised. There was no doubt in Barton's mind that Wilson was the man written about in the Dead Sea scrolls.

Pressing the switch, there was a *click* and the transport process engaged.

WILSON CRINGED. BARTON was looking at him from behind the relative safety of bomb-proof glass with an odd expression on his face. *You're right, Barton, I am an idiot*, Wilson thought.

With a loud *clunk*, the polished metallic hoops surrounding the Imploder Sphere began to oscillate. The lights in the mercury lab flickered. Wilson studied the faces of the mercury team, one by one, staring back at him through the glass. *I bet they all think I'm an idiot.*

'Is it too late to change my mind?' Wilson yelled out.

A single beam of golden light suddenly shone out of the darkness and Wilson squinted in trepidation. The first volley of energy had been fired in his direction. Think of the Rembrandt, he told himself—the sleeping baby and the angels.

'TWO MINUTES TO ignition,' Andre announced.

A faint smile crossed Barton's lips and he took a moment to marvel at the construction of the time machine. He'd done it, he realised. Scanning the master console readouts, he could see that everything was working perfectly. Just enjoy the process, he told himself. You've done everything you can.

The emergency door to the command centre suddenly sprang open and Jasper Tredwell appeared. With a long stride, he marched determinedly towards the master console, his arms raised in the air.

'Stop the test!' he called out.

'Get him out of here,' Barton yelled, pointing at the door.

'I said, stop the test!' Jasper repeated. Davin attempted to block his path, but he was physically no match and was easily pushed aside.

'Everybody continue what you're doing!' Barton said firmly. He turned to Jasper. 'Please *leave*! You have no jurisdiction here!'

GM suddenly appeared in the doorway. 'But *I* do,' the old man said. 'Stop the test.'

Barton's heart almost quit beating.

'Ninety seconds to ignition,' Andre called out.

WILSON WATCHED THE commotion unfolding in the command centre. *What are the Tredwells doing in there*? he wondered.

A constant thumping throbbed in the background as massive volumes of electricity surged from the electromagnets to the Imploder Sphere. Another volley of energy struck Wilson's body—he felt pins and needles all over as the collider lasers fired in an orchestrated sequence around the room.

Barton said the transport process wouldn't hurt ... but it suddenly occurred to Wilson that Barton simply wouldn't know. Another energy wave struck, the feeling even more intense.

'Stop the test!' Wilson yelled.

BARTON USED ALL his might to push Jasper away from the master console. 'You can't do this!' Barton pleaded.

'You've made a big mistake,' GM said, scornfully. 'You should have told us the truth.'

'I *have* told you the truth!' Barton said.

The old man pointed his walking stick around the room. 'Stop everything! That's an order!'

Glancing at the progress display, Barton realised things were critical. 'If we stop now,' he called out. 'Wilson will die! The colliders have already begun to deconstruct him! Everybody continue with what you are doing!'

THE SCHUMANN FREQUENCY

THE RINGS AROUND the transport pod spun furiously until they blurred together into a silver haze. Wilson could feel his skin burning as waves of energy continued to strike him. The lasers fired faster and faster. He was thinking, *Stop the test!* But his muscles failed to move and nothing came out of his mouth. He was frozen, as if locked in ice.

The walls of the chamber began to flicker.

Time appeared to go into slow motion.

Wilson's breathing stopped and everything went blank.

'FIFTY SECONDS TO ignition,' Andre said calmly.

The energy curves were rising, the trend lines coming into sequence. Everything inside the command centre began to shake as if an earthquake was rumbling beneath it. Glasses of water and coffee cups shimmied off the tables and smashed onto the floor.

'Commence EF procedure,' Davin called out.

It was time to open the electromagnetic field.

Karin hovered over the green EF button, but Jasper waved her back.

'Get away from there!' he said.

'Press it, Karin!' Barton yelled.

'You lied to me!' GM said accusingly.

Barton pointed towards the diamond-shaped scaffolding inside the mercury lab. 'Karin, open the magnetic field, now. Press it! Otherwise Wilson will *die*!'

Two security officers appeared in the doorway.

GM pointed at Barton. 'Keep him away from that console,' he ordered.

'I didn't lie to you, GM,' Barton said, backing himself away. 'It was information you didn't need to know.'

'Thirty seconds,' Andre called out.

'We know about the Mission of Isaiah,' Jasper said. 'We know what you're trying to do.'

'That was information you *didn't* need to know,' Barton said again. The guards approached warily, moving between him and the master console. 'There will be no harm to Enterprise Corporation. I gave you my word.'

'You should have told me about the mission,' GM said, obviously disappointed.

'Twenty seconds.'

The lasers inside the mercury lab systematically went to full power and Wilson's body exploded into billions of silver molecules. The sight of his sudden destruction caused everyone in the room to gasp. The scientists were all asking themselves *Have we failed?* Was it quark-gluon plasma they were looking at, or was it something more sinister?

Taking the opportunity, Barton lunged for the EF switch. He almost made it, but the security guards pounced, easily grappling his slender frame to the floor.

All the while, GM presided over the undignified mismatch. 'I'm sorry, Barton. I can't let you go through with this. There's too much at stake.'

'Press the switch, Karin,' Barton pleaded, 'or Wilson will *die!*'

'Ten seconds.'

'Press it!'

Karin's hand hovered over the green button, her index finger outstretched.

'Press it!' Barton yelled.

But she did nothing.

Sprinting for the first time in twenty years, Jasper leapt forward and pushed Karin aside.

Barton was pinned to the floor by two men, his contorted face gazing out into the mercury lab. GM took no joy in seeing his top scientist reduced to this. Nevertheless, he was resolute. 'I have to protect Enterprise Corporation,' he said. 'I have no choice.'

Barton couldn't understand why Karin had not done as he had ordered. If he could have stared a hole right through her, he would have done so. Instead, he watched the Imploder Sphere to see what would happen next.

Andre continued the countdown. 'Ten ... nine ... eight ...'

Stunned by the events of the last two minutes, the members of the mercury team stood motionless at their workstations. They didn't know what to do. The lasers inside the mercury lab abruptly extinguished and the vibration affecting the Enterprise Corporation building was gone. Everything was still once more.

Inside the lab, the shimmering plasma inside the Imploder Sphere splashed against the inner walls of crystal like ocean waves on a rocky shore. Everyone was about to witness the death of Wilson Dowling, they realised. A collective sense of remorse cut through each and every one of them.

Davin considered diving for the green EF button, but Jasper was guarding it as if his very life depended on it staying untouched.

'He'll die,' Barton whimpered.

GM watched the glowing molecules inside the transport sphere without remorse.

Andre's voice cut the silence, 'Three ... two ... one ... we have ignition.'

The diamond-shaped scaffolding inside the mercury lab began to glow, faintly. Then, with a blinding flash, the molecules from the Imploder Sphere blazed across the room. The interior of the diamond came alive with energy, shimmering like quicksilver.

The conductor banks went to full power.

Five petawatts. Ten petawatts. Fifteen petawatts.

Time distorted.

Thump.

The magnetic field opened and the quark-gluon plasma vanished.

Everything in the mercury lab was now cloaked in total darkness. Emergency lights suddenly flashed on to reveal the titanium rings around the transport pod swinging ponderously to a halt.

Jasper stared at the empty sphere, his mouth agape. 'What happened?' he said. He turned towards Karin for an answer, but she shrugged her shoulders in response.

'The electromagnetic field opened by itself,' Davin said, with a confused expression. He couldn't understand it, either.

'Are you saying it worked?' Jasper demanded.

Andre studied the data. 'Yes ... it worked.'

'How is that possible?' Jasper cried. 'No one pressed the switch. So, how?'

GM turned to the security guard. 'Release Barton,' he said. 'The time for panic is over.'

Climbing to his feet, the mercury leader took great care to readjust his clothing and neaten his hair.

GM smiled slyly. 'That was very impressive, Barton. You put an override on the EF switch, didn't you? As always, you prepared for the unexpected.'

'Thank you, GM,' Barton replied. 'It was the right thing to do.'

'We need to discuss this situation,' GM said seriously. 'And where this puts us.'

'Yes, GM.'

'You must be tired,' the old man conceded. 'Get some rest and we'll talk first thing tomorrow. You can explain everything to me then.'

'I'm sorry I kept information from you,' Barton said sincerely. 'I had no choice.'

GM turned to his grandson. 'It seems we've been outsmarted, Jasper. That's why Barton here is our top scientist.'

42

Somewhere over Southern France
Capriarty Private Jet
December 21st 2012
Local Time 12:45 p.m.

Mission of Isaiah—Day Twenty-Seven

BRIGHT SUNSHINE BEAMED through the circular windows of the Capriarty executive jet. In the background, a pair of Rolls Royce engines hummed in perfect unison. Wilson rolled his fate coin over the back of his fingers, his mind filling with cause-and-effect scenarios. This was an object that had been with him all his life. This *very* coin was in his desk drawer, in the future, and yet here it was, its journey to there just beginning.

Wilson and Helena were the only two inside the passenger cabin; she sat directly across from him and carefully studied his face. As the plane banked to the left, beams of sunlight slowly shifted across the wall. Wilson had on clean clothes—black pants and a white pilot's shirt. Freshly shaven, he looked well, although detached. In contrast, Helena felt tense. Their lovemaking on the Pharaoh's sailing boat had unearthed strong feelings.

'What are you thinking about?' she asked.

'About this coin,' he replied, but Wilson was reluctant to talk further about its place in his future. He gave her a brief smile to mask the inner turmoil that gripped him. Making love with her had been the most sensual, beautiful thing he had ever experienced. All he wanted was to hold her again, but he knew that was not wise. There was no future in it.

'You are the luckiest man I have ever met,' she said.

Wilson pressed his finger into the indentation on the coin. *Destined* was the word she was looking for, but it sounded arrogant to say so.

'You're right, I am lucky,' he said.

'One inch either side and you'd have been dead.'

There was silence for a few minutes. 'Wilson, I'm sorry about what happened with Visblat.'

'Please, Helena, not this again.'

She pictured the giant's face. 'I had him in my sights. I had him *right there.*'

'I told you, it's not your fault.' Wilson was becoming impatient with her about the subject. 'You did everything you could. Now drop it.'

'I feel like I let you down.'

He slipped the Egyptian coin into his breast pocket once again. 'You didn't let me down, okay?'

The pair had been talking on-and-off for more than three hours. And although Helena was perturbed by Wilson's aloofness, she tried to stay positive.

'Visblat must have been here for some time,' she said. 'He worked for the Houston Police Department for at least five years ... at least that.' They had already discussed the rumours that Commander Visblat was wanted for murder and that he had disappeared after a shooting in the police compound three weeks before.

It was clear to Wilson that Visblat was a time traveller, a Gen-EP—his amplified trackenoids proved that. But the question remained: who was he? Could he be the second candidate that Barton had spoken of? Strangely, there was a nagging familiarity in Visblat's voice that had Wilson second-guessing that particular theory; he just could not place the resemblance exactly, but he felt he knew him somehow. The thought led Wilson to wonder what it would be like when *he himself* returned home—to the future. What sort of reception would await him? How would his life be affected? Barton's words echoed in his ears yet again: 'Stay focused, be positive, be in the moment.'

Wilson's silent brooding finally caused Helena's anger to surface. 'We need to talk about what happened. You're acting like we've never even met before!'

The familiarity of Helena's body, the memory of being inside her, had Wilson in a spin. 'There's nothing to discuss,' he said.

She looked him in the eye. 'You can't deny what happened!'

'I'm not denying anything. You're the one making a big deal out of all this. I've got a lot on my mind, that's all.'

'You're *unbelievable*!' Helena gazed out the window at the blankets of puffy white clouds below them. 'Those special powers you have don't give you the right to be a jerk.' Minutes passed.

Wilson eventually tried to make small talk. 'What does your father do for a living?'

She took a deep breath, resigning herself to his evasiveness. 'He's a property developer.'

'This is a very nice plane.'

'I promised my father I was going to stay away from you.' Helena felt sick inside. 'I should have listened to him.'

Wilson was all too aware of the distress he was causing and it tore him up to act this way; but it was for Helena's own good. He stared into her blue eyes; the colour was unforgettable. His mind suddenly filled with questions: Why was this beautiful woman so compelled to risk everything to be by his side? He concluded that this must be her destiny also.

Not getting a response, she asked, 'What do you do for a living?'

'I'm a student.'

'*Really?*' Her expectations had him pegged as a spy or a government analyst or something like that. 'Studying what?'

'Law.'

'Lawyers are ruining this world,' she said, obviously unimpressed. 'They create nothing but conflict and paperwork. There has to be a better way. I was hoping you would tell me they didn't exist in the future.'

'We're as resilient as cockroaches.'

'Tell me honestly,' she asked, changing the subject. 'How do you deal with the stress of what you have to do? Opening the portals and everything. The time-travel part.' It caused her to shiver just thinking about the disassembly.

'I tend not to dwell too much on consequences,' he replied.

'You'll make a perfect lawyer then.'

Her comment amused him. 'That's funny.' Wilson liked her—he really did.

Helena considered the force of the weather they had seen over the Giza plateau. They had heard on the radio earlier that morning that it was the worst recorded storm ever to hit the region—massive flooding, thousands of lightning strikes, many deaths.

'How do you know the Schumann Frequency isn't fixed already?' she asked.

'If we had a cyber connection we could look it up,' he said in an off-hand manner.

'What the hell is a cyber connection?'

Wilson rethought his comment. 'A computer.'

She jumped up from her seat and slid open an oak panel above the desk, revealing a flat screen and a keyboard. 'This must be your lucky day.' Helena sat at the console and, without asking, typed 'Schumann Frequency' into the search engine and quickly hit the enter key. At the top of the results was the *Northern California Earthquake Data Centre (NCEDC)* web site.

'That's the one,' Wilson said, hitting the enter key for her.

Two graphs appeared with thick, jagged red lines that were trending upwards towards the right of the screen:

> Earth Ionosphere Cavity Resonance
> - Parkfield, California
> - Arrival Heights, Antarctica

He had seen them both before. On the left of each graph was the frequency in hertz; on the bottom, the date. For each completed day a smattering of tiny dots was added, reflecting the readings of the Schumann Frequency. There was ten years' worth of data in front of them—thousands of dots. And there was but one trend: everything was going upwards in steadily increasing cycles. Wilson checked the scale of the graph and his heart sank.

'What did you say the frequency is supposed to be?' Helena asked.

'It should be around 6.53 hertz,' Wilson said, despondently. 'In a perfect world.'

Helena moved her finger along the averages. The readings had been increasing dramatically for the previous seven years. It was now over eleven hertz, sometimes peaking to more than thirteen.

Wilson stared at the screen—it was a higher reading than he ever could have imagined. It explained why *this* world was so violent and unstable in comparison with the one he knew.

'Why is the frequency worse there?' Helena pointed at the graph for Parkfield, California.

'More people, more fear,' Wilson said simply. 'That's what drives the Schumann Frequency. It's always been that way.'

'If you succeed at Stonehenge, what then?'

'A magnetic surge will be reversed back through the energy portals. The Schumann Frequency will move from *there* ... to *there*.' He moved his finger down towards 6.5 hertz.

'Things must be different in the future,' she said thoughtfully. 'All the mysteries of life ... I suppose they're all figured out.'

'It's not that way at all,' Wilson said, trying to smile. 'The more you understand, the more you realise you don't know anything.' Seeing the readings on the screen should have spurred him onwards, but it only made him apprehensive. In rectifying the Schumann Frequency, Wilson knew he would be hurled back to his own time, never to see Helena again.

43

Gatwick Airport, England
Capriarty Private Jet
December 21st 2012
Local Time 1:52 p.m.

Mission of Isaiah—Day Twenty-Seven

THE BOMBARDIER GLOBAL Express descended through a blanket of clouds. Gatwick Airport, just outside London, came into view. It was raining steadily and the air was just a few degrees above zero.

The aircraft lined up with runway 08R and drifted downwards.

Settling on the smooth, wet tarmac, the engines clicked into reverse with a roar and the small jet slowed and turned into a private taxiway. It rolled purposefully towards a group of aircraft hangars and it came to a stop in its usual place, the engines shutting down.

A curved staircase dropped to the pavement and Wilson poked his head outside.

Captain Lewis closed his briefcase and handed Helena his passport. 'I could lose my job for this.'

'You won't lose your job.'

He gestured towards Wilson. 'I will if your father finds out.'

'I'm taking full responsibility,' Helena said. 'I'll deal with my father. You wait here until I contact you. Is that understood?'

'But, Helena—'

'I said, *wait here*!' She turned to Wilson. 'Come on, let's go.' Helena gestured across the glistening tarmac towards the aircraft hangar. 'It belongs to my father's company. He stores his plane here when he comes to England. There are cars inside.'

Wilson zipped up his jacket. 'Why don't we fly straight to Stonehenge?'

'We can't get airways clearance without drawing too much attention to ourselves.' Helena didn't look happy at all. 'If we do, Customs will want to search the plane. We have three people on board.' She held up the passports. 'And only *two* of these. Plus, we need a car, anyway.' Her expression was no-nonsense. '*I say* this is the easiest way.'

The rain was heavier now as Helena sprinted across the tarmac and huddled at the building entrance. She turned the key in an ice-cold padlock and pulled the door open. Flicking on the light switch, the hangar flooded with brightness. The air was frigid and still. In the distance, a trio of cars stood neatly parked at one end of the empty enclosure.

The sound of their footsteps echoed across the void as Helena and Wilson approached the vehicles: a red Ferrari, a silver Mercedes-Benz limousine, and a black Porsche Turbo. You could tell they were fast just by looking at them.

'This is exactly what we need,' and she opened the driver's door of the Porsche.

'Helena,' Wilson said, stopping her before she climbed inside. 'I've been an idiot since we, well … you know. I'm sorry. That whole thing between us took me by surprise. *You* took me by surprise.' His head tilted forward in embarrassment. 'Let's make a deal. I'll be myself again, and together, we'll get this over and done with.' He reached across the top of the car to shake her hand.

Helena stared at his open palm with a look of disgust. Her breath formed puffs of fog in the cold air. 'I agree: let's get this over with.'

Wilson lifted his glasses and stared into her eyes. 'Don't worry, Helena, I felt it too.' He was certain she knew exactly what he meant. 'And it kills me to think I will never get to touch you again. But there is no future for us. There can't be.' She held his gaze for what felt like minutes—expressionless.

'Are you coming, or what?' she said, and disappeared into the driver's seat. The engine suddenly roared to life. Wilson opened the passenger door and jumped in beside her.

'You're being as stupid as I was,' he replied.

'I know. Now do up your seatbelt.'

The steel doors of the hangar parted and misty rain swirled in through the ever-increasing gap. As soon as it was wide enough the

Porsche rumbled out into the deluge. The wipers whipped across the windscreen as they drove under the nose of the Global Express and accelerated towards the terminal building.

Captain Lewis stared out the cockpit window as the black sports car drove away.

Coming to a stop about two hundred metres from the airport exit, the Porsche idled menacingly in the rain. The security checkpoint had a guard booth in the middle of the road with two boom gates on either side: one for vehicles entering, the other for those making an exit. There were at least three men on patrol, all carrying automatic weapons. Metal tyre-slashers protruded out of the road like dinosaur teeth—when the boom gate went up, they disappeared.

'They'll ask for our passports,' Helena said. 'They're not stamped, so I'll do all the talking.' An image of how everything was going to play out ran through her mind. 'Our timing will be crucial.'

'I'm sorry, Helena,' Wilson offered.

'Shut up, Wilson. I'll help you get to Stonehenge, but shut up.' She took a deep breath. Two vehicles approached the exit, headlights on, and Helena accelerated in front of them. The rain was falling a little more heavily and the windscreen wipers automatically adjusted to a faster speed. The Porsche came to a stop at the boom gate first, the other cars pulling up just behind it.

Sheltering his paperwork from the rain, a guard approached the window. He was wearing a dark-green plastic poncho with a hood. A machine gun was strapped across his back. Helena handed him the two American passports. The guard didn't say a word as he briefly studied the photographs then glanced inside the cabin.

Helena held his gaze with a broad smile.

'These 'aven't been stamped yet.' The guard seemed perturbed about being out in the weather. 'You 'aven't been to Customs yet? Your vehicle paperwork, please.'

Helena looked surprised. '*Oh, no.* I was told to come straight here!' She stretched the extra paperwork towards him.

The guard checked the registration against the passport—this was definitely her car. He pointed towards the North Terminal. 'I can't let you leave without a stamp, madam. You 'ave to go to Customs first.' He handed all the documents back.

Helena tried to look bashful, which was almost impossible, then put her car in reverse. The white tail lights flashed on, but there were now at least three vehicles banked up behind her. It was going to cause a serious traffic problem, exactly as she planned.

The guard ordered her forward. 'Drive out an' come back in the other way, madam.' He indicated the way around the guard booth. 'Go *directly* to Customs. I'll see you on your way back.'

Everything was going perfectly to plan. The boom gate lifted and Helena calmly slotted her car into gear ... then planted her foot on the accelerator. The engine screamed, causing all four wheels to spin on the wet tarmac. The Porsche surged away in a cloud of vapour, down the ramp, left, and out onto the main road.

The guard ran after them in pursuit, but the vehicle was already out of sight.

Helena seemed amused.

'Why do I get the feeling you're enjoying this?' Wilson said, forced back into his seat by the acceleration. The car braked quickly and made a hard right-hand turn. His heart was in his mouth. 'Do you always drive like this?'

For the moment, Helena couldn't have cared less what Wilson was thinking. Travelling at twice the speed limit, they headed towards the M25 motorway. As if from nowhere, a police car slid out of a side street in pursuit, its roof lights flashing into the rain. Helena geared down and considered the best way through the congested intersection up ahead. Stopping was not an option. With her grip on the wheel quite casual, she drifted into the oncoming traffic and zigzagged her way through the vehicles at high speed.

'I've shattered the odd road rule in my time,' she admitted.

Wilson winced, near to terror, as they swerved away from multiple collisions, slid across the intersection sideways, and accelerated with a thunderous roar towards the onramp. A glance out the back window revealed that the police car was gone.

Helena smiled. 'Great move, don't you think?'

'I wouldn't know,' Wilson replied. 'I had my eyes closed the entire time.' They were now doing more than 200 kilometres per hour, weaving through the motorway traffic like it was standing still.

'We're a couple of hours away from Stonehenge,' Helena said. 'We can outrun anybody in this car, if we have to.'

Turning towards her, Wilson studied her profile. 'You're amazing.'

'Oh, I wish that were true.'

'The way you conduct yourself is so ... composed.'

'You mean my complete disregard for human life?'

'You know that's not what I'm saying.'

'What *are* you saying then?' she said with some annoyance.

Wilson was a little confused. 'I'm appreciative, that's all.'

Visblat's face flashed into Helena's mind and her jaw locked like rusted steel. 'I should've shot that bastard while I had the chance!'

'Why do you keep going on about that?'

'Because, I have demons!' she yelled. 'That's why!'

Wilson was stunned by her outburst. 'What's that supposed to mean?'

'I've been in that situation before,' she said, her words trailing off. 'Many years ago … and I *vowed* that I would never let it happen again.' Wilson put his hand on the back of her neck, reassuringly. Helena tried to pull away, but he refused to relinquish his grip. In truth, she wanted his hands on her—that was the only reason she didn't stop the car and step outside.

'Tell me what happened,' he said.

There was a long pause.

'I was seventeen,' she finally admitted.

'Go on …'

'My mother and I went to a show in the city, in Houston—at the Palladium—*Les Misérables*. How appropriate,' she quipped. Helena piloted the Porsche down the motorway, looking straight ahead. 'It's funny, I don't remember much about the production.'

Wilson listened and kept his mouth shut.

'We were so stupid,' Helena said. 'Our limousine was supposed to pick us up just after eleven. We walked through the back exit, to avoid the crowds, and we got stuck in the alleyway.' Helena's mind filled with visions of that night. It was like she was being transported there against her will. 'We were approached by a group of men—just local drunks, I thought at the time. They began harassing us.' A shiver shot down her spine and her speech became laboured, 'I don't know how it happened exactly, but my mother's handbag was thrown open and her pistol flew through the air. It landed at my feet. I can still see it there, lying against the concrete.' The vision of the Ruger 9mm handgun had haunted her for the last twelve years.

'I picked up the gun,' she said more quickly. 'I could have saved her …' Helena raised her right hand and pointed towards the windscreen as if she held it now. The Porsche rapidly began to slow. 'I tried to pull the trigger.'

Helena geared down, then began accelerating again. 'I panicked,' she said angrily. Then her face was momentarily devoid of expression. 'My mother screamed for me to run. I can still hear her voice.' Helena's features contorted in anguish. 'I tried to pull the trigger, but the gun wouldn't fire.' Tears began swelling in her eyes and her voice reduced to merely a whisper, 'I was such a fool. The gun wouldn't fire because the safety was on.'

His heart pounding in unison with hers, Wilson massaged the back of Helena's neck as her tears burst and rolled down her cheeks.

'I escaped because I had a gun. But not my mother. They found her the next day. She had been raped and murdered by those men.'

For Wilson, so much about Helena fell into place at that moment. It was like the vast blur of information he had about her had taken form: the guns, the need to be in control all the time—it all made perfect sense. He glanced in her direction and she stared back at him. The unquestioned compassion he felt for her made his resolve to rectify the Schumann Frequency stronger than ever. There was helplessness in her wet eyes—a vulnerability that Wilson had not seen before. He would never forget the sight—the way she looked at him, the intensity of her emotions ... the incessant rain outside ... the gloomy countryside flashing past the windows.

Wilson reached into his pocket and produced the Egyptian coin that had played such a vital role in his life. It represented the past being linked to the future. *Destiny*. He rubbed the damaged surface with his fingers. 'Helena, I want you to have this.'

Watching the road ahead, she somehow understood the significance of the moment. Wilson explained to her how the coin had been with him in the future and the role it played in his decision to go ahead with his omega programming.

'This coin,' he said, 'my fate coin. It's a way of ensuring that *your* future and *my* future are linked somehow. If I give it to you, our lives will be connected.' He paused. 'This coin is part of the reason why I'm here, and I'd like to think that you're part of that reason also.' Wilson placed it in the palm of her hand and closed her fingers around it.

Connected was not enough, Helena thought. *Why do you have to leave?* she wondered.

'Everything happens for a reason,' Wilson said, as if responding to her question. 'It's destiny. And for the record, I'm absolutely thrilled that you are part of mine.'

Helena turned off the M25 motorway and onto the M3. Raindrops were beading across the windscreen. The sky grew darker. For the next twenty minutes not a word was spoken. All the while, Wilson never removed his hand from the nape of Helena's neck.

44

Salisbury Plain, England
A344, Two Miles from Stonehenge
December 21st 2012—*Zero Point*
Local Time 3:49 p.m.

Mission of Isaiah—Day Twenty-Seven

THE SHORTEST DAY of the year in the northern hemisphere, December 21st—the Winter Solstice—was coming to an end. Through a narrow gap in the clouds the setting sun had the landscape awash with crimson. Travelling at high speed, a pair of car headlights scampered over the horizon. They dipped below the crest of a hill, into the darkness, then reappeared into the ruddy glow as the vehicle raced across the English countryside.

The engine of the Porsche whined as it decelerated through the gears and came to a halt at a pair of tall locked gates. Gently nudging its nose against the obstruction, it pushed forward with a touch of the throttle and the gates sprang open. Headlights burning against the early afternoon sunset, it swooped past a modern tourist centre and across a wide empty parking lot.

Standing in the middle of a flat grass plain was the legendary Stonehenge complex—a structure whose purpose had been clouded in mystery for thousands of years. The huddle of seventy or so upright megaliths was arranged in three concentric circles, one inside the other. The blocks of stone were up to eight metres in height, each reputedly weighing as much as fifty tonnes. Huge teardrops of solid rock, as Barton had described them. The largest megaliths were called sarsen stones, and some still supported lintels: rectangular stones suspended above a similar pair, forming a bridge. Only nine of the original thirty-four lintels remained in place.

Helena drove to the very edge of the bitumen, the car headlights lighting up the ancient structure. There were no other vehicles in sight. No people. She shut off the engine, leaving the cabin in silence. The eerie site of the third portal was directly beyond the front window, just one hundred metres away.

'The name *Stonehenge*,' Wilson said, 'comes from the Old English name *Stanhen Gist*.' He studied the formation against the fading light. 'It means: "hanging stones". When the construction began, the wheel wasn't even invented. It took more than 1500 years to build this place.'

Wilson imagined what it must have been like five thousand years before. The grassy landscape around Salisbury Plain would have looked much the same as it did today. And here, on this spot, Neolithic man, wearing only animal pelts for warmth, began building the structure. It was a task that would take many hundreds of lifetimes, the responsibility handed down from one man to another, even before the written word.

'Who built this place?' Helena asked. 'The Druids?'

'No,' Wilson replied. 'The megaliths here were already standing for two thousand years before the Celtic Druids even came into being. It was built by three distinct tribes in the course of its construction. First, by Neolithic Agrarians in about 3100 BC—they dug the first trenches and brought the first stones here. The Agrarians were subsequently invaded by the Beaker People around 2000 BC. They got their name because they buried beakers—pottery drinking cups—with their dead. And lastly, the Wessex People completed Stonehenge around 1600 BC, at the height of the Bronze Age.

'Some of these rocks,' Wilson continued, 'were hauled from the Preseli Mountains, near the southern tip of Wales, 250 kilometres away. The sarsen stones, the big ones, are from Marlborough Downs, which is about thirty-two kilometres north of here. They were brought overland using a roller and sledge: running the stone on top of six or seven giant logs of wood—a very labour-intensive process. It's estimated that up to six hundred men at one time would have been involved in moving a single stone—an astonishing number of people.'

Helena gazed out the windscreen. 'It is unbelievable.'

'Archaeologists have always had a difficult time explaining how they put those lintels in place. Raising a fifty-tonne object four metres in the air and setting it precisely is an extraordinary achievement using just human strength.'

'Most of the lintels have fallen down,' Helena said. 'Is that a problem?'

'Lintels once covered the entire outer circle—called the Sarsen Circle. And there were five lintels around the Trilithon—the middle circle.'

'What happened to them?'

'At one time, Stonehenge suffered terrible vandalism at the hands of those wishing to destroy its power.'

'Is the portal still going to work?'

'As I understand it, Stonehenge sits atop a natural energy fissure that leads to the very centre of the earth. The structure itself is just the activation point. It should still work.'

The sunset transformed from beautiful to spectacular as beams of crimson light speared the monument, forming a plumbline through the centre of two tall stones.

The sight took Wilson's breath away. 'You see the way the sun is setting,' he said excitedly. 'This is amazing! Do you see the way those beams of light are passing through there? That's called the Gate of Trilithon. Today must be the shortest day of the year.'

'December 21st,' Helena said thoughtfully. 'Yeah, I think that's right.'

It explained why the gates were locked and nobody was there: the British National Trust legislated that Stonehenge was closed on all equinox and solstice days, to avoid unauthorised rituals and protect the site from suffering further damage.

Wilson considered the significance of the date. He was exactly where he should be. 'First Stonehenge was built,' he said. 'Then the Giza pyramids, then the Yucatan pyramids. Together they are the workings of a complex energy system that has the capability of changing the very speed of time on our planet.'

Helena watched the megaliths against the darkening sky. It was clear that the end of Wilson's journey was at hand.

'We just need to activate the portal,' he said, 'and everything will be fine.'

'Should we drive out there?'

'It's very important that you stay out of the Sarsen Circle,' Wilson warned. 'It's a flat round section of grass about 115 metres wide. Around the perimeter is a ditch, and just inside that are fifty-six Aubrey holes. They're like indentations in the ground. Each one is about two metres wide and a metre deep. They're spaced evenly around the perimeter. My suggestion is that neither you nor your car want to be anywhere near them when the portal is activated.'

Helena sat quietly in the still air of the cabin. 'It looks cold out there.' She glanced at the display on the console:

Temp 4°C

'It *is* cold,' she added.

'I have to find a megalith called the Keystone,' Wilson eventually said. 'It's on the outer ring of those three circles, to the southwest.' As the words left his lips the last ray of sunlight disappeared below the horizon and an ebony darkness fell like a soft blanket. Wilson scanned the surrounding area. 'It looks quiet, doesn't it?' He reached for the door handle.

'Wait ...' Helena said. 'I feel like this might be our last chance to say goodbye.' An awkward silence grew between them.

Wilson didn't know what to say as a hundred scenarios flashed through his mind. He turned towards Helena, her face illuminated by the haze of the dashboard lights. Leaving her was something he didn't want to think about.

'Thank you for saving me,' she whispered.

'It's *you* that saved me.'

They stared at each other. Unfortunately, there was nothing they could do to change the future; their destinies were fixed. Helena leant forward and pressed her lips against Wilson's. The kiss was tender and brief.

Trying not to dwell on what was happening, Wilson stared through the window towards Stonehenge. 'That time-machine out there looks a tad more primitive than the last one I took a ride in.'

With a bashful smile, Helena reached out, grabbed Wilson's hand and held it firmly. 'This whole journey has been crazy, but I want you to know ... this has been the *best* time of my life. I'll always wonder what it would've been like if you'd stayed.'

Wilson watched the shadows as they angled across Helena's perfect skin. Her golden hair, her full lips. *So will I, Helena ... I promise you—so will I*, he thought, but not a word came out of his mouth. Wilson cracked open the door and freezing air flooded inside. He feared that if he didn't leave soon, he never would.

'You're right,' she said, frustrated by his lack of response. 'Let's get this over with.'

The headlights made long crisp shadows across the soggy grass.

Angry at not admitting how he felt, Wilson stepped outside. The cold air immediately whipped through his light clothes as if he was wearing nothing at all. With his hands stuffed into his pockets, he stomped directly towards the centre of the structure.

Having checked both her handguns, Helena did up her jacket and followed. The icy wind whistled past her ears, temporarily deafening her, and suddenly her senses were on alert—it felt like she was being watched! She sprinted past Wilson for the safety of the sarsen stones. 'We need to be careful,' she called out.

Plodding forward, Wilson was too upset to care. *Nothing can stop me from opening the portal*, he decided. By thinking this way he was breaking one of the fundamental rules Barton had given him: 'Never assume your destiny is assured. If you do ... everything will unravel.'

Wilson reached out and touched the four-metre-tall sarsen stone in front of him, one of a pair. An equally massive lintel was perched at their summit.

Helena nervously scanned the darkness. 'At the risk of sounding melodramatic, I have a bad feeling about this.' The icy wind gusted through the short grass—it was just strong enough to mask the sound of anyone approaching.

'If Visblat were here,' Wilson replied, 'we'd already know about it.' He went back to studying the stones. 'Have you noticed how every block is a little bit different?' He walked fearlessly through the shards of light.

Helena squinted into the car headlights. They were sitting ducks out here, she decided, and she eased herself into the complete blackness of a shadow.

'This is the Trilithon,' Wilson said. He was standing inside a group of upright stones that made up the ten metre wide inner circle. Stretching his arms in opposite directions, he looked to the left. 'The midwinter sunset goes down over there.' He looked right. 'And the midsummer sunrise comes up over there. And *that* is the Altar Stone.'

Helena watched him from the darkness.

'That would make the Keystone just about ... *there*.' Wilson walked towards a large chunky megalith on the outer circle of the structure. As he approached, his shadow crept along the ground and stretched up the craggy surface. His mind filled with information as he gazed towards the perimeter of the Sarsen Circle, looking for the Station Stones.

'RUN!' Helena screamed. 'WILSON—RUN!'

Wilson reached into his pocket and calmly put on his sunglasses. He turned to see the figure of a tall man silhouetted in the car headlights just behind him.

Her heart pounding madly, Helena watched Commander Visblat stride into view. She was careful to stay in the shadows—there was no telling how many men he had out there. To make matters more complicated, images from Wilson's eyes were flooding her mind through a red haze.

Commander Visblat nonchalantly slung his night-vision goggles around his neck, his gun pointing at Wilson's chest. 'You should be dead, Mr Dowling ... and yet here you are.' Gesturing towards the shadows, he said, 'Tell Ms Capriarty not to shoot. I'm only here to talk.'

Her gun sights trained on the silhouette of Visblat's head, Helena had one burning question: If I have to pull the trigger ... can I do it?

'Don't shoot, Helena!' Wilson called out. 'Let's hear what he has to say!'

'I'm not here to stop you from opening the energy portal, Mr Dowling.' Visblat lowered his weapon. 'Quite the contrary.' He looked relaxed, under the circumstances.

'What *do* you want?' Wilson asked.

'First ... how did you do it? A bullet-proof vest?'

'Yes. I was wearing a vest,' Wilson responded, as if it were true.

A contrived smile crossed the large man's face. 'So it seems. So it seems.' There was a long pause. 'Mr Dowling, I have an offer for you.'

'I'm listening.'

'Open the third portal and we *both* go back together.'

'Tell me who you are first,' Wilson said.

Shaking his head, Visblat replied, 'That's on a need-to-know basis, I'm afraid. You'll find out who I am when we get back. It'll be something for you to look forward to.'

Wilson felt he knew Visblat from somewhere. His gestures were so familiar. 'I know who you are,' Wilson replied.

'You know nothing,' Visblat scoffed.

'You said the second portal was sabotaged. You lied to me.'

'You have done irreparable harm, you fool! You've killed Barton Ingerson without even knowing.'

Wilson's heart sank into the depths of his stomach. 'What are you talking about?'

The reply was matter-of-fact. 'Barton is dead. That's the reason I'm here.'

'How did he die?'

'Let's just say he met with an unfortunate accident. Some say it was planned.'

'He was murdered?'

A smile came to Visblat's lips. 'Let me say this. My valuable services were re-engaged three days *before* he was killed. I've always thought that an odd coincidence. And now you've sealed his fate, Mr Dowling. You should've listened to me. You are such a fool! I hate fools!'

'Who sent you?' Wilson pleaded, 'Tell me his name.'

The question triggered a manic laugh. 'At this rate you'll never figure it out!'

'Don't trust him!' Helena yelled from the darkness.

'You stay out of this!' Visblat screamed back. 'You've done enough damage!' Prowling to his left, Visblat was moving in and out of the light streaming through the stones, trying to identify Helena's whereabouts.

'*Wait*,' Wilson said. 'I'm willing to consider your offer.'

Helena was defenceless against the commander and Wilson knew it.

'I could have killed you both if that was my plan,' Visblat said angrily.

'You almost *did*!'

The comment stopped him in his tracks. 'I wasn't shooting at *you*!' Visblat tried to laugh reassuringly, but again, it came across as manic. 'I was trying to *save* you!'

'You've been here too long,' Wilson said, boldly stepping towards him. 'You're saturated by the Schumann Frequency.' That was certainly the cause of Visblat's madness, Wilson concluded. People born in this time had a chance to adjust to it to a degree, but Visblat, coming from the future, had no such resistance. 'You waited too long before trying to open the portals. You tried to open the Giza portal—that's how you knew your way through the labyrinth. You tried to open it and you couldn't.'

'It's your fault!' he blurted. Visblat stared at his shadow against the stones, trying desperately to calm himself. 'You think you're so smart, don't you? And you're right, Mr Dowling. I can't open the portals. I waited too long.' He forced a reasonably benign tone of voice, 'Otherwise, yes, I would have done it already.' His expression hardened. 'That is why we will both go back together.' He remained calm: as calm as Cairo before the second portal had been activated.

'Out of interest, what's in it for me?' Wilson asked.

'You'll find out the truth about Barton Ingerson's death.'

'I'll find that out anyway.'

'If I stay,' Visblat seethed, 'you'll force me to be a monster.' He cupped his mouth with his hand as if whispering, 'There's no telling what I could do. Your girlfriend …' He looked towards the darkness. 'You know what I mean.'

Seeing through Wilson's eyes, Helena focused on Visblat's irregular features like he was right in front of her.

'Helena!' Wilson called out. 'It's time for you to leave! You must do as I say!' Wilson knew that anyone who was inside the inner circle of the Trilithon when the portal was activated would be transported. 'Get outside the Sarsen Circle, Helena. I mean it!' He imagined her running away.

'You have made the right decision,' Visblat grumbled.

A wall of mist slowly rolled across the countryside, making visibility a little blurry. Wilson was shivering, but he couldn't decide if it was his fear or merely the cold. He turned away from Visblat and faced the Keystone. Taking great care to investigate every notch of the tall megalith, he waited as long as he could.

For the portal to be opened, the Keystone had to be turned—swivelled—towards the Station Stone that marked the trajectory of the midwinter sunrise, in the east. There were five Station Stones—small megaliths about the size of a man—on the outer perimeter of the Sarsen Circle. Each stone indicated a specific point on the celestial and lunar horizon.

Visblat was becoming impatient. 'Get on with it!'

Stepping behind the Keystone, Wilson pressed his left palm against the surface. As soon as he made contact the megalith began to vibrate. Barely pressing against the cold rock, he gently pushed his hand forward and the stone rotated and locked into place. There was a crackling sound like popping corn as the keystone ignited with an ebony glow. Wilson peered towards the Station Stone on the outer perimeter; it too was shimmering.

The ground suddenly began to shake.

The vibration intensified, causing both Wilson and Visblat to struggle to maintain their footing. Then it began: the giant megaliths of Stonehenge lumbered from their positions in an uncanny dance of realignment. Groaning under an invisible force, they slotted into place, straightened, and combusted with a momentary glow before extinguishing again.

Wilson and Visblat retreated to either side of the Trilithon as the enormous rocks moved around them. The constant grinding unexpectedly amplified into a torturous reverberation that stung Wilson's ears.

Something was wrong.

A fallen lintel was jamming the alignment of the inner circle and the underground mechanisms were under ever-increasing strain.

'It's stopping everything from lining up!' Wilson yelled as he crouched over the megalith and felt the unnatural vibration. The stone was wedged so deep that only one third of its surface was above ground level. 'We have to do something!' he shouted.

Visblat threw down his gun and gripped the slab of rock with his powerful hands. Wilson looked into the eyes of the man crouched opposite him. The situation was something he couldn't have conjured in his wildest imagination.

'There are magnetic forces that will help us!' Wilson said. 'On three, lift this way.' He pointed to his right. 'One ... two ... *three!*'

With all their might the unlikely duo strained against the enormous weight of the stone. And while the lintel appeared to vibrate more vigorously under the force they exerted, it didn't budge. Visblat was the first to pull away.

Wilson listened to the magnetic energy building underground. It sounded like metal girders being twisted. 'One more try!' he urged. 'We have to work together! Give it everything!' Without question, Visblat threw all his effort into the task.

With a whisper, Wilson activated an Overload command. Gouging his fingers deep into the soil, he gripped the corners of the stone. The pair lifted in unison and the lintel slowly began to shift ... then suddenly popped free. Their combined efforts sent the enormous megalith tumbling end over end onto the grass.

To the sound of crunching rock, the last section of the Trilithon clicked into place.

Visblat lunged for his gun, then thrust it towards Wilson's chest. 'How did you do that?' he screamed, perplexed by what he had just seen. He tore the sunglasses from Wilson's head. 'Tell me how you survived when I shot you? I saw the blood! You weren't wearing a bulletproof vest! Your strength! Barton taught you something, didn't he?'

Flipping off the safety on her Colt handgun, Helena focused on Visblat's hysterical face. She wanted to shoot: her finger rested on the trigger, but it was as if concrete filled her body and she was frozen, unable to move.

Fear coursing through his veins, Wilson mustered his remaining energy just to sit up. 'Remember, I'm the only one who can get you home,' he said.

'The portal is open,' Visblat replied. 'I don't need you any more!'

Helena looked between the stones; at the same time she was looking through the red haze of Wilson's mind. There was madness in Visblat's eyes. She saw it. Absolute madness. Digging into her memories—into the terrifying circumstances of twelve years before—she fought the unnatural fear that paralysed her. Her mother's helpless face flashed into her mind and Helena somehow pulled the trigger.

Her bullet shot across the compound and the impact flipped Visblat over backwards.

But the commander's gun had also simultaneously fired.

Wilson was hit, Visblat's bullet passing through his torso, like a cold spear. He immediately clamped down on his stomach as streams of hot blood spurted through the fabric of his shirt.

Helena saw the blood gush from the wound. '*Wilson!*' she cried out. Able to move again, she cautiously stepped forward through the shadows, trying to make her way towards him. Two gunshots suddenly thundered from the ruins, shattering the car headlights and plunging everything into total darkness.

Visblat called out, 'You shot me!' He felt numb in his left shoulder and began laughing to himself. Strapping his night-scope to his face, he switched it on, illuminating everything around him. 'You shot me, you bitch!'

Imprisoned in the darkness, Helena closed her eyes and prayed.

Visblat gazed at his shoulder. 'You did well to shoot me! As your reward, I'm going to kill you … *slowly*.' Climbing to his feet, he stood over Wilson's unmoving body and nudged him with his foot. 'How did you shift that boulder? Tell me!'

Visblat scanned the Trilithon—Helena was nowhere to be seen. He called out to the darkness, 'You should have left while you had the chance!' With one hand pressed to his bloodied shoulder, he began to search, stone by stone. 'I'm coming for you, bitch!'

The threat echoed off the jagged rocks.

Helena stood with her back to an ebony megalith, her guns pointing helplessly into the air. Visibility was zero; not even a single star could be seen in the sky. She was blind—utterly helpless. At that moment, her mind filled with life-saving visions—she could suddenly see in the darkness, through Wilson. He had propped himself into a sitting position and activated the night-vision command. All the while, blood drained rapidly from his stomach.

Helena called out, 'This is your last chance, Visblat ... *Surrender!*'

'This is an interesting game,' he replied.

Helena yelled in different directions. 'I warn you, I can see you coming!' Both her hands were shaking. Sweat flushed her body. 'I'm not afraid,' she told herself. 'I'm not.'

'This is much like the evening your mother was killed,' Visblat yelled back. 'She was raped, wasn't she? Yes. I read about it in the papers. That must have been very traumatic for you.'

Helena's fear was suddenly gone and her hands steadied.

Visblat rounded each megalith, his night vision laying bare a green-tinged world. 'Yes, I know about what happened that night. The Palladium, wasn't it? Very sad. You and your mother went out into the laneway. I understand it was your fault ...'

Helena fearlessly stepped out from her hiding place, her guns stretched before her. She could see both herself and Visblat through Wilson's eyes. The giant loomed in front of her. Taking the best aim she could, she snapped off eight thunderous rounds without hesitation. In the illumination of the muzzle flash, she witnessed each bullet slamming into Visblat's chest as he was catapulted backwards against a sarsen stone, then to the ground.

'No one talks about my mother,' she said softly.

Unable to hold himself up any longer, Wilson buckled and fell.

The visions were gone.

Helena continued to fire shots into the air to get her bearings as she made her way towards her car and flicked on the hazard lights. A bright orange glow throbbed intermittently as she scrambled back to the Trilithon with only one thing on her mind: *Is Wilson still alive?*

As she had done twice before, she pulled his crippled body to her and held him tightly.

'Please be okay,' she said. '*Please* ...' Helena pressed her hand over Wilson's gunshot wound to stop the torrent of blood. 'Wilson, can you hear me? You have to start the healing command. Listen to me ...'

'I thought I told you to leave?' he whispered.

A distressed smile crept over her face. 'I *never* listen to what you say.'

Time appeared to slow for a moment.

'Use the healing command. *You've got to!*'

Intense pain stabbed through Wilson's lower abdomen. He coughed up blood, which ran down the side of his mouth. 'No omega commands,' he spluttered. Using a command now might negatively affect his transport, he realised—Barton had warned him of just that. Wilson grabbed Helena's hand. 'Take me over there.' He pointed towards a large slab of stone in the centre of the Trilithon: the Altar Stone. 'There's not much time.'

Guided by the pulsing glow of the hazard lights, Helena dragged Wilson across the grass and laid him beside the fallen megalith. 'You *must* heal yourself,' she urged.

Wilson coughed up more blood. 'You've got to go,' he winced. 'Get out of the Sarsen Circle.'

'I'm not leaving you.'

'You have to ...'

'I won't leave!'

'The portal won't work if you're with me.' It was a lie, but Wilson knew Helena would be killed if she was transported; only a Gen-EP could survive. He released his grip and pushed her away. 'Go, Helena!'

Her instinct told her to stay.

'Please, Helena. You must do as I say,' he said, groaning in agony.

Thinking this would be the last time she would ever see Wilson's face, Helena kissed him gently on the mouth. She backed up and stared into his eyes, committing his image to memory. Then she turned and ran, the taste of his blood still on her lips.

Wilson watched as she disappeared into the pulsing orange illumination. Waiting as long as possible, all the while flirting with his own unconsciousness, he lifted his hand and pressed his fingers against the pitted surface of the Altar Stone.

It ignited with a golden glow.

Thunder rumbled high overhead.

HELENA STOOD BESIDE her car on the outskirts of the Sarsen Circle. Through a red haze, she witnessed Wilson's hand activate the final portal. Above, sheets of red lightning flashed high across the misty sky. Wilson was just out of her view, lying injured on the grass. Reaching into her pocket, Helena rummaged for the coin he had given her.

A single bolt of lightning shot from the thickening clouds and struck one of the sarsen stones with a *bang*. In response, the megalith ignited with needles of light, like captive electricity released from the heart of the rock.

The clamour of thunder continued above.

In seconds, a barrage of thunderbolts rained downwards, striking each megalith in turn. One by one, each of the stones was ignited by the mysterious flickering glow.

The Trilithon began to hum.

Helena felt it in every cell of her body.

Suddenly her visions from Wilson were gone.

The clouds parted, framing a circle of stars in the night sky.

A beam of magnetic energy suddenly sprang upwards.

Startled by the luminescence, Helena turned away as another beam shot up beside the first. Then another, and another. Their source was the Aubrey Holes around the perimeter of the Sarsen Circle. In just seconds, all fifty-six of them ignited to form a broad coliseum of light stretching endlessly upward towards the heavens. The countryside lit up for kilometres. The tubes of light began to cycle on and off, the illumination rotating in an anti-clockwise direction.

Everything went into slow motion.

The portal was opening.

With a mind-shattering *thump*, north became south for just a microsecond. A wave of supernatural energy mushroomed from the structure—the golden luminescence flooding outwards in a continuously growing plume, in all directions at once, towards the horizon.

45

Salisbury Plain, England
Stonehenge
December 22nd 2012—Zero Point +1
Local Time 8:04 a.m.

Mission of Isaiah Complete

AS PROPHESISED, THE Age of Pisces had ended and the Age of Aquarius had begun. A new consciousness pervaded all things; it would be a time of renewed humanitarianism and friendship. Clarity of mind was again possible. The magnetic forces of the portal had been unleashed, reducing human levels of violence, suspicion and hatred that had built up through two thousand years of religious strife, two world wars, and many hundreds of other conflicts. Immune systems were recharging and people would sleep soundly once again. Time had slowed to previous levels, the average day feeling like it had almost doubled in length.

Helena opened her eyes and saw a faint band of colour on the eastern horizon. A midwinter's sunrise. She had been lying on the grass for more than fourteen hours and, strangely, she wasn't cold or tired. It was a peculiar feeling, as if she had been there for only a few minutes. A sense of well-being pervaded her entire body. Climbing to her feet, she noticed that the hazard lights on her car were still flashing.

Helena gazed towards the ancient megaliths of Stonehenge. The arrangement had returned to its normal position.

Did I imagine everything? she wondered.

Drawn towards the structure, Helena noticed that the Aubrey Holes around the Sarsen Circle were still smouldering, faint streamers of mist drifting into the crisp morning air.

As she approached the monument, she saw the barely distinguishable remains of Commander Visblat; his body, turned to white dust, was blowing away on the breeze.

The sight filled her with fear for Wilson.

The moment Helena entered the inner circle of the Trilithon, the sun crested the horizon with a burst of golden light. Her eyes squinted to adjust as the beams speared over the midwinter Station Stone, forming a long black shadow that stretched over the very spot where Wilson had been lying, wounded, the night before. There, imprinted on the Altar Stone, was the outline of a hand, etched smooth and deep into the surface. Helena fell to her knees and pressed her fingers to the indentation.

The portal had opened successfully and Wilson was gone.

46

California, The Americas
Mercury Building, Sub Level A5—Mercury Laboratory
June 20th 2081
Local Time 5:21 a.m.

28 Days after Transport Test

ALONE IN THE MERCURY lab, Davin scanned the barcode label with his laser pen. Having checked that the description was correct, he moved to the next device. Under a veil of complete secrecy, everything was being reassembled; they were on a tight schedule. Cables were coiled in piles on the floor and the five-terawatt collider lasers were stacked in boxes. The Imploder Sphere and magnetic-field generator were still in place—they had not been taken away because a special crane was required to remove them.

Davin felt a falling sensation in his gut when he looked at the cordoned-off section where the accident had happened. Yellow reflective tape was draped from makeshift poles. His mind filled with images of Barton's body lying on the ground, motionless.

What a terrible tragedy. Not only had he lost his mercury leader, but he had also lost a friend. In an effort to subdue his sorrow, Davin did what he knew best: he worked. Touching his handheld with his digital pen, he continued the audit and pulled up the next device.

A crackling noise began to emanate from the far corner of the laboratory. Davin couldn't understand what he was hearing. He drew himself upwards as the sound gradually became louder. Everything was supposed to be shut down. The noise was coming from the titanium inflator diamond suspended on the wall. The lights in the mercury lab suddenly extinguished and the inner surface of the diamond lit up with a blanket of mercurial energy.

An eerie luminescence filtered outwards.

The system was activating!

Davin ran towards the command centre, between the boxes stacked high around him, and frantically pounded his fist on the observation wall. Annoyance welled inside him. He wasn't prepared to accept any more foul-ups.

On the other side of the glass, a small team of mercury scientists were concentrating on the holographic screens in front of them. Even with Davin frantically hammering on the window, no sound could penetrate.

Andre eventually looked up. 'Who switched off the lights?' he said. Everyone inside the command centre turned towards the laboratory.

Davin was screaming at them at the top of his lungs, 'The magnetic-field generator is open!' He frantically gesticulated towards the time machine. 'Shut it down!'

Andre's eyes widened in shock. 'Did anybody activate the conductors?'

There was silence.

'Come on, did anybody activate them?' he said again.

'They're not connected,' one of the other mercury scientists replied.

Andre gazed at Davin through the glass and shrugged his shoulders. The situation was clear—no one inside the command centre appeared to have anything to do with it. Davin turned towards the shimmering blanket of energy. Everything was happening by itself.

Andre quickly dialled a number and spoke into the receiver, 'It's me,' he said. 'You'd better get down here. We have a problem.' There was a pause. '*Yes, it's serious!* I wouldn't call you otherwise!'

The Imploder Sphere hummed, louder and louder.

Davin clapped his hands over his ears to muffle the painful sound. The lights inside the command centre began flickering on and off.

There was no time to sprint for the emergency exit.

A narrow beam of energy suddenly leapt from the diamond, across the laboratory, towards the transport pod. Quark-gluon plasma—Davin had seen it once before. Feeling his exposed skin burning, he dived behind the very conductor bank that had been responsible for taking Barton's life. The imploder sphere gradually filled with a glowing translucent fog. As quickly as it had begun, the mercury lab was again cloaked in darkness.

A deathly silence reigned.

Davin lifted himself from the floor and scanned the transport pod.

Everyone inside the command centre looked on in open-mouthed awe. The mercury team were not accustomed to dealing with surprises like this.

Davin pounded on the glass again, his forehead and cheeks blistered by the intense heat. 'Turn on the emergency lights!' He pointed towards the master console. 'Turn them on!'

One of the mercury scientists clobbered the switch and a series of down-lights shone from the ceiling.

Davin tentatively made his way across the room, theories running rampant in his mind. The haze inside the Imploder Sphere gradually dispersed and the crouched image inside became clear—Wilson Dowling, naked, cradled in a pool of blood.

Turning towards the command centre, Davin crossed his arms high in the air, indicating he needed urgent medical assistance. The signal caused a frenzy of activity as everyone tried to do something to assist. Using the encoded release key, Davin unlatched the trapdoor on the base of the pod and Wilson fell unceremoniously to the floor in a red splash.

A TEAM OF MEDICS rushed inside as Andre looked on. Glancing at the clock on the wall, he took note of the exact time. *I knew this would happen*, he thought to himself. *We waited too long*. At that moment, Jasper stormed in through the door, making a beeline for him.

'What the hell is going on?' Jasper demanded.

'We've got a bit of a problem,' Andre replied.

Jasper scanned the mercury lab. 'What sort of problem?'

'It seems Wilson is back.'

'What do you mean, *he's back*?'

Andre folded his arms in resignation. 'He's here.'
'How is that possible?'
'The pod was filled with blood,' Andre whispered.

It was difficult to see what was going on because a medical team were circled around Wilson's body. Judging by the frantic pace of their activity, things were extremely serious.

'I told you this could happen,' Andre said, leaning closer. 'We didn't act quickly enough. And now we have an even bigger problem.'

47

Gatwick Airport, England
December 22nd 2012—Zero Point +1
Local Time 11:02 a.m.

Mission of Isaiah Complete

THE ENGLISH WINTER had given birth to a beautiful morning. There was not a cloud in sight and the sky seemed bluer than it had ever been. Helena drove up the ramp towards the security checkpoint, came to a stop at the boom gate and held out her passport to the security guard. She really didn't care if she was arrested. Adjusting the rifle across his back, the officer flipped through her documents.

There was no UK entry stamp that he could see. With a smile, he asked, 'Are you leaving the country?' His accent was Irish, the tone extremely polite.

Helena nodded.

Looking around to make sure no one was watching, the guard handed the documents back. His instinct told him to let her pass. 'Just make sure you're listed on the passenger manifest.' He looked her straight in the eye.

Helena did her best to smile, but her expression hardly altered.

'Have a nice trip,' he said.

The Capriarty jet was waiting on the tarmac where it had been the evening before. The hangar doors were wide open. Helena drove inside, shut off the engine and sat in a daze. So much had changed since yesterday and she felt numbed by her experiences.

I wonder if Wilson survived, she thought. *He must have.*

Captain Lewis's voice suddenly broke her concentration.

'I'm glad you're back. I was worried.' He stared at the shattered headlights. 'What happened to you?'

Helena didn't respond.

'Where's Wilson?'

For a few seconds, she thought hard about the answer. 'I'm not sure.'

'Are you okay?'

'It's been a long night,' she said, exhausted. Tears unexpectedly welled in her eyes, but they weren't tears of sadness. Helena knew it was time to let go—time to soften. The demons she carried about her mother's death, on some level, had been pacified at last.

Captain Lewis fumbled through his pockets and handed her a clean handkerchief. 'Have you seen what a beautiful morning it is? On a day like this it's hard to feel sad about anything.' He didn't know what else to say.

Helena's strength was fading quickly. 'Just take me home, Warren.'

Walking at a slow pace, Captain Lewis led her across the tarmac; he had never seen Helena emotional before. 'Your father called while you were gone,' he said, making small-talk. 'Don't worry, I covered for you.'

Helena was only picking up every second sentence.

When she didn't reply, he added, 'Did you see that electrical storm last night? It was amazing.'

Wilson would have been delighted, Helena thought.

Commercial jets were taking off every minute or so and the thunder of turbines rumbled in the background. Captain Lewis continued talking as they climbed the stairs, 'I'll inform customs that we're leaving. We'll be out of here in a jiffy. I've refuelled and everything is ready.' He disappeared into the cockpit.

Helena walked into the main cabin and went directly to the computer. When she pressed Enter, the screen came to life and a familiar image appeared:

> Earth Ionosphere Cavity Resonance
> - Parkfield, California
> - Arrival Heights, Antarctica

Wiping the tears from her eyes, she sat down and focused on the magnetic resonance graph. It was dramatically different from the one she had seen just the day before: the Schumann Frequency had plummeted, just as Wilson said it would, to less than seven hertz. It seemed that everything was in balance once again.

'You did it,' Helena whispered. But in truth, she had expected nothing less.

Sitting back, she gazed at the Egyptian coin in the palm of her hand. 'This is all I have to remember you by,' she whispered. There were traces of blood on her fingers—Wilson's blood. One day, Helena realised, the coin she was holding would find its way back to him again. In seventy-five years' time it would be in Wilson's desk drawer, waiting—an integral part of his life. It was comforting to know that everything was not over. In fact, in some ways, things were just beginning.

48

California, The Americas
Infirmary Building, Level 3 (Ward A3)
June 26th 2081
Local Time 11:45 a.m.

34 Days after Transport Test

WARM SUNLIGHT STREAMED in through the half-open windows of the third-floor hospital room. With it, a gentle breeze carried the delicate scent of summer blossoms. Wilson opened his eyes to see a lone figure standing at the end of his bed. Thinking it was Barton, Wilson focused, but the bushy hairstyle, short stature and unmistakable features belonged to his friend Professor Author.

'I can't wait to hear *your* story,' Author said with a quizzical expression. 'So tell me, how did you get injured like that?'

'Where am I?' Wilson said.

The Einstein lookalike gestured around him. 'Enterprise Corporation, of course.'

'What are you doing here? Where's Barton Ingerson?'

Author looked confused. 'I don't know any Barton-Ingerson, but one thing is for certain, the people around here are out of their minds! They think I'm your *next of kin*. Clearly, I'm much better looking than you are.' The professor sat on the edge of the bed. 'But let me tell ya, this place has its perks. They flew me here first class—limo, nice room, king-size bed. I had lobster thermidor last night.' He kissed his fingertips. 'Magnificent! Ya know, come to think of it, those *conniving bloodsuckers* are trying to manipulate me. They want something. And judging by *your* appearance, it has something to do with you.'

Wilson looked around the hospital ward. 'How long have I been here?'

The professor shrugged his shoulders. 'Mate, they forced me to come here three days ago. I have no bloody idea what's happening. I was hoping you could tell me. They've locked us in here, by the way. Not a good sign. Anyway ... where have you been these last few weeks? I've been missing our stupid conversations.'

Although Wilson felt utterly exhausted, the events that led him here slowly pieced together in his mind. Looking up, he saw two remote cameras pointing at him from the ceiling. Everything was being filmed—Professor Author was being used to get Wilson to talk about his journey, he realised. Why else would they be locked in?

'I want to see Barton Ingerson!' Wilson yelled out. 'Do you understand? I want to see him, immediately!'

'Who's *Barton Ingerson?*' Author looked up at the cameras also. 'Tell me what's going on ...'

'I want to see Barton, right now!'

THE NEXT HOUR passed with agonising slowness. Wilson was careful not to talk to Professor Author about anything related to Enterprise Corporation or the Mission of Isaiah. He found himself saying 'I'll talk to you about that later, Professor' at least a hundred times.

Author's frustration was growing to uncontrollable levels and he kicked the base of the door with his foot. 'I can't believe they locked us in here! *Bastards!* I hate being locked in! What do they want? I mean, what could they possibly want?'

There was a click and the door swung open.

Davin Chang warily entered the room, attempting to look poised, wearing his mercury labcoat. His face was severely sunburnt, his skin and lips badly blistered—it looked painful. The clear outline of his thick-rimmed glasses was the only unburnt area. Wilson suddenly remembered that Davin was the one who gave him the faulty contact lenses before he was transported.

'Nice of you to join us,' Wilson said, sitting up.

The reply was equally measured. 'It's nice to see you back, Wilson.'

Professor Author yelled, 'You didn't have to lock us in here! What sort of friggin' hospitality is that supposed to be? I hate treatment like—' He danced around the room, pointing in different directions and pulling strange faces. 'You people are bastards! Bloodsucking bastards!'

'Professor, that's enough,' Wilson said, putting a halt to the tirade. His gaze locked on to the mercury scientist. 'Where's Barton? I want to see him, immediately.'

'I'm here to answer any questions you might have.'

'*Might have?* Where's Barton? It's imperative that I talk with him.'

'I'm sorry,' Davin said, 'I'm under strict instructions.'

'Is he okay?'

'He's not available.' Davin tentatively adjusted his spectacles on his sunburnt nose.

Wilson studied the insignias on Davin's lapels—a black triangle with a star in the centre—it designated the rank of mercury leader. The same rank Barton held.

'I see you've had a promotion,' Wilson said calmly.

'I can only answer the questions I'm permitted,' Davin replied.

'How long have I been here?' Wilson asked.

'Six days.'

'How long was I gone?'

'You time-travelled for twenty-eight days.'

It was the exact amount of time Wilson had spent in the past—Barton's calculations were absolutely correct.

Professor Author's mouth fell open. '*Time-travelled?* What the fuck are you talking about?'

'Where's Barton?' Wilson said again. 'Is he okay?'

'I told you. He's not available.' Davin cleared his throat, obviously nervous. 'You've been back for six days. When you appeared in the transport pod you were suffering from a gunshot wound to the stomach. Our medics had you in an induced coma while they stabilised your injuries. First, a hyper-barometric chamber, then an ionisation cubicle to get your muscle tone back.' It was like he was reading from a script. 'We've amplified your trackenoids back to normal levels. When you appeared in the mercury lab, well, it caught everyone by surprise. The power to the magnetic field generator was supposed to have been disconnected. Yet the system went live.' There was a long pause.

'Is that it?' Wilson said impatiently.

Davin added, 'I'm here to inform you that everyone knows about the Mission of Isaiah.'

'That's plainly obvious.'

'The Tredwells are on their way to see you.' Davin adjusted his spectacles yet again. 'They wanted me to prepare you with the facts. They want some answers.'

'I want answers!' Author blurted. 'Sunburn-boy here is clearly delusional! *Time-travelled?* Will somebody *please* talk to me? I *deserve* to know what's going on—'

'Not now, Professor,' Wilson replied.

'A medical team is waiting to examine you,' Davin said. 'The Tredwells want to be sure that it's safe to meet.'

'So they sent you in first. Lucky you.' Although Wilson welcomed a reason to argue, there was no option but to co-operate. 'Fine, Davin, get the doctors in here. Then ... let's have a chat with the Tredwells. I'm looking forward to it.'

Professor Author leant in very close. '*Mate*,' he said with a whisper. 'If you don't tell me what's going on, I'm leaving.'

'I will, Professor. I promise.' Wilson parted his robe and looked at his lower stomach. The site of the gunshot wound was still pink. He winced as he remembered the cold, icy sensation of being paralysed from the waist down. It was a feeling he hoped never to experience again.

Three doctors eventually arrived and over the next twenty minutes they checked him from head to toe with all sorts of electronic devices. Wilson did his best to be polite, but his patience was wearing thin. He eventually snatched away his medical records and flicked through the data himself, then tossed the medical tablet to Professor Author as a diversion.

The three doctors tried to seize the digital document, but the professor scampered away to the other side of the room. It was like a *Keystone Cops* routine as the trio of men in long white jackets hopelessly stumbled over themselves giving chase.

'Please!' one of them said. 'You'll have to return that!'

'Stop him,' yelled another.

Professor Author ducked and weaved away again. 'Can't you see I'm reading?' Eventually, after three circuits of the room, they cornered him, but Author pretended he was going to smash the tablet if they came any closer.

'Give it back!' an authoritative voice called out.

Wilson turned to see Jasper Tredwell standing just inside the doorway, the stately figure of GM beside him. They were both wearing black pinstripe suits with rare black carnations in their lapels. Every indication was that Barton was in serious trouble.

GM lifted his ivory cane and pointed. 'You have a lot of explaining to do, Mr Dowling. Just exactly where were you for those twenty-eight days?'

'Where's Barton?' Wilson said forcefully.

'*You* will answer *my* questions,' GM said.

'I'm not talking to anyone except Barton.'

'Barton is dead,' GM replied, coldly.

'He was fatally wounded two weeks ago,' Jasper confirmed.

Wilson's legs immediately went to water. Although he had suspected this outcome since his arrival, it was still a shock to hear it confirmed. Visblat's prophecy had come true.

'How did it happen?' Wilson asked.

'In the mercury lab,' Jasper replied. 'A freak accident.'

Visblat's voice echoed in Wilson's head: 'If you open the second portal, Barton will die.'

'It was no accident,' Wilson said abruptly. 'Barton was murdered.'

Everyone stood there blank-faced.

GM turned to the group of doctors. 'All of you, out of here. You too, Davin.'

Wilson stopped Professor Author from leaving. 'Wait here, please.'

He whispered back, 'I'd rather go if that's all right,' and headed for the door. 'You won't tell me what's going on, so I'm going home.'

Wilson grabbed Author by the collar, yanking him back. 'I need a witness. Wait here!'

'Why would you allege that Barton was murdered?' GM said.

'Barton *was* murdered!' Wilson answered pointedly. 'Of that, you can be certain.' Although Wilson acted strong, in reality he felt like a lost child, searching for something. There were so many things to analyse, so many perspectives. His heart was racing; he felt panicked. It was a conspiracy that Wilson faced—Visblat had said as much.

'*You* want answers, GM, and so do I. But this is going to take time to figure out.' Wilson rubbed his forehead; it felt like his brain was going to explode.

'Do you know what this foray of yours has cost me?' GM said. 'You have meddled with *time itself*. Your presence here confirms that. And as a result, Barton has been killed. Did you ever consider that what you two were doing was *wrong*?'

An image of Barton's face flashed into Wilson's mind. 'Not for one second,' he replied.

The discussion went in circles for the next two minutes as GM unleashed a torrent of accusations. In return, Wilson tried to buy himself some time to think.

'Why should I give you more time?' GM questioned.

'Barton was my friend.'

'You only knew him for two weeks,' Jasper huffed.

GM speared the ground at Wilson's feet with his walking stick. 'I will not relent! You'll answer my questions!'

'You tried to sabotage my mission,' Wilson said accusingly.

'I did no such thing!' GM replied.

'You sent another time traveller to stop me!'

GM backed up half a step. 'I've sent no one!'

Wilson searched the old man's eyes. 'Then, GM, you don't have all the facts, *do you?*' Wilson's tone was as condescending as he dared. 'There was someone else sent from here,' he confirmed. 'Sent from *this* time. That's how I know Barton was murdered. In the past, I was told he had been killed, in no uncertain terms.'

'This is absurd,' Jasper said under his breath.

GM said to Wilson, 'You were told he was murdered?'

'That's correct. I knew before I transported back here.' Wilson paused. 'I see it this way, GM. You have two choices.' He raised a finger. 'You can trust me; that's how we'll both get the truth.' He raised a second finger. 'Or you can fight me, and I'll tell you *nothing*.' His gaze didn't leave the old man. 'I need forty-eight hours.'

'Why do you need time?'

'The mastermind of Barton's death is still here,' Wilson replied. 'If we play our cards right, we can expose him.'

'We will *not* negotiate,' Jasper said resolutely. He began whispering in his grandfather's ear, but the old man waved him away.

'I'm prepared to give you twenty-four hours, Mr Dowling,' GM said.

'Forty-eight,' Wilson replied. 'Two days is not long in the whole scheme of things. The truth is what's important here.'

There was a lengthy silence.

Eventually, GM said, 'I'm going to want to know *everything*. This arrangement means we are partners. *Understand?*' There was a look of great concern in his eyes.

On the face of it, GM was *not* in control. And from Barton's description of the Enterprise Corporation chairman, it was a situation he would not be comfortable with.

Wilson began thinking clearly for the first time in minutes. 'I'll need access to *everyone* and *everything* in the mercury building. The Dead Sea scrolls. Barton's files. The logs to the grade-one security system.' He paused. 'I'll need assistance from Professor Author, here.'

'How can we trust Mr Dowling with anything?' Jasper said, clearly frustrated. 'This is not right.'

GM turned to his grandson. 'The mere fact that the time machine was *connected* proves there's something going on that we are not aware of. Why else would the inflator diamond have powered up? Mr Dowling was *not* involved in that, was he?' GM turned to Wilson again. 'Do you need anything else?'

'I need to go somewhere I can think,' Wilson said. 'A helicopter. A helicopter to take me to Mount Whitney. That's what Barton would do.'

GM gave a subtle smile. 'Yes he would, wouldn't he?' But the smile abruptly vanished. 'A security team will be with you at all times.' GM looked at his watch. 'This is personal for me, Mr Dowling. I need the truth.' The old man hobbled out of the ward with his grandson tagging close behind. 'I will be in contact,' he called back.

As soon as the Tredwells were gone, Professor Author erupted: 'Time travelling! Missions! Murders! Do you know who those two guys were? They were the *bosses* of Enterprise Corporation!' He pointed out the door. 'You don't make deals with *them*! You don't threaten them!'

Wilson ushered Professor Author into the adjacent bathroom.

'We can't escape this way,' Author moaned. 'I've already checked!'

'Just relax.' Wilson said, trying to console him. 'There aren't any security cameras in the bathrooms.' The door clicked shut.

Professor Author grabbed Wilson by the shoulders and shook him violently. 'Tell me what the hell is going on! I'm gonna lose it otherwise!'

'I have a question, first,' Wilson said. 'If you had to name a command that allowed you to see in the dark, a cerebral command, what would you call it?'

'Have you lost your mind?'

'Please, Professor!'

The little man's face contorted even more than usual.

'What would you call it?' Wilson said firmly.

'*Possum!*' he whispered. 'You know that!'

The omega powers were something Visblat could never understand, and knew nothing about. It proved that Professor Author was not involved in the conspiracy of the second time traveller. 'Have you told anyone about my powers?' Wilson asked.

Author looked like he'd just bitten into a lemon. 'Of course not! I hate Enterprise Corporation! They want my research, *remember?*'

Over the next half hour, Wilson explained what he could. There was decoding to be done and Author was the perfect assistant—he was smart and Wilson knew he could trust him.

'You said someone else time-travelled,' Author said. 'Who was it?'

'That's the part *we* have to work out.'

'You don't know who it is?'

'Not exactly.'

'And you're sure this Barton guy was murdered?'

'I'm certain.'

'Out of curiosity, how are you going to figure out who did it?'

'By making them confess,' Wilson said. 'Barton's killer has no way of knowing how much information I have.'

'I wish we had some cigarettes,' Author said, thoughtfully. 'You know, the ones I like ... the *deadly* ones. They're so much more satisfying.' There was more silence. 'It's funny, but for some reason this conversation reminds me of that night we flipped your fate coin. Do you remember?'

'Oh, I remember.'

'Was your omega programming useful?'

'Professor, I need you to decode the Isaiah text,' Wilson said. 'It's absolutely critical. We need to find out why anyone would want to stop *all three* of the energy portals from being opened. That's the key to all this. We can talk about your omega programming later. Is that a deal?'

The professor leant in very close. 'What an amazing journey you've been on.' He rubbed his podgy face as if trying to subdue his enthusiasm. 'Time travel *is* possible! Amazing.' A crooked grin came to his face. 'I know you're telling the truth, Wilson ... cause there's *no way* you're capable of making up a story as entertaining as that.'

'Can you decode the Isaiah text?' Wilson asked seriously.

'If that Barton guy can apply the gigabit decoding algorithm, then so can I. No problem.'

But the professor could not have been more wrong.

49

California, The Americas
Mount Whitney, Sierra Nevada Ranges
June 27th 2081
Local Time 4:35 p.m.

35 Days after Transport Test

WILSON STRUCK A MATCH, cradled the flame and raised it to his cigarette. The wind was gusting from behind him and it blew a steady stream of smoke towards the mountain ranges stretching into the distance. He was not alone—a ten-strong security team, wearing dark-blue uniforms, were deployed around him and the Enterprise Corporation helicopter.

Perched high on the very peak of Mount Whitney, Wilson couldn't help but be philosophical. Barton had said that everything *here* stayed exactly the same. It seemed even more profound now because Barton was gone and only his memory lingered in this magnificent place. Wilson studied the tall green forest and the deep, slow-moving river carving through the valley below. A bank of white clouds swept quickly overhead.

At that moment, a vision of Helena dominated Wilson's thoughts. He had been trying not to indulge himself with memories of her too often, but as a result a smile found its way to his lips. He missed her. It was good just to think about her. Wilson wondered what her life would be like. He corrected himself: *had* been like. If she were still alive, she would be a very old woman now. He wondered if she had borne children, married, been happy. It would take all his resolve not to dig into the archives to retrieve her story. In one way, he didn't want to know what had become of her. As it was, she lived in his memories as the beautiful and amazing young woman he'd had the privilege to be with on his journey into the past.

High above, an eagle banked effortlessly against the high winds that swept over the mountain range. It reminded Wilson of what Barton had said: 'There is no use preparing for a mission like this if your *head* is not in the right place. Preparation is nothing if your attitude is wrong. You must remain positive at all times. You must remain in the moment.'

Inhaling another stream of smoke from his cigarette, Wilson refocused. He would need to be at his best if he was going to unravel the mystery of Barton's death. He nodded to himself. Stay positive, stay in the moment.

Wilson had a plan, but it was by no means foolproof. At GM's request he had sent a memo to everyone involved—detailing his mission and the journey he had taken. That was the first exchange in a battle of wits between him and the mercury team. But these were not ordinary people he was dealing with. They were some of the sharpest and most creative minds on the planet. The question was: could he uncover the truth with the information he had available?

Stay positive, he told himself.

Thinking through the scenarios like a chess player plotting checkmate, Wilson narrowed down the list of suspects. Only a select few had the wherewithal to thwart his mission, and a smaller group yet again the power to send another Gen-EP back in time. That was something that would take many people to accomplish—most likely, the entire mercury team. The fact that the inflator diamond was connected proved that the system could have recently been used.

Wilson thought again of his detailed memo. As a sideline, he had chosen to include Helena Capriarty, but omitted her real name. Her psychic link to him and her resistance to an optical trackenoid response was something he needed to understand. Disclosing her involvement was the only way of finding out more about the subject; otherwise the answers would certainly be classified.

Wilson continued thinking for more than an hour.

The greater the number of people involved, the greater his chances of uncovering the conspiracy of Barton's death. Sitting on the peak of the mountain, the wind whistling in his ears, Wilson recalled his journey into the past like he would a dream. There was no other analogy. The Schumann Frequency had been restored on December 21st 2012—the day Wilson transported back—and *time* felt expansive again, not rushed or out of control, as it had been in the past. His mission had been accomplished—he had done his part. But Wilson was determined to quash any feelings of complacency. He had to find out who killed Barton and why. Only then would he feel truly satisfied.

50

California, The Americas
Enterprise Corporation, Head Office, Level 12
June 28th 2081
Local Time 7:35 p.m.

36 Days after Transport Test

THE LAST TIME WILSON had stood at this spot he was with Barton, leader of the mercury team—a man who somehow controlled every aspect of his world. But this time Wilson was alone, without Barton's guidance and facing another great challenge. There was no one to fall back on now, and Wilson felt pitifully under-prepared. He took a deep breath and forced himself to remember the mountains of the Sierra Nevada Ranges. The outcome was certain, he told himself: the thirteen acclaimed geniuses on the other side of the door stood no chance against him. He smiled. There was a fine line between being positive and being ignorant, he decided.

He pushed open the double doors.

The executive boardroom was crowded with people, everyone neatly assembled in their chairs as requested. The chattering stopped immediately when Wilson entered the room. The atmosphere felt strained. Davin, Andre, Karin and Jasper sat four abreast in the front. Behind them, seated in two rows, were the other nine members of the mercury team. There were two empty chairs—one next to Professor Author and one at the head of the table, for GM.

The disarming scent of fresh flowers lingered in the air. Outside, the sun was dipping towards the horizon, the sky just beginning to take on a painted hue.

Wilson was deliberately more than an hour late. Each second counted and he stayed away as long as he dared—the professor needed all the time Wilson could give him to decode the scrolls.

Everyone in the room looked tense, having waited so long.

Every cloud has a silver lining, Wilson thought, knowing the conspirators had to be feeling the pressure more than most.

It was the first time he had seen the entire mercury team together since the transport test. They each acknowledged his presence in some way as he entered the room. Even Andre made a robotic effort to raise his hand in greeting. Expressionless, Wilson made his way to the far side of the table, pulled out his chair and sat down. He had to make them believe he already knew the truth.

A small holographic screen sat in front of Professor Author, pages of data flashing past on its display. Every few moments, the professor would type a new command, stare intently at the results, then type some more. Beads of sweat hung precariously on his forehead. Wilson had never seen him so stressed.

'The decoding,' Wilson whispered. 'How is it going?'

As a last resort, Professor Author was using Data-Tran to apply the gigabit algorithm from the Copper Scroll. The decoding had turned out to be much more complicated than he had anticipated. And although Data-Tran was not as secure as they would have liked, they were desperately in need of its processing power.

'I need more time!' Author whispered nervously. 'This is so embarrassing.'

Wilson's heart was pounding. Without knowing why Visblat wanted the second portal left open, nothing made sense. The information was critical. 'Do your best, Professor,' Wilson replied, attempting to sound reassuring. But in reality, his own anxiety was beginning to overwhelm him.

The door from GM's office swung open and the old man made an entrance worthy of royalty. He was wearing a black suit with a white tie. The blonde Amazon, Cynthia, strode beside him on his left, while an equally beautiful young brunette flanked his right. They made a striking trio—the incredibly healthy leading the incredibly old. The two young women led GM to his chair and without a word he sat at the head of the table. His female escorts silently retreated, closing the double doors behind them.

GM peeked at his watch, then glared across the room. 'This is not a very good start.' He sat menacingly forward. 'Mr Dowling, I don't like to be kept waiting. It's only my rampant curiosity that's letting this meeting take place, now.' Setting his walking stick between his legs, he gestured for the meeting to commence.

Upsetting the old man was a risk that had to be taken; nothing today should be comfortable for anyone. Wilson studied the team members sitting on the other side of the table wearing their prim-and-proper mercury labcoats. Then he noticed Jasper in an Italian suit of obvious quality, its grey fabric offset by a red tie and matching red carnation. Interestingly, it was the first time Wilson had seen the two Tredwells wearing different ensembles.

'It's too bad Barton can't be here to see this,' Wilson said.

He watched everyone's faces. *Nothing.*

'We've all read your memo, Mr Dowling,' Jasper said. 'You've made some extraordinary claims. I certainly hope you can back them up.'

GM gestured for Jasper to stay quiet. 'Get on with it, Mr Dowling.'

Wilson drummed his fingers on the tabletop before addressing everyone collectively. 'You're probably all wondering why this meeting has been called. And the answer is simple ... it is to find Barton Ingerson's murderer.'

'An investigation was conducted into Barton's death,' GM said, flatly. 'The findings were that he was involved in an accident, nothing more.'

'Not only will I prove that Barton was murdered,' Wilson said confidently, 'but I will expose who was responsible for killing him.' He traded glances with everyone. 'And that person is in this very room, *right now.*' The silence erupted into murmurs. 'That's correct!' Wilson reaffirmed. 'The mastermind of Barton's murder is in this room!'

GM came over the top of the crowd, 'Everybody *will* stay quiet!' The hushed voices quickly subsided. 'Mr Dowling has the floor until this situation is resolved to *my* complete satisfaction. But I'm warning you, Mr Dowling. I'm already in a bad mood. Your time is short and my patience thin. If you're wrong about all this, it will be *you* and your strange friend there who'll be the ones in trouble.'

Author's intense concentration was broken. 'What strange friend?' he said, looking about.

GM stabbed his cane into the floor at his feet. 'Get on with it, Mr Dowling!'

Under more than enough pressure already, Author went back to frantically typing on his small keyboard—he couldn't afford the time or the luxury of being offended.

'Barton was,' Wilson began, stalling for every second he could, 'the best of men. He was unselfish, a great lateral thinker and generous with his wisdom. The world is truly a lesser place without him here. In some way, each of us here owes him a debt of gratitude. All the more reason why we must take this situation seriously.' Wilson glared at the thirteen people sitting in front of him. 'As you read in my memo, I was transported back in time. Barton *did* tamper with the transport pod. My mission was to restore the Schumann Frequency.'

His words were met with silence.

Wilson tapped Professor Author on the shoulder. Taking the cue, he pressed a key and a three-dimensional image appeared above the boardroom table. It showed Schumann Frequency readings from the NCEDC. The graph went back more than 120 years. Wilson said, 'I would like you all to pay particular attention to December 21st 2012. *Zero Point*, as we now know it.'

On that exact date there was a sharp, almost vertical decline of the readings. It went from more than 11.2 hertz down to less than seven. Since then it had been rising gradually to its current level of 7.45 hertz.

'That graph hasn't changed at all,' Jasper said. He looked to Karin for confirmation. 'It's *always* been like that.'

'Jasper's right,' she agreed. 'That graph hasn't changed.'

Wilson pointed at the image. 'Exactly my point.'

Davin was nodding.

Wilson said, 'Would you like to explain, Davin?'

He cleared his throat. 'I'd rather not, if that's all right.'

'I insist that you do.'

Nervously wringing his hands together, Davin answered, 'I can only conclude that *this reality* is based on the portals being opened about seventy years ago. Everything that happened in the past—the storms in Mexico, Egypt and England, and all the dates—are consistent with Wilson's memo. It is therefore clear to me that the sharp decrease in the Schumann Frequency was triggered by the actions *he* took when he transported back to us.'

'But the graph was the same before he left?' Jasper questioned again.

'Davin?' Wilson said.
'The graph would only have changed if he *didn't* open the portals.'
There was another long silence. Wilson turned to GM. 'Barton told me you were concerned about meddling with the past ... and the effects that might have on the future. This graph proves that *this reality*,' Wilson waved his arm full circle, 'depends on things happening *exactly* as they did.'

'Tell me why the Schumann Frequency continues to go up,' GM said.

'Wilson is not an expert on any of this,' Jasper interrupted.

'I'm interested in what he has to say,' the old man countered.

'Fear,' Wilson answered. 'The Schumann Frequency increases because billions of people are *afraid* ... of the future ... of authority ... *of each other*.' Wilson remembered what he had seen and felt. 'Newspapers and television stations take all that is evil and unbalanced in the world, magnify it by a million and pump it into people's homes—as if the sickness was the norm. It's happening to us again—*here, now*. At the turn of last century, everyone I met was constantly wondering what they had to lose, pondering how evil the world was. They were all frightened and didn't even realise it. On an unconscious level they *all* lived in fear. And the more they sought to protect themselves, the more afraid they became.' He paused. 'The Schumann Frequency is unquestionably driven upwards by fear. The human mind—a very powerful electrical device—contributes. And in some instances, given the right volume and magnitude, it can overwhelm the very function of our planet.'

'I understand the subject of fear well,' GM said. 'If you can make people afraid, you have power.'

'I agree, GM. And *power* is the reason Barton was killed.' Wilson sat forward, trying to look confident. 'I was not the only one to travel into the past. Another Gen-EP was sent from Enterprise Corporation to stop me. I will identify the second time traveller in a moment.'

Wilson's overwhelming confidence had everyone looking at each other with blank faces.

'I need that information,' Wilson whispered in Author's ear. 'Without it, I'm screwed.'

Professor Author typed a message on the screen in front of him:

I need more time!

There was no choice but to take a gamble.

'Jasper Tredwell, you are undeniably involved in this conspiracy,' Wilson announced.

Jasper replied, 'Is that an accusation?'

'Simply a fact.'

Jasper turned to his grandfather. 'He's acting like a trial lawyer. This is not a court,' he said. 'I am *not* on trial here.' Jasper pointed. 'We should put a stop to this now, before Mr Dowling attempts to drag my good name through the mud.'

'You *are* involved,' Wilson said vehemently. 'And I'll prove it.' He tapped Professor Author on the shoulder. 'The second image please.'

But Author was fixated on the small screen, tension written all over his face. A single strand of data he was analysing appeared to implicate yet another scroll. It was difficult for him to understand how that was possible.

Wilson said again, '*Now, please.*' Finally hearing the request, Author hit a key and another hologram came to life. Jasper was on the screen and it was time-stamped May 21st 2081, two days before Wilson's transport test.

Jasper's eyes widened, but he remained outwardly calm. 'Stop this ridiculous charade, before you make a fool of yourself.'

But Wilson kept on talking, 'The grade-one security system revealed that *you*, Jasper Tredwell, swapped the contact lenses in Davin's preparation lab.' The digital video showed Jasper taking out the lenses marked 'Wilson Dowling' and replacing them with another pair.

Jasper pointed at the screen. 'You're taking this out of context.'

'Having my contact lenses changed,' Wilson continued, 'made me vulnerable to a trackenoid response. It should have cost me my life. Why would you do that?' There was a pause. 'I'll tell you why,' Wilson's voice tapered off. 'I know the answer. It's because you never expected me to come back and expose your part in this. You never expected this to be an issue for you.'

'That's correct, I didn't.'

Turning to his grandson, GM said with an icy tone, 'You acted without my approval, Jasper.'

'It's nothing to worry about, Grandfather. If Mr Dowling was travelling *forward* in time, like we authorised, there was no danger. It was simply a precaution.'

'So you knew back then what was going on?' Wilson said.

Jasper appeared to be completely unfazed. 'I suspected. Anyway, all this is irrelevant. This doesn't mean I killed Barton. And quite clearly *you're* still alive. So what is my crime?'

'Let's move on, shall we?' Wilson said, trying to look confident. 'It's time to reveal the second time traveller.'

Everyone was motionless—no one even blinked.

'Do you all remember Magnus Kleinberg—the second Gen-EP candidate?' A picture flashed up on the screen of a hulking redheaded man. Just seeing his face made Wilson feel nervous. 'Does anyone know what happened to him?'

Andre shifted uncomfortably in his chair.

'Mr Kleinberg went missing three weeks ago,' Wilson said. 'Three days before Barton died in the mercury lab. Interesting timing, don't you think?' It was a critical piece of evidence.

GM looked concerned. 'Are you suggesting that Magnus Kleinberg was the man sent back in time to stop you?'

'That is *precisely* what I'm saying.'

A group of images flashed up on the screen. Newspaper articles dated from 2008 to 2012. Photographs of Commander Visblat—the identical likeness of Magnus Kleinberg.

Headlines read: 'New Commander Appointed', 'Police Chase Serial Killer', 'Visblat Missing'.

'As you can see from these photographs and articles,' Wilson said, 'Kleinberg *is* undeniably the second time traveller. And that means only one thing.' He gazed at the mercury team. '*You* were the ones who sent him into the past.' The accusation was met with further silence. 'How long ago did you send him?'

They were all expressionless.

Eventually Andre spoke, 'No one else has been sent through the transport portal—other than you.'

Wilson stared at the holographic screens filled with information. 'What you see before you proves otherwise, doesn't it? Kleinberg *was* the man I met in the past.'

Davin said, 'It takes over twenty petawatts of electricity to open the magnetic-field generator.' He tapped on his palm device, transmitting a detailed graph of the day-by-day power usage in the mercury lab, to the screen above them. The last peak was during Wilson's transport test.

'No one else has been through the portal,' Andre said.

Jasper trumpeted, 'It seems no one else has time-travelled, Mr Dowling!' All the while his gaze was fixed on Professor Author. Jasper knew Wilson was missing something important. 'Your theory is in tatters. These two men,' he pointed at the screen, 'Kleinberg and Visblat, well, it must be a coincidence. They are not the same man.'

It had to be Kleinberg, Wilson reaffirmed to himself. And yet all the evidence showed he had *not* been sent back in time. How was that possible? Wilson was reeling ... then suddenly the answer came to him like a light bulb flashing on. 'Kleinberg hasn't been sent yet, has he? He's due to be sent into the past, but the transport hasn't happened yet. He's still here! That's why the magnetic-field generator was powered on ... you're *preparing* to send him, very soon!'

Wilson could see by the scientists' faces that he had struck upon the truth.

'This is preposterous,' Jasper said forcefully. 'Grandfather, I demand that we a get security team in here. I've had enough of these stupid theories about a second time traveller. Wilson has no proof—no proof at all. Look at the pair of them; they *clearly* don't know what they're doing. They're still searching Data-Tran for Christ's sake! We should be the ones interrogating them! Mr Dowling is the one who has broken the rules around here. In retrospect, Grandfather, we should have been patient. Yes. We should *never* have worked with a natural Gen-EP: an unknown, like him. We should have converted our own candidate—'

Jasper's ranting abruptly halted in mid-sentence.

Karin had ever so gently touched him on the hand, and their eyes met, briefly. It was only very subtle, but Wilson had seen Karin use that same sort of contact and expression before. It was exactly the way her hand had lingered against Barton that day in the command centre. Karin wanted Jasper to stop talking, *but why?*

GM pressed the intercom on his lapel. 'Cynthia, get a security team in here.' In seconds, two officers wearing blue uniforms burst into the boardroom. They must have been waiting just outside.

Jasper pointed across the table at Wilson. 'Arrest this man!'

The security team approached, as ordered, with their tazers energised and a pair of electronic wrist restraints at the ready.

GM's voice calmly redirected them: 'You men guard the door.' He gestured towards the entrance. 'That's an order.' The pair turned back without question and stood at attention.

Jasper looked bewildered. 'What are you doing?'

'Be quiet.' GM motioned with his hand. 'Please continue, Mr Dowling.'

Wilson said, 'The reason the inflator diamond is connected is because the mercury team are, right now, preparing to send Kleinberg into the past. Don't you see? They haven't sent the second time traveller yet.'

'He's still here?' GM said, trying to understand.

'If no one else has been transported, that has to be the case,' Wilson confirmed.

GM's gaze burrowed into the group of scientists. 'Are you preparing to send another time traveller?'

Professor Author suddenly thrust his clenched fists upwards.

'I've found it!' he yelled. There was a look of absolute relief on his face—Data-Tran had finally completed the calculations. 'I've found it, Wilson!' he blurted, again.

Wilson took a deep breath, knowing that so much rested on this moment. 'Why did Visblat want the second portal left unopened?' he asked, hoping to be given the critical answer.

'If the Schumann Frequency is out of balance,' the professor said excitedly. 'Time travel is *possible*. But if the Schumann Frequency is restored,' he pointed at the screen, 'and everything is in harmony—it says here, less than 8.1 hertz—time travel via the Stonehenge portal becomes *impossible*.'

Professor Author slouched back in his chair, exhausted—he had worked continuously for over thirty-six hours to find the answer. Mustering his remaining energy, he snared Wilson's attention by tugging on his shirt, and typed on the screen:

> By the way, Wilson ... I found something else.
> We need to talk!

Wilson ignored the professor's message. All he could think about was that—with the time-travel pathways now closed—he would never see Helena again. For the moment, he was unable to think straight. Helena was out of his life forever, he realised.

'Stopping the Mission of Isaiah is about keeping the time-travel pathways open,' GM said, understanding the situation perfectly.

Wilson's mind suddenly cleared. 'That's correct, GM.' He addressed the group as if he were their school headmaster. 'Andre,' he said. 'You know where Kleinberg is, don't you?' The boy was silent. 'Karin, would you like to tell me where he is?' She just sat there. Wilson shrugged his shoulders. 'Does anyone want to volunteer? Kleinberg can't be far from here. And when I find him, he'll tell me who secured his services.'

Wilson stared at each person in turn.

Andre was getting more emotional by the second.

'Andre, this is your last chance,' Wilson said. 'Tell me where Kleinberg is! There's no escaping the truth …'

Andre's gaze shifted to his left, towards Jasper and Karin, as if he was looking for some sort of guidance. 'We should tell him,' Andre said nervously. 'He's going to find—'

Karin leant forward and slapped the boy across the face, the impact cracking like a whip. 'Pull yourself together,' she hissed. 'Never forget you are a member of the mercury team. Never forget what's at stake.'

Andre cowered like a puppy.

'You'll keep your wits about you,' she added.

Across a hushed silence, Wilson held Karin's gaze—then he saw it. *Her eyes.* It caused the hairs on the back of his neck to bristle. Everything suddenly made sense. Wilson took a long cool drink of water, his hands shaking visibly.

'GM, would you like to know the truth?' Wilson announced.

The old man sat tall, preparing himself for any possibility. 'I would.'

Wilson carefully set his glass on the table. 'Kleinberg told me Barton would be killed if I opened the second portal. I now realise what that truly means.'

Loosening his tie, Jasper replied, 'Be careful, Mr Dowling.'

'Jasper, I'm sorry, all the evidence points *directly* at you,' Wilson said.

Jasper stood up. 'I'm not going to take any more of this.'

'You were the one who swapped my contact lenses.'

GM pointed his cane at his grandson. 'Sit down! I want to hear what Mr Dowling has to say.'

Jasper glanced at the security team. Huffing with frustration, he realised there was no way to leave and he reluctantly did as he was ordered.

Wilson said, 'Barton's diary was erased from the Data-Tran system. Everything was gone. That takes a very high access code and a great deal of skill. You have the authority to do that. Your motive was to undermine Barton's influence with GM.' Wilson was moving in for the kill. 'You asked Andre to decode the Isaiah scroll even before I was transported. We found his notes on the Enterprise Corporation system. And, it seems, you acted without your grandfather's permission. Therefore, you had the motive, the connections and the means to destroy me, Barton, and the Mission of Isaiah.'

Jasper was speechless.

'And yet you are *not* the one behind all this,' Wilson said. 'Everything points to you, yes. But you are *not* Barton's murderer.'

The tension in Jasper's face suddenly released. 'Oh, thank God.'

'Then who is it?' GM questioned.

'Someone who has the intellect to decode the Isaiah text. Someone with enough authority and knowledge to erase Barton's diary. A member of the mercury team with the technical ability to set a trap for Barton in the mercury lab that even Barton couldn't predict. And importantly, someone with enough ambition and cunning to see the advantages of time travel.' Wilson stared at the four people sitting in the front row, one by one. 'It's a person who would do just about anything to get what they wanted.'

Wilson pointed across the table.

'Karin Turnberry, you are the one who killed Barton Ingerson.'

Karin spoke softly in reply: 'That's ridiculous.' There was not a hint of distress on her face. 'You're just trying to confuse things.'

Wilson smiled in her direction. 'You're the one, Karin.'

'Why would I possibly want to kill Barton Ingerson?'

'You did it to solicit the mercury team's help.'

'Why would I need their help?' she said, coolly.

'That was the only way you could get them to conduct *another* time-travel experiment.'

'This is ridiculous—'

'You have the ability and the intellect to decode the mission notes,' Wilson said.

'Everyone in this room has that ability,' she replied, maintaining her outward calm.

'Who better than you to know the location of, and access codes to,

Barton's files? You could have erased them easily if you wanted to.'

'Anyone with enough authority could have done that,' she instantly rebutted.

'You had unrestricted access to the mercury lab. No one knew the electromagnetic generators better than you did.'

Karin raised her hands in the air, finally showing a degree of animation. 'So what if I did? That doesn't mean I killed Barton. And anyway, this is where your accusations fall apart. I had no reason to stop your silly little mission. Why would I?'

Wilson turned to Jasper with a question. 'That's why you swapped the contact lenses, wasn't it? Because Karin told you about them. She asked you to swap them, didn't she?'

Jasper said nothing.

'So what if I did?' Karin said. 'That doesn't prove a thing. The inquiry into Barton's death found nothing. Everyone here knows there are no surveillance systems inside the mercury lab.'

'You murdered Barton,' Wilson said. 'You made it look like an accident. Your goal was to get the mercury team to assist you in manipulating the past. Let me guess, you told them that if they helped you, *together* you could save Barton. That's why you sent Kleinberg to stop me—to keep the time-travel pathways open.'

'You have no proof,' she said.

'But I do, Karin. Kleinberg will confirm that *you* were the one who secured his services *before* Barton's death. That proves you planned everything. That's one of the critical errors you made.'

She remained composed. 'What good is time travel to me if I can't use it myself?'

'I'm so very glad you asked.' Wilson diverted his line of sight. 'Tell me Davin, how long would it take to genetically modify Karin into a Gen-EP candidate?'

'Six weeks,' he said sheepishly. 'Maybe less.'

'Is it an easy thing to do?'

Davin fidgeted with his spectacles.

'Keep quiet!' Karin snarled. 'He's trying to trick you!'

'Don't worry, Davin,' Wilson said. 'I can see it in Karin's eyes—the Gen-EP process has already been started, hasn't it?' The colour of her irises was different from the first time he had met her at Sydney University. 'We can go through the grade-one security tapes if you like.'

Davin had no choice but to confess. 'I started the Gen-EP conversion on Karin twelve days ago. She told me she wanted to time-travel so she could save Barton's life!' he said defensively. 'As a backup for Kleinberg! I had no idea what her real motives were.'

Staring in Karin's direction, just out of striking range, Andre said accusingly, 'You were the one who sent Barton into the mercury lab the day he was killed! I know what you did to the magnetic-field generator! I know how you tricked him!' Andre stammered, 'I'm—I'm not going to protect you any more.'

Jasper backed his chair away. 'I'm sorry Karin, you're on your own.'

Wilson had only one remaining question, 'Where is Magnus Kleinberg?' he asked.

'In the level-two testing laboratory,' Davin admitted. 'Studying.'

Karin began clapping her hands. 'I hope you're happy, Mr Dowling. *You* have ruined everything—you and your little secrets. Now Barton can *never* be saved. I intended to bring him back! I loved him! I was the one having an affair with him. It was only when he met you, that he started lying to me.' Then she realised that she had said too much. Karin turned towards GM and gave him a sparkling smile. 'We need to discuss this situation.'

The old man gazed back at her. 'Not a chance.'

Wilson stood from his chair. 'Karin Turnberry is responsible for the murder of Barton Ingerson.'

'Arrest her,' GM said.

The guards immediately clamped her with a pair of wrist restraints.

GM turned to his grandson. 'We are going to have a little talk, my boy.'

The guards ushered Karin towards the tall oak doors of the boardroom, but she stopped and wrenched herself free.

'You are all responsible for killing Barton!' she said accusingly. 'You are *all* responsible!' With those words she was forcibly led outside into the foyer.

Wilson pressed his fingers to his temples. Even if Karin *did* have plans to save Barton, there was no guarantee she ever could. And the realisation that she was prepared to murder him to get what she wanted was testament to her desire to time-travel. It was unusual, Wilson thought. In some way, he had *her* to thank for completing the Mission of Isaiah. If Kleinberg had not been there at Stonehenge, the third portal may never have opened. It was just like the Book of Esther, Wilson thought. This was about betrayal. Barton was betrayed by someone he trusted—like King Ahasuerus by his chief minister, Haman. The link was ironic. Then Wilson thought of Helena again. In reality, she was the reason Wilson had succeeded. Without her, he surely would have failed.

'I want to thank you, Mr Dowling,' GM said, 'for what you've done. Completing the Mission of Isaiah was an amazing effort. We are all very grateful.'

'We still have a problem,' Professor Author interrupted. Everyone turned their gaze towards him. 'What about Magnus Kleinberg?'

Davin understood immediately. 'He's right. Kleinberg was *there*, in the past, and yet we haven't sent him through the time machine yet.'

'It's a problem,' Andre said thoughtfully.

'We were due to transport him in just three days,' Davin said.

GM placed his palm on the tabletop. 'I'm interested in your answer, Mr Dowling. What do you think we should do?'

Wilson knew there was only one solution. 'Kleinberg must assume his role as Visblat. He *must* time-travel to the past—arriving six years before I do. For that to occur, everything that happened here today needs to be kept absolutely secret. In the past, Visblat knew nothing of my return to the future and you need to ensure that it stays that way.'

'All time exists simultaneously,' Wilson stated, repeating Barton's exact words. 'And we have an obligation to play our part in the past. There's no other choice.'

GM immediately ratified the decision. 'That's it then. We send Kleinberg back—top secret. We send him as if Mr Dowling had never returned.'

A contemplative silence hung over the room.

'I have a question,' Wilson asked, realising this may be his last chance to find the answer. He looked to Davin. 'The woman I met in the past. Why didn't she attack me when she looked into my eyes?'

Davin thought for a moment. 'Her eyes were blue, I assume.' He took off his glasses and studiously cleaned the lenses.

Wilson mentally stared at Helena's image like she was right in front of him. 'Yes, they were.'

Rubbing his chin, Davin said, 'It's an extraordinary coincidence, but I can only conclude that she too was a Gen-EP. That alone would void the trackenoid response. It's the only way I know it could happen.'

As soon as he heard it, Wilson knew it was true. In sending Helena away only seconds before the Stonehenge transport, he had made a critical error. She could have come back with him, and now he would never see her again.

'Does that answer your question?' GM asked.

Wilson nodded. 'Yes, it does.'

'You've impressed me greatly,' GM declared. 'We have *all* been impressed. Barton chose the right man to complete the Mission of Isaiah.'

Davin agreed. 'You were the perfect combination.'

'Far smarter than we realised,' Andre added.

How odd, Wilson thought. His only remaining secret was his omega programming. From the very beginning that was the one thing he wanted so desperately to keep from everyone.

Even Jasper reluctantly added, 'I concur ... Barton chose the right man for the job.'

GM pressed down on his walking stick and slowly stood up. 'Enterprise Corporation will honour its agreement with you, Mr Dowling. You are now a very rich man. And, as I understand it, there's also this ...'

Cynthia appeared in the doorway carrying a large rectangular Perspex container. Inside was Rembrandt's painting *The Holy Family*.

Wilson gazed intently at the framed image of a sleeping baby, so peaceful, being watched over by her mother—angels of protection secretly hovering above them in the darkness. His gaze was then drawn outside the Enterprise Corporation window where the sun was dipping towards the horizon, throwing a shimmering golden foil against the curve of the afternoon sky.

Sunsets can be breathtaking, larger than life. This was certainly one of those moments.

Thirty-six days after it had begun, the Mission of Isaiah was complete. The Schumann Frequency was restored and Barton's murderer had been exposed. But even so, Wilson's heart was heavy—with the time-travel pathways closed, he had certainly lost Helena forever.

Everything had come full circle.

Before Wilson could even clear his head, Professor Author leant in very close again, into his personal space.

'You are like a real-life Sherlock Holmes. Very impressive. *Really.* But before you let my compliments go to your head.' The professor whispered so that no one else could hear him, 'Data-Tran found something else in the translations.' He pointed at the screen, discreetly. 'A link to the Book of Ezra, the fifteenth book of the Old Testament.' His hushed words were deadly serious. 'It seems there's another job for the Overseer, Wilson. This isn't over yet.'

'In life, the greatest adventures
we face are not the ones we seek; rather,
they are the ones that seek us.'
—BARTON INGERSON